RED DIRT GIRL

GW00506041

C. A. LUPTON

RED DIRT GIRL

The Book Guild Ltd

First published in Great Britain in 2022 by
The Book Guild Ltd
Unit E2, Airfield Business Park
Harrison Road, Market Harborough
Leicestershire, LE16 7WB
Freephone: 0800 999 2982
www.bookguild.co.uk
Email: info@bookguild.co.uk
Twitter: @bookguild

Copyright © 2022 C. A. Lupton

The right of C. A. Lupton to be identified as the author of this
work has been asserted by her in accordance with the
Copyright, Design and Patents Act 1988.

All rights reserved. No part of this publication may be
reproduced, transmitted, or stored in a retrieval system, in any form or by any means,
without permission in writing from the publisher, nor be otherwise circulated in
any form of binding or cover other than that in which it is published and without
a similar condition being imposed on the subsequent purchaser.

This work is entirely fictitious and bears no resemblance to any persons living or dead.

Typeset in 11pt Adobe Garamond Pro

Printed and bound by CPI Group (UK) Ltd, Croydon, CR0 4YY

ISBN 978 1913913 878

British Library Cataloguing in Publication Data.
A catalogue record for this book is available from the British Library.

MIX
Paper from
responsible sources
FSC
www.fsc.org   FSC® C013604

*For my family
and other friends of the future.*

What are the roots that clutch, what branches grow
Out of this stony rubbish? Son of man,
You cannot say, or guess, for you know only
A heap of broken images, where the sun beats,
And the dead tree gives no shelter, the cricket no relief,
And the dry stone no sound of water. Only
There is shadow under this red rock,
(Come in under the shadow of this red rock),
And I will show you something different from either
Your shadow at morning striding behind you
Or your shadow at evening rising to meet you;
I will show you fear in a handful of dust.

T S Eliot

PROLOGUE

Some 300,000 years after they first emerged on the planet, homo sapiens discovered what they were made of – biochemically speaking. The architecture of human life – the 'mortal coil', they called it – had been prosaically distilled: four building blocks, twenty-four base pairs, three billion letters.

Armed with this blueprint, humans quickly mapped their species genome and set about dissecting its elegant codes and sequences. And the more they found out about how they worked, the less they could leave themselves alone. It would be inhuman, they agreed, not to intervene to prevent weakness and disease when they now had the means to do so. And anyway, they believed (at the start, at least) they were only tinkering with the 'batteries' of human life, not interfering with the main machinery.

At first, their attempts at modification were limited to snipping out the faulty genes. But as their scissors got sharper, their ambition grew bigger. Inevitably, perhaps, they took a further crucial step: not just to snip out the bad genes, but to replace them with good ones taken from another human being – to throw another egg into the genetic mixing pot, as it were. And with this move the sheath was well and truly off the molecular scissors. Before the end of the second decade of the 303rd millennium, the first 'three-parented' baby was crawling the Earth.

Many warned at the time that the move was reckless: that the science was too immature, too unproven and moving too fast, with significant potential risks to the individuals involved; that it would trigger the rise of consumer, or worse, state eugenics; that humans were behaving like the gods they used to worship. And more, that all this genetic tinkering would modify not just the batteries but the machinery of life itself – resulting in the beginning of the end for homo sapiens: the last remnant of the hominina sub-tribe of the hominid primates. Time will tell who was right, but one thing is certain: once this step had been taken, there would be no turning back.

1

A LOST CASE

A faint, metallic click. Or was it?

Detective Cooper-Clark listens, his breath light. Disembodied noise drifts from a distant pleasure dome, mixing with the soft, rhythmic swoosh of the overhead trans. The desolate shriek of a night bird rents the heavy sky.

He squints into the gloom, certain he's not mistaken. The suspects are grouped around what is almost certainly another victim. One seems to be standing guard; if she's heard anything, she's not reacting. He pulls at his sodden collar and listens again.

Another click. Then another. No doubt this time. He signals the men back into the shadow of the wall and flattens himself between them. Skin of their teeth. A brilliant beam of light turns the scene into a grisly shadow play: the silhouettes of the suspects ducking and diving as they scatter in different directions, chased by a volley of baton-wielding shapes; the fleeing bodies roughly felled and dragged off stage as a dark, lumpen mass is removed from the scene. Then the lights swerve away and the night reforms.

Stewards! He glares after the purple and sliver insignia on the departing vehicle, pulse racing. Weeks of careful work gone in a flash – literally. All that time; all that effort. And so close. He spits hard at the dull earth. *Typical Stews: no warning, no liaison.* That's what he dislikes most about the armed police of the Life Program – no bloody discipline. Just hired thugs throwing their weight around. Not answerable to anyone, apart from their Gencom bosses. He closes his eyes for a moment and takes a few deep breaths. Needs to keep it together; do him no good to lose it in front of the Uniforms.

'That'll be that then,' he says, turning to the men with a rueful shrug. 'Looks like the Stews beat us to it. Sorry, boys.' He tries not to look as if his economic future has just suffered a potentially mortal blow. The two officers give brief, empathetic grins and hasten away; eager, no doubt, to get home to their beds. No flesh off their noses; they'll get paid for the wasted time. Unlike him.

He makes for the nearest waterhole, rinsing the icy liquid around his mouth and spitting out before sucking the rest down his irritated throat. The car from the pool arrives fast for once and he strips off his mask with relief as he climbs into its chilled interior, gives his destination and switches the car to silent; he's not in any mood for 'conversation' with the driver. He's calmer now, more able to rationalise the situation. Had no choice but to give way: local police – and that's him by association – have to defer to the Program Stewards on any reproductive crime and he knew he was walking the line on this one.

It was a nasty case: a series of attacks on young males in the Banleus – the desiccated post-urban sprawl outside the Citi. Not seen anything quite like it before. He's got a strong stomach, but it turned a bit at the sight: each victim staked out naked, penis severed at the base but not, it seems, until after it had been employed sexually by at least one of the attackers. Could, probably should, have passed it to the Stewards from the off: the victims were Program recruits, after all, and, he gives a grim smile,

2

removing the genitals of a fertile male could arguably be seen to be a reproductive matter. But the Banleus are his patch and murder's his business. And anyway, the case was too enticing – and his coin too fast reducing – for him not to take the risk.

World knows how the Stews found out. Tipped off by one of the Uniforms, maybe – not exactly known for their loyalty – or one of Gencom's ubiquitous undercover agents. Whatever, it's well and truly lost now, that's for sure. Proverbial brick wall if he tries to follow up. Probably just as well – doesn't like to dwell on the fate of the female attackers once they reach the Program's holding pens. Most Stewards are ex-Program themselves and won't take kindly to the sexual torture of one of their own.

The car arrives at the central depot, subsiding with a small, deflated sigh, and he squints up at the cloudless sky as he climbs out. Spring's hardly over and it's warming up fast. Hottest summer ever, they're saying. He adjusts the rim of his hat against the bare-faced glare and takes the walkway that flows past the station. Boss is not going to like this. He'll be angry at the wasted time and effort; not just his, but Uniforms too. Resources are tight as a skinfit already, without losing the best part of a two-person week with nothing to show for it. Mind you, if he'd got more resources in the first place he could have beaten the Stews to it; his request for surveillance help having been met with one of his boss's trademark guffaws: *Gotta be joking, Coop. Can't have the men chasing round after Banni girls – can do that in their own time.*

Problem is, more and more's being spent on policing the outer-urbs, where people are struggling to make ends meet. Water's scarce, food's getting short and, top it all, the biting snits have blessed us with their early presence. Add in the burning resentment of the reproductively excluded and it's not surprising the human temperature is rising with the therms. He's sorry for the locals, but public order's not what he went into the job for. It was the idea of old-fashioned sleuthing – solving the puzzle, following the clues – that attracted him.

Growing up he'd sought out vintage detective stories in any shape or form he could find, mostly remastered Old-World 'movies' but also a small and precious number of physical facsimiles. Initially, he was smitten by the old-American private eyes, with their hats and hard-noses, but as he grew older he was drawn more to the methods of the ancient Europeans: their determination to build the theory from the facts, not vice versa. *Follow docilely where the facts may lead*, as the greatest, to his mind, of all the early scientific sleuths would say, *concentrate yourself upon details.*

As he enters the run-down offices of the central station, brushing the red dust from his beloved hat, his spirits take a dive: not been getting much of that sort of work lately. Not been getting much of any sort of work lately, matter of fact; if things don't look up soon, could find himself out with the Uniforms.

2

RED TIDE

As predicted, the boss is not at all pleased. He's standing in Don's large but overcrowded office, nostrils agitated by a lingering mix of stale food and fresh body odour. Possibly even his own.

'Should've got there quicker, Coop,' Don is saying. 'You can be too cautious sometimes, you know – too bloody methodical for your own good. I know you like to do things your own way, and…' he holds up a beefy hand, 'I know you usually get there in the end, but you've got to start speeding up. Fastee fastee, catchee monkee—'

'I think it's softly, softly, Boss.'

'Don't be a smartass, Coop.' Don frowns, eyebrows glistening like slug trails as they make for his nose. 'You know what I mean. We're all under pressure here. Upstairs aren't going to miss any excuse to replace you lot with that high-end kit they're getting in. Damned sight cheaper than humans and,' he swipes a fat finger across each of his sweating brows, 'a damned sight more reliable. Can't keep losing cases, Coop, or you'll be going out with the Upols.'

Just as he'd feared. The Upols (or the F-U pols, as the public likes to call them) are the widely detested street patrols. Their job is to keep the worst of human behaviour away from communal spaces; what goes on in private areas is not their business. *Sweeping the shit under the mat*, as Don describes it. It's unpleasant work and the Upols perform it in a reliably unpleasant way. Most are blatantly corrupt; their low-level of pay based on unspoken agreement that they're free to pursue any commercial 'opportunities' that come their way. A sort of 'dog eat dog' policing strategy.

Doesn't like letting the boss down – respects the hard-boiled male in charge of out-of-Citi policing: the Uniforms, the 'Contracts' like him (Don had refused, point blank, to let him term himself a 'consulting detective') and the vibrant network of street informants employed on a 'pay-as-you-get' basis. Doesn't look it, but he's smart. Knows the outer-urbs, and most of its criminal inhabitants, like the back of his hand. Straight, too. Tells it like it is, as they used to say when they still believed in truth. Some find his directness too much, but personally he likes to know where he stands.

And where he stands right now is not looking good. Could be worse: still got his remaining PA cases to work through – next one tomorrow – and that's better than street patrol, for sure. Unlike the Citi pols, local police have to prosecute their own cases. Most don't relish the job and few, to his mind, have the necessary capabilities anyway. But he likes the work, it's good coin, you get to spend time in the cool of the court, and he's good at it – colleagues say he has a lawyerly manner. Must admit he enjoys the formalities and, yes, the theatrics of it all. Used to get sent a lot of cases, but even this is drying up now they've opened it up to the latest generation of lawbots.

He walks back to his own, considerably less spacious, 'office' – if that's what you could fairly call the hot, just-short-of-a-cupboard he's been allocated in the underground station (bunker, more like). Not that he minds that much. It's a bit bare, admittedly, but that works for him: clear space, clear mind sort of thing. And anyway, his daily aim is to spend as little time in the place as possible.

He opens the casefile and absorbs the key facts: a sad, but increasingly common, situation. Male A signs Female A as Partner then jilts her last minute, at the Program equivalent of the altar, in favour of a younger model. Female A takes male to court for breach of contract, but Gencom, privileging youth, gets him off. Male celebrates with Female B in local bar, but Female A tracks him down, hauls him off his perch, out of the bar, and kicks him up and down the street. Wasn't a small woman either, witnesses said.

So much, so tawdry. Issue for him is that the accused wants to plead Not Guilty to the assault charge, so he's going to have to prepare the case against her. She's saying she entered the contract, properly registered at the Life Office, in good faith – only to be summarily rejected at the last minute. She admits she hit him – a few times only, and not very hard – but claims she was fully justified: deserved what he got for leading her on. Natural justice. Any reasonable female would have done the same in the same situation.

He has some sympathy for the woman, if not the logic of her case. This rejection will be a serious personal loss for her. Given the surfeit of female over male applicants for the Program and, yes, given her relatively advanced years, she probably won't get another chance at Motherhood now. And the publicity from the case won't play well for her either. She's clearly in a fragile mental state and a lengthy court battle's not going to improve things in that department. He'll need to persuade her that the best course of action is to admit what she did, express remorse and fall on the sympathy of the Court. Might get lucky, depending on the Host.

Seems pretty clear to him that her violence draws from the same deep well of female rage as the suspects in his previous case; the group attack was less personal but driven by a similar hatred of a system that is shutting them out. And they're not alone. There's a lot of anger at the Program: how it divides people into reproductive 'haves' and 'have-nots' and how the volume of 'have-nots' is rising fast – even in the Cities (forget it if you live in outer-urbs). Fewer and fewer are making the grade, and resentment of those who *do* get accepted – unfondly known as 'Proggos' – is running high.

For non-reproactive males, it's not the lack of sex (you never miss what you've never had, after all), as much as resentment at the repro-actives' cosseted lives. It's different for females; for them the resentment runs much, much deeper. Unlike males, sterilised pre-birth, all females are born fertile and those rejected by the Program have a very acute sense of what they're missing. The relentlessly rising tide of young female suicides, he's sure, is sourced from precisely that sense of exclusion – the *Red Dirt Cocktail*, they call it: a deadly mix of drugs, disease and despair.

The great irony is that the Program was sold as the ultimate liberation of the female sex. With the universal sterilisation of males, they told us, females would finally be free from sexual attack (at least by biological males). *The end of rape!* Males would benefit too, they said, able to have sex with as many females as let them without any reproductive kickback. *Free love at last!* But things didn't quite turn out that way – as they usually don't with plans that require humans to do what the modellers predict. Some bio females still want sex with males, even without the hope of pregnancy, but most bio males have lost the inclination, if not the ability, to accommodate them – or each other, for that matter. He gives a soft snort. Some might say it's a case of being careful what you wish for.

3

SATURDAY NIGHT

S eth scans the untidy space, checks his pockets and grabs his jacket. Decides against the mask. After activating the lock, he bounds up the stairs, and listens briefly at the communal entrance before leaving the old warehouse building. The night is warm and muggy, the slender light of a waning moon scarcely scratching the sullen sky. Tiny scuds of mist prick his face as he walks - *bad call about the mask* - and he pulls the jacket close. It's one of his father's old animal skins and the lingering smell of its previous owner triggers his guilt. Hasn't seen the old man for over a week. Maybe go around after band tomorrow. But first... there's Viki.

He's going to end things tonight. Finally decided. It's been good, they've had good times, but it's crystal, to him anyway, that they're after very different things: she wants to settle down, old-time marriage sort of thing, maybe a virtbaby or two, and that's the last thing on Earth he wants. He's got plans and she's not part of them. It's not that he doesn't like her; that's the trouble. She's a babe and the sex is cush – he savours the thought as he dislodges a scudflake stinging the corner of his eye – but good as it is, it's not enough. *Don't want to hurt her, but it's better to tell her sooner than later, isn't it – while she's still got time to find someone else? Not fair not to.*

He sees her leaning against the wall under the faltering streetlight – skinny legs in oversized boots; hair like a half-blown seed puff – and he can sense his resolve is about to make a run for it. He gives it a quick stiffening before he calls out to her, and she smiles and pushes herself up from the wall, strands of hair snagging on the crumbling brick. As he pulls her to him and kisses her soft, damp lips, a low stirring in his gut tells him just how much he's going to miss the physical closeness. He tries to linger in the embrace, but she moves back to the wall, smile slipping away.

'Got some news,' she says, clearly avoiding his eyes. 'Let's talk… over there.'

They walk, unspeaking, to an old sitting stone at the edge of the common ground, where he waits as she picks at her sleeve with thin, almost translucent, fingers; nails nibbled to the quick. *What's coming here? Something's up. Maybe she's going finish with me. Maybe she's got someone else.* He scoffs at himself for what he recognises as an entirely unjustified twinge of jealousy.

'It's good news,' she says at last, still not quite catching his eye. She hesitates again, then says in an almost-whisper: 'I'm pregnant.'

'Sorry?' He stares at her. *She didn't just say what I thought she just said, did she?*

She did.

'I'm pregnant, Seth,' she repeats more firmly, looking at him now, her pale violet eyes excited. 'We're going to have a baby. A real-life, human baby.'

'Yeah right!' He laughs out loud at this absurdity. 'Very funny, Vik – not.'

But something in her pale, eager face tells him she's not actually joking, and his scorn dries in his mouth. *What the fuck? Where's this come from? Has she taken something? Or maybe it's one of her 'how much do you love me' tests.*

'You sure about this, Vik?' he ventures.

She nods. 'Aunt Sis says it's about three months. I'm sure too...' She searches his face, but he can't – won't – disguise his disbelief and she drops her gaze again.

'But you know it can't be mine, Vik, don't you?' he says, taking her hand. 'You know that's just not possible.'

She reacts as if she's been slapped, getting to her feet and turning to him, eyes brilliant with hurt. 'So, what, you think I've been with someone else? That's what you think of me, is it?'

'Course not, Vik!' he says as he eases her back down and puts his arm around her thin shoulders. 'It's just that... well, can't see how it could've happened.'

'Well, it obviously did happen, didn't it? Or do you think I'm lying?'

'No, Vik,' he says quickly, 'but... dunno... couldn't you be mistaken somehow?'

'Mistaken how exacts?' She bristles, shrugging off his arm. 'Immaculate conception, maybe? Or d'you think I'm just fooling myself? Yes, that's it, isn't it?' she gasps, her eyes widening with anger. 'You think I want this so much I'm imagining it, don't you?'

'No, Vik,' he forces himself to say, 'course not.'

But this is precisely what he does think as they sit in silence, the restless night pressing in on them. That, and the fact that, if she's right, he's in some serious deep shit.

4

COMING HOME

'**Y**ou told him yet?'

Viki nods but focuses on the unedifying and, she now realises, largely ineffectual task of shifting the obdurate mass of skin colonising the severely overburdened feet of her aunt.

'So, how'd he take it?' the pedicuree persists.

Good question. And right now, one to which she's not sure she's got the answer.

'Yeah, okay; think he's pleased.'

She smiles to cover the falsehood: *hadn't looked pleased at all, had he? Anything but. Looked like he wanted to run a mile. Well, he can run all he likes, with that stupid band and his bestie friend, Queron. Got what I wanted, haven't I?* She knows he doesn't love her, if she's honest – not in the way she loves him – and that he was always going leave her one day. *But* – she allows herself a fleeting hope – *maybe he'll feel different now, with the baby...*

'He'll be worried about the risks, likely,' her aunt is saying, shaking her sparsely covered head. 'Can't say he's wrong there, hun, to be fair. Not heard of any who's tried it outside the system and lived to tell the tale.'

She says nothing, knowing that her aunt means well, and suspecting the likely truth of her words, but there's nothing her aunt or anyone's going to say that will change her mind. Not now. She smooths her hand over her scarcely swelling stomach with a shiver of anticipation.

'It's a dangerous business, childbirth,' her aunt is continuing, 'for all it's a natural thing. Aunt Sis has some of the old skills, but if anything goes wrong… And that's if you get as far as the birth. Not sure what we'll do when it starts to show.' She hesitates and leans forward to take her niece's hand, provoking a weary creak of protest from the chair beneath her.

'It's not too late to let it go, Viki, love. There's hardly anything of it yet—'

'I'm not getting rid of it, Aunts!' she says sharply, pulling her hand back, a little hurt that the older woman would suggest such a thing. 'Why in the World would I do that? Only chance I'm ever likely to get.'

She sees the slight protrusion of her aunt's lower lip and softens. 'I know it's a big risk for you, and for Aunt Sis. But we can go away. I've been finding out: there's groups, communes sort of thing, out in the Edgelands where you can bring up illegals. There's women there who've had illicit births themselves and know what to do.' She strokes the older woman's podgy fingers. 'I don't want to get you and Aunt Sis in trouble. You've both been so good to me—'

'Oh no, Vik, hun,' her aunt says quickly, 'that's not what I was saying. If you decide to go through with it, of course we'll help you. You can't be going off into the back of beyond with complete strangers. You need to stay close to your own at a time like this. They're welcome to do what they like to me and I know Aunt Sis feels the same. The chance for you to be a Mother…' She breaks off, her puffy eyes filling.

She gets up and kisses the older woman's powdery head. 'Love ya, Aunts.' She shakes the little pile of foot detritus into the combustor. 'So that's the feet done. Is there anything else needs doing while I'm here?'

'No, love. You've done enough. Can't have been the most pleasant of jobs,' her aunt says with a grimace. 'You're a good girl, Viki – don't know what I'd do without you. Have you time for a cuppa before you go, love? Got a bit of news…'

Viki makes the tea quickly, intrigued by the idea of news. 'So…?' she asks, as she sets out the cups on the table.

'Yes, well, no good beating about the bush,' her aunt says in a trying-to-be-bright sort of way as she pours the tea. 'Thing is… Naz is coming back.'

'Woah – talk about a bolt from beyond. For a visit, or for good?'

'For good, I think,' the older woman says. 'Had enough of it out there, no wonder.'

'Woah…' she says again, sitting back in her chair. 'Naz back. How long's it been, Aunts, five years?'

'Very nearly six. Went off in the autumn of '54 after that bit of trouble with the police.'

She tries to recall her only sibling. They weren't that close: he was six years older and wasn't at home much towards the end. He could be mean and selfish (although probably no more than she was to him) but he never physically hurt her, like she'd heard some brothers did, and he always looked out for her when she went out in public. But still, she's got very mixed feelings about his return. On the one hand she's intrigued to see what kind of man has grown from the boy she knew. On the other, much stronger, hand she's not at all sure about his coming back into their lives – especially now. Things are tight as it is: *Hard Coin Is Hard Come*, as the advirt says. They're only just managing on what she brings home from the market and the donations her aunt receives for her readings. And that's before the baby arrives.

'Is he planning to stay with us?' she asks.

'Well, yes, probably – for a bit, at least.'

'But where's he going to sleep?'

'Well, that's what I wanted to talk to you about, hun,' her aunt says, shifting in the chair. 'You'll need to double up with me for a bit; let him have your space—'

'No, Aunts! That's not fair,' she snaps, losing hold of a temper that's far too quick to get away these days. 'Why do I have to give up my space? Why can't he sleep downstairs?'

'Well, he'll need a bit of privacy – as a male—'

'Well, I need privacy too! As a female! Especially with the baby coming…' She closes her eyes to stem the tears of angry self-pity.

'Oh, he'll likely be gone by then,' her aunt says in an airy way. 'My friend says he can get him work at the allotments. That'd suit Naz; obsessed with growing things as a child – was always on at me to take him to the plant museum—'

'Yeah, cush for him,' she breaks in, 'but what they pay on the allots's not going to bring much in, is it?' She takes a deep breath; doesn't like getting cross with the old woman – hates it when her bottom lip trembles – but how could she agree to something like that without even talking to her?

'Look, Viki, love,' her aunt takes hold of her hand, 'shouldn't be saying this but, if I'm honest, I've got mixed feelings too. I like it just the two of us. I know Naz's like my own, but he's been away a long time. And…' she looks around as if fearing a listener, 'what if he's become hardened… brutalised? I've heard some terrible things about what goes on out there.'

'Well, that's just mad to think like that, Aunts,' she says, cooling down. 'Not everybody who goes to the Edgelands comes home a potential murderer, if that's what you mean. That's give a dog a bad name – Popnuze sort of stuff.'

Her aunt lets out a heavy sigh, triggering a rustling echo across the vast folds of her gown. 'Yes, you're probably right, Vik. Let's wait until we see him.' She gives her a sly look. 'Won't be long now, actually.'

'What? How long, exacts?'

'Well...' again the uneasy shift in the long-suffering chair, 'said he could make it for dinner tonight if he can get the early trans. Could be here when you get back...'

5

THE RESTORATIONS

Coop looks around the semi-circular arena – its tiered seats filling fast with brightly clad bodies. There's an anticipatory murmur swelling the cooled air and a tangible sense of collective gaiety. It's a paid day off work, after all, for the lucky few at least, so folks are inclined to make a bit of an outing of the whole event – despite its often-sober nature – stepping out in their best clothes and sunniest dispositions.

It's also one of the few occasions when Citi and non-Citi folks get together. All adults in the territory have to attend twice a year as part of their citizen duty or lose their right to the 'dal', the universal stipend. But there's limits to the extent of social mingling that actually goes on. The visually distinctive communities tend to accumulate in different sections of the stadium and, more often than not, on opposing sides of the moral debate. And VIPs, of course, can reserve the scenic seats – not exactly overflowing today – or indeed, attend virtually. Still, with all that, it's a rare opportunity for two very different social tribes to observe each other at close hand.

With any luck, it'll be a quick in and out today. He'd eventually convinced the still-angry Female A that a plea of Guilty would be very much in her best interest: humility, contrition and the full admission of guilt, he knows, always plays well with today's Hosts. *Favourable wind and all that, could be in for a lunch-time swim.*

He gazes at the stage where the Court motto – *To each according to their work* – is scrolling across the backscreen. The large, wrought-iron symbol of the Theists sits centre stage, surrounded by a horseshoe of finely carved high-backed chairs, in front of which are the virtual cages; can't see the walls, but they give the poor sods a hell of a shock if they touch them. Two sturdy wooden podiums face each other across the stage: on the left – a seat his backside has warmed many times – for the Public Accuser; on the right for the Public Defender. As it happens, the roles divide by binary sex: PDs are mostly female and PAs predominantly male; it's not old-fashioned discrimination – never get away with that – more an attempt to add a certain 'battle of the biosexes' nostalgia to the proceedings. The sexual Others routinely complain – to little effect.

There's movement on the stage. The Judges are taking their seats, wearing various guises of solemnity and sagacity. They're all certified 'high life-worth' individuals with exemplary records (or deep pockets) but most will sell their pardons for surprisingly little. Judges come from all sexes, but the session Hosts are always biological male – a red line for one of the larger sects that continues to this day to believe in the moral inferiority of the female and simply refuses to recognise the existence of any of the proliferating alternative genders.

Why they decided to give the Theists the job of managing the Low Courts is beyond him. Suppose they had to give them something to do, once their role in other human life events – the 'hatches, matches and dispatches', as they used to call it – had been taken under the Program's wing. They also needed to buy the faith organisations off, of course, to ensure their compliance with the New Reproductive Order: they were still very powerful and wealthy, even towards the end. Most likely, though, none of the Planners cared very much about the quality of justice dealt out to those in the outer settlements; any matter of importance to them and theirs would be handled by the Citi's High Courts.

The buzz of the crowd subsides as a small, brown-skinned male walks to centre stage. His almost perfectly round form is wrapped in purple and cut across by a wide, gold-embroidered sash; his small head is bald as an egg. A large silver replica of the Theist symbol hangs around his neck and another, smaller, version hangs on a chain secured in the vicinity of where his waist should be. He clears his throat with a dainty cough, welcomes the audience and introduces himself, with a small bow, as Host of the show. Each of the Judges, now looking suitably self-deprecating, is introduced in turn and acknowledged with varying degrees of enthusiasm by the crowd.

'The process of the Court is straightforward,' the Host explains, his thin voice belying his bulk. 'The Accused will be asked how they plead: Guilty or Not Guilty. If the plea is Not Guilty, the Accused, and any Witnesses to the crime, will be questioned, and the evidence addressed, first by the Public Accuser and then by the Public Defender. The Judges will then assess the arguments and verifiable facts and make a recommendation as to Guilt or Innocence.

'However,' he raises his arms, revealing tiny feet in high-heeled shoes, 'while you will of course wish to consider the informed advice of our valued panel of Judges, it is you, the People, who will make the final decision, by means of a direct majority vote, recorded' – he indicates two cylindrical light-tubes now appearing centre stage – 'on the Visual Verdicator. If the plea is Guilty,' he nods towards the panel of exemplary citizens, 'my esteemed colleagues will stand down and you, the People, will vote on the punishment to be given.'

Punishment. Coop shakes his head. *That's the bit the crowd likes – the more brutal the better. Flaying with branches is on a comeback and stoning is consistently popular.* Never fails to depress him how much human effort and ingenuity is expended on ways to give pain to fellow human beings, nor the appetite of supposedly decent people for the inhuman sights involved. Wasn't supposed to be like this. The Low Courts, or Restorations, as they're known, were set up to deal with local grievances and crimes against the community – a place for the public 'righting of wrongs', as it were. But in the hands of the old faiths, they've become less a forum for restoration and reparation than an outlet for collective revenge and retribution.

The crowd makes a sudden noise – half gasp, half hiss – as a young male is propelled up into the illuminated virtual cage at the front of the stage. He is small and rat-like; lank hair hanging in tails down his back; skinny body enfolded in a pink overall many sizes too big. His face twitches as he tries to conjure up a bravado he evidently lacks, and he shifts from foot to foot. As he registers the full spectacle of the event, he stands stock still, frozen in the unsparing gaze of the crowd.

'Are you Tomas Johnson, of Banleu 7, born on the eighth day of the tenth month of NL Thirty-Two?' the Host asks. The man starts in recognition and turns towards him, clearly struggling to take it all in. The question is repeated with a patient smile, this time eliciting a grunt and a nod of assent from the invisibly shackled man.

'Tomas Johnson,' the Host continues with as much gravitas as his thin voice allows, 'you are charged here today – in the Court of your fellow Citizens – that, on the third night of the sixth month of the year NL Sixty, you did unlawfully break into Banleu Four community store and steal five bags of rice and two sacks of potatoes. How do you plead: Guilty or Not Guilty?'

The small dark eyes of the Accused dart around him at the assembled dramatis personae and calculation creases his greasy forehead. The rotund Host addresses him again. 'I ask you once more, Tomas: are you or are you not guilty of stealing food from the common store?'

Calculation made, the man replies. 'Yes, your worship, honour, I took it, but—'

Hisses and boos emit from the crowd. Small objects skit and splink against the invisible walls surrounding the hapless man. Calls of 'Shame on you!' and 'Disgrace!' are joined by excited suggestions as to the nature of the punishment to be given. Flinching at the ineffective projectiles, the accused man brushes against the security wall and Coop cringes as he falls to his knees with a howl of pain.

The Host moves closer to the prisoner, his voice becoming shrill. 'Stand up, Tomas, and face your fellow Citizens.' The man does so, head held low, face hidden by sullen strands of hair. 'Did you do this thing of your own free will?' the Host asks.

The man looks up at him with a blank look.

'Did anyone make you take the food, Tomas?'

The rat-tails shake.

'Did you know that what you were doing was wrong, Tomas?'

Tomas gives a glum nod.

'Have you anything to say in your defence?'

The thin man shakes his head, clearly desperate to see the end of the whole proceedings.

'Not even that you are sorry for what you did?' the clerical compere prompts.

A glimmer of understanding shows in his feral eyes. 'Oh yeah... yes, your worship, honour...' he says as he snatches the lifeline. 'I'm sols... sorry. It was a, er... sinful thing and I want to, er, what's it? Repent. That's it. I want to repent, init?' He gives his inquisitor a sly look and turns to face the crowd, adopting a mantis-like stance. 'I truly repent and throw meself on the mercy of the Court. Melawd, Sir.'

The Host's upper lip twitches as he turns to address the audience. 'There you have it, my friends. The Accused admits to committing a grave crime, of his own free will and in the clear knowledge that it was sinful. He has nothing to say in his defence but wants you to know that he is truly sorry for his actions. As he has admitted his crime, we do not need to consult our esteemed Judges. It passes directly to you, the People, to decide the fate of Mr Johnson.' He looks out at the crowd with a solemn expression, bringing his fingers together over his protruding stomach.

'In reaching your Judgment you will need to know that none of the food was recovered. It had been consumed, or sold, by the Accused. You will also need to know that this is not the first time the Accused has stolen from the common weal. In this light, you will need to decide carefully how much weight you feel able to give to his claims of true repentance,' the Host gestures at the Menu of Punishment that has appeared centre stage, 'as you make your decision about the particular "dish" to be served up to this sinner tonight. In addition to the statutory punishments, and as is our privilege as Host, my organisation will be offering additional punishment options, at no extra cost to the community purse. You have five minutes to make your judgment, starting now. No conferring, please.'

Coop looks towards the stage where a series of differently coloured light columns has appeared, their relative heights fluctuating wildly – although purple seems to be edging ahead. The buzzer sounds and the Host teeters to the front of the stage, arms raised.

'Time is up; voting is now closed. If you use your vote now, it will be wasted.'

He turns towards the columns of light and then to the condemned man cowering in the invisible cage. 'Tomas Johnson, your fellow Citizens have spoken. It seems they feel, as indeed do I, that in the light of your past crimes, your profession of repentance rings a little hollow.' He points to the purple column, now the clear winner.

'They have selected, by a considerable majority, today's Special:

Abjection. You will be taken from this court and branded – on both your physical and virtual selves – with the indelible mark of the Thief. The World will be able to see you clearly – at all times and for all the time you have – for what you are.'

Tomas gazes at the Host, eyes wide, mouth slightly open, visibly struggling to understand the fate that has just befallen him.

'Take him away,' the Host says with a flourish of his embroidered sleeve, as the still-uncomprehending male is lowered through the floor.

Well, that's a new one on him: existential exclusion, poor bastard. He scoffs and shakes his head. Got to hand it to the Theists: you can always count on them for ever-new ways to create a hell on Earth.

He feels an insistent tugging at his sleeve and he looks down to see the placid countenance of a courtbot smiling fixedly at him. 'Detective Cooper-Clark?' the bot asks, although of course it knows him intimately.

'Would you like to come with me now, please, Sir? Your case is on next and you will need some moments to prepare. The accused has changed her plea to Not Guilty.'

He groans as the smooth-featured bot motions for him to follow. Can forget about that swim; worst-case scenario – there are no less than eleven witnesses to call – could be stuck here all afternoon.

6

FLESH AND BLOOD

She sees her mother, Ida, asleep under the old tree, its scraggy branches providing the only, and only just adequate, shade in the small patch of land her mother stubbornly calls 'the garden'. Ida is snoring, open-mouthed, eyes covered, outdoor gloves fallen at her feet. Bulging sacks of rubbish stand around her like silent sentinels. Lyse approaches without noise and looks at her sleeping parent, shocked by how aged she looks in the unforgiving morning light. *And so thin!* She bends down and pecks the time-traced cheek.

Her mother starts and looks up, shielding her eyes as she rises awkwardly from the low chair. 'Oh, hello, Lyse, love. Was I asleep? Only meant to sit down for a minute. Just tidying up after those wicked winds last night.'

'Well, looks good now.' She dissembles, scanning the sad little plot where, it is clear, her mother's Sisyphean struggle against the drying of the land is slowly being lost. She points to one of the few signs of sturdy life. 'They're pretty, Ma.'

'Ha yes, Lion's Teeth.' Her mother smiles. 'Used to pull them up as weeds; now we're pleased for the little bit of colour they bring.' She goes over to the yellow-headed plants and twists off a few stalks that she waves at Lyse. 'We'll have these for lunch. Are the others coming back, d'you know?'

As her mother washes the leaves, she wanders over to the cold store and examines the tab. *Just as I thought – zero activity since 7.00am. No wonder she looks so thin.* She frowns at Ida. 'This hasn't been opened since breakfast, Ma. You'll get ill if you don't get your daily quota.'

'Don't fuss, Lyse,' Ida says, her colour rising. 'I'm not a child; I'll eat when I want. Eat to live, not live to eat, that's what I say.'

'Yeah, well, perhaps you need to work more on the eat to live side of things, that's all I'm saying,' she persists, gesturing at her mother's insubstantial frame. 'There's hardly anything of you.'

Ida, warming to one of her frequent annoyances, ignores her. 'There's just too much of everybody minding my business, if you ask me. Not saying you, of course, dear, but there's spies everywhere in this house, watching everything, sending reports—'

'I'll get lunch,' she breaks in, familiar with the protracted length of her mother's diatribes once they get started. 'What's to eat – apart from the leaves?'

'There's some of that so-called cheese on the top at the back,' Ida says. 'World knows what they put in it, but its protein content is high, and there's a few of my tomatoes left, next shelf down. Not a great crop this year: bit small. Impossible to give them enough water, even with the amount you all use. There's the remains of the carb block on the bottom shelf – you'll find a little goes a long way – and the fat is in the cold store.' Ida examines her hands. 'I'll just go and have a quick wash, if you're okay doing this,' she says as she pads out of the room in her thick outdoor socks.

She has the food assembled by the time Ida returns, rubbing salve into her weathered hands. 'Found some pickles, Ma,' she says, 'and this sausage thing looks like it needs eating up. Sniffer says it's still okay.'

'Lovely,' her mother says, plumping up her thin hair as they sit down to their modest meal. 'I am a bit hungry, as it happens – perhaps the spies get some things right after all. Anyway,' she beams at her, 'I'm not getting cross about anything today. Not with your results!'

She gives an inward sigh. The results from their Sec finals came through yesterday and she, her brother Jai and adopted sider Ammi have all scored highly – herself much better than expected. She is pleased she's done well, but she knows this means her mother will try (yet again) to change her mind about going to music college, worried that she needs *something more reliable to fall back on* when it all comes to nothing, as she clearly thinks it will.

'Have you had any more thoughts about the autumn?' Ida asks, on cue. 'You'll need to decide soon. You could do a lot more than music now, you know, with your grades.'

'Don't start, Ma,' she snaps, more sharply than intended. 'I'm going to music college – end of.'

She's disappointed her mother doesn't seem to understand that music's the only thing she's ever wanted to do – hooked the minute her father showed her how to pick out the chords on his guitar. Real music, that is, not the formulaic junk churned out by algorithm-overdosing tunebots that passes for music these days. *But Ma's right; it's a tough field and many (most, probably) don't make it.* And her mother's doubts hit a deeper nerve. The heady excitement of the results has given way to an unexpected emotional flatness. A big part of her life has just ended and she's happy about that, but her eagerness to move on is not without a undertone of apprehension. She looks around the eatery, the bright and colourful heart of the run-down family home. It's a much quieter place now her father's gone and she and her siblings are old enough to enter public life, but the large, hard-scrubbed and much-scarred wooden table in the middle of the room has been the centre of her social universe for as long as she can recall. *Gonna be strange without it.*

They finish eating (Ida eventually) and sit without talking for a while, drinking their tea. She's planned a night out with Jai and Ammi to celebrate the results – live band she's heard about that's supposed to be kuru. Trouble is, it's over in the Bannies and Am, typically, is fussing about the biorisks, amongst other stuff. Had to get Jai to talk her round in the end but there's still a chance she'll get cold feet at the last minute – she's done that before. Lyse clicks her tongue; her adopted sister's over-cautious nature is extremely annoying. Ditto her tendency to hang on Jai's every word.

'So, about the other big decision?' her mother asks. 'Have you thought about that at all? Ammi's applying this year, as you know.'

'No, I didn't know that actually.' She's surprised and a bit hurt by this. 'Hasn't said anything to me. Thought she wanted to do Voyager stuff. Can't do that if she's starting on the Program, can she?'

'Well, perhaps I'm speaking out of turn here,' Ida says hastily. 'You'd best talk to her yourself. But remember, Ly, she's not like you or Jai. She lost her family very young. She's like a daughter to me, and a sister to you both, but we're not her flesh and blood, as it were. We can accept her as our own, but I'm not sure she can do the same for us. Maybe going on the Program is about having someone that's truly "hers", so to speak.'

'Woah.' She laughs, uncomfortable with the turn of the conversation. 'All a bit deep, Ma. Is the flesh and blood thing really that important? Does it matter who actually has the babies – as long as there's enough of them getting born?'

Ida doesn't reply and the distant look in her eyes prompts Lyse to ask – for the first time – about her mother's choice. 'Was that why you went for the Program? Because you and Pa wanted your own… "flesh and blood"?'

'Well… it was a big thing to do then and we were proud to do it. We were treated like national heroes. The *Mothers of the New World*, it was. There was a lot of media interest in us – you too.' Lyse recalls the image that went global for a slice of a second: her

27

chubby baby-self looking out from her mother's knee, startled but eager to please.

'I wasn't like you,' her mother is continuing. 'I didn't really have much idea of what I wanted to do. And I liked your father well enough.' She laughs. 'But it was a lot of pressure: all the weighing and measuring, poking and prodding. Testing for *this* and *that*—'

'You're not selling it, Ma.' She laughs. 'Anyway, there's loads of time yet.'

'There's not, actually—' Ida begins, but breaks off as the back door opens and Ammi enters, gently shaking the dust off a slender bunch of dark red flowers.

'One of the street vendors had got hold of these,' the new arrival says, handing the blooms to Ida with a wide smile, 'and I thought, I know someone who would like them.'

'How lovely!' Ida says, taking the flowers and kissing the proffered cheek. 'Haven't seen real tulips for years. What a sweet girl you are.'

Typical Ammi, Lyse thinks as she sees her mother's visible pleasure at the gift. *Little Miss Perfect: always doing the nice thing. Perhaps Ma's right with that stuff about family and belonging; maybe she feels she has to keep buying the likes.* She gives her adopted sibling a cool smile, but Ammi looks so genuinely pleased to see her that she instantly regrets her sourness, much of which, she knows full well, is cover for her own limitations in the 'doing nice things' department.

Her mother is gesturing at the remnants on the table. 'There's plenty left, Ammi. Come and sit down. Lyse and I were just talking about—'

'College,' she interjects quickly, not wishing to return to the Program discussion. 'Just saying I've decided to go to music college in the autumn. But you knew that already, didn't you?' She narrows her eyes at her adopted sibling. 'Because we tell each other everything, don't we, Am?'

7

FATHER AND SON

Seth is making his way to his father's house, taking – ill-advisedly, he now realises – the main route through the Citi's administrative centre. It's early evening and the autowalk is crowded with placid workbots returning to the central depots and only slightly less docile humans hurrying home or out to the pleasure plazas. He takes a few lungfuls of the cool air, enjoying the ease with which it slips in and out, almost without trace. One thing he did miss when he moved to the Banleus: being able to breathe easy – although, has to say, there's an undertone of something not quite so pleasant in the *mowed grass and honeysuckle* flavour of today's offer.

What he doesn't miss is the eerie quiet; apart from the soft sighing of the street cars and air trans, and the endless birdsong soundtrack, the streets – even in the heart of the Citi – are almost silent. No bot is able, and no human would think, to stop in public to talk to an unknown human – unless an emergency. And probably not even then.

He's mulling over Viki's news. *Can't be true. No-one gets*

pregnant off-Program. Just doesn't happen. That's the whole point of the effin' thing. Maybe the aunt's mistaken or maybe it *is* all in Vik's mind – a phantom of her desire sort of thing. Heard about that: when someone wants something so much they can make themselves believe it's happened. And totally no-one can want anything more than Viki wants a baby. *Or maybe,* he thinks as the walkway stops to let an emergency trans pass, *maybe there was (is?) another man.* Nah, he shakes his head, Viki wouldn't lie; most truthful person he knows – too truthful and trusting if anything. But what if it happened while she was out of it somehow – like drugged or deep in a virt? There's stories of otakus being robbed when they were, literally, out of this World. But who's going to do that? No repro's going to risk knocking up a Banni girl.

But what if...? He stops in his tracks, causing a badly reconditioned early era workbot to skid off course. *What if she's not got it wrong; what if, somehow, in some mad way, there actually is a baby? My baby.* A tentative flicker of excitement, swiftly doused in a flash-flood of anxiety: how'd that ever work? Stews would find them, sooner or later, wouldn't they? Or someone would talk – nothing gets missed round the Banleus. And World knows what'd happen if (when) they got caught. Kiss the band and the tour goodbye for a start. 'Nah,' he says out loud with a firm shake of his head, attracting looks of mild concern from passing carebots. *Get a grip. This isn't real. There is no baby. Or, if there is, it ain't mine, babe.*

He takes a turn off the central routeway towards the Citi's northern residential quarter. Used to be quite smart but it's pretty run-down now – out of fashion, mostly full of oldies like his father. Young families live in the Program's residential parks, and affluent singletons prefer the mobile prefabs near the ports and recreation hubs; no-one wants inflexible stone boxes parked permanently at the edge of the Citi. Those who would live here are put off by the cost of maintaining the ageing buildings, not to mention the skyrocketing taxes. The few trees still standing give the area an attractive Old-Worldly look, even if they're no longer alive in the technical sense, packed as they are with preservative and programmed to simulate the changing of the seasons – without the insanitary problem of fallen leaves, of course.

He sees the hunched shape of his father, Marcus, through the window of his childhood home and feels a tug of guilt. It's at least a week since they spoke, and much longer since they last had any real time together. He knows his widowed parent is lonely; doesn't have any friends apart from his card buddy Thelma and spends most of his time with his vinyl collection or in the memory lanes of Citernity clinging to the digital remains of Ma. Went there with him once, to the Arcade. He shudders. *Never again – total weird out. Better let the dead go, to my mind, than keep them hanging round like shadows.*

His father gives him a long, hard hug and he lingers in the embrace, breathing in the familiar old-man smell. 'Sorry it's been so long, Pa.'

'No worries, son,' Marcus says, patting him on the back as he lets him go. 'I know you're busy these days. Go and sit down and I'll bring us a beer.'

He establishes a seat-hold amongst the ill-assorted piles of stuff littering the ancient sofa and glances round the cluttered room. It is as it always was, as long back as he can remember. Not a speck appears to have changed in the five years since Ma died. Bit dirtier and dustier, though; even he can see it could do with a good clean. *Maybe I could offer to help*, he thinks for a brief, unconvincing moment.

'Oh, by the way,' he says, pulling a small packet from his pocket as his father returns with the beer, 'brought you this. Q got hold of some the other day and he knows you're a bit partial.'

Marcus looks delighted, eyes quickly scanning the room for the whereabouts of his beloved pipe. He opens the gold and green wrap and gives it a deep sniff. 'Oh my… that's good, that is. Best not to ask where Queron got it from, eh?'

'Yeah, Pa.' He laughs. 'Best not to ask.'

He watches Marcus stoke the pipe from the bright little packet, tamping the curly brown strands firmly down into the bowl, and catches the acrid whiff of phosphorous as the match is struck, the faint crackle of burning leaves and the first twisting lines of grey smoke. He enjoys the old man's visible pleasure, although it occurs, fleetingly, that he probably shouldn't be encouraging him in his illegal habit.

'And how is Queron – talking of the devil?' Marcus asks, taking a long pull on the pipe. 'And the band? Everything going well?'

He starts with the positives: that the band's been getting good crowds – bit of a following, actually (mostly girls for Queron, but still); that the management's agreed they can add some of their own songs to the set and that soon, six months, maybe, he reckons, they'll be ready for the tour. He sits forward as his excitement increases, causing a teetering pile of papers to spill onto the floor.

'Time's totally right, Pa, live music's exploding and we want to be part of that,' he says, gathering the fallen papers together. 'Only one problem…'

Marcus raises his eyebrows.

'Queron,' he says, sitting back on the sofa. 'Not putting in, keeps missing practice – even one actual gig. Keeps saying he's sorry and it won't happen again. Blah de blah. But then it does. If Q pulls out, Pa,' he says with an extended grimace, 'that'll be that; band's nothing without him.'

'Well, maybe he's got something going on in his life,' his father suggests, waving away the loitering smoke. 'Money problems, maybe, or a girl? Doesn't give much away, Queron, never did. Unlike you – heart on your sleeve, tell anybody anything. Maybe it's his work; what's he doing these days, anyway?'

'Bit of this, bit of that, like the rest of us.' He shrugs, not liking to admit that he doesn't really know what his oldest friend gets up to outside the band. 'Whatever turns up, mostly. Not much stable work outside the Citi these days.'

He doesn't think it is money – Queron always seems pretty

flush, and girls aren't his thing – so maybe it is the day job. *Whatever, I'm gonna have to pin him down sooner rather than later. But right now…* his stomach turns: bad as he feels about Queron, it's not the worst thing on his mind. There's Viki. He hesitates; even with his father it all feels a bit personal and he's going to look pretty stupid if she's lying, isn't he? But only Pa would know if there's any chance…

'Is there something else on your mind, son?' Marcus asks perceptively.

He's swallows his discomfort. 'Well, you're not going to believe this, Pa…'

Marcus very nearly loses control of the pipe in his mouth. 'That's not possible, Seth! You cannot possibly be the father. You were snipped pre-birth like all the rest. Mother didn't like it – no-one did. For the greater good, they said – and there was no avoiding it. Viki must be fooling you – or herself. Had relations with some other man and he's scarpered and left her to it. One of the old snip dodgers, I'd wager. Still a few of them around and Banni girls are doing desperate things to have babies. Not that Viki's like that, I know,' he says quickly, waving his pipe at him. 'But however much you trust her, you've got to make sure for yourself. There's tests they can do—'

'But I can't go to a clinic, Pa. I'm not on the Program system and there's nowhere else that does that sort of thing.'

'No, true,' Marcus nods, 'but I'll ask Thelma, she's some kind of medic – gives me something for my knee that seems to work, anyhow. She'll know how to get a test done, if anyone does. Got cards tonight and can ask her, if you like?'

'Yeah, great, thanks.' He drains the last of his beer, relieved finally to have got the weight off his chest, and stands up. 'Better be off. Sound check in an hour.' He pecks his father's smoky cheek. 'Thanks, Pa. Great to talk. Pin me if this Thelma woman can help.'

'Will do, son.' Marcus gives him another tight hug. 'Don't you worry too much about this, Seth, lad; I'm sure it's all a big mistake.

Mind you…' he says as Seth turns to leave, 'best keep the whole thing under your hat in any case. And make sure young Viki does too. Even if there's nothing in it, these things tend to get around.'

'Oh, cheers, Pa, just when I was starting to feel a bit better!' He grins, but he's calmer now as he leaves the house and hurries down the path. *Pa's right: can't make any decisions til I know the truth of it. Just have to hope the Thelma bird comes up with the goods.* His steps quicken. Not until he reaches the end of the road does he realise he never asked his father how he was.

Later, he's just about turning in when he gets a pinX – an urgent, self-destruct flasher that hangs around making an unearthly row until attended to. It's from Marcus, who sounds a little breathless, if not inebriated. Tells him Thelma's agreed to arrange the test but says it would be madness for them to try to go through with a pregnancy, whoever's the father. Someone would inform on them, she says, if there's coin to be earned, and not to mention the Gencom spies everywhere. If anything went wrong they'd have to go to a Program unit – nowhere else will touch human babies – and they'd find out straight away it was an illegal. No, his father says, his voice unsteady – his old friend was adamant they had only one option: if they have, against all the odds, started a baby, they must terminate it immediately.

8

THE BANLEUS

Lyse and her siblings are crossing over the North Bridge – one of the four great arcs spanning the vast human-made waterway separating the Citi from the surrounding settlements – on their way to the club Lyse had heard about. The expedition had begun in good spirits, despite Ammi's initial reluctance, but as they reach the end of the bridge, the three fall silent. It's the first time any of them has ventured outside the Citi and everything feels very different. Beneath the translucent structure the shining water lies still, as if waiting for something to pass, and the darkening sky, devoid of cloud, seems watchful. The ground around them – studded with sawtooth scrub and criss-crossed with thin, foot-beaten trails – is visibly poorer than the Citi's manicured banks, and the air is palpably thicker, much rougher than their young lungs are used to.

Lyse senses the shift in mood. 'It's not far,' she says, squinting at a hand-drawn map. 'Looks like it's through that archway over there. Let's go…'

The archway is dark and damp, its walls a ragged patchwork of text and images flirting for attention. Many are adverts for goods and services: to sell or exchange; people for hire (anything considered); people wanted – to care or be cared for; medical help sought, and remedies purveyed; information about meetings, events, activities. Others, more vividly graphic, are calls to action or warnings of one kind or another:

Lyse finds the one she was seeking and calls the others over, holding up a grainy image of a black-clad group of males that she's detached from the wall. 'This is the band. The Beatniks. Shuai, eh, Am?'

'Er, no,' says Ammi, her small, straight nose twitching with dislike, 'not my type at all – too glooms…'

Did she just look at Jai when she said that? And when did she get to have a 'type', anyway? Maybe it's something to do with starting on the Program. Maybe that changes the way you look at biomales. She gives a shudder of distaste. She hasn't talked to Ammi about her decision to sign up (hadn't wanted to give her any excuse to pull out of the trip) and still feels hurt about not being told, but she's not going to let that, or anything else, spoil things tonight.

They emerge from the dank tunnel to be hit by wafts of hot air carrying a pungent cocktail of aromas. Some are quite pleasant, enticing even. Others are curious, indescribable; many simply disgusting. The central thread in this tapestry of smells is a pungent musty-sour tang. 'Ganj,' Jai says, inhaling, his attempt to sound authoritative undermined by a rough burst of coughing. After her nose has adjusted to the olfactory ambush, Lyse's ears are accosted by the noise; the thick wall of sound rising from the mass of human beings around them, engaged, face to face, in all kinds of social and economic exchange.

'Woah,' Ammi exclaims softly, eyes wide. 'All a bit up close and personal, no?'

'Yeah, Antsville.' She nods, struck by the poor condition of the humans around her; the disrepair of the skin – even on the relatively young ones – and the general dilapidation of body. Some are thin and frail; many are massively overweight; few appear to be in the best of health. She watches an older male slowly navigating the crowd with the help of two poles, buffeted constantly in the human churn, and remembers her mother saying that many babies used to be born damaged in some way and couldn't be fixed. Had to get around with sticks and chairs, if at all. 'Disabled,' they'd called them, Ma had said. And many were treated very badly. Wouldn't happen today – that's the one good thing you could say about the Program: every baby's born perfect now.

Jai nudges her. 'Just seen some silverheads, sis. And loads of geez without any hair at all. Looks well nube – maybe I'll give it a go.'

'Well, I'll disown you if you do.' She grins, scuffing the back of his haystack of a hairstyle – a slightly less ruly version of her own. 'Where's Ammi?' She looks around and spots her talking to a tall, thin male who peels away fast as he sees her and Jai approach.

'Stupid idiot,' Ammi says, her colour high. 'Asked if I wanted anything for the night. Assumed he meant drugs. Told him only idiots do illegals.'

'Guess that's what brings Citi people over here,' Jai says. 'That and the bagnios.'

'Bagnios?'

'Yeah. Sex-houses – full of certified female steriles.' He grins.

'For Proggos to get a little "experience" before they settle down. Unsheathed, as it were. Don't blame me…' He mock-flinches in the face of a combined glare of disdain, holding up his hands. 'Only the messenger here.'

She walks with the others past lines of more or less makeshift stalls piled high with every imaginable and some, to her at least, completely unimaginable item. Each available surface, vertical as well as horizontal, is given over to the display of material things; every stall the hub of frenetic activity as people jostle together asking, offering, bargaining, pleading.

'Look at this, Ly,' Ammi says, pulling her towards a stall festooned in rubbery items, hanging like thick, black seaweed. 'Think it's from the stuff they used on the wheels of the old ground trans. There's all sorts – bags, bowls, shoes and, look there, bodywear even.'

'Ha. Maybe we should get Ma a new dress,' she jokes.

'Actually…' Ammi picks up a large rubber trug. 'This'd be really useful for her garden. She was just saying the other day—'

'Phew! What's that awful smell?' she interrupts, sniffing at the air. 'It's coming from there.' She points to a column of billowing smoke further down the line of stalls. The oily stench becomes almost overpowering as they approach its source, around which a small crowd has gathered. Ammi peers through the jostling bodies and turns back with a horrified look. 'Slaughtered animals!' she gasps.

'Zenban!' Jai says, joining them. 'Heard about that: combo of carbs, amino acids and oxidising fats. Sposed to be the perfect taste-bomb. Wanna try?'

'Yeuck, no…' she and Ammi respond in unison, utter disgust on their faces as they stare at the misshapen, pellicled lump of dead flesh rotating over a crudely fashioned stake. She can feel her mouth juices rising, however, even as she steps back in revulsion.

'Watch out!' Jai shouts as she narrowly misses a glutinous puddle in which the feet of some bird-like creature are floating.

'Oh, grotes,' she cries, looking down. 'Did that actually used to be a real thing?'

The greasy smell loiters in her nostrils as they reach the end of the first set of stalls. A small lane snakes off to the left. 'This is the turn, I think,' she says, peering again at the now near-disintegrated map. 'Come on, you two.'

Ammi hangs back, pulling at her sleeve. 'Wait, Lyse,' she says with an anxious look, 'are we sure we want to do this?' She nods towards a group of young males talking and laughing nearby. 'What if it's the wrong path; what if we get lost? It looks really deserted down there. It won't be long before it gets dark and I can't see any lights. Maybe we should give the Club a miss. We've seen the Banleus now.'

'No come on, Am.' She frowns, trying to keep a lid on her frustration. 'We can't pull out now we've got this far.' She looks at Jai for support, eyebrows raised.

'It'll be okay, Am,' Jai says, linking his arm through hers. 'I'll look after you.'

'Oh, nice,' Lyse jeers, relieved nonetheless. 'Loving that old-time machismo.'

9

BRIEF ENCOUNTER

The queue outside the door is youthful and largely female, its constituents strange and exotic to Lyse's eyes. Idiosyncrasies of person appear to have been deliberately accentuated: bodies and faces daubed in crude, but vivid shades; hair dramatically coloured and spun into gravity-defying shapes. The queue is excited and excitable; joking amongst itself but flinging occasional ruderies at anyone trying to gain advantage. *Like being in a flock of tropical birds*, she thinks. It all seems friendly enough, although she's seen a couple of sideways looks flashed their way – particularly from females and particularly at Jai.

They eventually reach the front of the queue, to find their path blocked by a hulk of a man. His moon-like face appears to balance, unsupported, on his sloping shoulders and its surface is as pitted and pocked as the moon itself, the eyes all but sunk into tiny lunar-like crevices.

'What can I do for you little lot?' He squints down at them.

'Don't look like you're from round here.' He speaks as if with considerable, and deeply resented, effort.

Lyse approaches him in a bold way. 'We're from the Citi, come to see the band,' she says, smiling and waving the flyer from the tunnel. 'We've got tickets.'

He ignores the tickets. 'Don't they have music in the Citi, then?' he asks with a sneer. 'Thought you had it all over there.'

She keeps hold of the smile. 'Well, there *is* music, on all the time, everywhere – difficult to get away from it, actually – but it's not real music, like tonight…' She trails off in the face of his stony gaze.

'Okay then…' He shifts his great bulk from one foot to the other with a heavy sigh. 'Whatya got?'

'Sorry?'

'For the entrance fee.'

'But we've got tickets.'

'That's the tickets, not the fee.'

'Well, what's the fee then?'

He scans them with an expert eye, his fat head moving up and down, tortoise-like, on his now-visible, multi-layered neck. His eyes form steely fissures in the flat, grey skin. 'Got any tech?'

She has a strong suspicion that, despite their agreement not to bring any valuables, Jai will have his Gamz™ in his back pocket and gives her brother a long, hard look. His internal tussle is visible, but brief. 'Okaay,' he sighs after a moment, holding out the small device. 'Got this.'

'Don't give him that, Jai!' Ammi jumps in. 'We don't have to give him anything.' She turns to the man. 'We've paid for these tickets,' she says with force, her pale cheeks flushed. 'We shouldn't have to pay again. We could report you.'

'Report away, girlie,' sneers the implacable hulk, shrugging his ox-like shoulders as he calls over her head to the next in line.

Jai looks at Lyse for direction. 'It's your call, Jai,' she says, frowning at Ammi.

'No, it's okay,' he sighs. 'It's only a toy, after all.'

His offer is accepted with a noncommittal grunt and the man waves them forward, eyes settling back into the bleak lunar terrain, normal torpor resumed. She glares hard at him as she passes – with all the impact of a snit on a stone.

Inside, they shuffle through a long, fust-smelling corridor lined with images of stars from the great rock and blues eras, and into a large, black-walled room with a small, raised stage at one end, in front of which a crowd is swelling fast. Giant misters line the walls, their cooling jets forming wraith-like patterns in the dull orange light. Lyse tries to keep her companions together, but a stream of excited bodies, abhorring any vacuum, packs in between and around them, forcing them apart. She lets the others go and moves with the flow until she spots a half-decent view of the stage and stakes her ground, legs apart, arms folded. There's not much to see: a mess of what she assumes are old electrical wires snaking out from stacks of black boxes, a battered old drum set, a keyboard and a couple of standing mikes. A young male, long hair tied weirdly in a bunch at the back, is wandering around adjusting knobs and dials attempting, from time to time, to coax the mess of wires to the back edge of the space. She glances around her: all eyes are fixed on the stage, the collective heartbeat almost audible.

The lights in the hall dim and the crowd lurches forward with a roar of excitement. Two young men have sauntered into the pools of dusty light circling the front of the stage, guitars slung low across narrow hips and tight-trousered legs. Both are dressed in various combinations of black on black, with metal trappings. The moving spotlights still and one of the males steps forward into their combined light. He is tall, with a smooth, slender body. His face, with its high cheekbones and rounded chin, seems almost feminine; but his hooded eyes are dark and soulfully male as they look out from under jet-black spikes of hair.

'Hello, Bannies!' he calls, staring out at the excited crowd with a smirk. 'You ready for a groovy night?'

As the crowd gives visible and vocal force to the affirmative, the second male moves forward into the pool of light, grinning broadly, prompting a renewed burst of collective enthusiasm. He's shorter than his bandmate and squarer, but just as lean. His open face is boyishly handsome and there's an energetic bounce about him that complements the louche languor of the other.

The second musician nods to the rest of the band as he strikes his guitar and she recognises the opening chords of a classic: one of the most distinctive three-note combinations of crotchets and quavers in Old-World rock history, and one of her all-time favourites. The bass builds for some moments before the taller male starts to sing. His voice is strong and fluid, easily handling the vocal sweep of the song and its tone of sneering rebellion. Drum and keyboards bring more enthusiasm than expertise to the mix, limited by the poor state of their instruments, to be fair, but it's not bad. *Not quite the jumping bassline or fuzzy guitar of the original, but not bad. Not bad at all.*

As the number comes to an end, she glances around for the others. She spots Jai, who looks as if he's having a good time. Ammi's standing near him, but she can't see her face – probably just as well. *Well, they can like it or not. Up to them. I'm going to enjoy myself.* The singer announces another favourite and shafts of light begin to strobe the crowd, giving visual echo to the thumping beats of the music; dry ice crawls out from the stage and fills her nose and throat, mixing with the heady smell of hot human skin as she's packed in on all sides by feverish bodies singing and swaying as one. Submerged in this full-sensory experience she loses hold of time and place and everything in-between. Only after the third encore, when she and the crowd finally accept that they've had the last number, does she look again for her friends.

Outside, once they leave the pink lights of the club behind, the night is velvet-dark, devoid of stars or moonlight. Lyse pulls her collar up as they start off fast towards the market square, heads down in the face of a tetchy wind that has bestirred itself all of a sudden.

'Well, looksie here…' a shrill male voice calls.

She looks up to find their path blocked by a line of moth-eaten young males, hopping like fleas on a carpet. One, the tallest, leads the taunts, grinning round at his scraggy mates.

'Looks like we've got us some Cities, here – slumming it down the Bannies.' He stabs a dirty corkscrew of a finger in Jai's chest with a snide laugh. 'Can't get what you want over there, ist?'

Jai starts towards them, but Ammi pulls him back. 'Don't, Jai, it's not worth it,' she says with force.

'You mean *we're* not worth it, dontu?' The lanky male turns on her with a nasty leer. 'But you're so worth it, arntu – you posh load of shite?' He grins again at his pals, who snigger snottily.

Ammi gets out her alarm and holds it out before her like a talisman. 'I've got an alarm,' she shouts at them. 'If you don't go away, I'll start it.'

'Oo lair!' a smaller, weasel-like male sneers, turning to the others. 'We're quakes in our boots, aren't we, cocks?' He preens at a pair of females who have stopped to watch the show then, with a sudden jump, swipes the device from Ammi's hand, scratching her wrist with his chains. 'I'll have that. Don't work down here anys, dinlo. Noth does; you're on your own, girlie.'

He pushes up close to her, his pimpled face close enough to touch, his mottled lips pursed in an ugly parody of a kiss. The rest of the jeering, jigging males close in, the rank smell of their bodies an assault in itself. She and Jai start pushing back at the encroaching males – one after another. *Like a real-life game of whack-a-molo*, she thinks absurdly. More practically, and effectively, Ammi starts to scream.

'What's going on here?' The moonface looms at the club door, its now-beady eyes sweeping over the group, seeming to size the situation up in an instant. 'Oi, I know you, you little shite!' he shouts, moving his large body surprisingly fast towards the tall ringleader. 'Told you lot to stay away from here! You and those other little gobshites.' The scrawny gang takes one look at the hurtling hulk and scatters like startled birds.

'What's up, Tiny?' a voice calls from the entrance to the club. She looks around to see two young males emerging from the door, trailing lines of vape, and her heart does a fancy little quickstep as she recognises them as the singer and lead guitarist from the band.

'Just some of the local scumbags, boys, trying to scare these good people here,' the big man says as he turns to the two young musicians, the moonface almost sunny now. 'Don't think they'll be back in a hurry. Good night tonight, lads, was it?' he asks as he lumbers back towards the door.

'It was amaze!' she finds herself gushing as she approaches the two musicians. They turn and smile at her; one briefly, the other more lingeringly. 'Glad you liked it,' the latter says. 'First time down here?'

'Yes. First time I've ever been to live music, actually,' she says, trying not to sound too breathless. 'It's my passion. Going to do it at college this autumn. With Live-ed… don't know if you've heard of them?'

He shakes his head, smiling, and something in his slate-blue eyes impels her on.

'Well, they're the best for live experience – you get to spend time with actual musicians, playing real music. Which is what I want to do – eventually.' She's gabbling now – slipping perilously close to the edge of foolishness. 'Sorry, going on a bit… Just wanted to say I loved the set. It's one of my college options: Mid to late twentieth-century rock music from the Old-World's northern hemisphere.'

'Blimes.' He grins. 'That's what it is, is it? Thought it was just good old rock 'n' roll.'

'Well, to be precise,' she grins back, adopting a portentous tone, 'it covers the seminal moment when the rock split from the roll.'

He laughs at this, moving closer and holding out his hand. 'I'm Seth, by the way.'

'Lyse,' she says, shaking his hand, appreciating the full mouth with the slight upturn at the corners and, now she sees it, the small dimple at the base of his chin.

'So, Lyse...' He is so close now that she can catch his scent: fresh and slightly salty, with a lower, muskier note that she finds rather disconcerting. Very different from Jai. 'You make music yourself, or are you just a fan?'

Her words seem annoyingly hesitant as she tries to tell him about her ambition to write and perform her own material one day. 'Not being immodest,' she says, probably being just that, 'but people say I've got a good voice. And I'm learning Pa's old sax, although way off performance level there —'

'You've got a saxophone?' He seems very interested in this, and appears to be about to say more, when there's a shout from the door.

'Van's all packed, Seth, mate. Beers at Mab's. Where's Q?'

'Over there, Mik.' Seth points to the singer, who is half-submerged in a group of animated females. 'Be right there.' He turns back to her and grins. 'Sorry, gotta go. Good to meet you, Lyse.' He fiddles in his pocket and brings out a stubby pad of tickets. 'Come again – on me. And bring your friends.' He makes to go but stops and smiles at her over his shoulder.

'And maybe ping me a demo...'

10

THE GOGIRL™

It's dark by the time Coop gets home and he's sweating; despite the best efforts of the atmosfers, the evening was uncomfortably close. But perhaps it's just him. *Been that sort of day – even the air's on my back.* He hangs his hat and strips off his shirt, welcoming the cool lick of air on his skin as he enters the small living space. He leaves the lights, preferring the noirish look of the room bathed, as it is, in amber glow from the neons outside.

Something soft brushes against his leg and he sees Arthur, his recently acquired 'catish', circling his feet. One of the latest animal haptics, extremely realistic. Wasn't cheap. Didn't go for real fur – not going to fuel that ghastly trade – but even the medium-grade simulated pelt cost an arm and a leg. Worth it, though – having something to come home to at the end of the day. He holds the warm body against his cooling chest, triggering a loud, although ever so slightly too rhythmic, purring sound.

He'd had a real cat once, but it was removed – rehomed, they'd assured him – like all the others, in the great depuration;

marmalade tabby (he's chosen the same colours for Arthur). Illegal now to keep live animals as pets, although there's a big underground market, sourced from the Edgelands. Anyway, the catish is a great improvement on the natural version; it feels, smells and sounds (almost) the same, but doesn't defecate, host blood-sucking pests or get very expensively ill. *Just wish I'd got the bug-attack model.*

The distinctive purple and silver branding of the package catches his eye, sitting on the table where he left it this morning. Bit smaller than expected; *did order the adult size, didn't I?* Anyway, he'll check that out later, right now he needs a drink. He opens the pouch he's bought on the way home, momentarily guilty: alcohol's forbidden – even for men – once you commit to the Program. *Well...* he pours a large cup of the aromatic spirit, *it's early days yet.* He takes his drink to the chair by the window overlooking the light-slickered streets and calls to Arthur, who climbs onto his lap and restarts the purring noise, pressing its front paws into his stomach in an insistent way. *Might all come to nothing. No point in getting ahead of myself.*

Talking of the Program, he'd better get some neuts in. He consults the set menu for the pre-concepts (that's him, apparently) and selects one of the base *prot'n carb* options – *Authentic Old Asian Taste!*, it claims (although, on past offerings, he's not optimistic) – adds a fruto-fibar and sends the order. He takes a deep sip of the drink and leans back, eyes closed, waiting for the soothing liquid to do its work.

Another dispiriting day. He'd won the case, but the whole thing had left him thoroughly depressed. Why she'd changed her plea again at the last minute is anyone's guess. Seemed she envisioned herself fighting some bigger battle. It was the right verdict, but the mercy of the Court was sadly strained and its punishment cruel. The woman was clearly suffering from a mania of some kind; didn't have to be a medic to spot that. Locking her in the stocks to be physically and verbally abused by all comers was a thoroughly inhuman thing to do.

And that's that; almost the last of his PA contracts. He takes another sip and lets the warm liquor trickle down his throat as he watches the iridescent trails of the transits streaking pass the window. He's got some coin to fall back on, but not much; if something doesn't turn up soon he's going to have to rethink things. This place, for a start. Can only just afford the rent on the low-end mobile prefab as it is. Would've been cheaper, much cheaper, to live in the Banleus – spends most of the day there, anyway – where there's plentiful space in the abandoned warehouses and retail parks. But life in the outer-urbs is hard: a constant struggle against the relentless dust and the remorseless advance of the insects. Doesn't like the twenty-four seven surveillance – who does? – but it's a small price to pay for the atmospheric equanimity of the Citi's streets.

He scans the compact living space with satisfaction. The only adornment is two (he hopes original) Old-Japon woodblock prints and an entire wall patterned with the muted hues of his book collection. The floor is bare, apart from a thick (and definitely *not* original) black and brown rug in the 'art deco' style lying in front of the cooler. Simple - just as he likes it. His strong inclination to minimalism is one of the many legacies of his early life with his Replacement Father. He swirls the viridescent spirit round the glass, thinking back. Must have been about five when his real father died and his whole world shifted in a heartbeat. The Replacement had arrived very quickly – too quickly – before, he can now understand, his mother's grief had time to play out.

It was never going to work – even if the Replacement had tried to make an effort. Which he hadn't. And even if he had, he wouldn't have let him get very far. From the start the man – he was never going to call him Father – filled their lives with himself: physically, with the clutter from his various, typically short-lived, enthusiasms, left scattered once the interest had waned (or his lack of ability became manifest even to him); but emotionally too, commanding more and more of his mother's time and shutting him out. The man wasn't allowed to lay a hand on him, but he lost no opportunity to make him feel small, worthless. And to use his perceived failures against his mother. *Mollycoddled*, he would snipe repeatedly, nodding his red-blotched face towards him. *That's his trouble.*

A siren screams and he looks up to see an armoured Gencom vehicle flash past in a purple haze, causing a few of the smaller cars to swerve violently upward. *Some poor sod's in trouble: illegal fertilisation – worse than murder in this brave new world.* He takes another sip of the alcohol and lies back, feeling the edges of the day finally begin to soften. His mother had changed towards him after the Replacement arrived. Rather than a source of comfort and security, she seemed herself to have become un-secured somehow, increasingly detached from him and everything around her. In the few intimate moments they shared after the Replacement arrived – when the man was inside one global sportvirt or another, or out at the pleasure domes – she'd talked of his real father, how much she loved him and how much she missed him, her deep brown eyes locked on to some very far distant point as she stroked his head. He recalls the touch of her long, soft fingers (so like his own) with a surge of longing.

He squeezes the last of the alcohol from the pouch and gives the door an expectant look. Used to promise *Food in Three or Food for Free*, but standards appear to be slipping – like pretty much everything these days. He takes a deep sip of the drink as he tickles Arthur behind its ears. His eyes sidle again to the unopened package: the 'welcome' present from the Program. Ball's well and truly rolling now; his Program 'journey' has officially commenced. He's not sure of the precise combination of emotions that thought has left him with.

He'd decided quite young that he wanted to go for Fatherhood, despite – or, perhaps, the psychs would say, because of – his own less than happy childhood, and despite his deep dislike of Gencom and its ways, had applied soon after grads. Hadn't wanted to leave it too late: used to be just females who worried about the biological clock; men could go on ferting as long as they liked – *and some did*, he thinks with mild disgust, *until they were very old* – but now all repro-active males are re-snipped at forty.

And anyway, doesn't want to rush things; suspects it might take time to find the right person. Knows the Partnership thing is more legal contract than bond of love in the old, romantic sense, but he wants something more out of the experience: a soulmate, not a brood-mate; someone to share his interests and pleasures even into later age, as they did in the Old-World.

'So… let's have a look at this thing, shall we?' he asks out loud, heaving Arthur off his knee, enjoying the extremely realistic look of haughty-cat outrage on its fabricated face. He opens the package and takes out an embossed compliments card – a strangely old-fashioned touch:

Welcome to GoGirl™ – your virtual playmate!

Enjoy a full sensory experience with 'state of the sci' olfactory boosters, full-audio authenticity and hyper-realistic feel!*

*Users participate at their own risk. Gencom takes NO responsibility for any physical or mental harms incurred, unless demonstrably the result of production error.

The contents seem impossibly small and doll-like but, as he unpacks and sets out each part in turn, placing a book beside the head to stop it rolling off, they begin slowly to expand with a faint wheezing sound. Once fully 'grown', the components fit well together; seamlessly, in fact – apart from the head, which he can't quite align, with the result that the GoGirl appears transfixed by something just over his right shoulder. Finally assembled, the thing seems almost human – perhaps a little too much so. The 'skin' feels extremely realistic, although is oddly sponge-like when pressed and, when he gets in close (as instructed), gives off a faint aroma of sweet vanilla.

He switches the thing on, its movements jerky at first as the limbs settle down, then quiescent apart from an annoying twitch in one eye, no doubt due to his failure to tighten the head fully. Switching off and twisting the head again has no impact on the twitch, but prompts a low-level humming, not unlike his parents' old refrigerator or a rummaging bee, interposed with soft sighs and a rhythmic opening and closing of the over-plumped mouth. He works out how to shut the eyes off, which helps with his growing sense of Other-intrusion, but he can't find to how to control the gulping fishlike mouth.

Following the operating instructions to the letter, he completes the first 'orienteering' stage easily enough. Spasmodically, the contented humming gives way to a burst of pelvic activity accompanied by a series of operatic moans as he succeeds in pressing the right buttons in the right order. Thankfully, he also finds a way to switch the sound off. He takes the suggested routes around the body, surprised by how much is in play (ears – who knew?), and manages the 'manipulation' stage quite well; his long, slim fingers proving adept at some of the more complicated manoeuvres. The final stage, however, requires a degree of physical cooperation that he's not yet fully able to provide.

He hears the tinny tones of the food delivery and collects and eats the unappetising contents quickly, without enjoyment. He gazes over at the GoGirl™ lying face down on the art deco rug, looking rather too much like a deceased body. Arthur seems to have recognised a kindred spirit and is curled up beside her plump pink bottom, snoring contentedly, but she – it – doesn't do anything for him. Can appreciate the ingenuity of the thing, but the whole exercise has left an unpleasant taste. *And anyway...* he drains the last drops from the cup with an unfamiliar flutter of excitement... *tomorrow it's the real thing.*

11

BAND PRACTICE

'But we'd only get the sax if we take the girl, that it?' Otis asks.

Seth nods, relieved to have manoeuvred his bandmates off the subject of Queron and his perceived lack of commitment. The possibility that they might get their hands on an actual functioning saxophone had been enough to stem the festering resentments – for a while. He'd had to admit that it wasn't a done deed but said he was pretty sure if they let her do a couple of numbers – needn't be much, just some backing or harmonies – he could get her to bring the sax along.

'Banni girls won't like it,' Mik mutters.

'You mean you won't like it.' Keif laughs, slapping him on the shoulder. 'Female of the species not your cup of tea, eh?'

'Girls just might like it, anyways.' Otis smirks. 'There's a lot of lez out there. Could go down well with a certain section of our crowd. If she's hot, that is.' He gives Seth a lewd grin. 'Is she hot, this chick of yours?'

'Couldn't be any less hot than you, mush,' Keif points out reasonably.

'Well, first thing,' Seth says, trying not to let Mik's constant negativity get under his skin, 'she's not my chick and, second thing, how she looks is not the point. It's about what she – and a sax – could bring to the band. Could give us a bit of an edge. Anyway,' he says, tapping the audipin, 'give it a rattle, see what you think.'

It's the opening song of their current set. She'd slowed it down, giving it a very different tone: less rebellious leer, more quiet menace. Her voice is strong and distinctive (its range greater, if anything, than Queron's), stretching without effort from breathy low to helium high. As they listen, he thinks about the girl herself. *Is she hot? There was something about the wide smile and the green-grey eyes, has to admit. Could get interested, very interested – other things being equal. But a new girl's not what I need right now; got to deal with the old one first.*

The song finishes and he can see the boys are impressed with the singer, quickly embarking on an animated discussion about particular tracks that could be done in a different way with a sax and a girl. Mik has a final worry, however: 'Is she expects to get paid, this bird? I'm okay for her to have a few spots. But not if it's going to cost us, man. I'm skint enough as it is.'

'No, Mik, mate,' he says with slightly less patience, 'she wants to do it for the experience. Nobody's talking coin.'

Consensus reached, the band gets down to the business at hand. It's a good session: some old numbers polished, a new one tried out. Queron not only turns up but seems to be making an effort, putting in ideas and encouragement – his disarming charm very nearly working. And he's in great voice: even in the practice room, and even after all this time, it's a voice that can send shivers down a person's back.

After band, the boys head up to Mab's bar. He walks with Queron, slightly behind the others. The sky is an obstinate blue and the air has an exhausted feel that he finds difficult not to echo. Queron, in contrast, who has stripped off his tunic and tied it around his waist, seems unusually upbeat.

'Pretty awes tonight, cuz,' he says, sliding his bare arm around Seth's shoulders, his body scent strong. 'New number's ice – good find, good find. Was that from Marcus?' He spins round to face Seth. 'Did he like the baccy I got him, BTW?'

He nods, and Queron grins and continues. 'Chick's pretty nifty too; there's loads of stuff we could use her on. Think we should get her in, bro. Try her out.'

This seems like a good moment to address the elephant dogging their tracks. He ducks out from under his friend's clammy armpit and pulls him to a stop.

'Yeah, but thing is, Q... must've noticed, atmos in the band's pretty shit right now. Boys're pissed off at you missing stuff all the time; saying it looks like you're pulling out.' He gazes at his friend's ever-unreadable face. 'So, you sure you still want in, Q, or you got better things to do these days?'

'Nah, bro,' Queron says, 'just had a lot on recents. All sorted now and course I'm in.' He gives a sinuous smile. 'You and me, Seth boy, we *are* the band.' He waves his arms expansively as he starts off again. 'Band of brothers, init?'

'Yeah, well, brothers talk to each other, Q,' he says, not unaware that he's not exactly sharing his own personal stuff at the moment. 'You sure there's nothing?'

'Nah, cuz. All ice with me.' Queron sweeps his hair away from his dark eyes and smirks at him. 'Far as I can see, it's you that's got the problem, Setho. It's you that's got the Viki bird round your neck. Can't have her *and* the tour – gonna have to choose. There's no way we can take her with us.'

'Yeah, well.' He shrugs, a little queasy at the ease of his disloyalty. 'Think it's pretty much over between us anyway.'

'What?' Queron snickers. 'Finally had enough of her? Or has she gone off you – fed up with all your bad habits? Always thought it was bit odd sticking with one chick anyway. Where's that going to go? The old horse-and-carriage stuff?'

'Yeah, well, no, it's not her. She's nube. Just don't want the same things. What she wants – *all* she really wants – is a baby.'

'Well, her and zillies of other Banni girls,' Queron scoffs. 'And she's barking up the wrong tree with you, nesepa? Needs to find herself a Proggo with his tongue hanging out – or get herself a virtbaby – sposed to be just like the real thing. Anyhow, Setho,' he says, patting him roughly on the back, 'that's not seismic, is it? Plenty more birds in the coop – especially when we get out on the road. Good-looking boy like you – have your pick. Why tie yourself to a single chassis, when there's a full fleet available – no diss to Vik, course…'

He's tempted to tell Queron what Viki told him; secrecy doesn't come easily, but something – his father's warning, his friend's recent detachment – makes him hold back. *And anyway, nothing's for real yet, is it? Got to keep that fact in focus.* He can't leave the matter entirely alone, however.

'Yeah, maybe, but… dunno,' he says. 'Viki aside, do you ever think about it, Q, the whole repro thing? Y'know – about being a father, maybe having a kid one day?'

'Shit no!' Queron's eyes widen in alarm. 'We're well out of all that. That's hell on Earth, bro. You have to give it all up to the Program – you'd have no life to call your own. Wouldn't go there, cuz – even if I could,' he says as he starts up a jog, causing Seth to follow suit. 'Not for all the coin on the Planet.'

*

He gets the pin just as they arrive at the bar. She's got some news. Needs to talk – at his place. He leaves Queron and the others grudgingly – could have done with that drink – and arrives back to find her waiting outside his door, her face a snot-wet mask of misery. The news is clearly not good. He motions for her to go down, but she shakes her head; got to get home. She wipes her nose with the side of her hand, spreading teary mucus across her cheeks, and tells him that the baby is lost. Miscarried. That the bleeding started at dawn and that she knew right away it had gone. She looks at him, ashen-faced.

'It just slipped away, Seth,' she whimpers, clutching him, 'like it was never really there.'

He pulls her towards him and strokes her hair as her small frame trembles. He's genuinely sad; sad for her and what she's had to go through, but also for himself. On a couple of occasions he'd caught himself imagining how it would feel to be a father, to have created an entirely new human being out of nowhere, and he'd quite liked the feeling. But his relief now at her news is overwhelming. *Whatever it was, whoever's it was, it's all over now. End of.* He tries hard to keep this emotion from his voice as he attempts to say something comforting.

'Perhaps it's for the best, Vik,' he ventures, taking her sticky fingers in his. 'Maybe some things're just not meant to be.'

He realises immediately he's hit the wrong note. She pulls away and stands facing him – eyes catlike with hurt hostility.

'How can you say that, Seth?' she squeals, hitting at him with a small fist. 'How can you say it's for the best that we could've been parents, could've had an actual, real-life baby, and that now we can't? That now we're back to exactly where we were. Which is exactly Nowheresville.' She gives him an angry stare. 'Don't you feel anything about that at all?'

He feels a lot of things but knows that most would be best left unsaid; he attempts a 'this is hurting me as much as you' tone of resigned regret.

'Yeah, I'm gutted, Vik. Would've been amaze. But was always a bit of a dream, wasn't it, if we're really honest? We'd never've got away with it. And that'd've been worse, wouldn't it? To have started a baby and then have it taken away?'

She says nothing for a while and he's beginning to hope that the worst has passed, when she reaches for his hand and says in a small voice, not looking at him: 'We could try again, Seth.'

The curveball catches him off guard. 'No way, Vik!' he snorts, dropping her hand. 'Why in the wide World would we do that? We were lucky no-one found out about it the first time; we'd be mad to risk it all again.'

'Oh, that's what it is for you, is it?' she gasps. 'A lucky escape?'

She slumps back against the door, staring at the floor, skinny arms wrapped around her like a sheltering bird. He tries to pull her back to him, but she shrugs him off and turns away.

Okaay, maybe now's a good moment to call it quits. Suggest we go our separate ways. But shit… he looks at her desolate face, *can't do that now, can I? Not while she's like this.* He watches as she visibly struggles with her emotions.

She looks up then, a more determined expression on her face. 'Okay, Seth,' she says in a quiet, but firm, voice, 'guess I knew that you wouldn't agree. That a baby's not what you want right now – or ever, not with the band and everything.' She puts her hand on his arm, 'But you could help me to do it myself – have a baby on my own. There's places I could go; you'd never see me, or the baby. No-one'd ever find out about it – or about you.'

Again the curveball; again it stings him into honesty.

'Whoa, Vik. No way!' he says with force. 'I couldn't do that. Couldn't start a baby – even if I could – and then just walk away from it.'

Her face is stony. 'But then you're just shutting me down, Seth. Giving me no chance. You won't let me have a baby with you and you won't help me start one without you. That's just not fair,' she cries, stamping a booted foot. 'You know it isn't.'

He says nothing, thrown by this new tactic.

'Please, Seth,' she cajoles, her tone softening, 'whatever your feelings for me, and I know they're not as strong as mine are for you…' She pauses, and he regrets the pain in her eyes as he fails to reassure her. 'But if you've got any feelings for me at all you'll help me do this.' She takes both his hands, her soft violet eyes pleading. 'Please, Seth, you know what it means to me. And you know it's my only chance. Say you'll think about it, at least?'

Great. Just when it all seemed sorted. He looks at her pale face, lovely even when scored, as now, with trails of salt and mucus. He's got feelings for her, sure, but those feelings are mixed up with a whole lot else. And he can't deal with any of it right now.

'Okay, Vik…' he says, stroking her wet cheek, 'I'll think about it. Promise.'

Best to say nothing about the test; she'll only take it as a sign I don't believe her. Which it is, of course. And I'd like to get out of here in one piece.

'So, after the gig tomorrow?'

'Okay,' she gives him a wan smile, 'after the gig.'

They exchange a brief kiss, newly awkward, and he watches as her small frame fades into the gloom. He wipes his fingers on his jacket with a sigh. Caught in the proverbial cleft stick, isn't he? Can't kick her when she's down but can't string her along and risk getting caught up in all that baby shit again. If, indeed, there is any baby shit. He shakes his head. *Just get the test done, Seth, and then you can let her down gently.*

As he turns to enter the building, he notices the dirty-green stratus slashing the evening sky and senses the change in the air: it's thicker, more agitated and laced with a sulphurous tinge.

Summer is revving up.

12

THE TEST

'**B**ollox,' he says out loud, checking the time and buzzing again. *All bloody deaf, these old people.* He sees a path running beside the house and remembers Marcus saying something about a greenhouse out the back. Sure enough: as he turns the corner he sees a large, wooden-framed construction covered in a transparent, plasticised material. Drawing nearer he can make out the shape of an elderly female, bending over a bench and spooning something into a row of small pots. *That's gotta be her.* Bit of a plantswoman, his father had said. He calls out and the body at the window straightens up and an apprehensive face looks out.

'It's me, Seth, Marcus's son.'

The face brightens. 'Oh, yes. Seth. Come around to the door, won't you?' She meets him as he enters the enveloping warmth of the plastic cocoon.

'How nice to see you.' Her smile forms deep, radial lines in the skin around her eyes. 'I've heard so much about you from Marcus. All good, of course!' She holds out a rather grubby hand and the strength of her grip surprises him. 'I'm really very sorry. I was, am, expecting you, but I've been running a bit late all day. I did pin Marcus to say, but I'm guessing he didn't pass it on?'

He shakes his head and they share a smile of recognition about his father's absent-mindedness. 'Never mind. If it's all right with you,' she says, waving a small trowel, 'I'll just finish off this little job. Need to get them off to market tomorrow.' She gestures to a pair of slatted wooden chairs. 'There's a seat over there and some akwa pods. Help yourself. I'll be as quick as I can.'

He lowers himself onto the rickety-looking seating with care and watches the quick, squirrel-like movements of the old woman. Must be really ancient – face cross-hatched like a dry riverbed – but her fingers are nimble, and her darting eyes are sharp. *Bet she doesn't miss much.* He recalls his father's mock-complaint about always losing to her at cards.

She waves at the lines of pots. 'My contribution to saving the Planet.'

'Oh, what are they? he asks, mildly interested.

'Basic crops, mostly: potatoes, carrots, beans and so on. Folks out here need to grow more of their own food; can't afford Citi prices. But it's not getting any easier.'

'Oh, how's that?' he asks, relieved to have a conversational prelude to the main business of the night.

'Can't get the seeds. Ones you get from Agcom, and there's practically nowhere else to get them, are sterile. So folks have to keep going back – paying again for new plants. These little beauties can reproduce; saving coin and saving themselves. Agcom...' she gives a derisory snort, 'Ag*con*, I call them, only bother with the profitable varieties.' She holds up one spindly-looking affair. 'This sweet little tomato would have been lost forever, if someone hadn't managed to preserve it. Mind you,' she gives a deep sigh as she presses the soft, brown earth around the fragile stem, 'it's probably all too little too late.'

She finishes the pots and leads him into the cool body of

the building, through a small, old-fashioned eatery and into an elegant, high-ceilinged room, its crowded contents dramatically striated by the strong afternoon light streaming through long, multi-panelled windows. Two plump armchairs sit either side of a large stone fireplace in the centre of the room. The walls are a faded ochre colour, hung with old paintings and drawings, mostly flowers of one kind or another: some with their roots and bulbs, some just foliage. Live plants, with strange and luxuriant leaves, sit in rows of ornamented pots underneath the windows. He doesn't recognise any of them, but then he's never been to any of the plant museums.

His eye is caught by a large heavy-looking fabric hanging on the wall opposite the fireplace, its intricate images drawn in threads of silver and gold, browns and greens. The subject of the cloth picture is strange. A man leans on the trunk of a twisted tree, surrounded by a pack of monstrous creatures, some half-human. All seem intent on doing him harm. A lightly dressed woman, holding what seems to be a weapon, also appears to have intent towards him, but whether as friend or foe, it is not easy to see.

'Oh, you like my tapestry?' she asks. 'I did it one year when I found I had a bit of unexpected time on my hands.'

'Wow. Must've taken lightyears. I'd never have the patience.'

'It's a copy of an old engraving,' she continues. 'They're not really sure who by. It's an allegory – a metaphor?' – she looks at him and he nods (just about remembers that sort of thing) – 'about the meaning of life. Or rather about the ultimate point of life – which is not quite the same thing.'

'Which is?' he asks, genuinely interested now.

'Which is, to strive to make the World a better place. And to not be defeated by the difficulties involved. Also,' she winks, 'to an ancient feminist like me, at least, it looks like the man is holding the woman back from this endeavour – to his likely mortal cost.' She gives him a quizzical smile. 'But you aren't here to talk about my tapestry, are you?'

'No…' he says, suddenly embarrassed about discussing his personal affairs with what is, after all, an almost complete stranger. *But I've come this far, can't chicken out now.*

'Don't know how much Pa's told you…?' he begins.

She suggests they start at the start and he sets out the situation as matter-of-factly as he can: about Viki and the baby she said was his and about how, even though she's lost the baby now, Marcus says he should get a test anyway just to make sure, and that she, Thelma, might be able to help with that.

'But it must all be a big mistake, mustn't it?' he asks, trying not to sound too pathetic. 'Pa says I was definitely snipped, along with all the others. Just isn't possible, is it?'

'Well,' Thelma replies, 'it is *theoretically* possible – although highly unlikely – that you could have been missed by the system somehow. Never been known, but that's not to say it could never happen. The only other alternative is even more unlikely: that your body resisted or overrode the procedure somehow. There's been rumours of such an event in other quadraspheres – a couple of flashes on the dark, but quickly doused – impossible to follow up. I know, I tried. But really, the most likely hypothesis is that the young woman was mistaken. She wasn't pregnant; or she was, but it wasn't yours.'

She goes on to warn him that a test won't give him all the answers he's seeking: while it will tell him whether, despite the best efforts of the Program's system, he has remained a fertile male, it won't tell him whether the baby Viki was carrying, if indeed it existed, was his. Even if the first is true, the second may not follow. And now the baby is lost, it will be impossible ever to know – unless he could get Viki here fast, today in fact.

'Oh, lor, no!' he says with feeling. If he is certain of anything in this whole surreal conversation, it is this. 'There's no way I could ask her. She'd just blow up. It's already fragile between us. And she wouldn't come anyway – she'd just see it as further proof that I don't believe her.'

'And there would be no convincing her?'

'No,' he says, 'no chance of that. Vik's very stubborn when she's made up her mind about something. There's no turning her around.'

'Well, perhaps it doesn't matter if you never know the answer to the second question. Perhaps it will be easier to accept the loss of the baby,' she suggests, her keen eyes on him, 'if you can make yourself believe it wasn't yours anyway?'

'Yeah,' he says, uncomfortable with the eyes – and the emotions they're stirring.

'So, will you tell Viki the outcome of the test?'

'Sure.' He gives a reflexive nod, although in fact he'll have to think about that. *Whatever the result, I could just say it was negative and that would be the end of it, wouldn't it? Kinder for Viki too; wouldn't feel so bad about breaking up...*

'And how do you think she'll react, if it's positive?' she persists.

'How d'you mean?' he asks, although he knows what she's asking.

'Well, she was very keen on this baby by all accounts. Would she want to try for another one, d'you think?'

'Yeah, maybe...' He smiles at her but allows his gaze to wander off to the enigmatic tapestry, sharing a degree of fellow feeling with the beleaguered male at its centre.

'She hasn't said?' she presses. 'You haven't had that conversation?'

'Well, yes, we have, but,' he shrugs, wishing himself out of this particular conversation, 'guess we've got a bit more talking to do.'

She pins him with her sharp little eyes. 'But you don't want to do it, do you,' she states rather than asks.

'No, don't think I do, actually,' he says, emboldened by the finality of her words.

13

DATE NIGHT

The meeting is booked for 6.00pm which he reckoned would give him more than enough time to write up and log the case, check in with Don, maybe clear a bit of admin, before nipping off mid-afternoonish for a nice long swim, then home to get ready. (He's bought a new tunic that he thinks sits well on him; nice tight fit round the back and shoulders but comes in snug at the waist – can't always get that in a tunic.) And enough time, more to the point, to give some serious thought to what might be among the most important questions of his life. What exactly do you ask a prospective life partner and child co-producer? In this regard, he hadn't been at all assisted by the *Prompts for Prospective Partners* pre-loaded on his confirmation pin, which included such gems of human communication as 'Who is your favourite virtstar?' and 'Have you had any upgrades yet?'

But the day hadn't quite worked out as he'd reckoned. Should have known. He'd completed the casework quickly enough, then got detained, almost at the point of leaving, by Don 'inviting' him in for a 'chat' about his work status. He'd been wondering, his boss told him, hands on hips, shirt hanging out, *why I should keep a self-styled 'consulting detective' on the books – especially one who seems to be doing a sight more consulting than detecting right now – when the bots could do the job better and for less cost – not to mention less lip.*

He made a convincing case for himself – not that difficult, Don knows he has many uses – and got a reprieve to the end of the month on the promise of two days' back office *World help me.* But by then it was really getting late.

Couldn't get a car from the station – not on any sort of promise – so had to take the walkway which got stuck, for what seemed like endless minutes, on the junction outside Gencom HQ; hemmed in, without warning, on all sides by angry protesters. For a couple of those minutes, he worried that they'd never get moving again, but the crowd dispersed in a flash, like a shoal of startled fish, as Stewards spilled out of the Gencom building, weapons primed. He looks around; was a time such an encounter would have been considered remarkable, but the humans beside him have barely looked out from their inner worlds. So much for the new normal.

By the time the pathway's moving again, it's seriously late; he's going to have to skip the wash and brush-up, never mind the swim, if he's going to make it on time. Not ideal: he'd deep cleansed this morning, but it's been an anxious sort of day – not least due to the niggling question of whether he's made the right choice.

He'd been sent a selection of genetically matched partners in his price bracket (couldn't quite afford the 'deluxe selection') from which to make an initial choice. The matchmaking is obligatory (otherwise he would have refused) and claims to ensure *Perfect genetic chemistry!* between prospective Partners: *High levels of romantic and sexual compatibility guaranteed!* Maybe it's necessary to prevent in-breeding (or an underhand attempt to curate the species, as some scientists have it), but he can't accept the idea that our genes determine how we feel about each other – that *love is no coincidence*, as Gencom has it. Humans, surely, are more than the sum total of their genes. And love is more than just physical attraction, isn't it?

He'd found it almost impossible to make a choice between the selected females on the basis of anything meaningful. Their *Partner Profiles* were fulsome on biophysical facts and academic or sporting achievements but were largely silent on anything that might illuminate their inner selves. Closest he could get to the 'lively mind' he's looking for, was the old chestnut GSoH – which seemed to come fitted as standard. In the end, he'd chosen – on an only just short of random basis – a female with an unusual combination of dark skin and sea-green eyes that he found visually intriguing, if not physically attractive.

Anyway, he's nearly ten minutes late when he finally arrives at the old faith building, absorbed like all the others into the sprawling Gencom estate, and his feet start cooling fast at the sight of the swirling purple banners of the Life Program either side of the metal-studded door. Resisting a strong urge to turn tail he walks stoutly into the building, to be met by an anxious white-coated receptibot and ushered without ceremony into a small, brightly lit, meet-pod containing the visibly annoyed figure of his first potential mate.

He removes his hat and takes a seat beside her, making profuse apologies for his lateness. Against her bare skin and glamorous gown he feels like a literal stuffed shirt in his day clothes. There's a cool smile, but he can see from the start that she's not much taken with him – and not just because of the lateness. *Hope it's not the lack of advance body preparation.* He takes her in as they exchange greetings. There is nothing about her that is not perfect: her face is as smooth and shiny as an old-fashioned china doll, her limbs like moulded silicone. Not a hair is out of place – in fact, not a hair is anywhere at all as far as he can see, apart from the long, dark mane on her head. The only slight 'flaw', and one that she's almost certainly going to get fixed, is the near-imperceptible gap between her two front teeth.

As the evening wears on, he tries steer the discussion into areas that might reveal something of her personality, but any effort to move into non-reproductive-related territory – with the exception of the question of her favourite virtstar, which she addresses in an animated way for some time – being politely repulsed. Having a baby, and the particular characteristics and aptitudes it should ideally possess, preoccupies her conversation.

And the more she talks, the less perfect she becomes, to his eyes, at least. She has a slight lisp, which takes no time to become annoying, and a tendency to end almost every utterance with an odd little giggle. And – if he's going to be pedantic – there's precious little evidence of the advertised good sense of humour. But it's not her 'faults' that are the problem for him (some might find them delightful verbal embellishment), it's the lack of them. It's the near-total perfection of her that he finds disconcerting.

Not really his thing, perfection; he distrusts the modern obsession with it and doubts it will end well for the species. Folks in the Citi, particularly young people, look more and more as if cast from the same mould. Peas in a pod. A form of biophysical regression to the mean: no feature too big or too small; no body part too fat or too thin; no asymmetry of face; no extremes (or, World forbid, misshapes) of form. A world full of perfectly perfect people. But beauty's not always about perfection, is it? The Old-Worlders knew this; recognised that imperfection can enhance beauty – or even achieve its own beauty – especially in a human face. Ugly-beautiful, wasn't it? Well, not anymore – it's 'beautiful-beautiful' all the way.

He gazes her with dispassion, as he might study a beautiful work of art (she *is* a beautiful work of art): her mouth could have been drawn by Botticelli; her striking green eyes from the brush of Rossetti. As she moves, her diaphanous dress affords almost unrestricted views of a body that he can see has been honed to perfection. Got to admit, she's physically stunning and presumably, when he starts reversal proper, his body will respond accordingly.

14

A DARK NIGHT

Viki is sitting on what now serves as her 'bed' – a reconditioned airmat she exchanged for a day's work – her two furry babies nestled in her lap. Impossible to get a good night's sleep on the mat – even without her aunt's snoring, which is resistant to any amount of nudging – physical or verbal. Getting past a joke now. Not only lost her bed, and her sleep, but increasingly her personal space. He's everywhere: huge dusty boots kicked off in the eatery, filthy outers hung over theirs on the hook, dirty clothes lying where they're dropped. Not to mention the all-pervasive smell of him. She strokes the stuffed toys roughly. Even started bringing plants home from the allotment – *brighten up the place a bit* – but doesn't think about how we'll water them, does he? So mostly they die, and Aunts has to get rid. Sure, he also brings home the odd bit of fruit or veg, but it's not very often and it's not in very good nick. And mostly it's him that eats it anyway – along with everything else.

She hears voices below: her aunt's soft mutterings, then his much louder voice. He must have come home early, probably looking for coin to spend on a pipe; she knows where he goes when he finishes his shift. She kisses the stuffed animals in turn and places them carefully against the wall at the end of the bed, then heads down the stairs.

'You'll get it back,' Naz is saying. 'It's only till the end of the week.'

Her brother is standing, red-faced and frowning, in front of her aunt, who is sitting, shoulders hunched, her white-tufted head shaking a little.

'What's going on?' she asks, walking around to see her aunt's face, which is just short of tearful. 'Why's she so upset?'

'It's nothing, sis.' Naz attempts a smile. 'Just a little misunderstanding, wasn't it, Auntie?'

The old woman sniffs and nods, dabbing her eye with a small cloth.

'Just wanted to borrow a bit of coin until I get me packet…'

She loses it then. Says that if he hasn't got anything to live on till payday, then he'll have to live without. She points at her aunt, who is looking down, twisting her fingers in her lap. 'She's given you a roof over your head – should be grateful for that, not start asking for more. You know she's none to spare – especially now she's got you to pay for.'

His face reddens further as he rounds on her, accusing her of always thinking the worst of him. Says it's clear she doesn't want him around – hadn't wanted him there in the first place and can't wait to see the back of him now. She doesn't deny the accusation; mainly because it's largely true, but also because she's feeling shit with Seth and one man is good as another.

'Well, don't worry,' he says, walking towards the door and pulling on his boots. 'You'll be rid of me soon enough.' He shuts the door hard behind him, causing the dishes, and her aunt, to wobble.

She regrets her outburst; not for what she said to Naz, but because arguments upset her aunt's fragile equanimity. She calms the old lady, makes her some tea and finds one of her favourite programmes on the enternet. Once she has her settled, she tells her she's going out for a while but won't be long.

'I'll smooth it over with Naz when I get back – promise,' she says, kissing the top of the older woman's head. 'But he's gonna have to do something about his stuff…'

She sets off to meet Seth, a swill of unease in the pit of her stomach. The streets are busy with higglers doing steady trade in the slightly cooler air of the evening and people milling around the bars and eateries. She keeps to the main areas which have some, albeit unreliable, street lighting. Been some attacks recently, southside; mostly on folks carrying food back from the market, but you can't be too careful these days; people are on the edge. She pulls her outers tightly around her; even though the evening is close and warm, she feels a chill in her bones.

As she makes her way through the moonless night, a medley of scenarios spools round her head: *the test will be positive, no question, but what's to stop Seth lying about it? Or getting this Thelma woman – his father's friend, after all – to lie for him? Say the test was negative. But I could call his bluff, couldn't I? If it's negative, he'd have no reason to stop the sex, would he? And he's not going to turn that down if he doesn't have to. But maybe he'll just decide to end it; use what he calls* the 'baby business' *as an excuse to break up.* She stops still, heart pounding, overwhelmed by the certainty that this is exactly what will happen.

There's a loud noise and she looks up to see a group of males weaving towards her, stripped to the waist, arms in the air (or round each other), chanting something short and repetitive. She presses back into a doorway; not that she's got anything worth stealing, but you never know who'll decide to take issue with the look on your face or the colour of your hair. The men pass by in a waft of alcohol-laced sweat, too preoccupied with each other to notice her and, as their voices begin to fade, she starts off again, returning to the spooling narrative. *I could make him do it, couldn't I? Got a trump card, haven't I? He's an illegal now, after all.* But would she really turn him in and get him imprisoned – or worse? She crosses the now-deserted market square, driving a pathway through the scuttling scavengers. But it wouldn't come to that, would it? *And anyway, why should I care about him? Clearly doesn't care about me.*

Her pace quickens as the pink neon lights of the club materialise from the murk. Several figures are silhouetted against the brightly lit entrance and she recognises him immediately. He's talking to a young female and they're standing close – very close. She's making obvious eyes at him and he's smiling in that way she knows so well. Spikes of jealousy dart in the shallows of her gut as she examines the female with an expert eye. Clearly a Citi girl; not from round here, that's for sure. Nearly as tall as him. Pretty, but in a plain sort of way. Nose a bit big, but then so's her mouth. And isn't she even a bit ginger? *Well, that's enough of that malarky.* She strides towards them.

Seth catches sight of her and waves, saying something to the girl that makes her smile before he comes over to her.

'Who's that?' she asks, evading his attempted kiss and nodding towards Lyse.

'Oh, just the new band member. Singer. Got a sax that she says we can use—'

'Yeah, yeah.' She's no time for this; wants to get straight to the point. 'So, have you thought about what I asked?' Her gaze is even, but her heart is skidding like a foal on ice. This is it: the moment that will change everything. She takes several deep breaths, steeling herself against the worst. But he says nothing as his eyes slide away from hers.

'So?' she challenges.

'So, what?'

'You know what, Seth,' she says, irritated now. 'Don't muck me about. Not on this.'

He glances at her but still doesn't catch her eye and her heart sinks.

'You're not going to, are you?'

He shakes his head, looking anywhere but at her.

She swallows, sick to her stomach. If she thought she had prepared herself for the bitter sink of despair that washes over her now, she was badly wrong. 'Please, Seth.' She clutches at his sleeve, trying to make him look at her. 'It's nothing to you – just bodily waste. But it could be everything to me.'

'Ssh, Vik.' He flinches, trying to move her away from the watching figures.

'Don't shush me,' she snaps, pulling away from him, self-pity turning to anger. 'That's what you want me to do, isn't it? Just shut up and leave you alone. Pretend all this never happened. Well, fuck you, Seth Marcuson. Fuck you!' She turns back to the figures at the door. 'And you lot can go fuck yourselves, as well.' She flicks a finger in their general direction and walks away fast, stumbling on the stony ground.

As she reaches the end of the road, she hears her name and turns to see Queron jogging towards her. She's not in the mood to talk and she's never been quite sure about Seth's best friend – there's something a bit closed off about him. But she's always found it difficult to resist the bottomless brown eyes. And so, when he gives her a hug and asks if she's okay, she begins, despite Seth's warnings, and almost despite herself, to tell him about the baby.

'So Seth's mad at you for going with somebody else? I'm not really surprised, babe. I wouldn't like it much—'

'No, Q!' she snaps. 'I didn't go with anyone else. Thank you for thinking that straight off. Typical male – you're all the fucking same. Well you're wrong, okay?' She looks him hard in the face. 'The baby was Seth's. I didn't "go" with anyone else, as you nicely put it.' She can see his scepticism but presses on. 'I know it's not sposed to be possible, but somehow it happened. That's the truth. Ask Seth if you don't believe me. But now it's dead, so that's the end of it.'

'What's Seth say about all this?'

'That he doesn't believe me; that I'm making it up. And that he doesn't want to be with me anymore.' She kicks at the stony path with a grim smile. *Hadn't actually said that, had he? But might as well have. I'm clearly just an embarrassment to him now, now he's got his new ginger girl.*

'Woah, Vik, you've got to go talk to him about this. He's gone with the others to Mab's – why not go find him? I'll come with, if you like.'

'No, thanks. Don't want to see his poxy viz again any time soon.'

'Okay – it's your call,' Queron says. 'Wanna go somewhere else?'

'Nah, you're all right, gotta get home and sort some stuff,' she says, the lack of sleep and the emotions of the day taking their toll. 'It's okay.' She smiles as she sees his hesitation. 'I'll be fine.'

As he turns to leave she pulls at his arm. 'You won't say anything to anyone about this, Q, will you?' she says, looking into his dark, expressionless eyes. 'Promise? Not even to Seth?'

'Not even to Seth,' he says with a smile she's tired enough to accept as reassuring.

15

BROTHERS

*G**otta be out of her head; scullies, maybe – heard they were having a moment. But she hadn't seemed stoned, had she? Angry, upset, yeah, but not out of it.* Whatever, he's got to tell Seth she's saying mad things about him, no matter what he promised. *It is mad, isn't it? Seth wouldn't – couldn't – keep something that big to himself. Only talked to him yesterday; he'd've said, wouldn't he?* Queron turns and sets off fast back the way he came. Something's going down here, and he intends to find out what.

'Setho!' he calls, pleased to find him on his own at the back of the bar. 'How's it going, cuz? Where's the others?'

'Yeah, okay. Boys're stashing the gear. Said I'd get the drinks in.' Seth grins, sweeping his hand towards the half-empty jug in front of him.

Looks like he's had a few already. 'Great, bro,' he says, filling a glass with the thick, green liquid. He raises it in salutation, downs it in one and looks at his friend. *Best get to it before the others arrive – and before Seth swallows much more of the old emerald nectar.*

'So, just caught up with Viki, didn't I?' he says.

'Oh yeah?' Seth asks with a sardonic smile, sloping in his seat. 'And how was that?'

'Not good, bro. She's saying some mad stuff about you.'

'What sort of stuff?' Seth frowns, trying to straighten.

He looks around the half-empty bar; doesn't want any listening ears. 'Okaay,' he says, refilling his glass and edging closer. 'Going to tell you this, even though she asked me not to. Case she's saying it around.'

'Saying what?' Seth asks, propping himself up on the table.

'That she'd got herself a baby – a real one, mind – but lost it. And, Seth boy, how mad's this? – that you were the daddy.' He sees the alarm in his friend's eye. 'I know,' he gives him a conspiratorial grimace, 'craze or what?'

Seth takes a long slug of his drink and sinks back. 'Not craze actually,' he mutters with a strange expression.

'What, she's been with another geez? You said she was desperate to get with a baby—'

'No!' Seth interrupts loudly. 'Well, I don't know…' he says in a softer tone. 'Maybe. Anyway, she thought she was pregnant but now she says she's not.'

'Does anyone else know about this?' he asks with an incipient prickle of alarm.

'No. Well, apart from Pa. And he'll not say anything. And,' Seth winces, 'I think he might have mentioned it to his friend, Thelma – y'know, his old card buddy?'

'Shit, Setho! What'd he go telling her for? She could've gassed it halfway round the Bannies by now.'

'No. She won't talk. Pa thought she might be able to help.'

'Help?' The prickle of alarm intensifies.

'Yeah, well…' Seth hesitates, taking another swig of his drink. 'She was going to get me a test. Y'know, to prove to Vik that I wasn't the daddy.'

The full import of this information suddenly hits him. 'Waay,

78

Seth boy! You've been keeping this to yourself all this time?'

Seth gives him a rueful smile. 'Guess I thought it would just go away somehow.'

'Oh yeah. The old head in the sand trick.' He gives a short laugh. 'Well, guess it's gone away now, one way or another. But, more seriously, cuz, you've gotta make sure Viki keeps her mouth shut. Doesn't go telling anyone else what she told me. And your pa and the old biddy. Don't want to let any baby rumours get started.'

Seth nods, but he's slumped back against the seat and he's not sure how much, if anything, his friend is taking in. And he's not convinced he'll be forceful enough with Viki. *Too soft, that's Seth's problem.* He'd better make sure she keeps quiet; could get Seth into a lot of trouble if she wanted to – and she seemed angry enough to want to. Even to be suspected of birthing outside the system can bring a man shedloads of trouble.

He knows that better than most.

16

COMING OUT

Lyse is having second thoughts. She'd agreed some time ago, reluctantly, to go to the Debuts with Ammi but, as they near the old Royal Palace, she's beginning to regret that decision. The event is a grand affair – designed to afford human coming-of-age all the pomp and ceremony of a State occasion. Held every year, the ostensible purpose is to celebrate the age cohort's formal entry into the public sphere. But it's sponsored by Gencom, the mega biocorp running the Life Program, and everyone knows the real aim is to shove its Partnership propaganda down impressionable young throats. Nevertheless, she's always been curious to see inside the Palace, its disgraced inhabitants long since removed, and she's not entirely uninterested in having a look at the male of the species *up close and personal*, as Ammi would say. Even so, she's not intending to stay for long.

She and Ammi feed into the animated throng being shepherded by liveried doorbots through a grand portal, along ornately decorated galleries and into the main Palace ballroom.

The splendour of the room takes her breath away; she'd heard it was impressive, but never did she imagine this. Glittering chandeliers hang from the gold-latticed ceiling like giant encrusted fruits, casting a confetto of brilliants across the room. Full-length mirrors line the walls, framed on each side by columns of blood-red marble, their coiled capitals like huge staring eyes. At the far end of the room, a grand ceiling arch, ornamented with plaster creatures, marks the Portal to the virtual arena, currently covered by long, vertical banners of purple silk, carrying the Program motto: '*Vivificans Vita*' – *Life to Life*.

Their fellow guests are forming small clusters along the edges of the room, scanning the scene, and each other, with hardly suppressed excitement, as upmarket waitbots circle around them with smoking drinks and small delicacies. It's the first time most will have been in the company of the differently gendered (outside their family groups or school teams) and the physical proximity of so many youthful bodies is creating an almost tangible frisson in the cool, perfumed air. She's impressed by the attention guests seem to have paid to their appearance – faces and teeth freshly upgraded, hair thickened and oiled, skins covered in the latest animated tattery – and briefly regrets her own lack of effort. She's borrowed one of her mother's formal gowns which had looked nice enough at home, and she knows the green suits her, but she can see it pales in the shade of the more elaborate outfits. Many females – including Ammi, she now notices – are wearing the latest motos. That'll be interesting: controlling the delicately spun gowns, and the emotions they reveal of the wearer, takes a lot of mind-skill. And a lot of years to master. She sniggers softly. Going to be a few here tonight quite literally wearing their hearts on their sleeves.

Some of the guests, roughly half, are wearing the looped cross of the Ank, the insignia of the Life Program, with different metals indicating the status of the wearer: brass for novitiates, silver for inductees and gold for whatever they call the fully processed. As far as she can see, the great majority of pendants appear to be brass with the relatively few gold versions all being worn by males. She finds the sight of so many young throats eagerly adopting the symbol of their reproductive entrapment thoroughly depressing and turns to her half-sibling with a frown.

'Are you really sure about that, Am?' she asks, pointing at the brass pendent hanging round her companion's slender neck. 'I mean, it's such a big decision to take so quickly.'

'Of course I'm sure, Lyse,' Ammi says, her colour rising. 'Or I wouldn't be doing it, would I? And it hasn't been quick, actually. I've been thinking about practically nothing else since finals. Worried that I wouldn't get the grades – not sleeping, not eating…' She regards Lyse with a cool gaze. 'Not that you noticed – too wrapped up in your own thing as usual.'

She says nothing, acknowledging the probable justification of this accusation.

'And they say the earlier the better,' Ammi continues, 'if you're going to get a good Partner, least.'

'Well, it's your life, I spose.' She shrugs. 'If you want to be an obedient Program-wife servicing some man who has who knows however many other so-called "Partners" and, once you're too old to breed, casts you back to where you started from, then go ahead.'

'Yes, thanks, Lyse, I know very well what you think about it,' Ammi says, her moto flushing dark purple. 'Don't need to go on. Can you see now why I didn't say anything to you? Would've been weeks and weeks of this. And anyway,' she says more calmly as her dress fades to lavender, 'males don't take other Partners now and—'

'Hang on, Am,' she interrupts, as her attention, already wavering, is caught by the sudden movement of the waitbots, arranging themselves into paired lines down the centre of the hall. Once arranged, do-si-do, they strike up a strident melody – soothing and unnerving at the same time, like metallic bagpipes. The mirrors on the walls flash briefly, then fill with a hi-spec holo of a dark-skinned female, beautifully formed and exquisitely costumed.

'Welcome, graduands,' the virtual woman says as she raises her arms wide to the assembled guests, the pearlised fabric of her dress slipping like milk over the slender slopes of her streamlined body. A sweet, musky fragrance fills the room and, she can tell by the collective inhalation, the nose of every watcher.

'On behalf of our generous sponsor, Gencom Global,' the image says with a slight bow, her voice mellifluous, her accent strange, indeterminate, 'I would like to welcome you to the 38th Annual North Europa Debuts.'

A few cheers and whistles erupt from the floor, but the crowd is largely quiet, watching expectantly.

'More importantly,' the image continues, her pale gown glowing a radiant yellow, 'I would like to welcome you to the threshold of adult life. You have reached a stage on your Human Journey when you will need to make many crucial decisions – about where, and with whom, you will live, for example, and how you will spend your time on our wonderful Planet. But one decision matters above all else,' she pauses and appears, unnervingly, to look directly into Lyse's eyes, 'and that is whether you wish to make your personal contribution to the future of our species.'

Lyse blinks hard and casts a questioning look at Ammi, who, pretty predictably, appears enraptured.

'You here are the lucky ones,' the female is saying with a slow, intimate smile, seeming to lean out of the mirror frame towards the listeners. 'Not everyone in your cohort has been given this wonderful opportunity. Some left the education system too early or developed unacceptable behaviours too young. Others failed to achieve the required level of socio-emoto maturity…' The image freezes as animated discussions break out across the room about those who expectedly, or unexpectedly, failed to make the grade.

'But all of you,' it restarts as the chatter dies down, 'are here because you *did* make the grade. You have all proved fit – in body and mind – to be the Parents of the next generation. Some of you, I know, have already made that momentous decision and, on behalf of our Sponsor and, indeed,' her sleek gown gives off a rosy-pink glow, 'on behalf of Humanity itself, I welcome you to the Life Program.'

A few self-congratulatory cheers and raised arms emit from the gold Ank-wearers, trailing off rather self-consciously in the otherwise hushed ambience of the room.

'To those of you who have yet to decide,' the virtual female continues, and again Lyse gets the uncanny feeling of being addressed personally, 'I would urge you to do so soon. You are all at your biophysical peak now, but you will stay so only briefly.' The pale pink of her dress fades to charcoal grey as she looks at the audience, her face grave.

'Delay too long and you could well find that you have left it too late to take part in Life's most amazing adventure.'

Ammi nudges her at this point, with a 'told you so' nod of her head – a flush of excitement in her usually calm face and a blush of scarlet tipping the edges of her gown.

'To help you with this momentous decision,' the woman is saying, 'the new, remodelled *Life and Loving* virtual will be playing in the Gencom arena tonight. It's a great show,' she says, her dress flashing a flirty tangerine, 'all your uncertainties uncovered and explored in a no-holds-barred, full-sensory experience. I recommend it to you all most strongly, but especially to those of you' – *was that another direct look?* – 'who remain undecided'.

'Whatever you finally choose, I would like to take this opportunity to congratulate you all on your splendid achievements. You deserve to be very proud of yourselves. And you should be very grateful to the Parents and Guardians, sponsors and supporters who have invested so much in you. I hope you continue to make them proud as you go forward in Life.'

'So, Worldspeed to you all,' the image says with a small bow, bringing her jewel-tipped fingers together at her forehead. 'Travel carefully – you have the future of our beloved Planet in your hands.'

She claps the crowd, which applauds her (itself?) enthusiastically in return.

'And now,' she says as the applause dies down, 'I leave you to enjoy the main event of the evening: the 2060 Ank Parade.'

The image flashes off and the waitbots restart their discordant fanfare as they set about dividing the room into two single-sex groups. She sees a few bots engaged in animated discussions with some of the guests who, she suspects, are protesting at the crude biological polarisation.

'Okay, Am,' Lyse says with a grimace as she looks at the visibly and audibly excited young people around her – their gowns flushing hot spectrum colours as they criss-cross the room. 'I'm not doing any of this bollox. Soon as Jai's done his bit, I'm off.'

'But you have to do it, Ly,' Ammi protests. 'They'll announce your name and it'll get noticed if you don't show. You'll get penalties—'

'Don't really care, actually,' she snaps, annoyed by the familiar moue of disapproval on Ammi's face. 'They can do what they like, but I'm not parading round the room like a prize animal. Everybody gawking. *You* may have signed up for this meat-market, but I certainly haven't.'

The males are called first to the Promenade, in alphabetical order. As each starts the circumnavigation of the arena, his personal details flash up in the mirror-spaces: vital statistics, biodata, age, notable academic, cultural and sporting awards. The level of applause each gets, added to their academic rating and multiplied by their current epop level, produces an overall score – the Livstat – the single most important determinant of an individual's future life chances. She watches Jai manage his turn, taking pride in his considerable accomplishments, and contributes loudly to his accolade, but turns to Ammi as the applause dies.

'Right. I'm off – try and persuade some low-grade doorbot to give me a sick pass.' She gives her companion a warm hug, feeling bad about her sharp words earlier.

'You'll be okay, Am?'

'Yeah, I'll be fine, Lyse, don't worry,' Ammi says in a light tone. 'Might go and find Jai – see if he'll come to the virts with me.'

'Well, good luck with that.' She grins as she sidles towards the nearest exit.

She's about to leave the building, having finally secured a passout from an annoyingly resistant doorbot, when she hears an unfamiliar male voice call her name. She turns and recognises the face. It's one of her swim team. Samuel something. A pale, pink man with weird hair; seen him at meets, but not really taken much notice.

'Oh, hi, Samuel,' she replies with a polite smile, noting the gold pendant dangling round his neck.

'It's Samael, actuals.'

'Sorry?'

'Samael, not Samuel,' he says, approaching. 'But don't worry, everyone gets it wrong. Pretty stupid name, really…'

'No, it's nice – unusual. Always good to be different.'

He moves towards her with a smile, thin lips pulled wide over small teeth. 'Not leaving already?'

'Yeah, think so,' she says, trying not to catch the odd look in his insipid blue eyes. 'Was good to see the Palace, but I'm not up for all this parading bollox. And this so-called "music",' she waves unspecifically in the air, 'is really doing my head in.'

He moves nearer and tells her that he's heard she likes real music and that he does too. 'Old stuff,' he says, 'like Elvish and the Rocking Stones.' She stops herself from laughing out loud at this but only because she can never resist an opportunity to talk music. He asks if she knows where he can see live bands and she tells him about BB's and how she's hoping to get a guest slot there as a singer. Rashly, she offers to get him tickets and he seems to take this personally. 'Maybe we could go together…?' he asks, sidling closer.

'Yeah, sure,' she says, regretting her hasty offer and uneasy at the closeness of his person. 'Usually go with my brother. I'm sure he'll be happy for you to come with us sometime.' She starts towards the door, but he moves to block her path.

'I like you when you're like this, Lyse,' he says, standing so close now that she can see the fluff on his upper lip and smell his pungent odour. 'Always thought you were a bit stuck up…'

Cheek! She takes a step back.

'But you're different tonight, somehow,' he says, coming up to her again, his thick fingers snaking her waist as he tries to pull her towards him, a sour tang in his heavily perfumed breath. 'You're my sort of girl, Lyse,' he lisps. 'We could make good music together.'

She does laugh out loud at this absurdity, but he seems not to notice.

'I'm already signed up,' he continues as he waves the pendant and starts to press something – at once both horribly hard and sickeningly soft – against her thigh. Something she doesn't like the feel of at all.

'Look, Samuel, Samael or whatever your stupid name is,' she says angrily, shoving him in the chest. 'Just because you've got yourself on the Program doesn't make you World's gift to women, y'know. Need to spend some time getting to know people before you start poking yourself at them.'

She stares at his pink flushed face, his thin mouth caught somewhere between a smirk and a snivel, and embarrassment and disgust flood over her in equal measure.

'For the sake of the team,' she says, forcing herself to keep looking at him, despite her squirming stomach, 'I'm going to pretend that nothing just happened. And I strongly suggest you do too. For now,' she says as she turns to go, 'just stay away from me, okay? And you can forget about the tickets – if, indeed, you even really like that sort of thing – which I very much doubt.' She walks away, heart thumping.

So much for the male of the species.

17

POST-MORTEM

'And he just kept edging nearer until he was right up close, grubbing my waist with his stumpy fingers, pressing his fat belly into me. Yeeuck and more yeeuck.' Lyse is lying across the end of Ammi's bed, getting into her stride.

'Honest, Am, it was the grotest thing I've ever experienced. How on Earth could he think that anyone in their right mind would want him to do that? Was only talking to him at all cos he's in my swim team – and he's not exactly the star of that. And the worst is…' she reaches a perfect pitch of indignation, 'he clearly thought I should be grateful – swinging his gold thing in my face, like it was some kind of medal.'

'Sounds like the sort of male they should be keeping off the Program,' Ammi tuts.

'Exacts. Not go winding them up and turning them loose on unsuspecting womankind. But that's just what they do, isn't it? There were others just like him. You saw them – the ones with the gold Anks. Buzzing around like king bees. Mind you, some of the females were well up for it too. Did you see that Danni from citizen club? Practically eating the face of that Mathewson kid. And as for Jai…' She sneaks a glance across at her companion.

'What about Jai?'

'Oh, nothing…' she says fast, but is unable to resist entirely. 'Just that I saw that plastic womanikin, Carli Angidottir, draping herself all over him as I was leaving.' She tries to sound casual. 'And someone said they saw them go into the virts together.'

'Oh, I'm sure she's not his type,' Ammi says in an airy manner. 'I'm sure he wants more from a mate than a toned body and a perfect face.'

'Yeah, you may be right,' she says. She's actually not so sure – he'd seemed pretty captivated by Ms Angidottir's thrusting décolletage – but something in her adopted sibling's tone suggests she should keep that thought to herself.

'Anyway, he's not interested in all that yet, is he?' Ammi half states, half-asks. 'He's got his precious Gencom job, hasn't he?'

'Well, those two things are not mutually exclusive for males, are they, Am? It's only females who have to give it all up.'

'He hasn't said anything to you, has he?' Ammi asks.

'About what exactly?'

'About going on the Program. Whether he's thinking about it?' She regards her companion closely, noting the blush. 'You like him a lot, don't you?'

'Well yes, ov,' Ammi says, picking at her shift. 'Would be odd if I didn't, as we've lived together for most of my life. He's practically my brother.'

'But he's not, is he?' she persists. 'He's not your brother, is he?'

'Well, no, not literally… but he's as close as I've got.'

She can hear the hurt in Ammi's voice. 'No, I didn't mean that, silly.' She reaches over and takes her hand. 'It's not a point about family, Am,' she says, recalling her mother's words. 'You're family as much as any of us. No, I just meant that you can like him in a different way, can't you, if he's not your blood brother, that is?'

Ammi stares at her picked-over dress, saying nothing, the sides of her sleekly bobbed hair hiding the expression on her face. Lyse knows that she should stop now. It's perfectly clear that Ammi has feelings for Jai. Does she really need to make her spell it out?

The incoming pin saves them both from the worst of herself.

'Talk of the devil...' She grins as it opens. 'What's he want?'

She can't believe what she hears. 'Blimes, Am!' she gasps. 'Jai says they've found a dead female down by the Club we went to the other night. Think she's been murdered.'

18

SMALL LIVES

'Here's one for you, Coop. Right up your street.'
Don is filling the small doorway, stuffing a protesting tunic into an overtight waistband. His colour is high. 'Dead girl,' he says in a cheerful manner, blotting his forehead with a pad. 'Found in a ditch, southern edge of the Bannies, down by the allotments.'

'Why's that up my street, Boss?' he replies in a mild tone. *Don't tell me he's putting me on road cleaning now.* 'Won't the sanitaries handle it?'

Don moves into the room; as he stands wide-legged, large hands spread on substantial hips, he seems drawn on entirely the wrong scale for the small space.

'Well, that's just it, Coop,' his boss says with a swift hitch to his trousers, as if to catch the frisky tunic unawares, 'doesn't look like a suicide. In fact, isn't at all clear what it *does* look like. Initial virtop shows no evident cause. Heart stopped suddenly, but not clear why. Possibly drugs, although none of the obvious apart from a mild cannabinoid. Some water in the lungs, but not enough to drown and no sign of suffocation. But before you say that sounds like natural cause,' Don holds up a hand, 'there's evidence of what looks like recent, and pretty brutal, sexual activity. Damage done – lots – but, again, not enough to kill her.'

His boss sits down hard on the lone chair in front of Coop's desk and looks at him with a grim smile. 'And then there's the body itself – very odd…'

He raises an eyebrow. 'In what way odd?' he asks.

'Well, have a look,' Don replies, flicking up a holo and enlarging to life-size. 'You're always saying how it's important to immerse yourself in the crime scene. So, there you are…' He jabs a stubby finger into the crystalline image. 'See what I mean? Decidedly odd. Looks like the body's been laid out quite carefully, not just dumped. There's plant matter in her hair and hands – looks like it was put there deliberately. Another odd thing too,' he says, dabbing a glistening cheek. 'Although the body was still fresh, baggers said it gave off a strong smell. Nasty, very nasty. No ID on that yet. But otherwise, she was strangely clean. Been penetrated – very roughly – but not clear with what; might get something if it was human. And that's about it. Lab's still looking, but not optimistic, given where the body was left.'

He looks at the pathetic figure lying in the plant-strewn ditch. Strands of dirty blonde hair straggle round a pale, oval face whose half-closed eyes and part-open mouth appear untroubled by death. *Seems almost peaceful.* Can't be more than twenty years old. And not much to her – hard to imagine she could have bothered anyone enough to kill her.

'So,' his boss is continuing, 'we don't know *what* she died of, rigor and vapor disagree, so we don't know exactly *when* she died and, of course, the biochip's missing, so we have no idea *who* she is. Apart from that,' he chuckles, 'we've got a lot to go on…'

Don snaps off the image and leans back in the chair, arms behind his head, a wide smile on his multi-layered face. Coop observes the patches of underarm damp with mild distaste. 'See what I mean?' Don grins. 'Just up your street.'

'Well, yes, but if it turns out that it's a sex crime, that'll mean—'

'Yes, yes, we'll have to notify the Stews.'

'And that didn't go particularly well last time, if you remember.'

His boss sucks his teeth. 'Well, we'll cross that cosmic corridor if we come to it, eh? Come on, Coop…' He leans towards him, the lashes of his insipid grey eyes beaded with sweat. 'What d'you think?'

'What do I think?' he replies – ignoring the fact that Don knows he's dangling a fresh kipper in front of a hungry cat. 'Well, what I think is that we have three key questions. First, whether the female killed herself – intentionally or not – or was killed by another; second, whether, and by whom – or what – she was sexually attacked and third, whether the attack and her death were related or, indeed, committed by the same person.'

Don beams at him, rising from the chair. 'Great, kiddo! Knew it'd be up your street. Lots of "ifs", "buts" and "maybes". I'll leave it with you then, Coop.' He gives a quick wave as he exits, the back of his ill-fitting tunic, having finally broken free, departing a triumphant nanosecond later.

He frowns at the closed door. Not sure about this; the sexual attack is worrying. Last thing he wants is to get mixed up with the Stews again. But if it *was* a human, it's likely to be a Program boy; non-repros don't have much appetite for sex. Most of their energies, outside scratching a living, are spent watching global sports or playing in the virts – when they're not sitting around getting stoned, that is. Males fight, no question, with each other and with women – over coin, food, whatever – but it's extremely rare for male violence to take a sexual form. Can't recall a case of a sexual assault by a male infert, on any sex, since he's been in the job. Might be a few of the old snip dodgers around, admittedly, who could still have the desire, but most would be too old now to take on a healthy young female – unless she was seriously weakened.

Could have been a female attacker, of course. Sexual crime

by women is certainly on the rise (his last case, for a start) and occasionally the victim is female, but the targets are typically the newly reversed Program recruits – mostly Citi boys – who venture across to the Banleus looking for sex. Difficult to feel sympathy for them, given how witlessly they invite their downfall. Think they're the hunters, but the incontinence of their sexual need makes them easy game for desperate young females seeking to mate. Or maybe it wasn't an attack; maybe the sex, rough though it clearly was, was consensual. Erotic asphyxia or some such…

He shakes his head. Getting ahead of himself. Needs to start at the beginning: find out who she was. Nothing more pitiful than a body without a name. She must have been someone to somebody – daughter, sister, friend, lover. Someone'll know something; they're a close-knit lot in the Bannies. He'll have to get down there and ask around face to face; no good trying to use the threadbare public web. Few but the orgs and the coms use that since the central control plane was set up. To protect people from crooks and terrorists, the government said; to snoop and sniff around more like, the people believed. The GIANT, they named it – the Global, Immersive, Ambient, Networked Territory. The SPYder, the people call it, and spend considerable effort trying to elude its inquisitive and intrusive presence. He checks the time; could get down there now – no time like the present. He stands and stretches his cramped frame. *What I really need is a long, slow swim. Tomorrow, definitely.*

He gets lucky with the name. After a hot and sticky couple of hours visiting the virthalls and bars, one of the market traders identifies her as a Viki Jansdottir: 'Used to work the clothes stall over there,' the man says, pointing to small stand nearby, shuttered and locked. 'Wondered why she hadn't been in recently, usually set your clock by her. Sweet young thing; nothing's happened to her, has it?'

He finds her on Edorg: Viktori Dotti Jansdottir, twenty-two and five months, last registered as living with a relative in the social housing blocks at the edge of Banleu North. It doesn't take him long to find the address; one of the more run-down streets in one of the more run-down parts of the urban sprawl outside the Citi's walls. The middle-aged female who answers the door is clearly in a very poor biostate. *How do people get so large when food's so short?* he wonders as he follows her into the small, terraced house. She moves with a slow, rolling gait and is visibly short of breath by the time they reach the cramped living space. He waits until her breathing has settled before showing her the picture of Viki and takes her hand when she whimpers in recognition and starts up a long, low moan, rocking backwards and forwards in her chair.

As she calms herself a little he manages to tease out some of the girl's background. She, the 'aunt' – he doubts she's a blood relative – had brought Viki up since she was about six (she thinks), supported by a small Program allowance. Her real mother had died young, 'some funny business there', and the biological father had scarpered soon as he found out the mother was pregnant, and before he could be officially registered. 'She was a good girl,' the aunt insists, gripping him with her doughy hands, 'always kind and helpful. Do anything for anyone, she would.' Her eyes fill with tears as she shakes her threadbare head. 'How could anyone do that to such a lovely wee girl?'

He lets her weep for a while, stroking her hand as her large body trembles, then gently encourages her on. Viki was a clever girl, she tells him; could easily have got on the Program if she hadn't dropped out of school. Last few years she'd been running a clothes stall in the central market. Didn't have many friends, the aunt sniffles, but she was mad about live music. Used to hang out a lot at a club near the market. Bee something, she thinks. Close with a boy in a band there, Seth someone, but not sure. Can't remember the name of the band. Last time she saw her was Saturday evening. Yes, think she was going out to meet the boy Seth, but she didn't say. And no, wasn't unusual for her to stay out all night.

He has a quick look round the sleeping space the girl appears to share with the aunt but there's not much to find. Like the dilapidated house generally, it's pretty bare: odd bits of face paint on a sideboard; a few clothes on the chair and floor; a row of small plants – dead, by the looks – on the window ledge. He checks the port. No sign of any virtaction as far as he could see; Webprint negligible; subscription expired many months ago. Mostly old adpins of one kind or another, or the incessant 'quick win' and 'good luck' offers. The only real sense of the occupant herself is a couple of hand-printed flyers for local bands stuck on the wall, which he pockets, and two small fluffy animals – one pink, one blue – staring out beadily from a neatly made bed.

His spirits are low as he leaves the aunt struggling with her loss in her bare little house. *Why is it always those with so little that seem to lose most?* Whoever does not have, even that will be taken from them. *Wasn't that from one of the old faith books? Well, they weren't wrong there, for once.* He thinks himself a modern man and is generally optimistic about human progress but sometimes it feels that just too many people are being remaindered, like yesterday's hardware, in the great race forward.

Back at the office, the news from the lab is both good and bad. Good because, while there was nothing on the body, they found two saliva traces on the victim's scarf. And the attack was definitely by a human male. The attacker used protection, so no semen, but with luck they'll find the make and origin of the sheath. But bad news because there's no further insight on cause of death; *instantaneous neurogenic arrest of indeterminate cause* is the unhelpful conclusion. What *is* clear, however, is that Viki Jansdottir didn't die where she was found; her body was moved after her death. She might have died accidentally, of course, and somebody moved her to the ditch for some inexplicable reason…

But no, he rubs his hands, *on balance, this is looking very much like murder.*

19

THE BROFRIEND

Coop had found the club the aunt mentioned easily enough – not far from the south end of the market square. The handbill he'd taken from the girl's room showed five young males posing, in what he assumes is considered a 'moody' fashion, above the legend: *The Beatniks: BB's Hip New House Band*. The big blighter at the door, however, had been less than helpful; only grudgingly parting with the information that: *Yep, there's a Seth in one of the house bands. Nope, don't know his family name or where he lives. Yep, could well be playing that evening, but haven't got the running order yet and, yep, bands usually have a run-through before the show. Maybe six or seven-ish.*

He'd extracted even less from him on the subject of the dead female: *Yep, was on the door Saturday night – on most nights, in fact. Pay's shite, given I'm here all hours dealing with an endless flow of low-lifes; on my feet, constant... Nope, don't recognise her; loads of girls hang round the club every night – all look much the same to me. Why? What's happened? Anys I should tell the management?*

He returns to the club just before six to find the big wooden doors firmly shut, and no sign of human activity. Knocking has no impact, except on his knuckles, and there is nothing to be seen through the dirty windows. He's about to give up when he hears the sound of laughter and looks up to see two young males approaching.

'You're too early, mate,' one of them calls out. 'Not open till eight.'

He gives them a friendly smile, showing his badge, and tells them he's looking for a musician called Seth. Wonders if he's playing tonight.

'Better be,' the two men exchange sniggers, 'being as how he's our dear leader, init?'

'Then I'll come in and wait, if that's all right,' he says, and follows them into the hall, flinching at the stale, deflated air of yesterday's fun. The men make busy on the stage, setting up stacks and stands and unwinding rolls of wires. A beep from outside summons them out, to return shortly with more equipment and what he assumes are two other band members. *Result!* He smiles as he sees he's been pointed out to one of the new arrivals.

The young male saunters over, holding out his hand. 'I'm Seth Marcuson,' he says. 'Hear you wanted a word?'

Handsome male, he thinks as he introduces himself, taking in the striking blue eyes and the open face with its distinctive chin-cleft. He watches that face intently as he shows him the image of the girl and asks if he knows her.

'Yeah, that's Vik. Viki Jansdottir.' The young man gives a broad smile, small dimples forming in the centre of his cheeks. 'We're...' he hesitates, 'good mates,' he selects in the end. 'Hangs round with the band. Why?' His smile becomes more cautious. 'Has something happened to her, Detective?'

'Well, yes, it has, rather,' he replies in a quiet voice as he closes the image and tells him about Viki.

'Dead?' The musician's fresh complexion blanches. 'No way! I only saw her a couple of nights ago. Can't be her.' He gives a firm shake of the head. 'Must be another girl. Lots look the same round here…'

He tells him that there's no mistake; that her aunt identified her body this morning. 'They're still determining the exact cause of death, but they're pretty sure she's been murdered.' He asks if Viki had any enemies, or had got herself into any kind of trouble, but the young man's response is as disbelieving as the aunt's.

'Okay…' He smiles as he takes out his notebook. 'You say you last saw her two days ago – that'll be… Saturday night?' The young man assents. 'And what time was that exactly?'

'Must've been close to midnight. We'd not long got off stage and were having a smoke. She arrived just after. We'd arranged to meet…' He stops, his open face clouding over. 'Can't be right,' he says with a doleful look. 'Only just saw her…'

He gives a sympathetic nod, then asks how Viki had seemed when he last saw her.

'Well, she was a bit upset, to be honest,' the young man replies, with an awkward smile. 'With me. Had a bit of a row, actually. Nothing major. Vik thought I was getting too close to the new girl in the band, that's all,' he says with a shrug. 'Bit of a misunderstanding.'

'Oh? But why would that bother her?' he asks, finding this odd. 'You weren't in a Partnership, were you?'

'Nah. Not eligible,' he says with a thin smile. 'But we were close. Known her since primes; almost like a sister.' For a brief moment, his eyes shift away and Coop thinks he sees a hint of colour on his cheek.

'Don't think she'd got anyone else much. Apart from her Aunt Dottie,' the young male continues, his restless eyes returning to his. 'Oh, and a brother who'd just turned up from somewhere. Wasn't very happy about that.'

'Oh?' he asks, making a note. *Strange the aunt didn't mention it. But then, didn't think to ask, did I? Immerse yourself in the scene, isn't it? If I'd done so, would have picked the signs of a male presence. Careless.*

'A brother? Are you sure?'

'Yeah, pretty sure. Said it was weird having a male around the house – didn't much like it…' His voice trails off and his eyes drift away again.

'So, had you?' he asks, bringing him back.

The musician frowns. 'Had I what?' he asks.

'Been getting "too close" with this new band member?'

'No!' the young man says with force, a full flush of colour on his cheeks now. 'She's – Lyse, that is – only just joined the band. We've been working on some songs together, that's all. You can ask her.'

'Well, I'll certainly do that.' He smiles, making another note. 'Is she on tonight, by any chance?'

The young man shakes his head. 'No, not until Friday. First gig.'

'Okay… so going back to that night, what happened after you and Viki argued?'

'Well, she stormed off. Was going to go after but…' He breaks off with an uncomfortable look.

Coop raises his eyebrows, with an encouraging smile.

'Just thought I'd let her cool off a bit,' the musician says with a slight shrug.

'Okay, and then?'

'Then,' he continues, his expression turning sheepish, 'I walked Lyse to the bridge, left her around one, then joined the boys for a drink at Mab's – our usual. Stayed there until, maybe three-ish, then walked most of the way home with Keif and Mik – don't know where the others went. Got in 'bout half an hour later. You can see the domlog—'

They're interrupted by a shout from the stage and the musician checks the time. 'Look, I've got to go now, Detective,' he says, with an apologetic look. 'We're on in an hour and I've got run-through.'

'Of course.' He gives him another sympathetic smile. 'Thank you for your time. Please stay close to home – I'll almost certainly want to speak to you again.'

The young male nods and Coop watches him walk back to his bandmates with a visible lessening of his earlier youthful bounce. Not quite sure what to make of him. His shock seemed pretty genuine, but he can't quite shake the feeling he was holding something back – that something important lay in what he *didn't* say. The argument suggests a possible motive – he'd protested rather too much that there was nothing going on with the new girl, hadn't he? – and he just about had time between leaving the bar and arriving home, although, admittedly, it would've been a bit of a stretch. Or she could have called round to see him later – there's still no verified time of death, after all, and logs can always be interfered with, if you know the right people. Maybe they'd met up later and argued again. Maybe she'd pushed him too far on the jealousy thing…

He shakes his head, enough of the maybes. *Unhelpful speculation is destructive to the logical faculties, as the man would say. Need to follow the facts – build on what we know.* Which is not a lot right now. But we've got some meat on the victim's bones, so to speak. It's clear she thought of Marcuson as her boyfriend, otherwise why would she be jealous of his relationship with another girl? But he seems not to see himself in that way. And he denies any relationship with the new girl although, as the sex worker said of the politician, *'He would say that, wouldn't he?'*

So, was the argument just a bit of a misunderstanding, or was it something deeper? Jealousy and anger are powerful motives, after all. Well… he adjusts the rim of his hat as he leaves the club, there's three people in this relationship. *Let's go and see what Mr Marcuson's 'other woman' has to say for herself.*

20

DEEP WATER

'Shit, cuz. Can't believe it. Viki? Murdered? Nooo... Shit!'
Queron exhales a slow stream of vapour through pursed lips.

Seth is leaning against the wall overlooking the orbital waterway. The gig hadn't been easy, but at least it had kept his mind off the cop's news. There's nothing to divert it now. He gazes out at the water, his thoughts blankly adrift. The moon is casting a shimmering path across the pale expanse, beyond which the Citi's towers stand in glittering relief against a darkening sky lightly dusted with stars, but the beauty of the scene is passing him by. He turns to his friend with a grimace.

'Cops think it's me, don't they?'

'What'd you tell them?'

'That it wasn't me – ov!' He tries a smile but isn't able to rise above his low mood. 'That we went to Mabs after the gig and stayed there till we got kicked out, what, a couple of hours after you left. Too pissed to walk straight after that, never mind murder someone. Boys'll vouch for that.'

'Did you say anything to the pols about the baby thing?' Queron asks with an anxious glance.

He shakes his head and turns again to the glimmering water. But it *was* all about the baby thing, wasn't it? He recalls the sour look in her eyes when they parted. Should have talked to her, tried to explain. Calmed her down before she left, at least. But too caught up with Lyse, wasn't he, to bother with Viki and her personal, possibly imaginary, dramas? He'd been pleased when she'd left, TBH. But now…

'Shouldn't have let her go,' he says, turning back to his friend. 'If we hadn't argued, if I'd gone after her—'

'Well, I went after her and she told me to piss off, basics. You'd've got worse, bro,' Queron says briskly. 'And you can't go beating yourself up about that. Vik had a mind of her own. When she sparked up she wasn't going to be mollied by anyone – not even you.'

'Yeah, guess so,' he says, scraping some solace from that fact.

'So, if Vik *was* pregs,' Queron continues, 'the murderer must be the daddy, no? Banged her up then shut her up. That'll be it.' He gives a short laugh, sweeping back his dark fringe and pulling on the vape. 'Well, whoever it was is going to get it. Stews'll be all over him like snot. Murder of a dirt girl's one thing – nobody'll be that bothered – blame it on some random chav – but ferting outside the Program – that's big shit.'

'But they won't know about the baby, will they?' he says, his stomach stirring. 'Unless I—'

'Unless you nothing,' Queron breaks in. 'It won't bring Vik back and it might just open up a stinking can of worms – with you in the middle. You gotta hope they *don't* find out about the "was it-wasn't it" baby. Concealing an illegal pregnancy's big doolies.' He takes a tight hold of Seth's upper arms and looks at him closely, his dark eyes intense.

'We've been through this, bro…'

He manages a weak smile this time. 'Yeah, okay.' He knows

he should be thinking things through for himself, but right now it's comforting just to do what he's told. And Queron's not usually wrong.

'Kay then,' Queron says, patting him on the shoulder, 'that's sorted. Look, I gotta be elsewhere. You ice?'

He nods and they exchange a brief hug before his friend starts to walk away.

'Oh, and Setho?' Queron stops and turns back. 'Did you say anything to the cops about me?'

'About you?'

'Yeah, about me going after Vik. Was only with her a split, so might just leave me out of it, 'kay?'

He gives his friend a curious look. 'Sure, Q, but—'

'Just in the middle of something right now.' Queron winks. 'Last thing I need is any pols poking round.'

'Okay.' He shrugs. 'No worries.'

'Cheers, bro. Appreciates!' Queron waves as he heads off towards the bridge.

Seth stands for a while looking out across the moon-slicked water, made more menacing now by a large bank of steely-grey cloud advancing from the west. Was Queron right? Was there was another man, and did he kill Viki because he got her pregnant? Kinda makes sense; about the only thing that does so far, anyway. So, he's got to tell the cops about the baby, hasn't he? Motive and all that. Bastard could get away with it otherwise.

But might they start wondering about him? Give him a test on the off chance? And anyway, most likely her death had nothing to do with the baby – if indeed there ever was a baby. No good putting your head in someone else's noose, as Q would say. Just Vik's bad luck. But then she never really had any other kind of luck, did she? And he hadn't exactly helped, had he? Some friend he'd been. He pulls his eyes, with some effort, away from the dark water, a pigswill of emotion in his gut, as the thuggish grey cloud makes its move on the sky's remaining light.

21

DINNER TIME

Carli is draped over a lounger, her long, sculptured legs clearly arranged for best viewing advantage. She's wearing one of the new skinfits, in shimmering salmon, the rubbery ribbing stretched so tight her body resembles a giant pink pupa. Much to Lyse's disgust, Jai has asked her to dinner to meet them all (or rather, she suspects, has been wheedled by the young Program wannabe into bringing her round – the approval of any living parent of a potential mate being essential for acceptance onto the Program).

'Well, anys,' Carli is opining, in a slow, slappy voice, wriggling as she talks, 'she must've brought it on herself in some way. They always do, girls like that.'

Lyse bristles (not for the first time that night). 'Girls like what exactly, Carli?'

'Oh, you know, red-dirt girls. Probs out of her skull. And why was she wanders around on her own at night? Asking for troubs.'

'No-one actually asks for trouble, Carli,' Ammi retorts, with some heat. 'Certainly not the kind that ends in murder.'

'Just saying as it is, girls.' Carli smiles sweetly at them both, patting the tight blue coils framing her face. 'Whatevs, it's not like we know her or anys, ist?'

'Well, I did know her, actually,' she says, and tells them she'd met her a couple of times – used to be close with a musician in the band she, Lyse, plays with. But before they say the obvious, she tells them she knows the musician didn't kill her.

'How can you be so sure, Lyse?' Ammi asks with a frown.

'Because,' she gives a small laugh, 'I'm his alibi. Well, part-alibi, least. He was with me on the night Viki died; walked me home. Pols interviewed me earlier – a Detective Cooper-Clark. Quite sleek, actually. Wears a hat, like in the old movies.'

'Who was wearing a hat?' Ida asks, bringing in a large, covered dish. 'Don't see so many of them these days – don't go very well with the blessed masks, I suppose.'

'Oh, just the detective I told you about, Ma,' Lyse replies. 'We're just talking about Viki.'

'Poor girl.' Ida shakes her head. 'Terrible thing. Sorry…' she nods from the dish to the messy table, 'can you make a bit of room, please; this is very hot.'

'Ma's famous fishy pie,' Jai says to Carli as Ammi clears a space in the middle of the table. Ida uncovers the pot and peers through the steam at their guest. 'Carli, dear, can I help you to some?' she asks, indicating the greyish lumpy mound. 'It's not real fish, of course,' she says as a slight wrinkle creases Carli's perfectly remodelled nose.

'Just a tiny bit for me, please, Mother Saldottir,' Carli replies. 'I'm not really big on fishalikes. And I have to watch my intake. That looks just a tingy bit calorifs.' She smiles round at the others as if certain of their interest. 'I'm always told I eat like a bird.'

'Prob is, Ly,' Jai says as he eyes his loaded plate cautiously, 'word is they can't nail the time of death – so your alibi might not hold up. Something to do with where the body had been left—'

'Please,' Ida says in a firm tone, as she sits down to her (tiny) plate of food, 'can we talk about this later? I really don't think it's an appropriate topic for the meal table.'

'Sol, Mother Saldottir…' Carli says with a cloying smile.

Ida frowns slightly. 'Just call me Ida, dear, would you? I don't like all that Mother nonsense.'

Lyse smiles into her plate.

They talk about other, lighter, things as they eat their meal. Jai's hopes for his Gencom internship, Ida's latest spy stories, but mostly Carli's ambitions to win the regional heats of the *Homo Perfectus* (Caucasian class) and the very precise dietary and exercise regime she will be following to that end.

Lyse – who has had just about enough of this tale, and its teller – rises as her mother begins to remove the dishes from the table. 'I'll help you with that, Ma,' she says uncharacteristically.

'What a total dope!' she exclaims when she and Ida are alone in the kitchen. 'What on sweet Earth does Jai see in her? Okay, she looks good, I'll give you that – although a stitch *too* perfect, if you ask me – but what a World-beating, self-centred melon – *Caucasian class.*'

'Lyse!' Ida admonishes in a half-hearted way. 'You're always very quick to judge people – often wrongly, as you know.'

'Well, I'm sorry, but Jai can do a lot better than that. Someone like Ammi's worth ten of her.'

'What's Ammi got to do with it?' Ida asks with a curious look.

'Well, you must know she's keen on Jai – and not in a sisterly way either.'

Her mother raises her eyebrows. 'Where on Earth did you get that idea? It's not surprising they're close, is it? They've spent nearly all their lives together.' She shakes her head with a tut. 'No, Ly, it's just your overactive imagination.'

'No, Ma, I'm not imagining things. Something's changed between them recents. She got all hot under the collar when I asked her about Jai the other day. And she's hating Carli being here tonight – you watch her when you go back in. See if I'm not right.'

'Well, you may be right. But if I were you, Ly, I'd keep my nose well out of it.'

Later, as the meal has been cleared away and they have moved to the easy chairs in front of Ida's rickety old cooler, the topic of Viki's murder is resumed.

'So, hun,' Carli is nestled against Jai, looking up at him with dog-like eyes, 'what's that you were says about the body being "arranged"?'

'Yeah,' Jai replies, with a slight grimace. 'Mate of George Danielson's found her on his morning physicals, in one of the irrigation ditches out by the allotments. Was really cut up about it. Said she'd been laid out, like in some kind of ceremony, with plants of some kind tied around her head – in a sort of crown.'

'Coronet weeds,' Ida says in a soft voice, almost to herself.

'What's that, Ma?' Lyse asks.

'Oh, just a line from an old play about a young woman found dead in a stream, a bit like this girl. A coronet was a sort of crown, you know. Now, how does it go again?' She narrows her eyes as she thinks. 'Something like: ... *on the pendant boughs her coronet weeds*, something, something, something... *when down her weedy trophies and herself fell into the brook.*'

'Had she been murdered, this girl?' Ammi asks.

'Well, no, she drowned herself, I think, after finding out that the man she loved had killed her father.'

'Oh, lair!' Carli gasps, wriggling closer to Jai. 'Just lurve these grues old stories.'

'And some think she might have been pregnant,' Ida continues, 'even though she was hardly a woman herself.'

'Weee!' Carli squeaks. 'Maybe the Viki girl was pregs too? But no...' she giggles, 'that's not going to work, ist? No Prog boy'd be stupid enough to go with a red-dirt.'

'Oh, I don't think you get anywhere underestimating the stupidity of the average Program male, Carli,' Lyse says, close to losing her temper with the vacuous female. *If she says any more about Banni girls, she might just get a slap across her perfect face.*

'Well, anyway, Ly,' Ammi breaks in, 'you can't seriously be thinking of carrying on with the band after this, can you? What if Viki's murder isn't a one-off? What if it's some madman on a killing spree and Viki was just in the wrong place at the wrong time? You were in the same place at the same time – could've been you instead of her.' Her clear blue eyes widen.

'And it could still be you, Lyse, if you keep going down there.'

22

THE RESULT

Seth descends the cracked stone steps into the basement of the abandoned warehouse, one quarter of which has been his dom since he moved out – three years ago now. Could've stayed living with his father, they rubbed along quite well together, but he couldn't stay living with his father's grief. Just too big. It's not much, his place; a bit dark, maybe, with its small, high windows (although that's bliss in summer), but it's near the Club and big enough for the band to meet. Most important, it's cheap as chips and there's nobody to complain about the noise.

He switches on the manuals, kicks the cooler into stuttering action and, with his usual reluctance, activates the *Buggo*™. Doesn't like it, knows it's poison, but once they sense the presence of a human, the advance of the creeps is relentless. And, anyway, don't look a gift drone in the mouth. Won't be long before this particular compound no longer works. He decons quickly, pulls on a lazesuit and finds a beer. Doesn't intend to go out again; fancies a quiet afternoon alone with his thoughts. And some sounds.

He selects a disc from a tall metal rack beside his worktable. It's a compilation by one of the most famous Old-World bands ever. Marcus had been beside himself with excitement at the find: *Deluxe edition, no less – all their greatest hits,* he'd grinned, the years dropping from his face. *Not a mark on it; sounds as fresh and clear as the day it was pressed. Can't think where it's been all this time, but someone's looked after it.* His father had stroked the only slightly yellowed cover with stubby, but tender, fingers.

Seth goes over to the old-electric turntable and raises its clouded plastic cover. After wiping the vinyl with a small sponge, he places it on the rubber platter, gently pulls back the metal arm then lowers it with care onto the edge of the now-revolving disc. He watches the arm undulate and enjoys the familiar hit of adrenaline as the crackle of static gives way to the low, sleazy screech of harmonica and the soft, rhythmic pad of the drums.

The song is… was… one of Vik's favourites. Easy chords; simple words, but she liked the old-fashioned romanticism. Wouldn't be his pick; although he appreciates the harmonies and the fact that the singer was his age when he wrote it. He'd taught her the song one evening, and her voice wasn't actually all that bad. Needed a bit more confidence, is all.

His spirits sink despite the jaunty sentiment of the tune. Deep down, he didn't believe her, did he? Much as some small part of him wanted it to be true. And worse – he recalls again her desolate look as she walked away – she knew he didn't believe her, didn't she? The depth of his self-disgust is further plumbed by the recognition that, even now, even with Viki's death, his overwhelming emotion is one of relief. But it *is* relief all the same. There's nothing – unless the cops get back – to get in the way now. Only a matter of time before the band'll be out on the road; leave all this shit behind. He breathes out deeply and allows the more primal beats of the next track to lift his mood.

He's hoping to persuade Lyse to join the tour – least until she goes off to college. She's going down well with the punters and, if he's honest, he quite likes having her around. But he's not sure how she feels about him now. It's possible she thinks he had something to do with Viki's death; he suspects some of the others are wondering. But she'd seemed okay with him today, hadn't she? Told him she'd been interviewed by a detective and confirmed his alibi. Said the cop had asked about his argument with Vik, but she'd said she was too far away to hear anything. He'd also asked whether Vik and Seth were 'a couple' in the old way.

And what did you say to that? he'd enquired, a little uneasy.

Just what you'd told me; that you'd been close in the past but not recents, and that you'd said Viki could get a bit jealous. She'd given him a wry smile then and said that the cop had also asked about whether she and Seth were in a relationship.

He'd said nothing at that, trying not to show how very interested he was in the answer to that question.

Said we were just bandmates, she'd grinned, *and that I'd only just met you and didn't know what to make of you yet.*

He'd smiled and, emboldened by her lightness of tone, caught her arm, pulling her towards him. *You know I had nothing to do with her death, don't you, Lyse?* he'd asked.

Well, yes, ov, or I wouldn't be talking to you now, would I? she'd said, moving quickly (too quickly?) on to the lack of progress being made by the cops. *Don't spose they're all that bothered,* she'd tutted. *If you're not a breeder, nobody cares.*

Riding on the back of his relief, he'd taken a chance and told her about his father's new music find – asked if she wanted to check it out; thought there could be a couple of new numbers for the band. She'd smiled (but had there been a slight hesitation?) and said she'd like to, but had a late swim practice – maybe another time?

His assessment of the positives and negatives of the discussion, which he is inclined, on balance, to find in his favour, is interrupted by the insistent tone of another pinX. It's from Marcus – clearly getting to like all the cloak-and-dagger stuff. Ma's bench. Half an hour. *Must be the result of the test!* His heart makes its sturdy presence known as he confirms the arrangement.

Ma's bench is down by the family's old allotment; just about still standing, although one of its central slats is missing and the little plaque of dedication had been prised off almost instantly. Thought it was a bit unwise – can get a good price for metal scrap – but his father was insistent that it's what Ma would have wanted. He built the bench for her when she got too ill to care for the plot. She went there a lot – said she was comforted by the sight of life's ceaseless energy, even if her own was stuttering to a stop – but he suspects this is the first time Marcus has been down there since she died. *Too many memories, son*, he'd said the last time he'd asked him about it.

He arrives before his father and draws up the mask against the snit-posse heading for his ears. The late afternoon air is still, thick with the diverse scents of living vegetation and, unusually for the Banleus, there's little noise apart from the excited buzz of insect life and the distant voices of the allotment workers. The sky is clear, save for a few puffs of pink-edged cumulus that appear to have snagged, like sheep's wool, on the bare tracery of the few still standing trees.

He spots Marcus, navigating the bedraggled path with obvious difficulty, face red with effort. They exchange a quick embrace before Marcus sits down hard on the bench, his breathing heavy. He observes the sheen of perspiration on his father's face with concern.

'Need to get a bit more exercise, Pa. Wilful self-neglect, they'll call it, when they come to take you away – and they won't be giving you your daily whisky at the Sunlit Uplands.'

'It's just this blasted heat,' Marcus complains, without his usual good humour. And anyway, he tells him, he is doing more, as it happens. Joined a real-walking group that goes out to the Wild Lakes once a week. Only takes an hour on the new speeders. Scenery's supposed to be better than any virt and the air's about as pure as you can get.

'Thelma found out about it,' he says. 'She's been nagging me too. *Start living life rather than visiting death*, as she puts it.'

'Yeah, well, she's not wrong there,' he agrees. 'So,' he asks, ignoring the fluttering in his stomach, 'talking of life…?'

'Ah yes…' Marcus reaches inside his tunic and pulls out a small white envelope.

He sees his name, written in a firm, elegant hand and looks at his father, who shakes his head.

'I've not been told, lad. You'll have to open it.'

He does so and scans the handwritten note inside, his heart jitterbugging. Its message is as stark as it is short: *Fertile*. He stares at Marcus in disbelief, tears pricking his eyes as he hands him the note. He's beset by a confusion of emotions: there's excitement, elation even, but also uncertainty and a low, unignorable, beat of foreboding. More powerful than any of that, however, is the sense that this is all happening to someone else; that he's not even here. He rubs his eyes as if doing so would somehow make whole situation disappear.

'What do I do now, Pa?' he asks after a while. 'Hand myself in, or what?'

'Not sure this is the best time,' Marcus says, 'not with…' He trails off.

'Yeah, shit, Viki.' He grimaces. 'But if I don't 'fess up, I'm going to have to spend my life pretending to be something I'm not. Or not something I am, more like. Not sure I could do that, Pa.' He gives a weak grin. 'Bit like having an original Les Paul and never being able to play it.'

'Yes, I can understand that,' Marcus says with a smirk, 'although who's to say you couldn't have a little strum on your own when no-one's looking, eh? But,' his face becomes serious, 'if you tell them, you'll keep the instrument but lose the desire to play. How would you feel about that?'

He shrugs. 'Can't really imagine. But loads seem perfectly okay with it. Take Queron. He's not really bothered. Mostly goes with girls to keep them happy – or to get them off his back. Always thought me and Viki being long-term was a bit odd.' He gives a soft snort. 'Well, he got that right, didn't he?'

'But maybe you don't miss what you've never had,' Marcus says. 'Much more difficult to have something and then lose it, eh?'

His eyes moisten as he tells him that Seth's birth was the most extraordinary experience: 'Best day of my life; no doubt about it.' And what a wonderful thing it had been to watch a tiny being, he'd helped to make, grow into a fine young adult. 'Nobody should be denied that,' he says, wiping the corners of his eyes.

He gives the old man's knee a gentle pat, unsettled by this show of emotion from his usually self-contained parent and by the ripples it's causing in his own, still volatile emotional state.

'It's a natural thing to want to pass something of yourself down to future generations,' Marcus continues, telling him how disappointed he'd been when Seth dropped out of Secs – although he was, and is, totally behind the music, he adds hastily – and at the thought he might never become a Grandparent. Says that part of him, a big part of him, hopes this miracle – he taps the envelope that he's still clutching to his chest – could be another chance for them both.

'That you could somehow hold on, keep quiet and one day, who knows, things could be different. Nothing stays the same forever, after all.'

He tries to find that thought comforting, although the conflicted look on his father's face suggests at the very least a struggle between hope and conviction. His own bickering emotions settle themselves down into a generalised state of low-lying anxiety.

The light is beginning to fade as they leave the allotments and walk to the bridge; There's a lot more people around now and they take a careful path, stepping round the beggars with their rough-looking dogbots crowding round the lift entrance. He watches his father safely into the lift-shaft then pulls up his mask and starts off home; better late than never for that quiet night in. And even more reason now, he pats the white envelope in his pocket, for some me-time with his thoughts.

Once home, he reclaims the lazesuit, grabs a fresh beer and stretches out on the old sofa; the large and careworn piece of furniture being the only thing he brought with him from Pa's. Not in great nick, admittedly – *struggling to retain its integrity*, Q had mocked – but it feels and smells like home. And he likes that at the end of the day – and particularly at the end of this particular day. He restarts the disc player and, as he listens again to the opening track – Viki's track – he's struck by a profound sense of loss: for her, for himself and for what might have been. *Could have been a father. A father!* He recalls Marcus's emotional words and thinks, with a fleeting stab of anguish, of the tiny human-to-be that he had started. *But no...* he thinks as he reaches for another beer, *got to believe it never would have been. Not with Viki and not with anyone anytime soon.*

23

A PROGRAM BOY

'A word, Boss?' Coop asks as he puts his head around the door. Don is sitting on the edge of his desk, frowning at a rather hazy visual. He's tried a new tunic and trouser arrangement – not entirely successfully; the firmer attachment of the parts giving the look of a sling round a melon.

'Sure, Coop. Come on in.' Don flicks off the holo and beams at him, smoothing his frontage with sweaty fingers. 'What's up?'

'Well, you're not going to like it—'

'Never do, Coop, never do. One day someone'll tell me something I want to hear. Live in hope. So, what's the bad news?'

'Okay, well, you know we found two human traces on the dead girl?' His boss nods. 'Well, I've got a match on one of them and it's a Program male. No surprise there, I suppose, but thought I'd check with you before I pull him in. Do I notify the Stews?'

'How d'you manage that, Coop?' Don asks in surprise. 'Local cops pulling biodata without a Special Order rings Gencom's alarm bells, y'know.'

'I know. I arranged for the request to come from inside – got a contact. Shouldn't we report up immediately if we bring in a registered?'

'Well, yes, but there's always a bit of wiggle room in these things.' His boss gives a sly smile. 'We can't officially report what we haven't officially got, can we? Anyway, what about the other trace?'

'That's even more interesting… Nothing.'

'Nothing?' Don looks astonished. 'Nobody matched? Impossible – the bioid of every legal human is in the Gencom bank. Must be a mistake, Coop. That insider of yours has got it wrong somehow. Can you get the test done again?'

'Could do,' he says, with a slow head shake, 'but I really don't think we need to, Boss. My contact's always been extremely reliable.'

'But if it's right – and I'm going to have to trust you on that, Coop – it means that we're dealing with someone off the system. Maybe one of those, what d'you call 'em, ghost kids.'

'Yes, possibly, someone born outside the Program or,' he says in an even tone, 'someone whose data are legally shielded.'

'Either way,' his boss grimaces, 'muchio shittio!'

He smiles in agreement.

'So…' Don slowly releases the air he'd taken into his cheeks, 'what else you got?'

'Well, we now know that the Program male was one of two people who had intimate contact with the victim before she died—'

'And he'll be the sex attacker?' his boss breaks in. 'You said the sheath was Program issue, right? So, it's a Saturday night on the razzle gone wrong, as we thought?'

'Yes, that's the obvious scenario, but the obvious is a slippery friend. It's equally possible that this other, unregistered, individual was the sex attacker.'

'And that the Program boy was the murderer?'

He nods. 'Indeed. Or that one or the other committed both acts. Or – unlikely, but not inconceivable – that both had physical contact with her, but neither committed either act. Problem is,' he continues, 'we still don't know if the two acts, the sex attack and the murder, are related. Or the two human contacts, come to that. The relationship between them could be absolutely crucial or,' he gives his boss a calm smile, 'totally meaningless.'

'Okay, okay!' Don holds up his hand in mock surrender. 'Thanks for that, Coop. I can see you've got your work cut out.' He sits back, arms raised, causing visible distress to the straining seams of his garments. 'So, what's the plan?'

'Well, if you're okay with it, Boss, I'll bring the boy in – see what he has to say for himself. How long have we've got before we have to tell the Stews?'

'Well… we'll need to make a formal application to Gencom for the bio test, just to cover ourselves. I'll do that. Keep it low-key: helping with enquiries about a local murder; no repro issues – that sort of thing.'

'Thanks, Boss,' he says, and turns to go.

'But, Coop…'

'Yes, Boss?'

'That'll give us a day or so – week max. Soon as the application goes in, clock'll start ticking. You won't need to hang around on this.'

'No, Boss.' He's already worked that out.

*

They pulled the reproactive in quickly and Coop enters the interview room to find a young male accompanied by what, he judges by the expensive attire, is almost certainly a Program legal.

'Mr Samson?' He holds out his hand. 'Detective Cooper-Clark.'

The young man nods but ignores his hand, staring down at

the table in front of him. His fleshy face has the bland, regular features that are standard for Program wannabes, his pink cheeks marked with the tell-tale blemishes of the newly fertilised. His knees beneath the table jig persistently.

Coop activates the session recorders and smiles at the dull face. 'Thank you for coming in, Mr Samson. We're investigating the death of a young female in the Banleus on Saturday night and we think you may have information that could help us find the person or persons responsible.'

The detainee says nothing; the Adviser gives an airy wave for Coop to continue.

He does just that. 'The murder victim was a Viki Jansdottir,' he says, bringing up her image.

The detainee makes a small noise and whispers something in the ear of the richly clothed person beside him. The response he receives is clearly short and to the point.

'No comment,' he mutters.

'Can I take it that you know this young woman?' he persists, watching him carefully.

'No comment.'

'Well, let me put it another way,' he says in a friendly manner. 'Can you tell me why, if you did not know her, a trace of your bio was found on her clothing?'

The already pale face of the young man is deathly now, accentuating the bulging pinkness of his eyes. Sweat beads his upper lip. He whispers to the lawyer again, somewhat more agitated, it seems to Coop. Again, firm words appear to be spoken by the woman, who leans forward and fixes him with cool eyes. 'Are you charging my customer, Detective?'

'No, not at this point, but—'

'Then he has no comment to make at this point,' she says with an expensive smirk.

He looks at the young man, who is still staring hard at the table in front of him. The jigging of his knees has intensified.

'It's Samael, isn't it?' he asks in a gentle tone. 'If something has happened that you didn't mean to happen, Samael, it will be best for you to tell us as soon as possible. We'll find out eventually, you know, we always do, and it will play very much worse for you if you say nothing now.'

The young man darts a questioning glance at the Adviser, who gives a firm shake of her head.

'No comment,' he says.

'Very well. But think about what I said, won't you, Samael? It will be very much in your best interest to talk to us – especially if, as it seems to me, you have something to hide.' He looks at the Adviser. 'Given the biomatch,' he says in a pleasant manner, 'we will be keeping your, er, "customer" for a few more hours; I will let you know when, if, he is to be charged.'

The woman gives him a curt nod of her well-coiffured head and, without a further look at the hapless male, moves swiftly towards the door, her young client staring wretchedly at her departing back. Coop gives him a reassuring smile and then nods at the two Uniforms standing by the door. 'Take him back down, please.'

He returns upstairs, frustrated. *That's got me nowhere fast. Shut up like a clam.* But Mr Samson's guilty of something, that's clear. The neuro shows a distinctive spike early in the interview that he's pretty sure will match the exact time he showed him the picture of the victim. Could just be shock at seeing a dead body, of course. But he thinks not. He lets out a sigh of exasperation. Even with the bio trace he's not got enough to charge him. He's got to find some way of opening him up; needs to speak to him without the legal eagle for a start. Well, it's pretty hot down in the cells; a slow stewing might make him more amenable.

Trouble is, I've not got a lot of cooking time.

24

THE FLY IN THE OINTMENT

Seth is sitting with Marcus in Thelma's outhouse, flanked on either side by rows of plants shifting sinuously in the breeze from a straining fan. 'Best in here,' she'd whispered when they arrived. 'Walls have ears, as they used to say.'

The air in the shed is very warm, and heavy with the pungent smell of fresh-turned earth. The only sound, apart from the faint wheeze of Marcus's breath and the deserted-dog whine of the fan, is the increased beat of his heart. Just when he thought he was out of the woods, she's telling him he's heading straight for the jungle.

'Thought you said it was too late for anyone to find out now?' He hates the pathetic note that's crept into his voice. 'Cops don't seem to have found anything—'

'Well, virtops are pretty cursory these days, especially for Banni folk,' Thelma says, handing him some tea. 'You'll have to hope that nothing prompts them to have a deeper look. As I said, they'll not be able to tell who the father was – too late for that now – but they could well find out that Viki had been pregnant recently. There'd still be signs of that, if they looked hard enough.'

'But it'll be okay now, though, won't it? Now that Vik—'

'Can't tell anyone?'

He feels a flush of shame. 'Yeah, guess so.'

'Do you think there's any chance she could have told anyone already?' Thelma asks.

'I honestly don't know,' he answers. 'Can't really be sure what she'd've done – never could with Viki. But she didn't have time, really. Thing is,' he gives his father an anxious look – *hasn't told him this*, 'last time I saw her, we had a bit of a row and she was pretty angry with me when she left.'

'Angry enough to tell someone about you?'

'Dunno, really. But, as I said, that was the night she died, so—'

'So, yes, as you say, not much time.' The old woman pauses, then asks: 'Would anyone else have known that Viki had been pregnant, d'you think?'

'Well... her aunt did, and her aunt's sister, I think, who'd helped when she lost it. Her brother, maybe. But if she told anyone else, she didn't tell me.' *Best not to mention that she had very much told Queron or that she was probably angry enough to tell the entire multiverse.*

'Well, I think we can trust them to keep quiet.' The old woman nods. 'They'll know better than to say anything; concealing an illegal pregnancy is an Earthly crime; everybody involved would face serious penalties.'

He registers this hardly comforting observation but still isn't wholly convinced. Surely it would be better for him to go to the authorities and explain things? he asks. 'Not my fault it happened, and I'm telling you soon as I found out, sort of thing?' He's not done anything wrong, after all, has he – if they don't find out about the baby, that is?

She gives him a thin smile. 'Well, that's a big "if" for a start, but let's put that aside. I really don't think you've any idea of the enormity of your situation, Seth. It's not just that you got a female pregnant outside the Program. That's bad enough – an offence against a founding principle of New Life: that no child would ever be born outside the sanctity of marriage. No, sorry, outside…' she adopts a chirpy, robotic tone, 'the *Humanity of Partnership*, as they now have it. But that's "merely" a social problem – they can deal with that. It happens from time to time – human nature being what it is, ha! But the fact that you have remained fertile despite having the universal snip, well, that's a very different cup of tea.'

'Can't really see that, Thelma, if I'm honest,' he says, although he can see that things aren't exactly heading in a favourable direction.

'Well, think it through, Seth,' Thelma says, taking a sip of her tea. 'Gencom's power derives from its absolute control of human reproduction. Of all human life. It was simply not possible for any legal male to breed outside the Program. Until now, that is. Until you. It could be that you were somehow missed by the system – a freak accident, from their point of view and, more importantly, a complete one-off. That could be easily managed. But there is another, much more interesting, possibility.' She leans forward, fixing him with her excited-squirrel eyes.

'Which is?'

'Which is, that you have a genetic resistance to the sterilisation process, which would make you a very special human being, biologically speaking – possibly unique, at this point in time, although there have been rumours of others – *and* a problem that cannot be so easily managed. As far as Gencom is concerned you'd be a significant threat to the whole shebang – a genetic fly in its ointment, so to speak.' She reaches for her tea again and sits back with a pleasant smile.

He glances at his father, who shakes his head, and then back at Thelma with a questioning look.

She leans towards him again, putting down her cup. 'Okay, let's take it slowly. If something's gone wrong in a human body the therapist needs to do three things to put it right. The first is to identify the "bad" gene – the one that's causing the trouble; the second is to find a "good" gene that can effectively replace the bad one and the third is to find a safe way to get the good gene into the body in question.' She looks at him with eyebrows raised and he nods – just about following her.

'So, while we have no problems with the first and the third actions,' she continues, 'scientists have long struggled with the second – the genetic code that could override the Gencom biolock. If your genes do indeed contain the key to that lock, once published they would enable any male to restore their fertility – in theory at least, although demand would hugely outstrip supply – and that, my dear boy, would be social dynamite.'

'So…' he's not got all the detail, but he's grasped the general thrust, 'if I'm like some sort of, what was it, mutant fly – what goes with that?'

'Well, what "goes", my young friend,' the old woman says in a calm voice, 'is you. If Gencom finds out about you, they'll not hesitate to track you down and neutralise you.'

'Swat the fly, you mean?'

'Exactly.' She nods.

'Even if I hand myself in?'

'Especially if you hand yourself in.'

25

A MUDDY DEATH

inally! Coop waits for his time slot, eyeing the ruffled surface with mixed emotions. It has the oily-grey tinge of water that's loaded with the outwash of excessive hygienics and churned by a constant stream of human bodies. But even in this miserable state, its pull is irresistible. His wristband flashes and he dives in – shutting the human echo chamber off like a light. The silence is broken only by the long, slow bubble-blow of his breath and the rhythmic slap of his arms as they cut through the surface. He relaxes into the watery solitude as if on leave from human time.

He swims hard, the repetitive beat of his stroke loosening his thoughts as he assesses the progress of the case which, has to admit, is not looking good. Lab's confirmed the sheath used is exclusive issue for new Program recruits. Same make can be got on the dark, so can't rule out the possibility of a snip dodger, but unlikely. So that's not looking good for Mr Samson, not least as he helpfully left his biological calling card. But is he also the murderer? That's the key question, and one he's got to answer before the Stews get wind of the case. Instinct says he's not and, much as he admires the solidity of objective fact, he's always had a soft spot for that fleeting, intangible sense that he's glimpsed the truth of the matter. *There's something pitiable about the repro*, he thinks as he approaches the turn. *Even if he had the capacity for murder, doubt he'd have the composure. Man like that would run and hide, wouldn't he? Not hang around toying with the body.*

He pushes off from the turn. But if it isn't Samael, then who? Rationally, it's not looking like the (non?) boyfriend. His alibi stacks up – at least until the early hours – surveillance data, such as exist, confirm his movements and there's no bio link. And he seemed genuinely shocked at the news of Viki's death. Even so, still got a sense he's not getting the full story from him; that Mr Marcuson knows something about the victim he's not telling. Not that he's lying; just that he hasn't been asked the right question yet. The nature of that question, however, is currently eluding him.

Then there's the girl singer, Lyse Idadottir, both alibi and possible motive – always an intriguing alignment. Could well be covering up for him, or in cahoots in some way. He'd tracked her down pretty easily: still living at home with her widowed mother. Nice house – shame about the garden – in a nice part of town. Mother was a bit odd, seemed to think I'd come to arrest her for some house crime, but the girl herself seemed pretty straightforward, amenable even. Like the musician himself, however, there seemed to be a certain 'doth protest too much' in her denial of any relationship. And she still hasn't sent the hub data. Might be worth paying Ms Idadottir another visit.

Her image stays with him as he turns again and strokes off through the water. Not beautiful by today's standards, people would say – features too irregular. Some would call her plain, but she has one of those faces that becomes more attractive when used. Some faces go the other way: perfect on the surface but, when activated, the features impress less. Nevertheless, he reminds himself as he flips the next turn and powers underwater, attractive or not, never assume a suspect doesn't fit the crime – basic amateur mistake. Everyone's guilty until proven otherwise. Even, perhaps especially, attractive young females.

His timer buzzes, signalling the end of the session, and he strokes hard down the final length, hanging for a moment on the end wall, panting softly, before hauling himself out of the pool. He checks his time. Not bad; faster than yesterday.

As he's walking towards the changing area, his breathing calmer now, he passes a young woman heading to the reserved lanes. He recognises her instantly, even with her hair caught up in a red swim cap, but she clearly has to do a double take on him:

'Lyse, isn't it?'

'Detective?' She raises her eyebrows. 'Almost didn't recognise you without your hat.'

They exchange pleasantries – and strong unpleasantries about the state of the water – and she asks if there's any more news on Viki. 'At least that I'm allowed to know about,' she gives him a challenging look, 'as a potential suspect, that is?'

'Well, everyone's a suspect until the culprit is identified, of course.' He drapes the small towel round his neck and smiles at her.

'Bit of a coincidence meeting you, actually.' He stops himself, thankfully, from admitting he'd just been thinking about her. 'Was going to contact you again; couple more questions. Could we meet briefly after your swim today. On the deck, perhaps?'

She agrees and, after dressing, he wanders over to the viewing platform. He spots the red hat and watches in admiration as its wearer powers effortlessly through the water, her elegantly arching arms entering at the perfect midpoint of her streamlined body. Seems almost to skim the surface. And breathes both sides. He's envious: taught himself to breathe one-sided and finds it almost impossible to change now, even though he's convinced it's hampering his improvement. Mind you – he takes a last admiring look in the pool – he could never swim like that, no matter how many sides of his face he breathes.

He sees her entering the deck and stands up with a small wave. She joins him in the booth, dropping her bag on the floor and flopping down in mock exhaustion. He offers her tea and they talk swimming for a while. She's in the Citi Squad, he finds. *No wonder she'd looked so good in the pool.* He says, perhaps a little immodestly, that his style isn't up to much – 'bit of an indifferent crawl' – but he's working on his speed. She says that she finds music helps with her stroke rate, ideally something with a strong, repetitive beat, and when she moves closer to show him her earplants, he catches a faint, floral scent of newly washed hair that lingers in his nose for a sweet moment. 'Impressive,' he says, handing back the tiny device with a slight flaring of the nostrils, but tells her he knows next to nothing about music; wouldn't know where to start.

She offers to make him a playlist – if he'd like. Water-themed, maybe. 'But only the real thing. Not the bot-driven noise they have the nerve to call music these days.'

He says, with complete honesty, that he's sure anything she suggests will be fine, and moves on from the topic, and the pleasure he's taking in the conversation, with reluctance. She raises her eyebrows as he takes out his notebook.

'Only way to keep your thoughts to yourself nowadays.' He smiles. 'Can't trust the pubweb with any secrets, that's for sure. 'So,' he says, opening the book, 'you last saw the victim—'

'Viki,' she interrupts. 'Her name was Viki.'

He nods, acknowledging the point. 'You last saw Viki Jansdottir, I think you said "having a bit of a ruck" with her boyfriend—'

'He wasn't her boyfriend,' she interrupts again. 'I told you – they weren't close like that anymore.'

'Well, okay…' He smiles. 'You told me you saw Viki arguing with Seth Marcuson outside the club?' She nods. 'Can you remember who else was outside with you all that night?'

'Not really, Detective, there were a lot of people milling about after the show. I think Otis and Mik were there for a bit.

And Queron – under a pile of girls, probably. Really not certain, though. Wasn't paying much attention, to be honest.'

'I see.' He looks up at her, controlling a smirk. 'You only had eyes for Mr Marcuson, is that it?'

'Ha, yes, no, I mean… he'd just told me I could try out with the band, and I was totally fixing on that.'

She grins at him and he wonders why he'd initially thought her plain; her features are strong for a female these days, admittedly, but the combination is striking; pre-Raphaelite almost, with that hair. *There's one painting in particular, Lady Lilith…*

She raises her eyebrows, and he realises he's been staring too long and looks quickly down at his notebook.

'So, you said that Viki "stormed off" after the argument, but that Mr Marcuson didn't go after her? He stayed with you?' She nods. 'Didn't leave you, not even for a little while, at any part of the evening?' She shakes her head. 'Okay, so this is important, Ms Idadottir, can you remember if anyone else went after Viki that night? Or left around the same time?'

'Not really, I didn't actually see her leave. It was all a bit awkward: she was making quite a bit of noise and we were all trying not to stare.'

'Yes, I'm sure. Well, let me know if anything comes back to you.' He hands her his card with a friendly smile. 'And talking of remembering, I think you were going to send me your hub data for the night in question?'

'Ah, yeees.' She takes the card with a sheepish look. 'Well, Ma's not so good on things like that. She hates all the personal security stuff. The *watching eyes*, she calls them. I've a nasty feeling that you may find that the hub's been disabled, and probably for some time now. But you're welcome to check with her, of course.'

'Of course,' he smiles, 'I'll need to do just that.' He looks at his notebook again. 'You live in the Citi?' She nods. 'Well, the hi-spies should also be able to confirm your movements. They've got the interior pretty well covered.'

'So, I'm still on the suspect list, then, Detective?' she asks with the challenging look he's beginning to find attractive.

'Well, as I said, everyone's a suspect, until we've got our man.'

'Or woman,' she says.

'Ah yes.' He nods. 'Or woman. Anyway, my final question's a bit odd, you may think.' He leans towards her, opening the odorpin. 'Bit of an off chance, but I wonder if you recognise this smell at all? We're pretty sure it's organic – some kind of plant, but it's not on Agcom's list, so we haven't been able to get a fix on it.'

'Phewee! Grotes,' she says, rubbing her nose. 'No idea, but it's pretty disgusting. How's it relevant anyway?'

'Well, maybe not at all,' he says, closing the pin. 'May be a red herring.'

'A long-dead red herring by the smell of it.' She grins. 'Tell you what, pin it me and I'll ask Ma. If it grows anywhere in the quadrosphere, she'll recognise it. And talking of Ma…' She hesitates and he gives her an encouraging look.

'Well. It's probably nothing really, but something Ma said when she heard about the body.'

'The body?'

'Yes, well, Viki, I mean… the way she'd been left. She said it was like an old play where a young female is found dead in a ditch with plants in her hair – a "weedy crown" or something, she called it.'

'*Coronet weeds.*' He smiles. 'Ophelia, I think she was called, climbed on to a tree branch overhanging a river – a *weeping brook* – and, *clasping her weedy trophies…* fell to a *muddy death.*'

'Yes, that's it. That's her. Well, it sounds a bit mad, but Ma says this Ophelia was pregnant and killed herself because the father of the baby wouldn't marry her. So I wondered, y'know, as Viki had been laid out a bit like her, in a "weeping brook" sort of thing, whether…' She hesitates.

'Whether Viki's story might have been similar?'

'Well, yes, and that could've been a motive if she was, couldn't it? Someone wanted to stop her having the baby...? Or to punish her for getting pregnant illegally?'

'You do have a vivid imagination, don't you?' The laugh slips out before he can stop it. 'But I can tell you that Viki was definitely not pregnant when she was found. And, as I recall, anyway, it isn't clear amongst scholars of such things whether Ophelia *was* actually pregnant.' He sees her embarrassment and regrets the laugh. 'But good thinking anyway – *little things can mean a lot* – as a famous detective once said.' He smiles as he holds out his hand. 'Let me know if you have any more ideas. And any suggestions for music would be greatly appreciated. Perhaps something by your band – or yourself, even?'

'Okay will do.' She picks up her bag and makes to go, before turning to him.

'Oh, yeah, so... wanted to ask... it's just that they're saying Viki might not be a one-off. Y'know, that it might've been a stranger, not someone she knew. That she was just in the wrong place at the wrong time and that...' She hesitates.

'...the killer might strike again?' he finishes for her. 'Well, I don't think it can be ruled out entirely, but there's absolutely no indication of that yet, no other recent deaths that can be linked. On balance – and at the moment, anyway – this is looking personal.' He smiles at her; the sun is filtering through the skylight and picking out the gold in her hair, and he wonders whether, if he breathed deeply enough for long enough, he could catch its delicious scent again.

'Talking of personal...' he collects himself, 'I assume you intend to keep going to the Club, whatever anyone says on the matter?'

She nods, with a firm set of her lips.

'Well, just take sensible precautions, won't you? Get an alarm that works down there. Most don't, you know. Or, better still – and I never said this – get a stunni, if you can get your hands on one. Don't get too out of it, which,' he holds up his hand, 'I'm sure you wouldn't and, most importantly, don't go off alone with anyone.'

She raises her eyebrows.

'Yes, not even with our friend Mr Marcuson,' he says in a firm voice. 'Maybe especially not with Mr Marcuson. I know...' he senses her defensiveness, 'you think he couldn't possibly be involved in murder. But, as I said, no-one's off the suspect list until we find the killer.' He smiles and raises his hat.

'Just be careful, Ms Idadottir, that's all I'm saying.'

26

THE POOL OF LIFE

Seth looks from Thelma to his father and back again, wide-eyed, trying to digest the unpalatable information he's just been given. The plant-heavy air of the old woman's outhouse is becoming oppressive, and his breath feels laboured. When she offers him a beer, he accepts with gratitude.

Perhaps sensing his discomfort, Marcus attempts to move the conversation in a more general direction. Tells them there's been more anti-Program riots over on the west side. 'Couple of people killed, although that doesn't seem to be stopping them. People don't seem to think they've got much to lose.'

'Wasn't always like this,' he continues, grinning widely at the generous glass of whisky Thelma is handing him. 'When they announced the Program they said all males would get restored once they'd Partnered up. No mention of any tests and conditions. But, bit by bit, they've raised the bar. Some say less than half who apply get in now. No wonder there's riots: people – perfectly bright, decent young people – being denied their birthright. Being shut out of life itself.' He takes a long, loving sip of the whisky, shaking his head.

Thelma agrees with a vigorous nod, loosing several strands of hair. 'It's a terrible, inhuman thing to do to people. Especially for the females refused the right to breed, but also for all the males being denied the right to experience sexual desire. Erotic exclusion, I call it.'

'But there's got to be a limit, hasn't there?' Seth asks, putting aside his own situation with some relief. 'Can't go back to when just anybody could have babies, can we? There were loads of babies born then that nobody wanted; used to give them away – or sell them even! Many got damaged or killed – sometimes by their actual Parents – before they'd had a chance to grow. Nobody checked if people were suitable to have them in the first place.'

'Well, yes, that's maybe so,' Thelma agrees, rearranging the several scarves lying across her knee, 'but the point is who decides? Who chooses who is "suitable" to contribute to the pool of human life, as it were, and who isn't?'

He shrugs. 'Well, everybody takes the same entry tests, don't they, and anybody who passes can get in, can't they? So that's kinda fair, isn't it?'

'Well, leaving aside the fact that those with enough coin can buy their way into anything, do you think the tests themselves are fair?' the old woman asks with a sour smile.

He senses that a positive reply is not anticipated and takes another grateful gulp of the cold beer.

'Well, they're anything but fair, let me tell you,' she answers herself. 'The tests were designed by certain kinds of people precisely to ensure the reproduction of the human race in their own image.' She gives a sardonic smile. 'In fact, humans aren't even in the process now. The advent of the Program means that entry to the human race is effectively decided by algorithms. Evolution by electronic selection, ha!'

'But that's all done and dusted now, isn't it?' he says. 'It's what people decided, wasn't it?'

'Only after a campaign of arrant lies, threats and bribes – funded by some of the most powerful interests on the Planet – did the people decide.' Thelma gives a mirthless laugh and shakes her head, jettisoning a small, woody sprig this time. 'In actual fact, the people didn't know what they were being asked to decide, so many lies were being told them. There was agreement, yes, that population control was needed, but very little consensus about what form it should take.' She looks at Marcus. 'Do you remember any of this, Marcus? I know you're not quite as aged as me.'

'Yes, well, a bit,' he replies, 'just a sense that the adults around me had agreed to something big and were beginning to panic about what they'd done.'

'Yes, just so!' She gives him an approving smile. 'Pandora's jar had been well and truly opened. What they'd done was to hand the control of human life over to a consortium of corporates with fingers in all aspects of the bio-business. So was born our friend Gencom – the biggest conglomerate on the Planet, with licence to control, and monetise, the entire process of human reproduction, from pre-cradle to post-grave. Talk about putting the fox in charge of the chicken coop!'

'Well, someone had to do it, Thelma,' Marcus says, 'playing devil's advocate here – after the waters rose. Better to limit the number conceived than to have babies born who couldn't be fed.'

'Well, you might well bring the devil into this, Marcus,' Thelma sniffs, 'but we'll come back to Gencom in a minute. No, the point is that it was never just about the numbers. As quickly became evident, the focus was on quality as much as, possibly even more than, quantity. The aim was not just to have fewer humans, but to have fewer of certain *kinds* of human. More of the "good"; less of the "bad".'

'But surely it's right to want to produce better humans, if we can?' Seth asks.

'Maybe, maybe not,' the old woman says, 'depends very much on what we mean by "better". It's not clear that the Program *is* making better humans, at least not if by "better" you mean healthier. It's difficult to find out one way or another, as Gencom owns nearly all the data – we're living through one huge secret experiment at the moment, in fact.' She looks from him to Marcus with beady eyes. 'But one thing we do know is that no apparent gain is without consequence. Take agriculture—'

'Oh no, don't get started on the crops, Thelma,' Marcus groans. 'We'll be here all night.'

'No, okay.' She grins at him. 'But there are important parallels, Marcus. Selective breeding results in loss of the biodiversity that's essential for the health of any species – plant or animal. We saw what genetic modification did to seeds. And we know how that ended…?'

'The Great Wheat War?' Seth dredges up a long-disregarded snippet of learning.

'Quite. So, my point is that the wholly unnatural selection taking place under the Program has the potential in the same way to reduce the diversity of the human gene pool – breeding humans from fewer and fewer male germlines, as it were – to the point where it may similarly threaten our species.'

'But as you say yourself, Thelma,' Marcus intervenes, 'there's no solid evidence one way or another.'

'Well, maybe not,' she concedes, 'but there are some early indicators. The data-commons are recording more miscarriages and stillbirths than at any period of the New Life. And, for the first time in the human story, people are no longer outliving their forebears. Humans today, especially mothers, are ageing faster and dying younger than at the end of the Old-World.' She inclines her head towards Seth.

'Just think how many of your friends have lost their mothers already.'

He nods, recognising the truth of this, at least, but resisting the wider implications of her words. 'But you can't seriously be saying that we should go back to when babies could be born damaged in some way,' he asks, 'not if we can prevent it?'

Thelma stops toying with the scarf on her lap and gives him a grim smile. 'But that's just the point, Seth. That's the sting in Gencom's forked tail. All those damaged children the Program claims to be preventing?' She fixes him with button-like eyes. 'Many scientists think they're still being produced – possibly in greater number – but that nowadays they're not allowed to survive. Just quietly and efficiently *deselected*, as Gencom would have it, before they get a chance at life. Parents sent back to do better next time.'

The old woman pauses now, a little breathless, and regards them with an apologetic smile. Marcus is shifting uncomfortably in his chair and rubbing his knee. And despite the beer, Seth is feeling thoroughly parched – in body and mind.

Thelma seems to sense that she's losing her audience and suggests a short break to stretch their legs while she 'freshens the drinks'.

'Did you follow all that, Pa?' he asks as the old woman leaves the room.

'More or less, son,' he says. 'It's not all new to me, of course.' He laughs. 'I've played cards with Thelma for long enough.'

'It can't be true, though, can it? That the Program gets rid of babies if they aren't perfect? We'd have heard about it, right, if something like that'd been going on? There'd have been an outcry, wouldn't there?'

'Hmmm, maybe,' his father replies. 'Although, I think Thelma knows what she's talking about. Used to be some kind of scientist. Ran a lab, I think, but something happened – not sure precisely what – and she left under a bit of a cloud. It's certainly the case that people want perfection these days – and are prepared to pay for it. Parents-to-be spend ridiculous amounts of coin to improve their offspring's biological value. And not just on physical things like intelligence or looks, or a specific talent, like sport, but also on particular personality types, like "extrovert", say, or "hardworking". There's sample books you can get – baby-building books. Bogofs even.'

'Bogofs?'

'Yes, buy one special attribute – say mathematical and get another – say musical, completely free.' He laughs. 'Only joking, but could soon be the case. Can't really see where it's all going to end.'

'Yeah, so everybody wants a perfect baby, I get that,' he says. 'It's unfair that some can pay more, I guess, but you can't blame people for wanting the best for their offspring, can you?'

'No, but the other side is that nobody wants a baby that's gone wrong… been badly made, so to speak.'

'But we're getting better at stopping things from going wrong, aren't we?'

'Yes, things we can predict, or foresee, that is. But Thelma's point is that all this "meddling", as she puts it, has unintended consequences. And unintended consequences, by definition, are unforeseeable and unpredictable.'

'So, she's saying that unborn babies may still be getting damaged, but we don't ever see them because anything less than perfect is, what was it she said… *deselected*, before birth?'

His father nods. 'Although I think "terminated" is the technical term.'

27

THE HERB OF GRACE

Her mother is balancing on a small floater that has clearly seen better days. She's scrubbing – with inverse result to the desired effect – at the greasy film coating the outside of the windows, flicking her cloth intermittently at the cluster of snits crowding in.

'So, he's going to come and see you this time, to check out my alibi,' she calls up to her, shielding her eyes from the glare.

Ida looks down at her with a worried face. 'You're not in any trouble, are you, Lyse?' she asks, descending carefully on the rickety board and shaking out the cloth – to the delight of the scrummaging snits. She starts to explain, but Ida interrupts.

'Ssssh, Lyse. It's far too hot to talk out here and,' she glances round, 'you never know who's listening.'

They move indoors and she reassures Ida that she's not in any trouble. Just that the police want to see the domlog to check the time she got home on the night of the murder. Her mother's shifty look confirms her suspicions: 'You didn't get it reset, did you?'

'No, I certainly did not. Blessed thing!' Ida says, her face – still rosy from the window washing – reddening further. 'Who says we need to keep a record of everyone who comes and goes – in our own homes. Bloody cheek!' Ida frowns at the windows as if she suspects them of having their smeary eyes on her.

She brings her mother back to the matter at hand, telling her that the lack of the dom data won't be a problem if Ida can verify the time she, Lyse, came back that night. Ida shoots her a doubtful look. 'I'm not sure I *did* hear you, dear. I sleep very soundly with those pills, you know.'

'Yes, but you could *say* you did, couldn't you, Ma?'

'I can't lie to the police, Lyse.'

'It's only a little white lie,' she wheedles, containing her impatience.

'You know I came home that night – you woke me up in the morning. It's not like I'm going to murder anyone, is it? It'd help the pols, actually – stop them wasting time. And,' she gives her mother a calculating look, 'it'd stop people gossiping. You know what they'll say about smoke and fires…'

She sees she's hit the mark. Ida sighs and supposes it wouldn't do any harm and that she probably did hear her, now she comes to think about it. 'It's criminal the way rumours fly around these days,' she tuts. 'Once a lie is spun, sticks to you like cobwebs.'

She smiles – grateful, for once, for her mother's antipathy to the modern world and tells her that the cops think the smell on Vik's body could be a clue, but they can't place it. 'I said if anyone could identify it, you could,' she says, opening the odorpin.

Ida takes a deep sniff, flaring her nostrils a few times, before saying she thinks it's from a plant called rue. Got some in the garden, although doesn't smell quite as bad as that – this must be the wild version. 'Used to grow everywhere. People called it a weed. Weed!' she sighs. 'They had that luxury then.'

Anxious to keep her mother's mind away from the lingering death of her garden – where she knows it can take root for some time – she asks why anyone would rub a stinking plant on a dead body. Ida shrugs and suggests maybe it was to keep predators away. Although,' she says with a small laugh, 'I suppose it could have a meaning…'

She regards Ida with interest, who continues: 'Well, in the old days, flowers were used as symbols for things, emotions largely, like love or hate, remembrance – that sort of thing – a "language of flowers", if you like. So, well, maybe rue has a meaning?'

She finds it quickly: '*The Historic Meaning of Flowers* – is that it, Ma? Yes, here it is!' she says, pointing at the image. 'Rue. Says *rue was used in ancient times to represent regret, sorrow or repentance.* And, and…' she pats her mother's hand excitedly, 'it mentions that play you told us about with the girl in the ditch. Ophelia – that was her name, right? Well it says here she was holding rue! In the ditch! Listen to this… *There's rue for you and here's some for me. We may call it Herb of Grace o' Sundays.*'

She looks at Ida, pulse racing. 'Don't know about the last bit, but it all ties up, don't you see? The ditch, the flowers, the rue. The killer is using the play to send a message—'

'Oh, Lyse.' Her mother shakes her head. 'There you go again. I'm sure it's all one big coincidence. And it doesn't all fit, anyway. The girl in the play wasn't murdered, for a start. And most likely,' she says in a firm voice, 'the plants don't mean anything at all. They just happened to be growing nearby and the killer used them to hide what he'd done.'

They both jump slightly as the back door opens and look up as Jai enters. He slumps down on the chair by the table and gazes, in mock desperation, at Ida. 'Any chance of a drink, Ma? Hot as hell out there.'

She looks hard at her brother, whose normally rude health appears ruder than usual; his perma-bright eyes even brighter. 'So, whatsup?' she asks. 'Looking very pleased with yourself.'

He turns to check that Ida has left the room and tells her he's decided he's not going for the Program. Just done the introductory session and it's put him right off. 'You'd have practically no life of your own, Ly. Not to mention being pumped full of drugs – and not for pleasure either. And…' he leans back, eyeing the door, 'worst thing, you're tied to one female for the duration. I'd be mid-age by the time it's all over. Lose my best years.'

'Ah, but what about the sex, Jai?' she teases. 'Sposed to be zenban when you have the reverse. Better than any drug. Used to write songs about "doing it" all the time or, particularly from the males, about *not* doing it when, or as often as, they wanted.'

Jai grins and shakes his head. 'Nah, that's all just Program propaganda, Ly; nothing can be that good.'

They talk for a while about his plans to do the cross-world challenge once he's got enough coin together from the Gencom job. She's full of misgiving about this. Lots of young people do it – it's a sort of global rite of passage and she's heard of the wonderful sights, better than any virtual, but there's also tales of bandits, inhumans and dreadful ends. She says nothing, however; he's her brother and she knows that, like her, he'll not easily be blown off course. *And anyway, there's a bit of a silver lining here, isn't there?*

'So that's it for you and Carli, is it?' she asks, keeping her voice neutral.

'Well, yeah. Think you could say that.' Jai laughs and confesses that actually Carli's blown him out. 'Found someone a whole lot keener on the Partner thing. Relief, to be honest, Ly, got a bit of a bore about it.'

'Well, that does surprise me,' she says in a sardonic tone.

'Don't say anything to Ammi yet about this, eh, sis? She's been on my case about the Program, as it is.'

'Well, you know why that is, don't you?' she says, narrowing her eyes at him. His blank look gives her pause. *Ammi ought to be the one to tell him, shouldn't she? Best to keep my nose out, like Ma said, isn't it? But, hey, no harm in oiling the wheels…*

'Because she wants to Partner up with you,' she says in a matter-of-fact way.

'What? Don't be mad!' Jai starts in surprise. 'Are you kidding?

Me and Am? She's my sis – almost! Er… no, Ly. That's just too weird to think. You're making this up. Did she say this to you, actually?'

'No, not in so many words, but—'

'Thought so. It's your overactive imagination, sis, like Ma always says.'

'Maybe, but maybe it's your under-used eyes, *bro.*'

'Nah, Lyse.' He shakes his head. 'Maybe you should stop seeing things that aren't there. Whatever…' he says, firmly disinviting any further discussion, 'I'm not going near the Program – not with Ammi or anyone else.'

'What's that about Ammi?' her mother asks as she returns with the drinks.

'Oh, nothing, Ma,' she says quickly. 'Where is she anyway?'

'Well, I ought to let her tell you herself,' Ida says, with an excited air, as she settles herself between them, 'but I'm sure she won't mind. And she didn't say not to…' She looks from one to the other with a broad smile and tells them that Ammi started on her Program induction this morning.

Lyse directs a raised-eyebrow glance at Jai, who keeps his gaze fixed on Ida. 'Well, that's very good for her, Ma,' he says, raising his glass. 'Well done, Ammi!'

Predictably, this prompts Ida to ask after Carli, and Jai says in a 'don't-make-too-much-of-this-Mother' kind of way that it's pretty much over between them. 'Not a good choice – on Carli's part,' he says with a rueful smile. Ida's obvious disappointment at this news deepens visibly when he adds, rather too brutally Lyse thinks, that the experience has put him off the whole thing.

'The whole Program?' Ida exclaims, eyes wide. 'Oh, surely not, Jai? It's just that you made the wrong choice, this time. You just need to find the right young woman—'

'Nah, not going to happen, Ma,' he says, shaking his head slowly. 'Any time soon, anyways. Want to live a bit first.' He sees Ida's crestfallen face and slips an arm round her. 'But that's not saying never, Ma. Never say never! Who knows what the future will bring?'

'Me getting too old for grandchildren, that's what,' Ida sniffs, brushing microscopic particles roughly from the table.

'There's Ammi, though, isn't there?' she says, trying to cheer her mother up.

'Yes, but she's not…' Ida stops herself.

'Flesh and blood?' she finishes with a quizzical look at Ida, who looks down at her tea. She lets it lie, still finding the whole blood thing a little weird, if she's honest, and asks Jai if there's any news on Viki's case.

'Nah, nothing official. People saying it's a Proggo out on a bamazi.'

'Bamazi?' Ida asks with a frown.

'Girl-hunt, Ma. Program boys' last fling, sort of thing, before they get tied down.'

Ida screws up her nose. 'There you are, Lyse. That's your big mystery. Some newly reversed boy lost control of himself. Let's hear no more about secret messages.'

'Secret messages?' Jai raises his eyebrows, with a grin. 'Sounds interesting…'

She ignores her mother's sigh of vexation and tells him about the rue and how Ida had said it could be a message in flower language…

'Don't bring me into it,' Ida interrupts with a frown. 'This is all in your head, Lyse.'

'…and that it must mean,' she continues undeterred, 'the murderer was saying sorry for having killed her, mustn't it?'

'Or, as I said,' Ida interjects again, rising from the table with an exasperated sigh, 'the bloody plant just happened to be growing nearby.'

'Or…' Jai looks thoughtful and she can see his interest is piqued. 'There could be another interpretation—'

'Jai!' Ida cries. 'Don't you start, please.'

'What other interpretation?' she asks in an eager voice.

'Well, one of the old faith tribes – early Cathols, I think – used to sprinkle rue over their dead to wash away their sins.'

'Yes, that's it!' She looks from one to the other, her excitement rising. 'It all fits, don't you see? If Viki *had* been pregnant, like you said, Ma,' she ignores Ida's squeak of protest, 'that's sinful, isn't it – in some people's eyes anyway?'

'This is all getting far too fanciful,' Ida cuts in again. 'And anyway, didn't you say your policeman pooh-poohed the idea that Viki was pregnant?'

'He's not my policeman, Mother,' she says, although the dishy detective had said just that. She squirms a bit at the thought of their last meeting: made a bit of a prat of herself, hadn't she? World knows what he made of her. She recalls his slender fingers as he opened his notebook. No Ank-ring. But pols can get Partnered, can't they? Maybe he's not into all that Program stuff – or maybe he's just not into the female of the species…

'Well, then; there you are. That's your theory out of the window, isn't it?' Ida says with a sniff of triumph.

'But,' Jai says in a quiet voice, 'maybe it wasn't personal. Maybe it was nothing to do with Viki but was, still is, someone on a mission against women in general. A deranged religio, p'raps – you saw some of the nutters down at the Court. There's lots still about. Maybe one was on the lookout for a female – any female – to punish.'

Her eyes widen. 'You mean…?'

'Yeah. Maybe he'll be back.'

28

UNDERCOVER

The air inside the room is almost as bad as that outside. Moist, foetid almost, with the animalistic tang of the sexually active male. Queron sees the men themselves clustered, roach-like, around one of the Program virtports. No need to guess what they're viewing.

One of the men, tall Piet, looks up and grimaces. 'Hey, boys,' he calls to the others, 'look who's graced us with his presence.' Piet unfurls his lanky self and nods his sharp nose towards him. 'Mr undercover himself. Or should that be "Mr under-the-bed-cover"? What dark hole you just crawled out of, Flowers?'

He smiles in resignation. The work culture is an ongoing war of attrition, as his inexactly named 'colleagues' hustle ceaselessly to improve their place in the all-male, predominantly repro, hierarchy. Few females are willing to take up this area of work – not surprising, really. But it's a pity, as it means there is nothing to dilute the endless flow of grubby verbal jetsam that clogs up his working day. But he's got to play the game. The worst offence, and one guaranteed to slide you fast down the greasy pole of respect, is not to take the bait; not to make the snappy comeback.

'Let me see, Piet,' he gives him his most lascivious smile, 'Thursday, is it? Must've been your sister. Nothing special, mind,' he says, licking his lips, 'your ma was way better.'

As the others snigger, he suppresses the slightly soiled feeling such encounters always provoke. Before Piet has time to form a riposte, the Chief of Section enters the room.

'Quick briefing, boys,' she calls. 'Gather in.'

Chief Eddi Sandidottir is the exception to the rule about the job being a male preserve. She's tall and elegant in a bony sort of way. Long, thin hair round a long, thin face, enlivened by an unexpectedly full, red-lipsticked mouth. Difficult to judge these days, with all the upgrades, but he suspects she's no spring chicken. Not bad nick, though – if you like that sort of thing.

He positions himself out of her line of vision behind the generous bulk of his colleague, Hiro. The chief glances around the assembled men and spots him immediately.

'Do join us, Flowers,' she says in a sarcastic tone. 'How nice to see you again. Was beginning to forget what you looked like.'

'Ugly bastard, that's what,' Hiro says, turning round and grinning at him.

He smiles at the chief, who is one of the few colleagues for whom he has some respect. Seems like someone trying to do right in a job they increasingly find to be wrong. He suspects she has a bit of an eye for him and gives her his winsome look.

'Yes, Chief. Sorry to have missed the last meet – was out on a job.'

'Flowers is always on the job,' Piet snarks, to low-level tittering.

'Okay, okay – settle down,' the chief says. 'Had a call from datacor... Yes, yes,' she acknowledges the groans of the gathered men, 'I know, but it's not one of their normal jobs. Banleu South have put in a request for ID on two different samples – both found on a dead female. Murdered, they think.'

He starts. *Not Viki, surely? How's that come here?*

'Why's this our problem, Chief?' Hiro asks, echoing his thoughts. 'Local police'll sort it, won't they?'

'Normally, yes, but there's also mention of a possible sex attack, although that's not exactly clear from the request—'

'Ay up,' Eido leans forwards, his sly grin exposing long teeth, 'what do you call a sex attack on a Banni girl?'

The others snigger expectantly.

'An oxymoron, that's what, heh-heh.' Eido laughs.

The others give him blank looks.

'Look it up, fuckwits,' Eido snaps. 'Improve your vocabularies, why don't you?'

'Thank you, Eido,' the chief says in a firm voice. 'We'll have the language lesson another time, if you don't mind. And let's have less of the so-called "jokes" about females from the Banleus, shall we? So...' she says, opening a vidpin, 'they pulled two bios off the victim and one of them... this boy,' she says, pointing to the image, 'is one of ours. A Samael Samson, 18.5 years. Latest batch of Program intakes. Currently living at home with an abandoned mother in Citi Zone E10.'

They all stare, some wistfully, at the smiling image of a healthy, if a little plump, young male standing optimistically on the threshold of adulthood.

'Thing is,' the chief says, smoothing back strands of hair behind long-lobed ears, 'upstairs want us to keep a lid on this one. Possible reputational damage. Not a good time, as they see it, with all the protests. Last thing they want's a repro seemingly out of control, attacking females, wherever...' she gives Eido a hard look, 'they're from. So, we need to find out what's going on – and engage in a bit of damage limitation, if necessary. See what we can get on the female. Maybe she's the sort that seeks out repros, in the hope that something'll come of it. Maybe she encouraged this one but got cold feet at the last minute.'

'Yeah, "prick teaser", they used to call it, init?' sniggers Eido.

'It's the boys that's the victims these days, if you ask me,' Jebb interjects. 'They pump their bodies full of drugs and stuff their heads with porn to the point where they just can't control themselves—'

'Sounds like bliss to me!' Piet smirks. 'Where do I sign up?'

'Yes, Jebb, that's the sort of line,' the chief says, giving Piet the kind of look she might cast a pool of sick. 'If there was illegal sex, and this man Samson is responsible – and we need to make sure the area pols've got their facts cast-iron on that – let's see if we can't encourage them to see our man as the real victim of the piece.'

'More victim than a dead female, Chief?' he finds himself asking – despite a creeping disquiet.

'It's not my personal moral compass, Flowers,' she says, pursing her plump red lips. 'I'm just repeating what I'm told. Upstairs're not trying to protect the boy; they're trying to protect themselves. Anyway,' she nods at him, 'as this is all going on in your patch, you'll need to get down there and have a look around. Case's being handled by a contract – Cooper-Clark. Odd name, odd man, by all accounts. Wears an old-style hat.' Her smile broadens and a slick of the red lip colour catches the edge of her perma-whitened teeth. 'You may need to use all your reputed charm, Flowers, to bring him round to our way of thinking.'

'Will do, Chief,' he says, ignoring the riffs of derision behind him. 'What about the other bio trace?' he asks, trying to keep his voice calm. 'You said there were two requests?'

'Yes, well,' she pushes the escaping strands of hair behind her ears again, 'that's another reason why we need to keep the noise down. There's no accessible data on the other bio – seems like we've got us a ghost.'

'One of our beloved UCs, maybe?' tall Piet asks, with a snide grin.

His stomach tightens, but he gives his smirking colleague a benign smile, trusting that he doesn't have the wit to realise just how close to the mark his careless little snipe may have landed.

'Possible, but more likely one of the VIPs,' the chief is saying. 'We'll need upstairs clearance to find out, whatever, so best left alone until we're told different. See if it's an issue for this Cooper-Clark chap, Flowers. If not, let's hope it goes away; likely to be trouble otherwise.'

'Yes, Chief.' He feels himself beginning to sweat. 'What's the name of the female?'

'Erm, Viki something...' the chief flicks up the details. 'Jansdottir. Viktori Dotti Jansdottir. 22.9 years. I've sent you all we've got on her, which isn't much. Lived with a so-called aunt in one of the Projects.'

He swallows hard, manages a pleasant enough smile. 'Okay, great. I'll get going on that, Chief, unless you want me to stay for anything else?'

'No, you're okay to go, Flowers,' she says, smiling at him with red-smudged teeth. 'Just don't come back empty-handed, will you?'

'Or with the pox.' Piet grins as the others snicker softly around him.

Shit, fucking shit, he thinks as he travels across the bridge in the midst of a silent group of carebots returning from the Sunny Uplands senior community. *How the fuck did that happen?* He's totally careful, paranoid even, about his fluids – never even shares a vape. He slows his pace, receiving several warning beeps from the ever-smiling bots. *Nah, calm down, wasn't with her that long. Gotta be a coincidence.* He enters the downshaft quickly, not wanting to get crowded in with the glassy-eyed carers. Anyway, it's good news for Seth; the sex attack gets him off the hook. Just hope they get the Prog for the murder too. *But, but, but...* his gut's telling him his old buddy knows more about Viki's death than he's letting on. Never been good at hiding things, Seth. *Just needs the right sort of encouragement. From the right sort of person.*

He finds his friend in low mood, half-dressed and bleary-eyed. And, he glances at the untidy pile of old records on the floor, *wading through his misery-rock collection by the look.* While Seth goes to get some beers, he picks up the earphones and is completely unsurprised to hear the sparse, almost parched vocals of one of the great late twentieth-century poet-songwriters. *Too friggin' dark by half; needs something a little lighter than an old man singing his last.*

'What about that new find of your pa's?' he asks when Seth returns. 'Got that here? Could do with a listen.' As Seth unearths the disc in question from the near bottom of the pile, Queron slips two small black and silver vials from his pocket. 'Have a pull on that,' he says as they settle together on the aged sofa. 'That'll smooth your spirits.'

And loosen his tongue, with any luck. He takes a deep, satisfying pull on his own vial. Even in his drug-hardened brain, the bespoke ingredient soon works its sweet little tricks.

'Woah...' Seth gasps as he exhales the vapestream, 'that's reached the parts alright. Where d'you get this stuff, Q?'

'That's for me to know and you to find out,' he says with a theatrical tap of his nose. 'What you don't know can't give you grief.' He slips his friend a sideways glance. 'Even brothers have secrets, no?'

He fancies that Seth flinches a little at this and it seems like a good moment to make a move. 'So, what's new, cuz?' he asks, edging closer. 'Gotta be good they pulled a repro in for Viki? Gets you off the hook, no?'

'Yeah.' Seth nods, laying his head on the back of the sofa and closing his eyes. 'Relief.'

They sit in silence for a while and Queron pulls back, allowing the bluesy notes of the new album to play around with his emotions. He looks over at his friend's handsome face, relaxed – serene even – and resists the urge to stroke his cheek. Some time passes before he can bring himself back to the task at hand.

'So, looks like Vik did go after Proggos?' he starts up again after a while. 'You said she was fixed on trying to have a baby. Maybe—'

'No, Q,' Seth grumbles mildly, eyes still closed. 'She didn't "go after" Proggos – or anybody.'

'But, look, bro… you can't keep saying that, can you?' he presses, sensing he's on the rabbit now. 'Fair do, know you want to be loyal, and respect for that, but how else did she get herself a baby? Gotta shag a repro to get one of those.'

Seth shakes his head and takes another pull at the silvery vial – a faraway look on his face.

'But Setho,' he persists, 'unless she was lying about the baby, and you said she wasn't, then she clearly went with at least one repro. Case closed, nesepa?'

'No. You're way off,' Seth murmurs as he sits up slowly, opens his eyes, face flushed, and takes a tight hold of his arm. 'We've got each other's backs, haven't we, Q?'

'Yeah, course.' He gives his friend's hand a reassuring pat. *Here it comes – just one more little tug.* 'So, what's up, Setho?' he asks, stroking the hand. 'Spit it out.'

Seth puts the vial down, a complex expression on his usually straightforward face. 'Viki…' He stops, as if the words have stuck. 'Viki,' he tries again, 'was telling you the truth.'

'About losing the baby? You told me that, bro.'

'Yeah, and about the rest.' He gives him a sheepish look.

'The rest? You mean…?'

'Yeah, about the baby being mine.'

'Wha?' He's completely thrown. Hadn't expected this of all things. 'But… you're not… you can't…' He stutters to a stop. But of course, totally makes sense: Seth and Viki long-term. How could he not have seen?

'Thelma got the test done,' Seth is muttering. 'Says I'm a genetic freak, a mutant fly or something.'

He's surprised at this. *How'd the old bird get a fert-test done? All that's got to go through Gencom labs. And they'd be on her case in a split. Unless…* He stops himself; he'll come back to that interesting question later.

'This is seismic, Setho,' he says with feeling. 'Terra… no zetta shitbomb!'

'Yeah,' Seth says with a slow grimace. 'Thelma says it could be *social dynamite.*'

'Well, she's not wrong there, repro boy,' he says, internal alarms cutting shrilly through the calmative effect of the drug.

'Thing like this could blow up in everybody's face.'

29

PATERNITY

Well, I never. Coop smiles as he reads the lab report: signs of early abort/hi prob spon. *So she was right after all.* He cringes at the thought of how he'd reacted. Hoped it hadn't seemed like a put-down, but all that stuff about the old play was a bit fanciful, wasn't it? He'd got it checked out anyway – just in case he saw her again – and, against the odds, looks like she's put her finger on something: Viki had been pregnant, it seems but, intentionally or not, had lost the baby. *So much the worse for poor little Viki, but maybe not for me. Time for another word with Mr Samson, I think.*

He enters the interview room with a jug and two cups of fresh water, pleased to find the suspect without his Adviser, and nods to the Uniforms to wait outside. He places one of the cups in front of the wretched man and smiles. Twenty hours in the oven has turned his face to sweating dough, his red-rimmed eyes inset like currents.

'Just an informal chat, Mr Samson,' he says in a friendly manner. 'Nothing's being recorded yet. You are welcome to ask for your Adviser, but I think you might want to hear what I've got to say before you decide on that.'

Samael nods and gulps the water down, excess trickling from the corners of his white-crusted lips. He offers his own, untouched, drink, which Samael takes with unsteady fingers.

'We have some new information,' he says as he watches the young man take a long draught from the second cup, 'about Viki Jansdottir.' He waits for him to put the cup down. 'It seems that she had recently been pregnant.'

Samael's face is impassive.

'Do you know anything about that, Samael? Was the baby yours?'

'Whaaat!' Samael splutters. 'You think I'd be so stupid as to make a Banni girl pregnant?' His indignation appears to have overcome his enervation – and his circumspection. 'That's what got me into this mess in the first place…' He stops himself.

'Oh, how so?' He smiles.

Samael shakes his head, saying nothing.

'What was it that got you into this mess, Samael?' he presses.

'No comment,' he mutters.

One more attempt at Mr Nice and then the gloves come off. 'Look, Samael, if you have committed any part of this terrible crime, it will go very much better for you in the Court – and don't doubt our ability to get you there – if you admit it now. Confession and repentance. That's what the People want to hear.'

Samael looks at him in sullen silence.

'Okay. Well, now, let's see,' he says, leaning back in his chair and spreading his fingers across the badly scarred table. 'The thing I was struggling with, if I'm honest, was the motive. Just why would you do it? Why would anyone do it? Young girl like that.'

He leans forward, eyes narrowed, but still smiling. 'But Viki's pregnancy changes that, doesn't it? Provides an obvious motive. You had sex with her and, when she told you she was pregnant with your illegal child, you killed her to keep her quiet.'

'No! It wasn't—'

'It wasn't what, Samael?'

No answer.

'Wasn't like that?' he persists. 'Is that what you were going to say?'

He leans forward again, keeping his eyes steady on the young male. 'Okay, Samael. Then think about this. As you will know, any attempt at off-Program fertilisation must be reported immediately to Gencom. And you will also know that the penalty if you're found guilty is irreversible sterilisation. Even to face suspicion of this Earthly sin could see you expelled immediately from the Program.'

'Being accused of sex assault and murder's not going to go great for me either,' Samael says with asperity, pink spots breaking out on his pasty cheeks.

'You have a point.' He nods, surprised at this spurt of spirit. 'But,' he continues in a firm voice, 'these are crimes that can be dealt with at a local level, at the Restorations. They aren't Notifiable unless…'

'Unless what?' Samael asks with a suspicious look.

'Unless we feel we have a particular reason to send up a Notification.'

An uncomprehending look this time.

'Well, let me speak even more plainly. Reporting to Gencom – with the severe existential penalty that holds for you – is at our discretion. Unless the pregnancy can be clearly attributed, of course. Then there is no choice. But that's not the case here. Too much time has passed.' He smiles as pleasantly as he can and continues in a calm voice. 'So, I would suggest that we could help each other out, Samael – you and me. You tell me exactly what happened that night and I might feel less compelled to inform the Program of what may prove to have been an insignificant matter.'

Samael sits, frowning as he visibly digests this information. 'And if I say nothing?' he ventures after a few moments.

'Then we'll have to move to instant Notification, I'm afraid,' he replies. 'Just to cover our backs.' He's hoping this all sounds more plausible than it actually is. And that the young man is too tired and hungry to call his bluff.

'Okay.' Samael appears suddenly to decide. 'I'll talk.'

Coop activates the input mode and asks him if he would like some more water, before they get going. The prisoner assents with a vigorous nod.

'Right then,' he says as he places the refilled cup on the table and opens his notebook. 'Let's begin at the beginning. How and when did you first meet Viki Jansdottir?'

'That night. That's the first time I saw her – honest. First time I'd been to the Bannies, actuals. Wish to the World I hadn't gone there at all…' He falls silent, his face gloomy.

'When was this, Samael?' he encourages.

Samael drinks the water, more slowly now. 'After the show – at the club… BB's?' He looks up at Coop, who nods in recognition. 'Was on my way home when I saw her, near the bridge with one of the singers from the band. Seemed really upset. He left her and she just carried on crying and walking. Felt sorry for her and went over to see if she was okay. Honest,' he says, looking up at him with plaintive eyes, 'I only wanted to see if she was alright.'

'And then…?' He steels himself. These are the narratives he's come to loathe: the slow build of cruel happenstance and banal detail of which they are invariably comprised. In this case, it's the age-old sexual transaction gone wrong – boy thinks girl consents to sex; girl changes her mind; boy refuses to accept the change – and the same old tired and tawdry justification: she led me on.

'When I said no way I'd do it without protection,' the boy is saying, 'she goes mad, starts shouting at me to get off her, leave her alone.'

'But you didn't get off her, did you?' he remarks in a quiet voice. 'Didn't leave her alone?'

'No, no, I didn't.' The young male has the decency to look

shamefaced. 'Dunno, guess I was just too far into it by then…' He gives him an expectant look. 'Y'know, how it just takes you over?'

'I'm afraid I haven't had that pleasure,' he replies, with a thin smile. *If indeed that's what it is; sounds more like pain to me.*

'So, you carried on, even when it was very clear she didn't want you to?'

'No, well, yes, but she *did* want it to begin with. Wasn't fair to change her mind, not after we'd got started, was it?' Tears are welling in his puffy eyes; whether from self-pity or regret, Coop's not sure, but neither does anything to lessen his distaste for the pathetic individual.

'So, you killed her to shut her up – after you'd had sex with her?' he asks, working hard to keep that distaste from his voice.

'No!' the young man squeals. 'Yes, I made her carry on with the sex when she didn't want to, but I didn't kill her. I really didn't.' He looks at him, face earnest, eyes filling with tears. 'She was alive when I left her, Detective. You must believe me.' He lets out a sob, shaking his head. 'I didn't kill anyone.'

He lets him weep for a while. Wear himself down. It's difficult not to feel any pity for the hapless male. Too much; too soon, that's the problem with the Program system. Minds and bodies too immature to cope with it all. But can there really be urges that are unstoppable, once triggered, or was this young male just tragically weak? He gives a soft snort. *Guess I'll be finding out for myself someday soon.*

'Okay, Mr Samson,' he says after a few minutes. 'Let's say I believe you. And that Viki was alive when you…' He is tempted to say, 'finished with her', but selects 'left her' instead. 'What time was that?'

'Not sure, wasn't really looking at the time…'

'No,' he gives a curt nod, 'I'm sure you weren't.'

'…but I went straight home – got in around one. It's about half an hour from here… You can check with the hub and Mother.' His eyes water again at the mention of his only parent, and he gives him a pleading look. 'She'll be worried about me. Have you told her? Can I talk to her?'

He shakes his head. 'All in good time, Samael. Let's get to the end of the story first, shall we?' He looks at his notes. 'You said she was with a young male when you first saw her – one of the singers from the band, I think you said?' Samael nods. 'Can you remember which one? I believe there were two singers, weren't there: a tall, dark one and a shorter one with fairish hair?'

'I think it was the taller one, the main singer. But I couldn't swear to it.'

He sees Samael's eyelids begin to droop and his head start to sag; he's clearly had enough. And there's probably not much more to come. He informs the young male that they'll check his alibi and decide whether, and with what, he is to be charged, then knocks on the door. 'Take him back down,' he tells the Uniforms as they enter. 'And keep him hydrated, please.' He watches dispassionately as the deflated youth shuffles out of the room.

So... all very interesting. He gets back to his office, fixes himself a long, cold drink of purified and puts his feet up on the desk. That little exchange would seem to suggest two main possibilities: either that Samael is lying, and he killed the girl, possibly without intent, at the time of the sex attack. An accidental killing is plausible; he looks like a boy who doesn't know his own strength. But why all the palaver with the body? If the surveillance data (and the mother!) check out, he wouldn't have had a lot of time to hang around.

Or, other possibility, Samael is telling the truth. Viki survived the sexual attack and bumped – fatally – into someone else that night. If so, was it someone she knew? Or just a random encounter: wrong place, wrong time – with someone who could strike again? Despite the reassurances he'd given the challenging Ms Idadottir, a serial killer remains distinct a possibility.

He sighs. It'll be up to the boss whether to charge Samson with the murder as well as the sex attack. And Don'll be tempted; will want to tidy this all up as soon as possible. They've got a biomatch, after all and, with the time of death so slippery, they could probably make something stick. But, got to admit, the possibility that the Program boy is not the murderer is gaining traction. The lost baby has to be the key, he's sure, and the repro-active male is the obvious candidate. But there's nothing more deceptive than the obvious. Call it a hunch, but he doesn't think Mr Samson's the father – or the killer.

He leans back and stares at the flaking ceiling, across which a spindly insect is traversing slowly on long, delicate legs. For some unfathomable reason – who knows what goes on in insect brains – it decides to stop and turn back, equally haltingly, the way it had just come. *Know how it feels: one step forward, two back.* He sighs again and pivots forward to open his messages.

One makes his spirits rise. The young woman, Lyse, has sent a swim playlist, including some tracks by her band. Says they're playing Friday night at BB's club; if he wants to come and hear them, she'll put his name on the door.

The other makes his heart sink. It's from an Agent Flowers, Program Steward. Wants to talk about a murder.

30

VISITORS

Coop is looking at an extremely handsome young male; smooth and sleek as an otter. The face is an intriguing mix of the binaries – the dark, hooded eyes and aquiline nose are strong, but the lines of the cheeks and mouth are soft and rounded – and the combination is intriguing. They exchange virtual greetings.

'Colleagues call me Coop, if that would be easier,' he says.

'Okay, Coop, great,' the man says with a friendly smile. 'Hear you've arrested one of our boys?'

This smile, though disarming, doesn't quite reach his eyes. *And isn't there something familiar about him?*

'Yes, a Samael Samson,' he replies. 'We intend to charge him with the violent sex attack and murder of a young female. He's admitted the attack but is denying the murder.'

The agent's first question is whether the attacker used protection. *No surprise there: one-track mind, the Stews. As long as it's not illegal sex, they don't care about the damage.* He confirms protection was used, and that it was standard Program issue.

'Seems to have had the presence of mind to do that at least,' he says, 'even though he claims he lost control in every other respect. Says the victim was willing at first, but then changed her mind.'

The man's curved lips snake into a smile. 'Oh, yeah. The old "she led me on" defence?'

'Yes, that's about it.' He nods. 'He's adamant the victim was alive when he left her and the chrono – such as they are – suggest he'd have been pushed for time. Especially as the body had not only been moved but had been, shall we say, arranged?'

'Arranged?' The dark eyebrows slide upwards.

'Well, yes, I think that's the right word. Have a look.' He calls up the death scene and they both regard the pitiful tableau for some moments. His revulsion at the pathetic sight replays and when he sees that the agent also seems moved, it's his turn with the eyebrows.

'Oh. Just my first dead body,' the visitor says with a slight grimace. 'We deal in birth, Coop, not death. Bit of a shock to see someone so young… like that.'

He feels better disposed towards the man as a result of this confession. Not quite as brash as the other Stews he's met, at least. 'So…' he continues, easier now, 'I'm inclined to believe your Mr Samson. Call it a hunch, if you like, but I don't think he's our murderer.'

'Oh?' the agent says with a slight frown. 'And what else do you have, Detective?' he asks.

He tells him about the second bio trace and how they've drawn a blank on it. 'Told it's off-limits – "ghosted", I think you call it?' He asks if that's something the agent, as an insider, could help with. The agent agrees to have a look around but doesn't sound particularly optimistic and moves swiftly on. 'There's a boyfriend, isn't there?' he asks, sweeping back a loose-hanging slick of hair. 'Isn't that your usual suspect?'

'More likely a girlfriend these days.' Coop smiles. 'Although as it happens, the victim, a Viki Jansdottir, *was* involved with a young male. But, for the moment at least, he appears to have a reasonably strong alibi.'

'Maybe there was more than one boyfriend?' the agent suggests. 'Maybe she liked to go after Program males? Heard some of the Banni girls do that sort of thing.'

'Maybe.' He nods, but tells him that, unless he gives him a convincing reason not to, his boss will want to charge Mr Samson with both crimes. 'He's keen to put this to bed as soon as possible.' He looks into the dark, unrevealing eyes of the image. 'Assume you'll have no problem with that?'

'Nah, suits us.' The eyes slip, for a fraction of a second, away from his gaze, but just as quickly return. 'We don't want a lot of noise around this. If there's no foetal crime, we don't need to be involved. Murder's your department, thank the World.' The virtual visitor rises to go.

'Good to meet you, Coop. Keep us in touch. I'll get back on the ghost – if I find anything. But don't get your hopes up. A ghost is a ghost for a reason, after all.'

Could have been worse, he thinks, as his eyes adjust to the afterimage, *bought a bit of time – although likely not much. The agent will find out about the baby when the case gets to court, if not before. But, for now, he looked almost relieved to leave the case to me. Perhaps the Stews dislike working with us as much as we dislike working with them. Pleasant enough man; just wish I could figure out why he looked so familiar.*

He's just started updating his notes and anticipating a swim when there's a sharp knock and a badly hair-restored head appears round the door.

'Got an old female here, Coop. Says she's got important information about the Jansdottir murder.'

The uniformed man stands back abruptly as a small, wiry old woman pushes past him into the room. The wind has whipped the blood into her aged cheeks and scrambled her thick, grey hair into a child's scribble. She looks ever so slightly mad. She tilts her head and gives him a bird-like look. 'Detective Cooper-Clark, I presume?'

'Indeed it is,' he says as he shakes her small, rather dirty, hand. 'So, how can I help you, Mother...?'

'Not Mother anybody,' she says sharply, taking the seat and arranging her many layers of colourful clothing around her. 'Name's Dr Linsdottir. Thelma Linsdottir. You can call me Thelma.'

'Very well, Thelma,' he says, amused, 'how can I help you?'

'Well, you should rather ask how *I* can help *you*, Detective.' She nods. 'I've got some information about the murder of Viki Jansdottir. Understand you've arrested someone?'

'We have a suspect, yes, whom we are about to charge.'

'Yes, that's what I heard. Well, I'm here to tell you that you've got it wrong, Detective.'

'Oh?' His heart sinks; *another mad old crystal gazer.* 'And how would you know that, Thelma?' he asks, failing to disguise his scepticism.

'Don't patronise me, young man,' she replies with asperity. 'I'm not here to waste your time – or mine. I know you're wrong because I saw Viki after that man had finished with her, poor thing.' She shakes her head and tuts. 'Men are no more than beasts when all's told, Detective, are they not?'

'I can't agree with you on that, Thelma,' he says with a calm smile. 'Most of us do manage to resist our baser instincts – such as we're still allowed to have them.'

'Well, not this man, that's for sure,' the old woman tuts again. 'He didn't resist anything, by the state of her. Left her there – in the middle of nowhere – vulnerable to all and sundry. Such a small thing, too; hardly anything of her. I nearly didn't hear her at first, the knocking was so faint. Thought it was those feral cats again, if I'm truthful. They've been getting worse lately and nothing's being done about it. The smell's disgusting—'

'Okay, Thelma,' he interrupts. 'Let's go a bit more slowly, shall we? And start at the beginning.' He stands, smiling. 'Can I get you some tea, first?'

'That would be very nice, thank you, Detective. It's another exceedingly hot day.' She unwinds the scarf from her reeded neck, folds it over her lap and gives him a sweet-old-lady smile. 'Green, please, if you have it.'

He returns with the tea and she takes the cup and blows on the surface, nose twitching in the steam, before taking a hesitant sip and returning to her narrative.

'She was in a terrible state, Detective. Absolutely filthy. And shivering – despite the heat of the night.' She puts the cup down and fixes him with sharp eyes. 'I washed her damaged body. And treated her wounds – the physical ones, anyway.' She dabs her eyes with the edge of her scarf. 'Anyone who could do that to another human being really is no more than an animal.'

'I couldn't agree with you more on that one, Thelma,' he says. 'And I can assure you we will do our best to bring the perpetrator to justice.'

'Justice, ha! You mean the old Theists in their fancy dresses on their moral high horses?' She shakes her head. 'Beyond me how they've managed to worm their way back into things again. Thought the whole point of the New Life was for us humans finally to stand on our own two feet.'

'So... getting back to that night?' he asks, resisting a discussion that, other things being equal, he'd quite like to have.

'Yes. Yes, well.' She pats her hair and seems to compose herself. 'I gave her some painkillers and a mild sedative, then made up a bed for her. Assumed she would sleep until the morning. Best thing for her, I thought. Sleep is the great healer, after all, Detective, isn't it?'

'It is, indeed, Thelma. It is indeed.' *Wouldn't mind getting a bit more of it myself.*

'But she didn't sleep for long,' his visitor continues. 'Heard her moving around a few hours later. Turned out she was setting off. I tried to persuade her to stay, to rest up some more, but I couldn't stop her. Had to go and put something right, I think she said, although she wasn't making a lot of sense. In no fit state to leave the house, in my opinion.'

'No, I'm sure not, by the sounds of it,' he says with a sympathetic nod. 'What time did she leave, Thelma, can you recall?'

'Not really, Detective. It was early – before birdsong came on. And no, before you ask, I don't have one of those surveillance hubs; nobody's business but mine who comes and goes.' She narrows her eyes at him. 'Anyway, when I heard you'd arrested someone, I had to let you know she wasn't killed in the sexual attack. She survived that – just. If it was the same man who murdered her, he would have had to come back for her later. And that seems unlikely to me, given the speed with which he scarpered.'

He nods. *Not as daft as she seems.* 'She had no idea of the identity of the attacker, I assume?' he asks.

'Only that he was a "slimy fat grote" – I think those were her exact words – and that he was definitely a Program boy. She was especially disgusted by that.'

After showing the old woman out he returns to his notebook with a frown. If she's telling the truth – and she'd have no reason not to, would she? – then he really is back to square one. He's got the domlogs (from a near-hysterical mother; had to be restrained, apparently) which confirm the time Samael arrived home and show no further exits until 7.30 the next morning. So he didn't kill her in the attack and it doesn't look, on the balance of probability, that he went back for her later. All of which adds weight to the conclusion he was beginning to reach: Samael's not his man.

But if young Samael moves out of the picture, for the murder at least, who's left in the frame? Aside from the 'ghost', and he's not holding his breath on that one. He flicks through his notes and gives a slow smile, tapping at an entry. A brother, that's who's left. One that the musician said the victim wasn't too happy about. And one that the aunt omitted to mention.

31

THE ALLOTMENTS

The aunt looked very much worse than Coop remembered: dark shadows around her eyes and a greyish tinge to the corner of her lips. She'd got very flustered when he'd asked why she hadn't mentioned her nephew.

Hadn't thought about it, she'd sniffed, shifting heavily in the manifestly ill-equipped chair. *And you didn't ask me anyway, did you... whether anyone else is living here? If you had, I'd have mentioned. Obviously. Wasn't trying to hide anything. Haven't got anything to hide, have I? Anyway, he's not here anymore. Only stayed with us for a few days before moving on. Been out at the Edgelands a long time and wasn't settling back. Friend found him work on the community allotments, but not sure if he's still there; haven't seen him for days. It's possible, but unlikely, he's gone back to the Edge.*

He's decided to have a look round the allotments, see if he can find any trace of the man. Curious to meet him, has to admit. Not many come back from an Edgeland tour – alive at least. And those who do generally keep very quiet about it. The male volunteers (no other sex is allowed) build strong bonds out there, close as blood ties: 'biomates', they call themselves. Few enlist who have any sort of foothold in the Civilised World. It's a bit of a stereotype, admittedly, but the EdgeForce is seen to attract a certain kind of personality: the sort of male who has a short fuse and a predilection for trouble. What's it Don calls it? *A place for those who've run out of bridges to burn but can't let go of the matches.*

He walks fast, perspiring in the late morning heat. Should have called a car; thought it was nearer than this. He's just about regretting the whole expedition when he sees the large wrought-iron gate to the south end of the allotments and makes his way over. Stopping at the entrance for a long drink and a quick lick round with a coolie, he surveys the large area of reclaimed land set aside for the public allotments. Rows of plants, many in flower or heavy with fruit, form a multi-coloured living tapestry as far as the eye can see and a pungent, ripe-vegetative smell hangs heavy in the air: a "dinner-gong for primates", he recalls someone describing it. Hovering over this feast, a thick veil of insects simmers in synchronised gluttony. Takes him a moment to realise that the intense and insistent vibration in his ears has an external rather than internal source.

The allotments are, quite literally, the lifeblood of the Banleus; the only place most folk ever get to see, never mind taste, food in its near-original state. Produce is sold on a first-come, first-get basis, with protected allocations for the old and vulnerable. Prices are kept as low as possible, sufficient only to cover the cost of new seeds and – the never-ending problem – water, bought from the Citi only when unavoidable. Mostly, the allotments are fed by the aquashare scheme, whereby people exchange used house water for crop vouchers. He gives a little snort; water – how things change. Used to be, just poured it down the drain.

A group of males at the far-most edge of the fields appears to be engaged in clearing the drainage ditches. Most of those doing the digging are youthful, but there's a thin, rather stooped, older man standing on the higher bank who seems to be supervising the work. He picks his way gingerly towards this man, avoiding the scattered heaps of sodden debris, calling out a greeting as he approaches. Several pairs of unfriendly young eyes turn towards him.

The older man slides his gaze away from his young charges with obvious reluctance and fixes them on Coop, shaggy brows raised.

'Looking for a man called Naz. Nazri Janson.' Coop smiles, showing his badge. 'Supposed to be working here with you?'

'Oh ay, Naz.' The man nods, eyebrows relaxing. 'He's usually on the graveyard. Won't be in till later – if he comes in at all, mind you.'

'Oh? Why do you say that?'

'Well, he's had a bit of a blow. It was his sister, y'know, the girl killed the other day. Taking it very badly, by all accounts.'

'Oh? In what way badly?' he asks, taking out his pen and notebook.

'Dunno, just seems to have knocked him for six. Was getting on all right to begin with. Kept himself to himself, but reliable, like. But now he doesn't turn up most nights. And Stan, Night Super, told me he caused a bit of a ruck last time he was in. Got a bit nasty, Stan said. Didn't say what it was about; you'll have to ask Stan.'

The man sighs, scratching his thinning hair. 'Reflects badly on me, this does. I was the one put him up for the job. Don't want to be too hard on him, especially after… all that, but if he doesn't shape up we'll have to let him go. There's too much to do to carry a man and there's plenty others keen to take his place.'

He gives him a sympathetic smile. 'So, you knew him before he got the job here?'

'Yeah, well, I know his aunt Dottie quite well. Go way back, Dot and me. She was a cracker when she was young.' His gamey grin exposes large, age-yellowed teeth. 'I know, I know,' he says as he catches Coop's look of surprise, 'she was a bit slimmer then, heh-heh.'

'So, how well do you know Mr Janson?' he asks.

'Oh, only as a young lad. Was generally polite and well-behaved, as I recall. Bit soft, if anything. Went off the rails as a teenager but show me a lad who doesn't these days. Heard he'd gone away under a cloud, like. Not sure why; Dot's never told me the full story. Anyway, when she told me he was back and looking for work, offered to help, didn't I? Remembered he used to spend a bit of time up here as a kid; really liked the plants. I know Dot doesn't have much from one end of the week to the other, so got him some night work. Not the best paid of jobs, true, but one that meant he could pretty much be left to himself, which is what he seemed to want.'

The supervisor casts a quick glance back at the young diggers, most of whom appear to have seized the opportunity of his absence to rest on their shovels. As they swiftly return to their labours the old man grunts and resumes his story.

'Told me that he can't fit in back here; misses the men out there. Spose it was the only family he'd ever really had, poor bugger, since his old man scarpered.' He shakes his threadbare head. 'There was a bad 'un if ever there was one. Knew more about the death of Naz's mother than ever came to light, to my mind. Strange how she had the fall just as she was about to go to Court. Too much of a coincidence, if you ask me. You need to have a look into that one, Detective,' he says with a meaningful nod. 'Tell me there's not a wrong been done there.'

'I'll certainly look into the matter when I get back to the office, Mr…?'

'Tonkinson, Wil Tonkinson.'

'It does sound a bit of a coincidence, Mr Tonkinson, and I'm always rather suspicious of those. Anyway, as you were saying, Naz's father ran off—'

'Yeah, well, a lot did the same then. No excusing, mind, but it was a worrying time for men, especially those not yet started their families. You'll be too young to remember. The Program was just finding its feet – spreading its ugly roots more like, given what we now know – and men were getting wary. Especially when it came out it was all going to be compulsory.'

He nods, recalling his father's outrage at the idea of conscription. That wasn't what he and his generation thought they'd voted for. No-one had said anything about sterilising grown men – voluntarily or otherwise. Everyone just assumed, indeed, were strongly led to assume, that it was all going to start with the next generation of newborns.

'Told me he can't get used to civilisation,' the supervisor is continuing. 'Likes to sleep with the smell of the earth in his nose. Between you, me and the stars,' the man bends towards him, prickling Coop's nostrils with his pungent breath, 'thought he'd been kipping out in the sheds at the end of the lots.' He nods his head in the direction of the possible location. 'But had a gander this morning, and it don't look like anyone's been there. And Stan hasn't said anything about it, so,' he gives a bony shrug, 'maybe not…'

'He could always go back, I assume?' Coop asks. 'To the Edgelands, I mean. If he misses the life that much.'

'Nah,' the supervisor says with a short laugh. 'Funny thing, that. Naz said he'd been released for health reasons. Said he had… what was it, now?' His already creased forehead creases further. 'That's it,' his brow relaxes, 'said he had a problem with his "masticatory coefficient". Lost too many teeth, wernit? Can't do the job without them, apparently, heh-heh.' The man's thin shoulders jerk up and down like an old cartoon character.

Coop suspects that's as much as he's going to get here and closes his book, smiling at the man. 'Okay, well, if you see him, Mr Tonkinson, could you tell him I'd like to speak to him? Tell him it's in his interest to get in touch, especially if he's in trouble in any way.'

'Trouble?' The man's wiry eyebrows shoot up. 'Why'd he be in trouble, then?' The realisation shows on his face. 'You don't mean…?'

'No, no. I don't mean anything at all,' he says in a firm voice, cross at his misspeak. 'Just need to talk to him about a matter. So, if you do see him, I'd be grateful if you could ask him to call me as soon as possible.' He hands him his securpin. 'Or, even better, let me know where he is – there'd be some coin in it for you.'

He calls a car to take him back; he's had enough of being snit bait. It arrives quickly, and he relaxes into its soft seats, breathing in the cool, filtered air. Hasn't come away with much from that little escapade. The man had agreed to pass the message on but hadn't seemed very confident about seeing the brother again. And if Mr Janson's no longer coming to the allotments, to work or sleep, it'll be very difficult to find him – even in the out-of-Citi areas he, Coop, has come to know quite well. And worse, if (dental incapacity notwithstanding) he does go back to the Edgelands, that'll be that. He'll never find him. That's the whole point of the Edge: the only place in this endlessly interconnected and relentlessly surveilled World for a human soul to hide.

32

DISAPPOINTMENT

They've finished the show and she's buzzing. First live performance. And people actually clapped; some even cheered. Her heartbeat is furious and she's high as a kite. She looks around, struggling to focus on her material surroundings, and sees Seth walking towards her, a wide smile on his face. 'Smashed it, Lyse,' he says, giving her an enthusiastic hug. 'Totally smashed it!'

'Yeah, wasn't bad.' She grins, pulling away.

'Not bad?' He pats her on the back. '*Cooking with gas!* as Oat would say. Biggest clap of the set. Gotta celebrate. Go for a drink?'

'Sure,' she says, twisting slowly down to Earth.

'See y'later, boys,' Seth calls to the remaining members of the band, as they leave the club and step out into the night air. 'Woah,' he groans. 'Still roasting out here. If we don't get some rain soon it's all going to burn up. And this effin' dust's shit; gets in everywhere.'

'Yeah. Thank the World for the atmosfers,' she says, taking out her mask. 'Don't need to cover your face everywhere you go.'

'Yeah – okay for you lot in the Citi,' he says, wrapping his scarf tightly around his nose and mouth, 'but the shit the Citi chucks out just makes it worse for us outside.'

They walk on, conversation hampered by their face coverings, until they reach the bar and enter its darkly lit interior. An old blues lament she vaguely recognises smooches in the background and the steely blue smoke of old-time niccos writhes in the air. A barbot dispatches their order with a smile of benevolent servitude, and they head to a small table at the back of the long, low-ceilinged room. 'Used to come here with Q a lot,' Seth says as they slide into their seats, placing their smouldering drinks on the greasy table in front of them. 'Not so much, recents.'

'So… it's the trial tomorrow,' she says, as the smoke from their drinks clouds the air between them. 'You okay about that?' she asks, waving a hand to clear the view.

'Yeah, guess so.'

'You heard he's pleading not guilty?'

'Yeah. Cop told me. Asked if I knew someone who'd Testify for Vik at the trial.'

'Why Testify for her?' she says, taken aback. 'She's not the one on trial.'

'Well, that's just it. Cop said they'll try to make out she brought it on herself in some way.'

'Oh, for World's sake!' she snorts. 'That's such bollox.'

He nods in agreement but says nothing.

'Well, you could do it, couldn't you?' She looks at him, eyebrows raised. 'You've known her longer than anyone else, apart from her aunt, haven't you?'

'Maybe… I don't know. It's complicated.' He gives a brief smile, avoiding her gaze.

'How so, complicated?' She follows his eyes.

'Dunno…' He stops and shrugs. 'Just not sure it'd do any good, really. Nobody's going to listen to me, are they?'

'Well, someone's got to stand up for her,' she says, surprised at what she's hearing, 'and you'd be better than no-one. You could tell them she didn't go with other men for a start.'

'Yeeah,' he circles his glass slowly on the greasy surface, 'that's the complicated bit actually.' He looks out across the bar, where a few isolated individuals are nursing glasses of steaming green liquid – their 'occupied' signs reflecting redly on the undersides of their mournful chins – then turns back to her and says in a quiet voice: 'Seems she did go with other men. Q says the cops found out she'd got pregnant.'

'Pregnant?' she gasps. 'No way! Who by?'

'Well, that's what the cops want to know.' He gives an awkward laugh. 'Not by me, ovs.'

'No, ovs.' She smiles a little, but she's thrown by this. 'So, that means Vik *was* sexing around?' she says.

'Yeah, looks like.' He shrugs. 'So, I didn't think there was much point me trying to say she wasn't like that.'

'But that creep could get off if no-one speaks up for her. No, what am I saying?' She gives a snort of derision. 'She shouldn't have to be spoken up for – she's the one who got murdered.' She slaps her hand on the sticky table, causing startled jets of smoke to erupt from their drinks. 'This is so Oldsville, can't believe it.'

'Yeah.' He takes a long swig of his drink and gives her a wry smile. 'Guess some things don't change very much.'

She lets it go but is surprised at his reluctance. And disappointed, if she's honest. If he'd cared about Viki at all, he'd want to stick up for her, wouldn't he? Whatever people thought. Would want people to know that she wasn't a bad person. And anyway… she clicks her tongue, even if she *had* been with another man and got with a baby, that didn't make her a bad person, did it? Can't believe anyone still thinks like that. Especially not him. She glances at his passive face behind the thinning curls of smoke and realises how little she actually knows Seth Marcuson. He has the look of someone who would be brave and loyal but maybe he's not what he looks; *seems pretty disloyal and cowardly right now, doesn't he?*

The smooth detective slips unannounced into her mind. He'd

have spoken for Viki, wouldn't he? He wouldn't have found it 'too complicated' to stand up for a friend. Seth's a bit older than her, but he's just like one of her mates, or Ammi and Jai: same ideas and interests, same approach to life. The detective is very different. Can't actually be a lot older, late twenties, maybe, but seems more like an actual grown-up; someone who's seen a bit of life, knows a few things. And not bad on the eye either.

'So, Lys,' Seth asks of a sudden, as if aware of the unfavourable comparison, 'what's your take on the Program?'

'The Life Program?' she asks, uninterested. 'Why bring that up? You're not thinking about signing your body away, are you?' She starts to snicker but cuts it off; there's no way she wants him to think she's okay with him.

'No, it's just that Pa and his friend Thelma were talking about it the other day. How it controls the whole birth thing – you know, decides who can and who can't have babies.'

'Well, I guess it has to be done somehow,' she says, with a frown. 'Can't just go back to people having babies all over the place – no offence to Viki, ovs.'

'No, that's what I said, but Pa was saying that too many's being shut out now.'

'Well, he may be right.' *Although maybe they should've worked a bit harder at school.* 'But it is what it is. Can't see it being changed any time soon.'

'No, but what if the Program wasn't there anymore?' he persists. 'What d'you think would happen?'

'Well, I don't know exactly, but chances are it wouldn't be good news for the female of the species.'

'Yeah?'

'Well, yeah – if it meant that all men were like that Samael creep, it'd be a nightmare. More sexual attacks. More Vikis discarded by the roadside.'

'But,' he still persists, 'it could mean more females got to be Mothers.'

'Yeah, or have Motherhood forced upon them, whether they wanted or not,' she snaps, tired of the conversation and tired of him right now. 'Ending the Program's not going to allow females to control their bodies. New ways would soon be found for males to take charge of that little problem again. I don't like Gencom – no-one does – but I honestly think that ending the Program would take womankind back to the Bad Old Days.'

*

Coop has also been to the club that night and is returning to the Citi alone. She'd sent him the tickets as promised and he'd rather enjoyed being nodded in, like he was something to do with the band. And, once his ears got used to the noise level and the smell of unwashed human, he'd enjoyed the raw energy of it all, the beats of the music still a faint echo in his ears. And she was very good, even if she didn't get to do much – and certainly looked the part in the retro dress, what there was of it anyway, and the white ankle boots with the slots in the side.

She'd also sent him a rather breathless vizpin about the smell from the body; something about it being a plant called rue, which has a number of different meanings – all of which she took to support her theory about it being a message from the murderer: *saying sorry for what he'd done, maybe – or for something, some sin, he thought Viki'd committed. And also…* she'd rushed on excitedly, *the female in the play had sacrificed herself for love and could it be true of Viki too – that she was some sort of sacrifice?* His instinctive scepticism at her theories is tempered by the fact that she'd been right before – and also by the enjoyment of watching her expressive face expound them. Probably unnecessary to view the pin quite so many times, however.

He'd waited behind after the band finished, leaning on the wall across from the entrance as the crowd dispersed, hoping to compliment her on her performance and, yes, maybe walk with her a bit. But, before long, he saw her leaving with Seth Marcuson. From the body language they'd looked quite close and he'd felt the grip of what he'd assumed must be sexual jealousy. *But band members would be close, wouldn't they? And she's a naturally friendly young woman, after all, isn't she?* He'd turned away, resisting the desire to follow them as being one that was not entirely driven by professional motives.

But the evening hadn't been a complete washout. He now knows where he's seen the androgynous agent before. He pulls the flyer from his pocket and scans the promo. Lead singer: Queron Brandonson. It's definitely him. Unmistakable face. So… not only is our Agent Flowers a singer in the same band as the ex-boyfriend but, if Mr Samson is to be believed, he was one of the last people to see Viki alive that night. And the fact the agent didn't think to mention either of these things is interesting to say the least. He's not inclined to coincidence; something more is going on here than meets the eye. As the man himself would say: *the Universe is rarely so lazy.*

33

THE TRIAL

'So, you still going through with the Program thing, Am?' Lyse asks, determined to show interest in her adopted sister's chosen path (she can't think of it as a 'career' no matter how much Program propaganda she hears). They arrived early for Viki's trial and secured good seats with a clear view of the stage. People are packing in around them, quaffing festive drinks as they exchange gossip and small delicacies.

'Yeah, course.' Ammi bristles briefly but then subsides with a small sigh. 'It's all a bit scary actually, Ly, now I've found out more about it.' She hesitates. 'I knew about the health side – the monitoring, the drugs and stuff. Wasn't happy but saw the reason for it. But, turns out, there's other stuff you have to do – or not do. How to be a good Mother, sort of thing.'

'Oh yeah… and a good wife, spose?'

Ammi nods. 'Sort of. There's these ten pledges—'

'Ah ha! The dreaded terms and conditions.'

'Exactly,' Ammi says, turning down the corners of her neat little mouth. 'If you don't stick rigidly to your *Personalised Progenitor Pathway*,' she says in a sardonic tone, 'you're put back nine months and have to start again. But that's not the worst of it,' she says, pulling the front ends of her hair as she becomes more animated. 'I knew about not being allowed to work – you get a Mother's wage, which is quite good, actually – but there's other, more personal, things…'

Lyse says nothing, trying to show no trace of any 'told-you-so' satisfaction.

'Like, you can't be alone with a male who's not a relative and you've got to wear what they call modest clothes at all times. And,' Ammi's blue eyes widen, 'you've got to commit totally to the man, your Partner… you know, sexually; you can't refuse him in your fertile phase unless the medics have signed you off. And, worse, even if it's all broken down between you – even if you've come to actually hate each other – you have to stay together until the childs are old enough to go public.'

'Woah, Am!' she says, as if any of this surprises her. 'Sounds like a big ask to me. You'd have to be sure you'd got the right man. And you know what they say: *a good man is hard to find. You always get the other kind.*'

Ammi laughs. 'Swear you've got a line for everything, Ly.'

Movement on the stage attracts their eyes. Various persons are beginning to take their positions. Some, presumably the Judges, take the Highchairs. 'Look at that.' She nudges Ammi. 'All male. Must be the ones Jai told me about – don't think women are intelligent enough to judge men. Thought he was joking…'

She stops as she sees the detective walk to the front of the stage, removing his hat as he steps up to a podium. He places his notebook in front of him and gazes at the audience with a calm smile. Looks very distinguished with his smooth, dark skin against the white tunic. She resists the urge to wave at him and points him out to her companion.

'Yeah, nice,' Ammi says, 'but he'll already be taken – or not interested.'

'No, I don't think so.'

'You don't think so, which – not taken or not interested?'

'Both.'

She falls silent as she sees Samael slowly rising up into the virtual cage. He casts a brief, unseeing, glance at the audience, then stares down at his feet. She gives an involuntary shudder.

A tall, elderly man in a long white robe walks to the front of the stage and holds up his hand to silence the crowd. 'Good morning, friends.' He bows with a restrained sweep of an arm. 'For those joining us after the break, I am Dr Farquason, your Host for this Session of the Court, brought to you today by the Hismoli Brothers. We have moved very swiftly through the cases this morning and I'm hopeful that we can keep up the pace.' He nods towards the scrolling information banner. 'The next case is the People versus Samael Samson.'

He moves closer to the crowd, hands clasped behind him, nodding slightly. 'This is an interesting case. Mr Samson, Program recruit Z4273, is being charged, very unusually, with the Old-World crime of rape. To wit, that on the night of Saturday, June 11, in the 62nd year of our New Life, he did forcibly have sexual intercourse with a Viki Jansdottir, against her will.'

'Oh, not her murder, then?' Ammi asks, looking at her. She shrugs, also surprised.

'The Accused is pleading *Not Guilty* to the charge,' the Host informs the crowd, so the Court must move, as a result, to Full Trial. He instructs the Judges to prepare and asks, with a theatrical wave: 'Who makes the Accusation for the People?'

She sees the detective rise and hold up the palm of his hand. 'Detective Cooper-Clark, he says. 'Working with the out-of-Citi Division of the community police.'

'And what is the basis of the People's case, Detective?' the Host asks, as he settles himself on the highest of the Highchairs, smoothing the wiry hairs underneath his bottom lip.

The detective walks towards the front of the stage with a

pleasant smile. A few wolf whistles emit from females in the front rows, and she nudges Ammi and grins.

'Good morning, Citizens,' he begins in a clear, calm voice, bowing slightly to the audience. 'The People accuse Mr Samson of committing the cruel and unusual crime of "rape" on a young and vulnerable female. Many of you will be unfamiliar with this ancient statute, which defines the crime as the penetration – by a human body part, or foreign body – of another person, without that person's consent and under threat or use of force.' He waits a moment to allow the ripple of disgust to run its course before continuing.

'By the Accused's own admission, "rape" is precisely what happened on the night of 11/7. *By his own admission*, I repeat again, Samael Samson, penetrated Viki Jansdottir with his penis extremely forcibly, against her clearly expressed wishes.' He looks solemnly out at the audience. 'S.4 of your evipak describes the considerable external and internal physical damage his actions caused the victim.'

He pauses again to give the audience time to absorb the vivid graphics, then continues. 'Unfortunately, the Victim herself is now sadly deceased and cannot bear Witness to the crime committed against her. But there is significant circumstantial evidence: Mr Samson's genetic matter was found on the Victim, the protective sheath used in the attack was standard Program issue and a pack of six such sheaths, with one missing, was found at the house of the Accused. But most centrally,' he looks out at the audience, 'as I have already said, we have a recorded confession from the Defendant himself that he raped Ms Jansdottir that night.'

'We must be clear that this confession has now been retracted, has it not?' the bearded Host interjects, as he sees the Public Defender rising from her seat.

'Yes, true.' The detective inclines his head to the Host. 'But we must also be clear that Mr Samson's is not – even now – denying that he committed this terrible crime.' He turns towards the audience. 'Nor is he denying that his actions inflicted considerable pain and suffering. What he *is* denying,' he looks out, eyebrows raised, 'is any responsibility for his actions. Put simply, he did rape Ms Jansdottir, but it wasn't his fault.'

Cooper-Clark moves slowly back to the centre of the stage. 'On extremely bad advice,' he nods towards the Defender, 'Mr Samson is now casting around for other things and other people to blame, including – I'm sure you will hear shortly – the Victim herself. However,' he turns back on the audience, 'I put it to you most strongly, that Mr Samson has no-one but himself to blame for the tragic events of that night. By his own admission, he penetrated Viki Jansdottir against her will and for that violation – that rape, as we must now name it – he must be found Guilty as charged.'

He bows slightly to the seated Host. 'That is the opening case for the People, Sir.' Loud clapping and cheers from the crowd accompany further she-wolf whistles as he returns to his seat, face composed. Lyse takes a vicarious sense of pride in his performance.

'Thank you, Detective,' the Host says, standing, 'for setting out the People's case so succinctly. You will be allowed final remarks following the arguments from the Defence.' He looks to the other side of the stage. 'Who amongst you is Defender of the Accused?'

A smoothly corpulent middle-aged woman, clearly the beneficiary of many facial updates, rises from her seat. She is expensively, if rather carelessly, costumed in a cream two-piece (antique silk, as far as Lyse can tell). 'Mog Reesdottir, Sir, on behalf of Gencom,' the woman says, rising, ignoring the loud hisses erupting from the crowd at the mention of the much-despised behemoth. She turns to the crowd with a wide smile on her expertly coutured face.

'Let me take you back to that fateful Saturday night, my friends,' she says, holding out an upturned palm, metal armlets glinting. 'My client – a young man barely out of his teens – had travelled across to the Banleus to hear some live music. He does not deny that the possibility of finding a female willing to have sex had also crossed his mind – he is a healthy young male, after all. Conscious of his moral duty, however, he was carrying a pack of sheaths.' She gives the audience an oily smirk. 'You could say he was being a little optimistic there, although we all know there's no shortage of Banni girls willing to have sex for money – or even for free.'

'Thank you, Ms Reesdottir,' the Host interrupts, hand raised. 'The Court would be grateful if you would stick to substance rather than supposition.'

'Apologies, Sir,' the Public Defender says with an unctuous bow, 'just keen to establish a little local colour. So, as I was saying,' she turns back to the crowd, 'our Mr Samson had recently started reversal and it is well known that this process has an immensely powerful impact on young male bodies. Many describe the almost uncontrollable nature of the forces unleashed within them; how they become so highly sensitised that almost any stimulus, visual or physical, triggers unbidden and undesired arousal. They are cocked, we could say,' she winks at the crowd, 'like loaded pistols – primed to shoot off at the slightest provocation.'

She pulls a jewel-studded flask from the pocket of her tunic and drinks, her chin raised like a fat-throated bird.

'It was in this, shall we say, "loaded" state,' she continues, sliding the flask into her ample, silk-covered bosom, 'that Mr Samson left the music club and was on his way home when he chanced upon the female in question. She appeared visibly distressed and the Defendant went over to see if she needed help. His intentions at that point were entirely honourable. He did not approach the young woman with sex in mind and he did not initiate the sexual activity.' The PD takes another sip from the glittering bottle, wiping her mouth with the back of her beringed hand.

'However,' she continues, scanning the crowd, 'Mr Samson tells us that the young woman quickly made it clear that that sex was very much on *her* mind. In his words – I refer you to S.6.1

of your evipack: she *suddenly came on strong* and was *all over me.* She seemed experienced – seemed, as he put it, *to know what she was doing*, and he quickly became aroused. It was only at a point, fairly – or, indeed, unfairly, you could say – late in the proceedings, when Mr Samson tried to use the sheath, as is his moral duty, of course…' she flashes the Judges an ingratiating smile, 'that the female changed her mind and tried to make him stop. By then, however, she had pushed him too far. Provoked him indeed, we would argue, to the point of no return.' She regards the audience with evident satisfaction at the weight of her argument.

'So, this is the truth of what happened that night, my friends,' the elegantly costumed Defender continues. 'There is no dispute about the facts. As you have heard from the Public Accuser, my client admits to the encounter. But I put it to you that we have to look at the behaviour of *both* those involved, not just those of my client, and ask the central question,' she pauses and adopts a kind-to-be-cruel expression, 'of how far the alleged victim can be seen to have brought her unhappy fate upon herself. Was she indeed an innocent victim, as the smooth detective suggests, or did she in some way invite – some might even say deserve – the fate that befell her? Might it be possible, indeed, to see my client, not the female, as the real victim of the encounter?'

'Told you so,' Lyse hisses. 'They're putting Viki on trial – just like Seth said they would.' She looks around for Seth – *maybe he changed his mind* – but sees no sign of him. *Some friend, eh? Maybe…* she entertains a thought that her conscious mind has been resisting stoutly, *maybe he* does *know something about Viki's murder. And maybe that's why he's not showing his face today. Maybe he's got more to hide than his mutation.*

'We don't know much about this young woman,' the PD is saying. 'She seems to have lived almost entirely off-grid and, unlike Mr Samson, had made very little of her Life. But we do know one very important thing about her, something that my esteemed colleague,' she smirks across at Cooper-Clark, 'omitted to tell you. One piece of information that may be absolutely crucial to understanding her motives on the night in question.' Her slick smile spreads wider as she approaches the audience in a confiding manner.

'The key fact about Ms Jansdottir that the detective failed to tell us is that she had been made pregnant illegally and, willingly or not, had aborted the unborn child.'

The crowd gives a collective gasp at this news that appears to hang in the air for an infinitesimal moment before breaking down into a multitude of animated individual conversations.

'Wow! Did you know that, Ly?' Ammi asks, eyes wide. 'That Vik'd been pregnant?'

'Yeah.' She shrugs. 'Seth told me.'

'But if she was pregnant,' Ammi says with a moue of disapproval, 'that means she was having sex with other men, while she was sposed to be with Seth.'

'Yeah, guess so. No biggies, though – they weren't joined at the hip, after all.'

'But you said they'd argued the night she died,' Ammi presses. 'Maybe that was what it was about? Did you ask him?'

'No, I didn't ask him, Am,' she replies testily. 'I'm not a pol, y'know.'

'Is that why he didn't want to speak up for her today, d'you think?' Ammi persists. 'Because he's angry about her having sex with another man?'

'Well, yes… no, I'm not sure, to be honest. He just said it was complicated.'

'Well, whatevs,' Ammi says with a sniff, 'doesn't really reflect on him very well, does it? Bit cowardly, don't you think?'

'Yeah, guess so. But maybe he's got his reasons,' she says without much conviction. A bit cowardly is exactly what she thinks – at the very least – but she's not going to admit that to Ammi. 'Anyway,' she says in a firm voice, 'no-one should have to speak up for her, should they? She's the victim here, remember.'

The smooth PD is continuing. 'So, we have a sexually active young woman walking alone, after dark, in a deserted area of the Banleus. We know she had been drinking and had a cannabinoid substance in her system,' she gives Cooper-Clark a smug smile, 'which is something else the charming detective omitted to tell you, by the way.' She turns to the audience with raised eyebrows, her full lips slightly pursed. 'So exactly what, we have to ask ourselves, was the young woman after that night?'

She pauses to let the question register, before answering it herself. 'I put it to you that Ms Jansdottir was actively looking for an illegal sexual encounter. An encounter of the kind, indeed, she thought she had found with Mr Samson, a repro-active male. There is no other way to interpret the fact that it was only when my client, quite properly, refused to have unprotected sex that she decided to end the encounter. Had he been willing to break the law that night, and copulate without protection, I contend, she would have allowed – indeed, energetically and enthusiastically encouraged – him to continue.'

The white-robed Host rises partially from his seat. 'That is speculation on your part, Ms Reesdottir. There is no evidence, apart from the testimony of the Defendant himself, to corroborate the version of events that you have just provided. Without Witness, we cannot truly know what passed between these two unfortunate young people that evening.'

The Defender concedes this point with a stiff bow and takes another sip from the jewelled flask before turning again to the audience. 'Nevertheless, I suggest to you, my friends, that it was Mr Samson, not Viki Jansdottir, who was the real prey that night. Caught tight,' she brings her thumb and first finger together to give visual emphasis to the point, 'like a hapless grub in a pincer. Between the powerful push of the forces unleashed within him and the irresistible pull of a sexually predatory female.'

She casts a triumphant look at the restless crowd. 'So, if

you consider, as I do, that the provocation experienced by this vulnerable young man that night,' she gestures towards Samael, 'was such that no fertile male could reasonably be expected to resist, then you must accept my client's plea of *Not Guilty* on the basis of severely diminished responsibility.'

'Thank you, Ms Reesdottir,' the bearded Host says, rising again from his Highchair. 'As there are no Witnesses to the alleged crime and no person to Testify…' he looks enquiringly in the detective's direction, who shakes his head, 'we will move swiftly on. I therefore call on the People to make its – ideally brief – concluding comments.'

'Thank you, Sir,' the detective says, rising and turning to face the crowd. He has a pleasant smile on his lips, as always, but she thinks there's a steelier cast to his smooth features than she's seen before.

'Much has been made here today of the fact that the Victim had become pregnant,' he says in an even tone, 'with attendant insinuations about her moral character. But let us be absolutely clear on this: the sexual history of the Victim is wholly immaterial to the case we are considering today. I put it to you that, even if Ms Jansdottir had sex with a different male every day prior to, and every day following, the attack by Mr Samson, it would not change the fact – attested by the Accused himself – that she did not want to have sex on that particular night with that particular man. And even if she did initiate this particular encounter, that does not mean that, in doing so, she forfeits the right to change her mind. No, as they used to say, means no – at whatever point in the proceedings it is said.'

He moves to the front of the stage and regards the crowd with the calm-but-firm expression of an experienced teacher. 'The Defender is suggesting that the actions Mr Samson took would be those of any "reasonable biomale" placed in the same situation, but not for a very long time has sexual assault been accepted as the action of a reasonable man (or woman); nor that a male can be irresistibly driven to violent crime by the sheer force of his desires. Such an idea – the old *crime passionnel* – harks back to a darker period in human history, when much of the female sex was effectively enslaved by the male.

'The Defender is asking you to see the situation from the perspective of the Accused,' he continues. 'Well, I think we can all do that, can't we?' He raises his hands, palms upturned, in reasonable-man mode. 'We can all understand that the young man's body was experiencing powerful emotions that he'd never felt before. We can even understand that the Victim's actions may have fuelled those emotions.' He scans the crowd slowly as he speaks, lowering his arms. 'But understanding is one thing and excusing another. Understanding the reason for Mr Samson's failure to control himself does not diminish the fact that lose control he most certainly did. Nor, most crucially, that it was his loss of control – and not the behaviour of his Victim, nor the drugs in his system – that was responsible for the terrible crime committed that night.

'In conclusion,' he says as he hears the Host clear his throat. 'The facts of this sad case have been set out before you today – simply and clearly. On the night of July 11, Ms Jansdottir was brutally raped by Mr Samson. Mr Samson admits this crime and it is for this crime that he – and he alone – now has to answer. We can see no mitigating factors that can be taken to lessen his guilt nor diminish his responsibility and urge you to reach a *Guilty* verdict.' He gives a small nod to the seated Host. 'That concludes the People's case, Sir.'

'Well said,' Ammi cries with a small clap, amidst much applause and cheering from the crowd. 'Rape, that's a good word for what he did.'

'Thank you, Detective,' the Host says as he turns to the PD. 'Does the Defence wish to make a final response, Ms Reesdottir?'

'Only a short one, Sir,' she replies with a smug twitch of her over-plumped mouth. 'I cannot hope to match the eloquence of the People's Accuser, but I have no need; the kernel of our case can be simply set out. A crime was indeed committed on the night in question, but it was not one for which my client can be seen to have the sole, or even the main, responsibility. *It takes two to tango*, as the old saying has it.' She gives a wide smile and reaches again for the bright flask, taking a slow draught before continuing.

'The esteemed detective suggests that to focus on the behaviour of the female is to turn the clock back to the dark age of paternalism and misogyny. But maybe,' she says, replacing the flask and raising her expertly arched eyebrows, 'maybe it is his view that is the more backward-looking? His is a view of the female as a sexually powerless creature, without desires and drives of her own. But this is to deny the full agency of the female, is it not? In the New World it is rightly accepted that the sexual appetite of the female is equal to that of the male. Indeed, so much so,' she simpers towards the crowd, 'that today it is the male, not the female, who is more likely to be the sexual prey.'

'So...' she says with an over-sweet smile, 'I want to ask you, one last time, to put yourself in Mr Samson's shoes. He's on a night out, looking for some music, maybe a little fun. He stops to help a female in distress and she turns on him sexually. His excitable young body is aroused, almost to breaking point, then suddenly – and, to my mind, cruelly – rejected when the female doesn't get what she wants. My client does not deny he did wrong; he admits he lost control and is heartily sorry for it. But I put it to you that he lost control because he was provoked beyond endurance. And it is on this basis – the Accused's diminished responsibility in the face of irresistible provocation – that the Court must, in all fairness and compassion, reach a determination of *Not Guilty* today.'

The PD moves back from the front of the stage and inclines her artfully coiffured head towards the Host. 'That concludes the case for the People's Defence, Sir.' She looks expectantly at the crowd and receives a smattering of applause, as well as many hisses and cat calls.

The bearded Host rises again. 'Thank you, Ms Reesdottir.

And you, Detective.' He nods towards Coop. 'I think we have had sufficient exposition of the evidence and the issues involved. You may both resume your seats.' He turns towards the crowd. 'We will take a short break of half an hour while the Judges decide on their recommendation to the Court. The hospi-hubs will be open for the duration.'

'Phew, thank the World for that,' Ammi says, breaking open a water capsule. 'All trey heavy. What d'you think about him saying he just couldn't stop himself, what with all the drugs and stuff? D'you think that's true for all repros?'

'Don't know, Am,' she says, diverting her eyes with reluctance from the rear view of the detective leaving the stage. 'You've met more Prog boys than me. Samael was a full-on sexpest, but maybe he was a bit extreme. Maybe they're not all like him. You'd better hope so, anyway.' She sniggers.

Ammi says nothing, her lips set in a firm line.

'Well, Jai's not about to find out, anyway,' she continues with a sideways glance at her companion. 'He's decided against signing up after all – with or without Carli.'

'Oh?' Ammi starts, lips parting slightly. 'He's actually said that, has he?'

'Yeah, told Ma and me the other day. Thinks it'd get in the way of things he wants to do. Says he wants to travel – see the "real" world. And,' she sneaks another sideways look, 'says there's no way he wants to be hitched to a single female for the rest of his life.'

'Oh,' Ammi says again, the disappointment clear in her voice.

Their conversation is interrupted by the return of the white-robed man to the stage; the noise of the crowd quietens to an expectant hush.

'Thank you for your patience, my friends. I hope you have enjoyed the refreshments, generously provided by Gencom. Please note that the hubs are now closed.' He ignores the grumbles of discontent and clears his throat. 'I have consulted with my esteemed Brothers and we have reached our – unanimous – recommendation.'

The Host swells his chest to give more force to his words. 'You have heard the case for and against the guilt of the Defendant,' he declaims. 'Rape, as it was traditionally defined, is a very grave crime in our eyes – involving serious transgression against a woman's honour. But we must hold centrally in mind that universal law says a person is innocent until proven guilty. And that guilt must be established on the basis of clear proof or strong circumstantial evidence.' He takes another deep breath and turns to the audience with a solemn look.

'In the absence of any direct Witness to the event in question, it is impossible to determine exactly what took place that night. Was Ms Jansdottir a vulnerable young lady who suffered an unprovoked sexual attack from a predatory male, as the Accuser would have it, or a sexually experienced female toying with an inexperienced, and sexually vulnerable young man, as argued by the Defender? Both narratives are equally persuasive,' he continues, 'and equally without clear evidence. So reaching a Determination has not been easy.'

'However, on balance, and considering the behaviour and character of the two protagonists, my Brothers and I concur with the People's Defender that it was the young male who was the victim that night – provoked by powerful forces beyond his control, and by the female herself, to a point where he could no longer be held accountable for his actions. For this reason, we recommend that the People accept Mr Samson's plea of *Not Guilty* due to significantly diminished responsibility.'

Boos and hisses emanate from parts of the crowd and the Host holds up his hands with a calm smile. 'As I said, this is the collective view of our distinguished Panel. But you, the People, will of course be the final Judge. As the Defendant has denied his guilt, you will have two votes. The first will be a simple choice between *Guilty* or *Not Guilty*, taking account, I respectfully request, of the recommendations of my learned friends. If the former is selected, the second vote will be to choose an appropriate punishment for the crime.

'Please cast your first vote now – on the Guilt or Innocence of the Defendant. No conferring, please.'

34

THE PAVVI

*N*ot even here – typical! He was the one asked to meet – said it was urgent. So what happens? I get here as fast as I can – part run, part trans, part duck and dive – and just about make it, and whatd'ya know – no sign of him.

He enters the solid brick building in cautious steps, recoiling at the musty-urine smell of the entrance. Long time since he's been here but doesn't seem to have changed much. Not much to change, to be fair. The rows of metal lockers rusted away years ago, but the stone benches lining the sides and centre of the room are mostly still standing and, while much of the black and white tiled floor is missing or cracked, its striking fish centrepiece is largely intact. A raised platform has been erected over the sunken bath that runs the full length of the back wall and various large objects have been commandeered into makeshift tables – arranged, with little apparent care, in front of the benches. Small bottles of long-dead flowers make a pitiful stand on a few of the tables.

There are signs of recent human activity: an old bed pod with its guts hanging out, nicco stubs strewn across the floor, food wrappers, alcohol pouches and best not to investigate what else, thrown into the empty bath. The Pav – the old Sports Pavilion – is a favourite haunt for newly emerged young adults: it's cool in summer, warm in winter and out of sight of most human habitation. There's a live musician at the weekends – world-folk mostly – sometimes just a singer, occasionally a poet. Queron and he both did sessions here early days; acoustics were shit. Probably still are. The building is 'maintained', in an ad-hoc but just about sufficient way, by the Pavvers – fans of Old-World contact sports and self-appointed caretakers of the building.

He brushes the debris off one end of a bench and sits, examining the sporting images lining the walls, some of which have been updated, with enthusiasm, if not expertise, by the Pavvers. Apart from the early scenes of humans racing animals, sports in the ancient world mostly appear to have involved spherical objects of varying sizes being hit with a stick, thrown or kicked, at a target or even just into the air, by people wearing very little clothing. Highly dangerous – even lethal – some of it, from what Pa said. Who in their right mind would willingly get punched in the head, or anywhere, frankly, on a regular basis – or play with a ball so hard it could kill them? The few Old-World sports he'd watched seemed nearly as dangerous as virtgames: ears bitten off, eyes gouged, testicles twisted (where available) and bones, sometimes necks, broken – and that's without the long-term structural damage from routine and repetitive physical combat. Marcus told him the players were lauded as heroes (although many resented the amount they were paid) but often at significant cost to their minds and bodies.

He hears the crunch on the gravel outside and looks up as Queron enters, without his usual wide smile, and perches on the edge of the bench opposite.

'Sols, bro. Just got back from the Trial, haven't I? Thought you'd want to hear soon as.'

Seth's stomach drops as he looks across at his friend.

'Proggo guilty...'

He gasps with relief.

'Nah, bro,' Queron says quickly. 'Guilty of the sexual attack. Wasn't charged with the murder in the end. The old biddy Thelma – of all people – said she saw Viki alive after the attack. Claims she patched her up and Vik left some time in the early morning.'

The relief drains away. 'So... what? That's me back in the frame?'

'Nah.' Queron shakes his head, his thick fringe falling forward. 'They'd've picked you up by now, if so. Looks like they think your alibi is solid. Reckon they've got their eye on someone else or they'd have charged the Prog out of desperation. Anyway, Setho,' he says, sweeping back the fallen fringe, 'it's not the cops that's the problem.'

Queron goes over to the door and peers out before coming back to stand in front of him, jiggling the coin in his pocket. 'It's the Stews that's the problem,' he says. 'Now they know there was a baby, they'll start looking for its Daddy. Told you: murder's one thing—'

'I didn't—' Seth says.

'I know, I know. Just saying, murder's one thing; illegal ferting – as you well know – is something else entirely. And Gencom will be looking for something to take the public's mind off the Proggo's conviction.'

'A nice little fly to swot?' he says miserably.

'Something like that,' Queron says with a grimace.

'Great... effin' great.' His mind's racing, chasing its tail. He turns to Queron. 'So what do I—'

'Do? You disappear, bro,' Queron says, his eyes locking on his. 'That's what you do. Don't be findable if anyone comes looking.'

'Disappear? How?' He pulls away from Queron's gaze and scans the walls as if they might provide an answer. 'Where would

I go? Can't afford the trans to the next state, never mind the cost of staying there.'

'Well, I could lend you coin. Enough to get yourself settled, or…' Queron goes to the door again and returns, eyes excited, 'or, you could hide at mine, bro. Be my basement buddy.' He sniggers, sitting on the bench beside him. 'No seriously: got a new gaff – loads of room. Wouldn't need to be forever. Couple months, six max, and the Stews'll give up – pin it on a random snip dodger – or a roamer. There was no live baby, after all, and they have bigger fish to fry. You're only small fly, ha ha.

'Sorry, not funny,' Queron says as he sees Seth's stony face. 'You'll need to tell everyone – including your pa and this Thelma-gets-in-everywhere – that you're leaving but can't say where. Tell them you need to get away – put all the Vik stuff behind you sort of thing. I'll cover with the band; say you're making contacts, sourcing venues, that line of chat. Going off on a, what's it they used to call it, busman's holiday, no?'

Queron turns to him and clasps his forearm. 'What d'you think, Setho, mate? Do some serious writing – get some new material together? Sound set-up at mine's pretty good, even if I say so myself, flat's got all the mod cons – latest virtgim, newly upgraded gamz – and I can keep you supplied with all the essentials, including some damn fine home-grown. What more could a boy want?'

Well, Lyse, for one thing, Seth thinks. Maybe he could tell her; she wouldn't tell anyone, pretty sure. Although that would put her at risk, wouldn't it, if someone thought she might know? But she'll just think he's running away again otherwise won't she? Which he is. Be the second time she'll think he's failed to stand his ground.

'Won't it just make me look guilty if I disappear now?'

'Maybe,' Queron says, 'but, just said, it's not the cops you gotta worry about. I'll keep my ear out; if they're sniffing round again I'll hear. But it looks to me like they've lost the trail. Don't forget, they'll be looking for the Daddy – which they will assume can't possibly be you. Really, bro, trust me,' Queron says, 'mine'll be perfect.' He gives a soft snigger. 'Stews'll never think of looking for you there – I promise you.'

He's not totally convinced about Queron's plan, but he really doesn't have much choice. And it could be ice. Bit of time out; do some writing, maybe recording. He agrees to bring his stuff over after dark tonight. Only essentials, Queron tells him: all tech, any original docs, especially biodocs, a few clothes (he won't be going out much) and his guitars. Have to leave with what he can get on his back, can't risk getting tracked in a cab. He'll send a lugbot for the vinyl tomorrow.

Later, once Seth's finished getting his things together, he takes the last three beers from the cooler, stuffs two into the top of an already-straining backpack and takes the remaining pouch to the old settee to wait for nightfall. As he looks at his guitars, cased and ready to go, the doubts creep in. Not only about Lyse, but his pa's going to worry, isn't he? And what about the band? He takes a long slug of the beer. *Is Queron really right about this?* He knows Marcus thinks he's too easily led by his old friend; blames him for Seth's brief period of 'going astray'. Told him he could lead himself astray, didn't need Queron to do it for him. But if he was honest it *was* usually his friend who did the leading.

It was Queron who got him into music, for sure. Sent him a live recording by the Old-World's king of rock 'n' roll and he was hooked straight off. Worked out how to pick out the tune on his first guitar and that was the start of his musical 'career'. (He'd been gutted to discover that his own thick, but fine, hair couldn't be coaxed into a frontal quiff with one moodily escaped strand – no matter how much fix was applied.) Soon as they were old enough, he and Queron started meeting up and planning the band. Didn't take them long to recruit the others and, when they got their first booking, he'd dropped out of secs to play full-time. *Maybe Pa was right; if Queron hadn't already left, I'd have stayed on and taken the exams…*

He's hit with a sudden longing for those uncomplicated days. Before any babies and mutant flies. Before any Viki. *Just me and Q building the band, living the life.* The streetlights stutter on – and off and on again – and he can see through the small windows that the sky is darkening. *Nah, didn't mean that last bit; none of this is Vik's doing. But why on Earth didn't she stay at the old woman's after the Proggo got her? Would've been safe there. And what possessed her to leave that time in the morning? Wasn't exactly an early bird. What was so important it couldn't wait for daybreak?*

He picks up his bag, hangs his guitar across his back and heads up the steps. As he sets off to Queron's, head down into a spiteful wind, his spirits are laid low by a relentless beat of remorse: *if I'd reacted differently; if I'd not been drunk; if only she'd stayed at Thelma's.*

If, if, if...

35

GAME ON

'So guilty, eh? Well done, Coop,' Don says with a wide smile. He's returned to the earlier split costume arrangement, more successfully anchored this time, although, when he removes his outerwear, it's clear that the underarm damp has proved less tractable. 'Heard you made a good case at the Court. What was it – a big female turnout?'

'Yes, that,' he replies. 'But there's not a lot of public sympathy for the repros these days. And the fact that Gencom paid for his defence didn't help matters.'

'Well, whatever. Good news. What'd he get?'

'Forty swipes, I'm afraid.'

'Actual or virtual?'

'Virtual. I don't think they're allowed to do actual anymore, are they?'

'Well, it hurts just as much, either way,' his boss says cheerfully, as he eases himself onto the only other chair in the room. 'You've got to do something about the state of this place, Coop,' he complains, looking around in distaste. 'There's nothing in here: nothing to sit on, nothing to lean on and nothing to look at but your ugly mug.'

Coop gives him an indulgent smile and continues. 'Crowd didn't much like the Judges' recommendations, but they did like the look of the special punishments offered. He was lucky not to get a public stoning then and there.'

'So,' his boss eases back into the chair and regards him with half-closed eyes, 'you've got the sex attacker. Now all you've got to do is find the murderer. You say the boyfriend's in the clear?'

'Well, it doesn't help that we can't pin down time of death, but he's pretty well covered, apart from the odd half-hour between leaving a bar with some friends – very much the worse for wear, by all accounts – and being clocked by his building log. Just about possible. But there's no obvious motive, apart from a possible love triangle. Could have been a mindless act of jealously or anger, say, but there were no fatal injuries to the body. People who kill on the spur of the moment usually leave their mark.'

Don grunts. 'So what about the second trace? Getting anywhere with this ghost of yours?'

He tells him the agent promised to investigate but hadn't seemed particularly motivated. Seemed quite happy to leave the case to them, in fact. But now the pregnancy is out he suspects he'll change his tune. And they'll have to send the case up to the Stews anyway now, won't they? His boss considers this for a moment, rasping the bristles on his chin with the side of his thumb. Coop knows he won't want to lose another case to the Stews if he can help it and is relieved, but not surprised, when Don says he thinks they can hang on till the end of the week.

'Make us look sloppy, but can live with that. I'll say we've got a lot of work on – not wrong there, either – but any longer and I'll get it in the ear. In fact, we'll be lucky if they haven't started sniffing round already.'

'So, I've got what, just over seventy-two hours?' *No pressure then.*

'Yeah, not much time, Coop. You'll have your work cut out; need to speed up a bit. What else you got to go on? Didn't you say something about a brother? Ex-Edger? Sounds promising.' He leans forward with the trace of a sneer. 'You know what they say: you can take the man out of the Edgelands, but you can't take the Edgelands out of the man.'

'Yes, they do say that, don't they?' he says with an even smile. 'Maybe unfairly, don't you think?'

Don makes a noncommittal noise.

'Anyway, not got much on him, I'm afraid. Went back to the aunt, who'd somehow forgotten to mention him first time round, but he's no longer living there and she doesn't know where he's gone. Was working nights at the community allotments but – significantly, maybe – didn't turn up the night of the murder. Came back once since, caused a bit of trouble and hasn't been seen again.'

'Probably slunk back to the Edge,' his boss says with a grimace. 'You'll have to contact the Edge Lodge see if they know anything about him, although they look after their own that lot, suspect you'll not get much out of them. Not for the death of a Banni girl, anyhow.'

'Well, if he's gone back there, I'm not going after him,' he says with conviction. 'You'll have to send the boys with the hardware.'

Don gives a throaty snort. 'It's a long time since we had the coin for that sort of caper, Coop. If that's where he's gone, then he's gone. Punishment enough, I'd've thought, to grow old and die out there.' He rubs his perspiring eyebrows. 'Anything else?' he asks.

'Well…' he hesitates, knowing this won't go down well, 'there's the smell.'

'The smell? What smell?'

He reminds him about the foul smell on the body and Don gives an uneasy nod as if the very mention of it might summon up the noxious pong. It's a bit of a long shot, he tells him, but apparently it's from a plant that has a meaning in the language of flowers…

He should have known better. His boss lets out a loud guffaw. 'Flower language? What the feck's that, Coop? I know you like to approach things a bit leftfield, but this takes the biscuit. More like – if it was actually used deliberately at all, which I doubt – it was just to keep the scavengers away.'

'Yes,' he nods but perseveres, 'but even that would be a bit odd, Boss, wouldn't it? Why bother to protect a dead body – and take time to do it – unless it was for a reason? Just doesn't add up.'

'Nah.' Don shakes his head firmly. 'Know you like to get down to basics, Coop, but there's a danger here of not seeing the wood for the trees. Or the body for the weeds, in this case.' He grins at his self-perceived wit and grasps the arms of the chair to rise. 'So, is that it now?'

'Yees,' he replies, smoothing the top of his desk with his fingers, 'although there is something a bit odd about the agent himself.'

'Odd? How?' his boss asks, settling back in the chair.

'Well, quite by chance, I came across him playing in a music band under a very different name. The same band as the victim's boyfriend, no less. Bit of a coincidence, don't you think? And you know—'

'Yes, yes… you don't trust coincidence. But people used to do that, didn't they – use a stage name, sort of thing?'

'True, but I think it's more than that. Think he's leading some kind of double life. Didn't say anything about knowing the boyfriend – and maybe even the victim herself. At the very least, that's a bit odd, isn't it, given that we're liaising on the case?'

'Well, it is odd, I'll admit,' Don says, heaving his large frame up from the chair and grabbing his outers. 'Highly unprofessional. But the Stews are a law unto themselves, as you well know. I'd ask him about it – see what he says. Mind you,' he stops suddenly, one arm half in one sleeve, and turns towards him, 'have you thought that maybe he's your ghost, Coop – the agent? You say he's got a double identity. If he's undercover for the Program, he won't be found on the public system.'

'Hmm, yes, that's true,' he says, brightening. 'Not a bad thought, Boss.'

'Yeah, well, I do have them sometimes, Coop – not just a pretty face, y'know,' he says with a wide grin. 'You'll need to find a way to get his bio off him. Not easy these days, although you could try the old biodegradable cup trick, if you could get him in the right place.'

He gives him a questioning look.

'Thought you'd know about that, Coop,' Don says, keen to leave but detained, Coop suspects, by the pleasure of knowing something his 'clever-dick' junior doesn't. The cups at the water pods biodegrade, Don tells him, but the rim takes a little longer than the body. If he can bag it within a few minutes of using, he says, may be able to collect a trace.

'Worth a try – he's obviously not going to ID himself.' His boss grins, stuffing the other arm into the remaining sleeve. 'Go see this Flowers chap. See what he has to say for himself and get his bio if you can. Forget the other flowers. Try the Edge Lodge about the brother – he seems a likely suspect. But get a move on, Coop, clock's ticking.'

He sits for a while, considering Don's suggestion. Could the agent really be the ghost – and possibly the murderer? But what on Earth could he have as a motive? Because of the foetal crime? But if he knew about that, why not just have her arrested? He's a Stew, after all. But maybe it was personal; maybe she was blackmailing him; he clearly has a past. And could he be the father? Maybe he got her pregnant and she threatened to report him? Mind you, it would be unusual for a Partner to take on undercover work, and he gets no sense at all – just the opposite – that the agent has any sexual interest in females. Still, whatever the motive, if he has skin in the game, it would explain why he's been dragging his feet on the bio trace.

He's interrupted by an incoming message. For a moment the name means nothing, then he recalls: Tonkinson, the allotment day supervisor. Says that Naz Janson has just been seen down at the allotment sheds – *looking a bit out of it*. If he comes quick, might catch him.

Game's afoot! He grins, grabbing his hat, and, after a moment's hesitation, his stunni. He looks out of the window, where a high sun blazes in a cloudless sky; he'll get a car to the edge of the allotments this time, but he'll still have to walk the final part. Recalling the veil of hovering insects, he picks up a new can of Buggo™.

And the Buggo™ is the first thing he reaches for as he arrives at the allotments, removing his hat and spraying the repellent round his head and neck as he scans the row of sheds at the edge of the plant beds. Most seem well secured, windows shuttered, doors visibly locked, but a couple at the far end look a bit worse for wear. He replaces his hat and edges down the line until he can see through the broken window into the first of the dilapidated huts: completely empty; looks as though it's been cleaned out recently.

He moves on to the second hut, which has a swathe of rough material drawn across its window. A long rent in the bottom corner of the fabric affords a partial view of the dim interior. Full of junk, as far as he can see. Tools, pots and other garden paraphernalia stacked high against one wall. Piles of what look like old sacks against the other. *Can't see any movement.* He creeps around to the front, where the door is hanging slightly ajar, and pushes gently, fingering the stunni.

The door gives out a rusty shriek and the pile of sacks explodes, shedding its many skins to reveal a wild-looking male wielding a sharply pointed garden implement. The man is tall and strongly built, with tufts of red hair sprouting from his shaven scalp that give his sharp features an almost vulpine look. But his legs are unsteady and his eyes dull.

'Who're you? What d'ya want?' the male shouts, poking the spiked tool towards him.

'Detective Cooper-Clark, local police,' he says in a calm voice, taking a step back and showing his badge.

'Wha'dja want here?' the man asks again.

'I'm looking for a Mr Janson.' He keeps a smile on his face and a tight grip on the stunni. 'Would that be you by any chance?'

'Yeah, that's me.' The hollow eyes are hostile. 'So? Not doing anything wrong. Got a right to be here. Night shift, init?' His hands tremble as they clutch the weapon.

'Okay, good to meet you, Mr Janson.' He releases his grip on the gun and smiles at the agitated man. 'I'd like to ask you a couple of questions, if that's all right with you.' He pauses. 'About Viki Jansdottir – your half-sister, I believe.'

'Viki?' the man says in a hoarse voice. 'You know she's dead, don't you?'

'Yes, that's why I'm here… Naz, isn't it? Can I call you that?' He gets a suspicious nod. 'I'm trying to find out who killed her, Naz. I've had reports that she was on her way to see you, the night she was… the night she died.'

The man gives a little groan and falls to his knees, dropping his weapon beside him.

'So did Viki find you that night, Naz?' he asks in a gentle voice.

The man looks up, his grey face abject. 'No… no she never got to me,' he whispers. 'Wish to Earth she had.' He takes his head in his hands, shoulders trembling.

He waits a few moments before asking, 'So, when was the last time you saw your sister, Naz?'

With some effort, the man gets to his feet and stands, legs shaking. 'That night. Saturday. Before she goes out to the club. Was both at the aunt's. Been staying there since I got back from the Edge…' A challenging glance accompanies this last snippet of information.

'But you're not there now, at the aunt's, I understand?' he asks, ignoring the challenge.

'Nah. Wasn't working out. For them or me. Been kipps here since. Suits me better.' The man gives Coop a baleful look, right eye twitching. 'Spose you think like the rest. That it was me?'

'I'm not sure what I think, Naz. That's why I've come to talk to you,' he says with a smile. 'See if you might know anything that could help us get to the truth of it.'

'You want talk to that bloke of hers,' he says, rubbing his eyes with a grimy hand. 'That's who she went to meet that night. Musician in some band. Knocked her up and then told her to get rid of it. Like to get my hands on the bastard.'

'We have talked to him and are keeping our eyes on him,' he replies, 'but it wasn't him who knocked her up, as you put it. He's a certified infert. So you can forget about that. 'Anyway,' he gives an encouraging smile, 'you didn't see Viki again after she left for the club?'

The man shakes his matted head.

'Stan says you didn't turn up for your night shift that night?'

'Nah.' He gives a sheepish grin. 'Had a pipe or two under the bridge – knocks me out, don't it?'

'Is there anyone who can vouch for you being there, Naz? Maybe there were others there when you when you smoked the pipe? There's usually a few under the bridge on any night, aren't there? Think, Naz,' Coop presses, 'it could be important. Very important.'

'There was others, sure, but you minds your own down there. Don't ask, don't tell, init?'

He tries another tack. 'So how was Viki when you saw her? Did she seem worried about anything, anybody?'

'Nah. She was just regular. Although we had a bit of a ruck, before she left. That's why I went for the pipe.'

'Oh? A ruck about what?'

The man shrugs. 'Dunno, really. Nowt serious. Thought I was taking the piss coming back and staying with them – y'know, taking advantage of the old bird.'

'Of the aunt?'

'Yeah. As if she's got anything I'd want. You been round there?' Coop nods as the man glances up at him. 'Well, you'll know she's got diddily squit.'

'So why did Viki think you were taking advantage?'

The broad shoulders shrug again. 'Give a dog a bad name, init? No-one trusts us Edgers – not even my own, seems. But look, mate, I'm not going to hurt my baby sis, am I? Only just found her again.' He stares at Coop, tears forming in his clouded eyes. 'Was going to get sorted, wasn't I, so I could look after her and the aunts.' He gives a bitter laugh. 'Well, that worked out, dinnit?' He rubs his eyes and sniffs. 'Should've been there. Should've been there to protect her from the scumbag what killed her.' He shakes his head and sinks to his knees again, grimy hands covering his face.

He feels some pity for the pathetic man. But he has a potential motive and no verifiable alibi, so he's going to have to take him in. Can't risk him disappearing. Do him good, anyway, to clean himself up and get some food in him. 'Okay, Naz,' he says in a calm voice. 'I'm going to have to ask you to come back to the station with me.'

'You taking me in?' The man picks up the pronged tool and gets unsteadily to his feet. 'I'll get the sack if they hear cops've picked me up.'

'No, Naz.' He stands his ground, fingers on the stunni. 'I'm not arresting you. I just need you to come with me for a bit. I'll clear it with Stan. Tell him you're just helping us with our enquiries.'

'Yeah, well, we all know what that means,' the man says, squaring up to him. 'Wasn't me, mate. You've got the wrong man. You need to go after the cheating scum boyfriend.' He pushes his face towards Coop, the twitch in the eye furious now. 'Wasn't me,' he repeats, brandishing the weapon. 'I ain't going anywhere.'

He takes out the gun and points it at the agitated man. 'I think you are, Naz,' he says, his voice steady. 'I think you're coming with me.'

36

CORNERED

'You're in for it now, mate,' Piet creases his grey slab of a face into a spiteful grin. 'She's not happy. Not happy at all. Wants to see you ASAP.' He sniggers. 'Whatcha been up to, Flowers?'

'Don't know, mate. You know as much as me.' He tries to sound nonchalant, but his stomach tenses as he knocks on her door.

'Come!' a harassed-sounding female voice calls.

She looks up as he enters and smiles. *Good sign*, he thinks, relaxing a little.

'Ah, Flowers,' she says, 'thanks for coming in. Just a quick word. Take a seat, won't you?' She sweeps her thin hair behind her ears and appraises him with cool grey eyes. 'How'd the Banleu Trial go?'

'Afraid we lost that one,' he says, sitting as instructed. 'Guilty as charged. Crowd didn't go for the whole "rapist as victim" thing. No sympathy for Program boys who step out of line these days. Anyway, that's that. He'll be expunged now, no?'

'Maybe not.' She gives a grim smile. 'He used a sheath and that's the main thing. We can be quite indulgent about the sexual peccadilloes of our boys – as long as there's no accidental fertilisation.'

'Old-fashioned rape's hardly a peccadillo, Boss.'

'I know that, Flowers,' she snaps, a trace of a frown on her high forehead. 'Don't need you to tell me, but you know how they think upstairs.' She relaxes the frown into a smile. 'So, local pols still looking for their murderer, eh?' The smile widens. 'And still asking about our little "ghost"?'

His heart's speeding as he tells her he told the detective there was almost no chance of finding the identity of someone ghosted. 'Seems to have accepted that; hasn't mentioned it again, anyway.' He smooths his hair back from his face and keeps his eyes steady on hers. 'That was right, wasn't it?'

'Well, I don't know about that, actually, Flowers.' The chief gets up and walks around the desk until she's standing in front of him, bending slightly, her hands on the arms of his chair. The closeness of her person is unnerving.

'What if I was to tell you that we know who the ghost is?'

'You do?' he asks, keeping his voice as neutral as he can. *Starting to feel like a fish on a hook here.*

'Yes, we do, Flowers.' She leans forwards and whispers in his ear; her perfume is overwhelming. 'And I think you do too, don't you?'

'Sorry?' He blinks to provide some momentary relief from the relentlessness of her gaze. *On a hook alright and just about to be reeled in.*

'Oh, I think we're past sorry, Flowers,' she says, drawing back, her black-edged eyes fixing his. 'Let's give up the pretence, shall we? We both know you're the phantom the cops are after. Did you really think I wouldn't check it out?' she says with a mock-hurt expression as she straightens up. 'You underestimate me.'

He says nothing. His normally fast-running brain stuck in its tracks.

'Question is,' the chief pulls up a chair alongside him, brushing his thigh as she crosses her legs, 'what exactly am I going to do with this information?'

He shrugs, trying to cover his agitation. *Well and truly caught: hook, line and sinker.*

'Well, it would help if I could understand how your bio got picked up on the dead girl's body in the first place,' she says in an emollient tone.

'Okay,' he says as he pushes his chair back and arranges his thoughts. 'Long story short: I'm an old friend of a friend of hers who's in the band with me. It's a good cover, actually,' he grins, 'the band. Hiding in plain sight and all that. Anyway, after the gig my friend Seth and Vik, the victim, had a big row, and she stormed off. Seth was with another girl, so I went after Vik to see if she was okay. She was a nice kid, and I felt a bit sorry for her.' He looks directly into her slate-grey eyes. 'I really don't know how my bio got on her, Chief. Maybe I gave her a peck. I really can't remember. Wasn't with her more than ten minutes, max.'

'Nothing more? Just a peck?'

'No. Nothing more – then or ever. Didn't see her again that night.' He withstands the intensity of her eyes and says in a quiet voice. 'I had nothing to do with her death, Chief, believe me.'

She sits for a few moments, considering him. He thinks she must be able to hear the sound of his agitated heart.

'Well, I believe you, Flowers,' she says after a while, 'I really do. Trouble is I'm not sure anyone else will.' She hesitates, shaking her head. 'I really should send this upstairs. Apart from anything else, you're far too close to the case.'

She rises from the chair and walks round to sit on the front of her desk, facing him.

'I like you, Flowers,' she says. 'You're one of my best agents, but if you're mixed up in this – in any way,' her eyes scan his face, 'upstairs'll come down hard and I won't be able to protect you.'

She considers him without speaking for a moment, twisting

the escaped strands of her hair. 'I could be persuaded to leave it alone, however. To ghost the ghost as it were.'

He gives her a hopeful look.

'Yes, I could do that little thing for you. And maybe also see about getting you released from your current, um, "bondage", shall we call it, to our Gencom bosses. I know how much you want to get out. So, I might do those two things for you, Flowers…' she pauses and gives him a challenging smile, 'if you're prepared to do one small thing for me.'

'Oh?' *Somehow don't think I'm going to like this.* 'Guess that depends on what you had in mind Chief,' he says with an uneasy laugh.

'Nothing illegal, of course.' She sits on the chair beside him, pulling it close. He tries not to flinch as she touches his knee with scarlet-tipped fingers. 'I'll speak plainly, shall I, Flowers? No point in beating around the bush. As I said, I like you. Who knows why, but I do. So…' she looks him squarely in the eye, 'I'd like to offer you the position of my personal sex-partner.'

'Sex-partner?' he echoes.

She is continuing, in a calm, measured voice. 'Yes, my PSP. Paid, of course, and you'll find I'm a very generous woman. Once or twice a week – nothing too onerous – at least to begin with. See how we get on. But regular. Own room, if you wish to sleep over. Maybe Wednesday and Saturday nights, if that would suit? What nights does your band play?'

'But I can't. I'm not…' His brain won't deliver the words.

'Oh, don't worry about that,' she soothes, leaning into him, giving him yet another heady hit of perfume. 'I can provide all the stimulation you'll need.' She strokes his thigh with her crimson-nailed fingers and looks deep into his eyes. 'You'll find I'm very experienced.'

He says nothing. *Not only caught and reeled in, but now landed, flat on my back with my legs in the air – possibly literally.*

'I hope the idea's not too repulsive?' she asks when he says nothing, removing her hand as a deep crease scores her forehead.

'No... no.' He gets himself together. 'You're a very attractive woman. And if I was... I mean, it's just all a bit... well, unexpected.'

'Oh, come now. You're a beautiful male, Flowers. You must've had females ask you before now? Especially when you're out playing with that band, lots of groupies, no?'

'Yeah, but I don't work with them, Chief,' he says, attempting a sardonic smile. 'They're not my boss.'

'Well,' she says, rising, 'if our little arrangement works out, I won't be your boss for long, will I? If it seems to be going well, I could see to it that you had a very generous release settlement. Set you up nicely for a new start. Get away with that band of yours, perhaps. See the World. What d'you think?' She seats herself on the edge of the desk again and gives him a candid look.

He cannot see how 'no' is a possible answer here. The best play he can make is for extra time to consider his options – if any. 'Can I let you know Monday morning?' he asks with his best effort at endearing. 'Need a bit of time to think about it. Bit stunned, to be honest. But flattered, of course,' he adds hastily.

'Don't know what there is to think about,' she says in a stiff voice, returning to sit behind her desk. 'But very well then,' she nods him towards the door, 'first thing Monday morning.'

He walks back to his desk, deflecting the attentions of his colleagues with a pretence of urgency, feeling well and truly fished and filleted. He opens his messages, and his mood is not helped when he sees the pol with the hat's after him again. Wants to meet as soon as possible; says he's got something new. *Oh, why not? Day can't get any worse, can it?*

*

He spots him on the bench by the waterhole, brushing the dust off his hat, and saunters up.

'Ho Coop! How's things?'

'Oh, Agent Flowers, hello.' The detective says, picking his hat up from the bench and resting it on his knee. 'Thanks for coming. You heard the news on the Trial?'

He sits down beside the detective, impressed, now he sees him in the flesh for the first time, by the good physical shape of him. Swimmer, he wouldn't mind betting, with those shoulders. 'Yeah. Guilty, wasn't it?' He grins. 'Right outcome. Think we went over the top with the old blame the victim stuff.'

'Yes.' The detective gives him a wry smile. 'Suspect it rang a little hollow to those without the repros' opportunities in life.'

'Yeah. Guess so. Anyway,' he smiles, 'imagine that's not why you wanted to meet up?'

'Well, yes and no. You heard about the victim being pregnant?'

'Yeah. Got the Report. Should've told me, Coop,' he says, giving the detective a hurt look. 'That's my neck of the woods.'

The detective apologises; says he didn't find out until after their last meeting and, if he was honest, was rather hoping it wouldn't come out until after the trial. Knew it wouldn't play well for the victim. As it is, he assumes the agent will want to take over the case now, given the foetal crime.

'Oh, don't think there's any rush about it,' he says in a casual manner. Taking over the case being just about the last thing he wants right now. 'You're the man for murder, Coop. Not me. Might as well see it through now you've started. Keep me informed, sort of thing.'

To his annoyance, the detective shakes his head and says he's going to have to decline the offer, even though it would have been helpful – very helpful. 'Boss says we have to hand over by close on Friday at the latest. And you can't argue with the boss, can you?' he asks with a rueful smile.

'No, guess not,' he says. *Not with mine anyway.* He winces at the recall of the red-nailed fingers.

'So I'll need to press on with the little time I've got left.' The detective smiles. 'And, to that end, I was wondering if you'd made any progress on our ghost?'

'Nah, 'fraid not,' he says with a light smile. 'Not getting any movement on that, Coop. Not at all. I'll keep on it, but don't hold your breath.'

'I suppose you've got an interest in that not coming out, haven't you?' the detective says, looking at him directly with his calm, brown eyes.

'What me?' he says, with a sudden sense of unease. 'Why would I—'

'No, not you personally, of course,' the detective reassures. 'No, I meant Gencom. That Gencom'll not be wanting any more bad publicity at the moment.'

'Oh yes,' he says, covering his relief with a smile. 'No, you're not wrong there. But I'll do my best, anyway, Coop. You got anything else to go on?'

'Not really, although the pregnancy opens up a whole other can of worms. The victim's brother says she told him Seth Marcuson was the father. But that's not possible, of course, and there's no way to find out who was, now.'

Shit, and bigger shit. So she told Naz about the baby. Bad news; very bad news.

'Well, sorry to hear that, Coop,' he says, trying to hide his distraction as he starts to rise. 'So, are we just about done here?'

'Well, yes, nearly. Just one other thing while I've got you, so to speak?'

'Sure,' he says, sitting again, with reluctance. *Could've told half the allotment boys by now…*

'Air seems to be getting hotter every day, don't you think?' the detective is asking, wiping his cheeks. 'D'you mind if I get a quick aqua?' He smiles. 'And can I get you one?'

'Okay, yeah, great, thanks. Wouldn't say no.' *Need to find him ASAP, make sure he keeps his mouth shut.* He has a contact down at the allotments owes him a favour; could call that in. Better still, heard the Nazzer likes a pipe or two; knows where to find him, if so.

'So, what's up, Coop?' he asks as he takes the water cup.

'Well, you are, actually,' the detective replies, sipping his drink.

'Me?' He gives a short laugh and downs the refreshment in one. *What the eff's this now?* His expectations of the day just continue to outdo themselves in the lowering department.

'Yes, you.' The detective takes another sip and tells him that he went to a show at BB's the other night and is pretty sure he saw him there – in the band. 'At least, that is unless you have an exact double, and I thought they avoided those these days.' He narrows his eyes at him. 'It was you, wasn't it?'

'Oh yeah,' he says, trying to sound casual. 'The Beatniks – sing with them sometimes.'

'Under an assumed name? Presume that's because you don't want the rest of the band to know the business you're in?'

'No. Just like to keep work and play separate.' *Play it cool, play it cool.*

'So that means you knew the boyfriend of the victim, Seth Marcuson?' The detective turns to him with a frown. 'And the victim herself, presumably? Seems like the very opposite of not mixing work and play to me. Why did you not think to mention any of this to me?'

'Didn't feel it was relevant, Coop, to be honest.' He shrugs, losing the smile. *On the friggin' hook again.* 'My only interest was in the repro side of things and that didn't seem to be an issue – at that point, anyway.'

To his relief, the detective seems to accept this and holds out his hand. 'Well, thank you, Agent Flowers. That was all I wanted, really. Sorry to take up your time. I'll trash that with mine,' he says, relieving him of his cup. 'Have a good weekend.'

'Yeah, you too, Coop,' he says, walking away as fast as he can, heart pounding. *Shit, and double shit.* If Viki had told Naz that Seth was the father, who else had she told? And never mind the local quiddies, what if the detective starts to wonder about Seth?

Starts seeing the truth staring him in the face.

37

CONFESSION

Seth's been to band practice. Plan was to explain himself to the boys, have one last drink at Mab's and possibly, just possibly, a night with Lyse later – say goodbye properly. All went okay as far as the boys were concerned – *although they didn't have to be quite so enthusiastic about possible replacements, did they?* – but something's not right with Lyse. Been avoiding his glances and keeping her distance all night. Now they've finished she's clearly heading straight off; no last drink and definitely no 'later' at his.

He picks up his bag and calls after her; to his relief, she stops and turns, not much of a smile on her face. He asks her what's wrong, but she says it's nothing and makes to go. He pulls her back, his hand on her arm; says he knows something's up, can see it in her face.

'I think you know very well what's *up*, Seth, don't you?' she says in a hostile tone, shaking off his hand.

'You mean Viki?'

'Yeah, I do mean Viki. Did you hear what they did to her? Not that you even bothered to turn up. Made her out to be a red-dirt slag, chasing repro boys for sex.'

'Yeah. Heard it was pretty grues.' He gives a rueful smile, hoping that would be enough to close the conversation down. It wasn't.

'Yeah, well, it was pretty *grues* that no-one spoke up for her, don't you think?' Lyse continues. 'Not even her closest male friend?' She stares at him, lips pursed

'Yeah, but—'

'I know, *it's complicated*,' she interrupts. 'And now you're running away again, aren't you? I don't believe all that crap about sourcing venues, BTW, and I doubt the others do either.'

'But it *is* complicated, Lyse,' he says, sounding pathetic even to himself. 'Really, seriously complicated. You've no idea.'

'Well, give me an idea then,' she says, her expression close to dislike. 'Tell me what's so complicated about standing up for your friends?'

He realises he'll say anything to stop her looking at him like that; even something that might drive her further away.

'Okay, Lyse,' he says, scanning the milling crowd, 'I'll tell you. But not here.'

They leave the hall and walk, unspeaking, to a low wall looking across to the market square, in the scant shade of one of the maintained trees. It's mid-afternoon but the traders are already packing up; people start out early these days to get the best picks and by now most stalls have been stripped bare. The nearby tea houses, brownbars and coffee shops surrounding the square are buzzing with shoppers seeking out their shaded comforts – *just a quick one!* – taking their refreshment with one hand and keeping the other firmly on their purchases.

They sit side by side, but she makes a show of maximising the space between them before turning to him with a decidedly unfriendly: 'So?'

'Okay,' he says, taking a deep breath. *Here goes.* 'So, the cop told me that Vik's pregnancy would come out at the Trial—'

'What and you didn't want to speak for her cos she'd got with another man's baby?'

'No, that's just it.' He pauses, looking down, his mouth as dry as the dust beneath his feet. *It's gotta be now, hasn't it?* If he doesn't tell her now, he's never going to tell her. And if he never tells her, they can't ever be together that way.

'It wasn't another man,' he says, holding her gaze, and his metaphorical breath.

She gives him a blank look. 'What d'you mean – can't have been a female, can it? Or, I know, one of those angels they used to say went round making women pregnant.' She laughs, then stops as she sees his face. 'Oh, you don't mean…?'

'Yeah.' He laughs to cover his embarrassment. 'It was me. I'm some kind of mutant, appaz – a fertile infert.'

'Woah!' She looks at him, wide-eyed. 'Galla, or what?'

'Yeah, you could say that,' he says, trying to read her expression without being caught doing so.

'So, what… wait, this is unreal, so you couldn't go to Court because that'd come out?'

'Yeah. Only thing that would make any difference was to tell them it was my baby and that Vik and I'd been going steady together. Just saying I thought she was a good person was never going to cut it – not when the illegal baby suggested otherwise.'

'And that would've meant big trouble for you?'

'Yeah, Lyse. Crime against Humanity, isn't it? Probably cut my balls off.'

She gives a short laugh but says nothing and he can't bring himself to look at her face again just yet. Telling her has brought relief but also new anxieties: what if it changes things between them? What if she feels uncomfortable being around him? Or, World forbid, feels repulsed by him.

'So, you don't want to be "reversed"?' she asks, interrupting his thoughts. 'Even if you can never ever use this... er,' she sniggers, 'special power of yours?'

'Well, I guess I'm hoping I might be able to one day – if things change,' he says, relaxing a little at her laugh.

'Don't think anything's going to change in the Program department any time soon, if that's what you mean,' she retorts.

'No... maybe not. But it's more than just the making babies thing. It's part of what I am; what I've grown up with being.' He gives a self-conscious laugh. 'I'm the natural one. They're the ones creating mutants.'

She looks up at him, a provocative smile on her lips. 'So, would you really miss the "more than making babies" bit – that much?'

'Yeah,' he nods, thinking how very much he'd like to run his tongue along those lips, 'guess I would.'

'Were you sad when Viki lost the baby?' she asks, moving closer and placing a hand on his thigh that fires a bolt straight to his groin.

'Yeah, a little.' He shifts his position to one, slightly more controllable. 'Relieved, mostly, if I'm honest. Never wanted us to be long-term. She was nube, don't get me wrong, but we were rolling on different tracks.'

'Talking of Vik,' she says, removing her hand, 'cops don't seem to be getting any closer. Stuck for a motive, seems.'

'Yeah, that's the bit I don't get,' he says, thankful for this shift of focus (less for the shift of hand). 'Why would anyone want to kill Vik? Wouldn't harm a snit. And why do all that stuff with the body?'

'Yeah. Told the detective my theory about it being the killer sending a message, but he just laughed at me.'

'Well, let's hope he comes up with something soon – taking long enough. And meanwhile,' he says, shamelessly seeking sympathy, 'that effin' great cloud of suspicion I thought had moved on has slunk back over my head.'

'So the cops still think you're a suspect?'

'Maybe, but Queron says it's the Stewards, not the cops, that's the problem now. Says if they find out about me, they'll make a meal. Best make myself scarce, he reckons. Says he's found a place I can stay where they'll never think of looking. Wouldn't need to be longer than six months, max, he says – Stews'll give up after that, appaz – and meanwhile he can look after the band.'

'Sounds like Queron's got it all planned out, hasn't he?' she says, shifting away from him. 'But you don't have to do what he says in everything, do you? Maybe it's up to the rest of us who caretakes the band, for a start. And maybe he's not right about you leaving. You've done nothing wrong, well, I mean, you didn't *mean* to do anything wrong, did you? – it's not your fault you're a freak of nature, after all, ha ha. But disappearing might just make them decide to look for you even more.'

She's putting her finger on some nerves, and he's beginning to see the holes in Queron's plan, but he's committed now, isn't he? *Told the boys, cleared the flat of anything valuable – only Pa to sort. And don't want to look even weaker than she obviously already thinks I am by changing my mind again.*

'Guess it's all kinda sorted now,' he says with a shrug. 'Won't be so bad, I can write some new stuff, work out the itinerary for the tour. It'll go quickly. Queron says…' He stops and grins, acknowledging her sardonic smile. 'Okay, fair enough, but he does seem to know about that sort of thing. Anyway, says I could be back before winter. But…' he tries to look upbeat as he gets to the bit that's really worrying him, 'I guess you'll be gone by then, won't you? College starts in October, doesn't it?'

She tells him that she'll stick with the band through the summer, not to worry and even when she's away at college, she'll be able to do some sessions with them – at least until they set off on tour. Either way, she'll see him again before he leaves. Relieved at this, he asks if she wants to come back to his for a bit now, maybe pick up a pouch on the way, and tries hard to cover his disappointment when she tells him she's got an evening practice session. 'Three-line whip. Can't get out of it, coach'll go ape.'

She gives him a few pats on the knee and rises to go before leaning over to kiss him on the cheek. 'But I could come back after,' she whispers in his ear, 'if you'll still be up, that is?'

He'll still be up, he tells her.

38

ACCIDENTAL HERO

After Seth mentioned the illegal test, Queron had looked up
Thelma ('Dr', actually) Linsdottir. Found out a few interesting
things: that she'd been something of a rising star in the international
scientific community – the youngest ever to manage a government
genlab – then had a very public fall from grace when she was
sacked for releasing classified information; that she was arrested in
the Referendum riots and the later anti-Gencom protests – given
six months virtjail and ebranded for life; and that, since then, she'd
pretty much disappeared from view.

*But what if she hasn't disappeared, politically; what if she's still
active? Once a terrorist, always a terrorist, they say; you don't stop
believing, do you?* His bosses have long suspected the existence of
a network of scientists working to break Gencom's grip on human
reproduction. Just the sort of people who'd be very interested
in someone who appears to have slipped that grip. The old bird
would've had to use a dark lab for the fertility test, and he's pretty
sure they've all got links to the science underground. If she's told

them about his mutation, Seth could be getting caught up in something way out of his league. *Let's give the old bird a visit – see what she has to say for herself.*

They've met before, when he went with Seth one time, but her look when she opens the door is not one of recognition. He introduces himself and apologises for calling so late in the day.

'No matter. It's not quite my bedtime.' She gives him a quizzical look. 'Is it about anything we wouldn't want anyone to overhear, by any chance?'

'Well, yes, it is, actually,' he says, feeling a bit spooked by her prescience.

'Then we'll talk in the shed.' She nods towards the back of the house.

'So, what kind do you want?' she asks as they enter the shed. 'I've got some tasty little mixes, depending on what you're after. All home-grown, of course. No pesticides or fertilisers.'

He laughs out loud at this. 'Oh no, Thelma, I'm not after weed, ta.'

She looks dismayed and apologises for assuming that young people would only be wanting one thing. He laughs, says it's fine. Explains that he's come because Seth told him about the baby and he's worried about what his friend might be getting into - in particular why she said his mutation was "social dynamite".

'There's really nothing to worry about,' she reassures. 'Seth will be fine. The test was done on the dark, so no possible trace. If Seth doesn't say anything about it, no-one else will.' She looks as if she considers the matter dealt with and makes to rise.

So much for the concerned friend approach. Need to activate plan B. He takes out his Gencom badge and sees her flinch at the blue and silver insignia.

'And what does the old devil want with me?' She darts a sour look at the badge.

He reassures her that he isn't there for Gencom – even though, he says, still smiling, he could arrest her for performing an illegal test. But he isn't interested in small matters, he tells her. Seth really is his main – and only – concern. He can see he's got her attention and starts to bluff it up a bit: says he's aware of the scientific importance of Seth's mutation, how it could put a mighty spanner in the Program's works and that he strongly suspects she's passed his friend's bio sample to her underground contacts.

She starts to protest but he cuts her off. Tells her he doesn't want to know all the ins and outs, the whatever/whoever, just whether anyone is planning to ignite the 'dynamite', as she called it, anytime soon. And whether Seth is going to get hurt in the blast.

She stares at him for a while before nodding and conceding that, yes, *in principle*, Seth's mutation could be the catalyst for which the so-called 'terrorists' – that is, she insists, the great majority of scientists on the Planet – have been waiting. Its publication would enable dark labs to overwrite the genlock and restore the fertility of any male anywhere in the World. And, yes, it is *theoretically* possible a network of labs is primed and ready to move once they have access to Seth's genetic 'key'. But, she insists, if any of this were to be true – and she's not saying it is, mind – it wouldn't endanger Seth; just the opposite. Gencom would be too busy firefighting on too many fronts to bother with small fry like Seth. He'd be irrelevant – an accidental hero.

'But what if this theoretical move against the Program failed. What then?' he asks.

'Well, then it would be all over anyway,' she says, 'for all of us. Stupid humans would have lost their chance to reclaim their biological destiny. In the face of such a loss, the fate of any one individual would be immaterial.'

She appears to get stuck in this thought for a while, making several squirrelly shakes of her head, before returning to the thread and saying that, should the plot against the Program fail, Seth would just need to plead ignorance: an innocent victim whose biodata were stolen against his knowledge. He'd get readjusted, yes, but that would have happened eventually, anyway – as she'd told his father enough times.

Something seems to shift in her at the mention of Marcus, and she grasps his hand with bony fingers, fixing him with earnest eyes.

'If you are the friend to Seth you say you are,' she says, 'then you must see that the end of the Program is his only hope. He's got far, far more to gain than lose from its downfall.' She gives his hand a firm squeeze and urges him to ensure that Seth says nothing to anyone. 'At least for a short while. If a move were being planned against the Program,' she says with a knowing look, 'it would not be long in coming.'

They part on reasonable terms: he agrees to make sure Seth keeps quiet and she agrees, whatever happens, to keep Viki's pregnancy out of it. Their common interest in the fate of Seth Marcuson establishes a working level of mutual trust, although neither is unaware of the hold the other now has over them. He could pull her in for the illegal test and concealing an illegitimate pregnancy – not to mention clearly being up to her grizzled neck in a plot against the Program. But she could blow his cover, and his whole world, apart.

In his eagerness to tell Seth he catches a pubtrans, first time in ages. Usually avoids them like the virus. In fact, the overcrowded, direct-entry passenger vehicle that careers erratically along the Banleus' congested streets is probably the ideal place to make the acquaintance of a virus. *But time's short and needs must.* All private capsules being occupied, he takes a standing slot in the central core, as near the door as he can, wraps his scarf tight round his nose and mouth, activates his occupied sign and shuts his eyes to any visual pleas from fellow travellers – the noisome wafts of whom are less easily evaded.

She's right, though: Seth handing himself in is a lose-lose scenario. What could he say? That someone stole his genetic identity? Not his to steal: Gencom owns the blueprint of all legal humans. But that's precisely the danger for the plotters, isn't it? They'll be hunted down for patent theft. And it won't take the omniscient corp long to find them – dark labs or no dark labs. Gencom's got trackers tracking the trackers, that are tracking everybody on the planet. In fact, we've probably got an eye on Thelma and her gang already, waiting for them to show their hand.

But if the old bid's to be believed, it's worth a punt, isn't it? There's a lot riding on it – for him as well as Seth. Could be a way out for them both. Opposition to the Program is growing, and not just amongst scientists – politicians too. The streets are full of angry people. If it all ended tomorrow few would mourn. And if the plot succeeds, he could be a free man. Out from under Gencom's thumb at last. *Mind you*, he thinks with a grim smile, *if it fails, I'll more likely be a dead man.*

39

COINCIDENCE

Coop decides to visit the old woman again, see if she can recall anything else the victim said that night. She may have been the last person to see her alive, after all – apart from the murderer. And possibly the brother. But he's not going to get anything else out of that particular individual – not for a while, anyway. Last he looked, Naz Janson was curled on the stone floor of the cell, sweating and shivering simultaneously. Maybe he should've left him where he was, in his sack cave. Whatever – his immediate destination now is the barren and brutal state of cold turkey.

It takes him longer than usual to get a car and the light is beginning to fade as it draws up at the end of Thelma's lane. He's half-considering returning tomorrow when he sees the figure of a tall young male standing at her door. Interesting. He steps back into the lengthening shadows. Even more interesting: the light from the opening door reveals the man to be none other than Agent Flowers – in Queron Brandonson mode. *Oh ho, what's our friendly Program Steward doing visiting Dr Linsdottir at this time of day?*

Thelma leads the agent around the side of the house and he follows, watching as they enter a large wooden-framed building in the back garden. He can just make out their shapes through the semi-transparent structure and sees them settle by the far wall. By crawling around the outside and tamping down a large clump of vegetation, he manages to manoeuvre himself close enough to hear voices. He can make out a few words: Seth's name – a couple of times, he's sure – and something about the Program. But that's about it.

He sits back in frustration on the now-flattened foliage and is about to retreat when he sees the two figures rise and move towards the entrance. He edges slowly back around the building in time to see them exchange farewells, before the agent sets off down the road and Thelma returns indoors.

He waits a few moments then walks up to the old wooden door and gives it a hard knock.

'Who's there?' a sharp voice calls.

'It's Detective Cooper-Clark, Dr Irisdottir. I wondered if I could have a word with you?'

The door opens a smidgeon. 'It's a bit late in the day for a house call, isn't it, Detective?'

'I'm sorry to disturb you,' he says in a polite voice. 'I was just passing and saw your visitor leave, so I thought I'd take a chance you'd not yet retired for the night. Just wanted to ask you a couple of further quick questions about young Viki.'

'Well, I'm not going to be long out of my bed, so you *will* need to be quick about it.' The door opens a little and a venous hand beckons. 'You'd better come in; I'm certainly not talking to you on the doorstep.'

He's ushered into a large, brightly lit room whose walls are almost entirely covered with large, black-edged prints and etchings, and a good part of whose floor is filled with potted plants of various kinds. Too cluttered for him, by far; the visual overload would drive him mad – although the large tapestry almost filling the wall opposite the fireplace is pretty spectacular.

'*The Dream of Raphael* isn't it?' he says, nodding at the cloth wall hanging.

'You know about art, Detective?' she says, clearly surprised.

'Well, only a little.' He's not taking her surprise personally; he knows no-one thinks much of his chosen profession. 'Did some art history after grads and *Roman High Renaissance* was one of them. I remember this image – very enigmatic. The woman is supposed to represent reason, I recall, which the old man is hoping will rescue him from his plight. Something like that?'

'Possibly.' She inclines her head. 'Although I think there are many layers of meaning. The more you look, the more you see, sort of thing. But I think the clue is in the legend at the bottom: *Sedet aeternum qui sedebit infoelix.*'

'Is that old Latin? Never did that, I'm afraid.'

'Yes, from the *Aeneid* – an ancient epic poem. Loosely translated it means: *He will sit forever who sits unfortunate.* She tilts her head at him, her sharp little eyes chestnut bright. 'What d'you make of that, Detective?'

He thinks for a bit. 'That self-pity can be incapacitating?' he suggests.

'Yes that,' she nods, 'and, more broadly, that the point is not to accept the bad things that happen in this World; the point is to try and change them.'

'Oh, so it's a call to action, you think?'

'Yes, you could put it like that,' she says as she reconnects several unravelling strands of hair. 'Everyone moans endlessly about the injustices of life, but no-one wants to leave their precious little bubbles of self-interest and do anything about any of it, do they?'

'No, maybe not,' he nods, acknowledging the truth in her words, 'but don't we have to accept that some things just can't be changed? And that sometimes we can do more harm than good by trying to change them?'

'Don't pick fights you can't win, is that it?' She gives a short laugh. 'Well, you may be right, Detective. But sometimes I think we give up too easily. Sometimes it seems like we humans have no fight left – apart from those we ceaselessly pick with each other over meaningless things.'

'Are there any particular fights you think we should be having, Dr Linsdottir?'

'Oh, too many to mention,' she says with a small laugh. 'Now's not the time of day for what I can promise you is a very long list.' She turns her squirrelly eyes on him. 'So, what was it you wanted to talk to me about, Detective? It really is getting rather late, and I need my beauty sleep, as you can see, ha!'

'Well,' he smiles, 'as I said, I wouldn't usually have called at this hour, but as your visitor had just left… He looked vaguely familiar to me, by the way, your visitor?'

'Oh, I doubt it would be anybody you would know. Just a friend of a friend.' She gestures to one of the soft chairs by the fireplace. 'Do you want to sit or do you want to stand there all night?'

He positions himself on the edge of the chair, places his hat carefully beside him and gives her a pleasant smile. 'You will have heard that Samael Samson was convicted of the rape of Viki—'

'Good thing too…' she interrupts. 'And good to see they're using that old term again. Just making an act unspeakable doesn't make it undoable.'

'Yes, although he tried to argue that she had consented—'

'Oh, that's so ridiculous.' She slaps a hand on her knee, with a loud snort. 'You only had to look at her afterwards; no-one in their right mind could think someone would consent to that.'

'You would think so, wouldn't you?' He nods with a grim smile. 'But I find you can never overestimate people's capacity for wrong-mindedness. Anyway, thanks to you, we know we're looking for someone else for her murder. So,' he takes out his notebook, 'I'd just like to go over again exactly what Viki said to you before she left that night. You said she mentioned getting back to her brother. Did she say *why* she wanted to see him?'

Her brow furrows. 'I think it was something she'd done… or said, that she wanted to put right. But really, Detective, she wasn't being very coherent – about that, or anything.' She gives him sharp glance. 'You don't think it was him, do you, the brother? I heard he was in the EdgeForce, and you know what they say…'

'Yes, I know people tend to make assumptions about the men who've been out there,' he says with a thin smile. 'But I prefer to judge people as I find them.'

'And you've found him, have you?' she challenges.

'Yes, he's sitting in our cells as we speak,' he says, and, when she makes no response, asks: 'Was there anything to suggest that Viki was still frightened – in fear for her life?'

'No, she didn't sound frightened. Anxious, maybe – if anything. But she wouldn't have gone off on her own in the early hours, if she was afraid of someone, would she?'

'No, I wouldn't have thought so, but, as you said, we can't assume she was thinking straight.'

The old woman gives a vigorous nod. 'No, I'm sure not. Who would be? But I suspect it was all just rotten luck, wasn't it? The poor girl was in the wrong place at the wrong time – and for the second time that night – a truly terrible coincidence.' She gives a loud sigh, clasping her hands and setting her many bracelets jangling.

There's that word again. 'I'm not a great believer in coincidence,' he says, 'but you may be right. The strongest probability is she was just tragically unlucky.' He leans a little closer to the old woman. Maybe she's tired or just keen to see the back of him but he's getting a strong sense that she's got her shutters down.

'So, there's nothing else you can tell me about that night, Dr Linsdottir, that might help us find Viki's killer – no matter how small or insignificant?'

'No, not really, Detective.' She shakes her head. 'Not that I can think of. Pretty sure I've told you everything. I was tired too, you'll understand; it was the middle of the night, after all. And my memory's not what it was, you know…'

'Okay,' he says as he closes his notebook and reaches for his hat. 'Thank you for your time. Much appreciated. You've been very helpful. You have my securpin, if you have any further thoughts – once you've had a chance to sleep on it.'

'And that's precisely what I intend to do now, Detective, if you don't mind.' She gets to her feet and holds out her hand. 'Goodbye and good luck. I hope you get your man.'

Or woman, he hears Lyse saying. He makes to go but stops and turns back.

'Oh, by the way, almost forgot. You know a thing or two about plants, don't you?' He opens the odorpin and holds it out to her. 'Have you any idea what this might be?'

She sniffs and recoils slightly, with a decisive shake of her head.

'No idea, Detective. No idea at all.' She gives a little laugh. 'I clearly don't know as much as I think I do. Mind you, they're producing new hybrids all the time; it's difficult for an old brain to keep up.' Her bright smile seems ever so slightly forced. 'Why do you ask?'

'It was found on Viki's body; her skin appeared to have been rubbed down with it.'

'How very odd,' she says, her nut-like eyes holding steady on his.

'Yes, indeed. Very odd.' He smiles as he dons his hat and takes his leave.

He'll walk back; it's a poor substitute for a swim, but at least it's exercise points and he needs to up his monthly average. He pulls the brim of his hat down against the grainy fug that has started to accumulate of late in the curves and corners of the Banleu streets, putrefying as it lingers. Been a long day, but not an unproductive one – especially that last little encounter. There's something more to the agent's visit than a friend passing by. Why go outside to talk, if so? Hadn't sounded like a conversation between friends, had it? Perhaps the old woman's working with the Program Stewards on something. She was a bit of an expert in her day, after all. Unlikely, he thinks, as he recalls their conversation about the tapestry. Or maybe she's under investigation. Maybe the Stewards think she's up to something and the agent has been sent in undercover…

Or maybe, he grins, it was just Queron the singer, friend of the son of the man the old woman plays cards with, trying to score some of Thelma's finest home-grown.

40

SITTING UNFORTUNATE

'Only me, Daddy-O!'

Seth is relieved to hear Queron at the door. It's day three of his self-imposed exile and he's missing human company. Probably would have been fine staying in if it wasn't that he knows he can't go out. But, as it is, he's going stir crazy. Not that it's not comfortable here; he's on a brand-new airbed in what Queron calls the 'games room'. Playing non-stop was fun for the first day or so, but even that's begun to pall now. Suppose he thought Queron would be around more, do some jamming, possibly writing, but his friend's been going out early on the *places to be, people to see* ticket and not coming back until late.

Queron is visibly excited, a glint of light at the bottom of his depthless eyes. He grabs two beers from the icer and comes over to perch on a chair beside him, handing him a bottle. As he takes a long swig of the cold beer, he says he's got some news. 'End-to-all-your-trouble-type news.' Tells him he went round to Thelma's to score some green – he chucks a bagful of the pungent flowers on the table in front of him – and they had a smoke or two and got talking. When he'd told her that he knew about the baby and was worried about Seth, she'd strongly hinted that something was about to happen that would change everything.

'Turns out old bird's got links with the science underground, and your genes, bro, are just what they needed to prise Gencom's mitts off the whole birth thing.'

He leans forward with his trademark cat-got-the-cream grin. 'Just think, Setho, that'd be ice – deep fried! If they destroy the Program, you'll be in the clear – could end up a hero: Super Mutant Saves the World!'

He looks at Queron in astonishment. Can this be real? Thelma has links with terrorists? Who are planning to overthrow the Program, using his bio? Sounds like the script of an old sci-fi movie. *But it's not fantasy, is it? It's real life – my life – and I don't like people playing fast and loose with it.* He turns on his friend, his slow-to-rouse anger beginning to stir.

'So the old bird's given my bio to terrorists, that it? Without saying anything to me? And that's okay with you, is it?'

'They're scientists, bro, not fanatics,' Queron tries to reassure him. 'And I've told you before, they're not your data – *you* don't belong to you; *you* belong to Gencom.' He leans back with a relaxed smile, pulling a couple of vials from his pocket. 'Have a little toke of this, Seth boy – calm things down a bit?'

He shakes his head, tempted though he is. Needs to think clearly.

'Okay. Well, anyway…' Queron smirks, pocketing the vials, 'think it's all a done deed, from what the old bird said. Too late to stop it now.'

That just about does it. All a done deed? His anger has fully roused itself.

'I'll tell you what's a done deed,' he shouts. 'I'm the effin "done deed" – done over by an old biddy who calls herself a friend.' He gets up from the chair, heart pounding. 'Well, it's not too late to report the treacherous old bat, is it?' He stares down at his friend. 'I've got to do something, Q,' he says in a quieter voice. 'What if people found out we knew an attack was being planned, and did nothing? And never mind other people,' he shakes his head, 'how could we live with ourselves, knowing that we did nothing?'

'Setho, Setho!' Queron soothes, catching his arm. 'That'd be suicide. Look, bro...' He finds himself being eased gently back into the chair. 'Think it through. If you go to the Stews now, the old bid'll tell them about the baby, and you'll be right up shit creek. Just sit tight. Do nothing. If it all goes tits up, which it won't, you can say she took your bio without asking, which is true, and that you knew nada about any plot. She's not going to say any different.'

'But people'll get hurt, Q, won't they, if the Program collapses? Lose their chance to have kids, be a family—'

'Yeah, well, a lot of people are losing that chance now, by all accounts,' Queron says, his voice smoothly reasonable. 'That's what your pa thinks, no? If this plot comes off, loads more'll get a chance to drop their sprogs. And you'd be safe, bro – be able to stay your own man.' He squeezes his arm and grins from under his fringe of hair. 'What's not to like?'

He nods, seduced by the certainty in Queron's voice as well as his ingrained inclination to please him, and the talk turns to other things while they drink the beers. He tells Queron he's got a start for a new song and wants his reaction and is disappointed when his friend says he has to go out again: *see a man about a dog*. Won't be late, though, Queron reassures him; they can have a little playtime when he gets back.

'Main thing, bro.' Queron looks at him, his dark eyes shining. 'We've got us a way out, no? All we gotta do's sit tight. Like the three little monkeys, init: hear nothing, see nothing, say nothing.'

After Queron leaves, he does sit tight – for a while, anyway – turning over his friend's words. Regrets not taking the toke now; could do with something to calm him down. He's gotta do something to stop it all, hasn't he – no matter what Queron says? Pa and others may be right about the Program being unfair, but that's not the fault of the people on it, is it? And it's them that'll suffer. Young people trying to start their families, older adults on a last chance and, if Lyse is right, the female population generally. *Lyse...!* He flinches at the thought of her. She already thinks him weak and indecisive. If she found out about this, she'd look at him the way she'd looked at him before, wouldn't she, when he didn't stand up for Viki? *Not so much three little monkeys as one cowardly lion.*

But he's promised Queron, hasn't he? Doesn't want to make things bad between them – especially now he's let his own gaff go. Best to sit tight, like he says. Path of least resistance, after all; the one he usually likes to travel. He selects an album, makes a consolation spliff with the flowers and climbs onto the hydrommock *How does Q afford all this stuff?*, where he lies, gently undulating, as the melancholy notes of a blues trumpet twist around him. From nowhere, the image of the beleaguered old man in Thelma's tapestry comes into his mind, leering, as if to taunt him. Is he like the man: timid, cowering – *sitting unfortunate,* wasn't it? – waiting for others to sort his life out? Too afraid to be the agent of his own destiny?

He takes a long draw on the smoke, blowing a series of white rings into the air. Maybe Lyse is right (and doesn't she even look a bit like the female in the cloth picture?), maybe it's a message: time to start making his own decisions; take control. *It's my soddin' life on the line, after all. Queron's not the fly in the ointment, is he? It's me with the wings in the grease.* And while we're at it, he takes another deep pull on the joint, what was Q doing talking to Thelma about his personal stuff anyway? He's only met her a couple of times. Why would either of them think he's any of their effing business? And Thelma, a terrorist! He snorts out the smoke. People are so not what they seem these days. No wonder she was so keen for him and Vik to keep quiet about the baby. Needed time for her stupid little plan to work. And Vik went to her – of all people – for help that night. Ironic, that's the word, isn't it?

He sits up suddenly, causing the hydro to undulate violently. But what if Thelma didn't help her? What if she thought Viki was going to report the baby and told her terrorist buddies, who sent someone to shut her up? *Nah.* He lies back, eyes closed, the combination of the weed and the rough swell of the chair making him feel slightly nauseous. *That's just mad; old Hollywood movie stuff. She's just an old lady who plays cards with Pa, for fuck's sake. Hardly a master criminal.*

The thought has staying power, however, turning itself round and round in his agitated mind like a settling cat.

41

A TRIFLE

Coop is waiting in the 'offout', as the agent has named their usual meeting place, enjoying the play of the atmosfer's new 'iced zephyr' feature on his uncovered face. It was he who had asked to meet, convinced now that the enigmatic male is a crucial piece of what is starting to feel like a nearly completed puzzle. Whether that piece comes from Queron Brandonson or Agent Flowers he's yet to determine. As he sits, he becomes aware of a singularly unpleasant, but oddly familiar, smell. Seems to be coming from his person, which he scrutinises, locating a suspicious-looking stain on the hem of his outers that appears to be the source. He rubs the mark, heightening the nasty aroma. And then it hits him: the smell on the body. *How on Earth...?*

A cheerful voice calls out and he looks up to see the agent approaching with a wide smile. 'Gotta stop meeting like this, Coop,' the arrival says. 'People'll start to talk.'

He returns the smile.

'So, what's up, Dec?' the agent asks, sitting beside him and draping a languid arm along the back of the bench.

'Well, thing is,' he replies in a neutral voice, 'I've had a bit of a breakthrough.'

'Great, Coop. Got your man?'

'No, not quite,' he smiles, 'but I've just realised that all this time I've been chasing after a phantom when the real thing is standing in front of me.'

'Sorry, you'll have to run that by me again,' the agent says with an uncertain laugh, slicking back a wing of hair.

'Okay, well... let's start with what we know, shall we? Two males left a trace of themselves on Viki Jansdottir's body the night she was killed: the wretched Samael was one and the other is the one we called the ghost. When the first proved not to be the murderer, my suspicions naturally turned to the second. The ghost in your machine, as it were.'

'Haven't got any further on that, Coop,' the agent breaks in. 'Did say it'd be difficult.'

'Yes, and I can now understand why it would have been difficult.' He holds him in a steady gaze. 'Particularly for you, Agent Flowers.'

'Oh? Why me in particular?' The agent is still smiling, but he thinks he detects a twitch of anxiety around his mouth.

'Because you are the ghost, are you not?' he says in a calm voice. 'It was your bio that was left on Viki's scarf that night, wasn't it?'

'What makes you think that, Coop?' his companion asks, his smile tightening.

'Oh, I don't think it, I know it. You left a bio trace on the water cup when we last met; I caught the rim before it fully degraded. Surprised you didn't know about that little trick.' He smiles. 'Anyway, your bio matched the trace left by our so-called "ghost".'

'Okay – it's a fair cop!' The agent gives a short laugh, leaning back against the bench. 'So, you think I'm your murderer, do you?' He leans forwards, face composed. 'It really wasn't me, Coop.

243

You're barking up the wrong tree there. What possible motive could I have for killing Viki? She was my best friend's girl, after all.'

'Well, that's what I asked myself.'

'And what did you answer yourself?' An amused look has crept into the agent's eyes.

'Well, I need to go back a bit before I tell you that,' he says. 'To the point where I became convinced that Viki's lost baby was the key to the murder. Accepting that, the central question became the identity of the father.'

'Well, you can count me out of that one, Coop,' the agent says with a small laugh. 'I'm not daddy material; you can check that easily enough.'

'No, I realise that but,' he holds on to the now-restless eyes of the other, 'I think we both know who the father is, don't we?'

The agent says nothing, his deep eyes unreadable.

'The obvious contender for fatherhood,' he continues, 'was, of course, your good friend Seth. He had a long-standing relationship with the deceased that, even you commented, is unusual in this day and age. He was also very adamant, on her behalf, that she was not the type of young woman to have sex with other men. I had eliminated him initially – as a non-fertile male. However, as a famous detective once said: *when you have eliminated the impossible, whatever remains, no matter how improbable, must be the truth.* Or more accurately in this case,' he smiles to himself, 'when you have eliminated the improbable, what remains, no matter however apparently impossible, must be the truth.'

'And?' The agent gives a languid shrug. 'The impossible truth of all this is?'

'That Seth Marcuson is not infertile at all. That he was indeed, by some fluke of nature, the father of Viki's baby.' He smiles at him. 'As I think you well know.'

The agent nods but says nothing.

'As I think you also know,' he continues in an even tone, 'it was the motive that always bothered me. But if Seth was the father, that opened up new possibilities, didn't it? The strongest being that Seth killed Viki to prevent anyone finding out about his illegal sexual status. When his alibi held up, and you were revealed as the ghost, my next hypothesis was that you had killed her, on your friend's behalf – or behest – to stop her informing on him.'

The agent gives a short, mocking laugh. 'You're way out there, Coop, I'm not the murdering kind. And also – ask Seth – I've only just found out about the baby myself – days after Vik was killed.' He narrows his hooded eyes. 'Anyway, you said I *was* your next suspect…?'

'Yes, I now think you had nothing to do with Viki's death. Although,' he gives him a pointed look, 'you did nothing to allay suspicion by your lack of openness. The ghost proved to be quite a red herring, to mix a metaphor. Wasted a lot of time. And,' he sighs, 'you're still not telling me everything, are you? You're still holding something back.'

'How d'you mean, Coop?' the agent asks with an uncertain smile. 'Holding back on what?'

'On the reason for your visit to Thelma Linsdottir last night, for a start. Is there really nothing I need to know about that?'

The agent straightens and looks at him in surprise. 'How on Earth…?'

'Did I find out? Coincidence, actually.' *Sometimes even I have to accept it happens.* 'I was on my way to pay Dr Linsdottir a visit myself last night when I saw you at her door. I confess I followed you into the garden and overheard some of your conversation, which appeared to be about Seth Marcuson…' He breaks off, discomforted to see the agent grinning at him.

'Well done, Coop – Ace Detective! You got there in the end.'

'Oh?' he says, unsmiling. 'And perhaps you'll be kind enough to tell me exactly where it is I've got?'

'You've got to my undercover case, Coop. That's where. We've had this Linsdottir woman under surveillance for some time now.

Known terrorist sympathiser. Got evidence that she's part of a terrorist cell, planning an imminent attack on the Program.'

'And what does that have to do with Seth Marcuson?'

'Come on, Coop, think it through. You gotta see the risk that Seth presents: a young male with a genetic resistance to the universal snip. Undermines the very basis of Gencom's control. Once the override code's out there, any male can get reversed; simple cut and paste job. Well, any male with enough coin, anyway. Cheap enough to make the copies, but those few with the skills to do the job will charge a high price.' He leans back, re-draping his arm along the back of the bench, a sinuous smile on his lips. 'Nevertheless, it'd be a fatal crack in the Gencom dam, and they, we, believe the Linsdottir woman is at the centre of things. I've been going in UC to try and flush them out. Not easy; she's a wily old bird and still suspicious of me.'

He sits for a while, twisting his hat in front of him, considering the implications of the agent's information. The noxious smell drifts up to him again, like a child not wanting to be ignored, and he inhales a few times more before he remembers. Thelma's garden, that's where he picked the smell up. Outside the greenhouse. Yet she claimed she didn't know what it was…

'Yes, of course! That's it!' he says, standing, hat in hand. 'Why didn't I see it before? Right in front of my nose. Literally, in the case of one vital clue,' He gives a rueful laugh: should have known better, *nothing so important as trifles*, after all.

The agent is looking perplexed.

'Okay, so… we know that Viki went to Thelma after the attack. What if she gave Thelma reason to believe she was going to tell the authorities about Seth – that would upset the terrorists' applecart, wouldn't it?'

'It would indeed, and you think someone wasn't about to let that happen?'

He nods. 'And what's more, I think that "someone" was Thelma Linsdottir. All that stuff about Viki leaving to find her brother was just to throw me off the scent. To cover the fact that Viki never left her house again that night – alive, at least.'

The agent looks uncertain. 'Well, as I said, she's a wily old bird, but you really think she's capable of murder?'

He recalls the intensity of Thelma's eyes as she talked about the need to take action against the wrongs of the World. 'Quite honestly,' he says with a grim smile, 'I think she'd be capable of pretty much anything – if the cause was right.'

'Okaay… so how d'you want to play this?' the agent asks, getting to his feet.

'Well, I'll need to bring her in immediately.'

The agent gives him an anxious look. 'Any chance of giving me a couple of hours on that, Coop?' he asks. 'As I said, I'm getting closer but still haven't got to the bottom of the plot. Bit more time would give me one last chance to go in as Seth's friend and winkle out the rest of it. She'll just seize up if you bring her in and word will spread in a split. Plotters'll scatter and,' he gives him a plaintive look, 'I'll have wasted weeks of hard work.'

He hesitates. 'Not sure I can do that, Flowers. As I said, Boss says we've got to report up by close today.'

'But you have reported it, Coop – to me,' the agent presses. 'I can give you an affi on that and anyway, we still have a few hours left. What d'you say, Coop?' he entreats, his smile on maximum wattage. 'It'd be win-win, no? Couple more hours and I get my terrorists and you get your murderer.'

He examines his fingers, thinking. He knows the agent could just tell him to back off if he wanted – the Program's work being paramount at all times. And he appreciates the man's attempt to serve both their interests, which suits his own disposition.

'Go on, Coop,' the agent cajoles, seeming to sense a crack in the door. 'It's no skin off your nose, is it? Couple of hours and she's all yours.'

Agent Flowers has the kind of physical magnetism that makes other humans generally inclined to please him; himself not excepted. He sighs in mock surrender. 'Okay, but I want that affidavit ASAP, Flowers – cover my back with your lot.'

'Great, Coop,' the agent says, his dark eyes eager. 'I won't let you down. You'll get Thelma Linsdottir before the day ends – trust me.'

Trusting him is the last thing he feels like doing. But the agent's right – another, what, he checks the time, six hours is not going to make much difference. And he could get the report drafted meanwhile. Boss'll live with that, he's pretty sure. Especially if he gets a result on the murder *and* earns some brownie points with the Stewards.

He's so busy reassuring himself about the logic of his decision that he fails to listen to the small, but sharp, inner voice of doubt. The one that's always on the button.

42

SACRIFICE

Queron's bought himself a bit of time, but maybe not very much. He's not sure the cop with the hat totally trusts him. Can't blame him, really; he wouldn't trust him either. He feels sick about Thelma. Did she really do it? An old bid like that, with all her years of life, stealing those of a young girl who'd hardly had any? He spits the idea out with the dust in his mouth. After midnight, they can do what they like with her. But right now, he's going to warn her. *Eye on the prize, as the song goes.*

The evening air is grittier than ever; filtering down the back of his throat, despite the multiple layers of scarf. He wipes his eyes and pulls the scarf high over his nose. *Not looking forward to seeing the old woman again, TBH. If Coop's right about her, it'll not be easy to be civil. Talking of which...* he spins round and peers into the sweaty gloom behind him but sees no sign of a following detective. Still, it's with a deepening sense of unease that he turns into Thelma's road.

Her smile when she answers the door is conspiratorial. 'Hello,

Agent, or is it Queron today? Nice to see you, whichever way. Come in, come in.'

He stays at the door, eschewing the pleasantries. Nods his head in the direction of the greenhouse. 'Can we talk out there, Thelma?' She frowns, perhaps sensing a change of tone, and leads him through to the wooden structure without speaking. They enter the pungent-smelling space and she gestures for him to sit.

'No, I'll stand, thanks.' He's brusque. 'Haven't got long.'

She also remains standing, clearly wary now. 'Has something happened to Seth?'

He tells her the cops know she killed Viki and are coming for her. She stares at him, eyes flicking like a startled rodent, and disgust creeps slowly up his throat. He's bought her a bit of time, he tells her; persuaded the detective to give him a few more hours…

'How long exactly?' she asks in a sharp voice.

'Well, he said midnight, but I don't think he trusts me altogether, so it could well be sooner. He overheard us talking in here the other night, by the way – was listening outside.' He scans the blank-eyed apertures of the shed quickly and the old woman follows suit, nostrils twitching in mouse-like alarm.

'So, it's started?' he asks, as her eyes return to him.

'Yes.' She gives a short, excited nod. 'Midnight tonight the deed is done; the die is cast. That'll be the end of it. Well, the beginning of the end of it, anyway. No going back.' She looks at him with bright eyes, hands clasped to her cheeks. 'I can't believe we've done it – after all this time.' Her smile freezes as she sees his smile-less face, and she raises her wispy eyebrows.

'Okay, Doc,' he says. 'Hope the plan comes off – for all our sakes – but however it turns out,' he narrows his eyes, 'it wasn't worth a girl's life. If it *was* you killed Viki,' he makes no attempt to disguise his disgust now, 'I hope you get everything you deserve.'

He's making to leave when he hears a noise and turns to see a figure entering the greenhouse door. 'Get down!' he hisses to Thelma as he ducks behind the potting bench. The figure quickly delineates, and he recognises it immediately.

'Seth!' He stands up to greet his friend. 'What y'doing here, bro? You're not supposed to be—'

'Where is she?' his friend shouts, ignoring him. 'Murdering bitch! Come out if you're in there!' he calls, with a challenging stare around the room.

'She's not here, Setho,' he says, catching his arm, uneasy now. 'No-one's here. I was just leaving. Let's go. Get a beer back at mine.' He tries to encourage his friend in the direction of the exit, but Seth rounds on him, pulling his arm away. 'What you doing here, anyway, Queron?' he asks with a suspicious look.

'Just came to score a bit more weed, bro. Had to, rate you're hoovering it up. But no-one's here. Might as well split.' He puts his arm round Seth's waist and starts to edge him towards the door again. 'How come you're so sure about the old bird being the killer, anyway?'

Seth halts his already infinitesimal progress exit-wise and turns to him. 'Was you, actually. Made me think when you said about Thelma and the plot against the Program. Always had a problem with *why* anyone would want to kill Vik. I mean, why would they? But Thelma had a reason to shut her up, didn't she? Viki went to her after she was attacked, we know that, and must've told her she was going to turn me in. She was angry enough to do that, we know that too. So, Thelma had to stop her – or the plan was fucked. And all that stuff with the body, that's gotta be Thelma.'

He's unsure how to play this; thrown by the uncharacteristic volatility of his friend and unsure, for once, about his ability to calm him down. He wonders in passing what Thelma's up to; hasn't heard any movement behind him.

'Have you been to the pols about this?' he asks, hoping to get Seth to talk it out.

'Nah, wanted to have it out with her first – see what she had to say for herself.' Seth stands, red-faced. 'But I'm going to tell them right now. The cops can dig her out from whatever stone she's hiding under.'

'Wait,' he catches Seth's arm, 'if you go now, Seth, bro, you'll bollocks up the whole plan. And you'll be arrested, straight off.'

'Fuck the plan. Fuck the lot of it. I never asked for any of it.' Seth shakes off his arm and glares at him, a storm in his slate-blue eyes. 'She killed her, Q, I know it. What'd Vik ever done to her?'

'Got in the way, I guess.'

'Yeah, well, I'm going to get in *her* way now,' Seth says, turning to go. 'Stick the fly right back in her ointment – see how she likes it.'

'But that means Vik'll have died for nothing,' he says, taking hold of Seth's arm again. *Even if he's right about the old bird, can't turn back now.*

'At least if the plan works,' he tries again, 'it'll have meant something, Setho.'

'Whose side are you on here, Queron?' Seth splutters. 'You think it was okay that Viki was killed, do you? Because she got in the way of something more important – some big plan that might not happen anyway?'

'No, of course not, bro.' He tries again to restrain him, but Seth shakes him off.

'Don't "bro" me, Brandonson,' he shouts as he starts for the door. 'That vile old bird got Viki killed and I'm going make sure she pays for it.'

'Stay where you are, young man!' a shrill female voice calls. 'You're not going anywhere – not for the next few hours anyway. Not going to let you ruin things at the eleventh hour.'

Thelma is standing at the end of the bench, waving a gun at Seth. 'Sit down here with us, like a good boy. You, me and this charming friend of yours, and we'll chat nicely until it's all over. Just a few hours and you can hand me in to the police yourself.'

'I'm not sitting down with you, you murdering bitch!' Seth cries, charging at her.

'No, Seth!' he cries, lunging after him.

There's a single shot, a female cries out and a figure crumples, then falls.

A pool of dark crimson spreads across the greenhouse floor, discarded seedlings spinning in its viscid flow.

43

BRIGHT STAR

Seth is heading to the Citernity Plaza with Marcus, the periwinkle sky mockingly bright for such a day. As the trans snakes a smooth path though the glassy-eyed streets, he unloads his self-loathing onto his long-suffering parent: how everything's his fault; first Viki, now this; how he was the one got her into trouble and then pulled Q into it all; how it's because of him that Queron was there and his fault Thelma shot him – he was the one that rushed at her, not Queron… He looks at Marcus, blinking fast.

'Just can't believe I'm never going to see him again, Pa. He's always been there…' He wipes his nose on his sleeve and makes a pathetic attempt at a smile.

'Yes, I know, Seth,' Marcus says, patting his son's arm. 'Not easy, I know.'

He sniffs and sits back in his seat, staring at the succession of featureless buildings speeding by as the nagging loop of self-recrimination starts up again.

Marcus cuts it off. 'What did you bring for his Virtuosia?'

He swallows hard. 'Holo of him doing one of his favourite numbers - *rock and roll frees the soul*, sort of thing. Band got the coin together; bit of a scrape and it's not very long, but think he'd like it.'

Marcus tells Seth he's found an old video of Queron as a young child; wanted to make it into a holo but couldn't afford it in the end. 'Price has shot up since your mother's day.' But he's brought the video anyway; hopes it'll play okay. 'Such a beautiful boy,' he says, shaking his head.

They are entering the central financial area and the trans slows to pass through the checkpoints as armed guards with tense faces and ever-ready fingers scan its contents. He looks away from their shielded squints and thinks of the dark, hooded eyes and slow, sensuous smile of his lost friend.

'So how does it work, the Resomation?' he asks as the trans pulls away from the checkpoint.

'Well, if it's like your mother's,' Marcus says, 'we'll have about an hour to play our mementos and say our goodbyes. As we do that, his body will be reduced to dust, then fast-compressed into hundreds of little brilliants. "Ashes to ashes, dust to diamonds" sort of thing. As I recall – it might be different now, mind – they provide little glass urns for people to take the gems home with them.'

'Hah, yeah,' he gives a soft laugh, 'that's about right; *crazy diamond*. Q would've loved that.'

*

Cooper-Clark is also walking towards Citernity, for the same purpose, full of regret about not having prevented the agent's death. If he hadn't listened to him, given him the extra time, if he'd gone and arrested Thelma then and there… But Agent Flowers was a difficult man to resist when he turned up the charm. As it was, he did go after him in the end, and was nearly at Thelma's when he heard the shot. It was a grim spectacle: the agent almost certainly dead; Seth lying with his arms around him, blood-slathered and whimpering. He shudders as he recalls the grisly struggle to prise the two men apart.

He's sorry he's not brought anything for the Virtuosia. Still has the records of their meetings, but those were with Agent Flowers and somehow he doesn't think the deceased, aka Queron Brandonson, would want Seth and the others to know about his double life. *Wonder how someone like him ended up as a Steward? Didn't seem the sort to have joined the Force willingly. Maybe that was it, maybe they'd got some sort of hold over him; he did at times seem like a man whose life was not entirely his own.* He's still not clear if the agent was working for or against the Program. Went to see Thelma straight after their last meeting, that's clear at least, but whether to warn her or incriminate her he's not sure. Instinct says the former – maybe he had something himself to gain from the downfall of the Program – but he'll not find out for certain now, not unless they catch the old woman – which he strongly doubts.

Removing his hat as he enters the Funeria, he walks through an arch and down into a small, oval-shaped room. Tiers of white seats, covered in what looks like real animal skin, line the walls and a large silvered canister rests centre stage. Rolling images of the agent, qua Queron, are playing across the walls of the chamber and the vaulted ceiling is glowing respectfully, in muted pastel shades. The air is filled with a sweet, almost cloying, melody. *Like being inside a softly boiling egg*, he thinks.

There are fewer people than he expected, although there's still time before the start. He spots Lyse sitting with several young males – band members, he assumes – and goes over.

'Hello, Lyse,' he says, ignoring the sniggers and raised eyebrows. 'Would you mind if I join you?'

'Of course not, Detective! Be my guest.' She smiles and he thinks she looks pleased to see him. 'There's plenty of space.' She gestures around her.

'Yes, I'm surprised. Thought it'd be packed.'

'No. Seth was clear that Queron would want it private. And wanted it here – loved all the vintage stuff…' She breaks off and he sees she's spotted Seth entering the other side of the chamber with his father. She waves and he tries not to notice her disappointment when the musician fails to respond. Doesn't seem to be registering anything much, by the looks.

'Who's that, d'you know?' he asks, largely to divert her eyes from Seth, whose visible melancholy, he suspects, is likely only to enhance his attractiveness. He indicates a tall female with striking red lips entering the other side of the arena. 'Some relation, d'you think?' he asks. 'Can't see any family resemblance.'

Lyse studies the thin-haired, tall-boned female who takes a seat across from them. 'Never seen her before,' she concludes. 'Don't think Queron had any family – not that he talked about. But then, he never talked much about personal stuff anyway – to me at least.'

'A girlfriend, d'you think?' he persists.

'Nah. Queron wasn't into girls. He liked all the flattery and attention – of both sexes – who wouldn't? But it was only ever Seth for him.'

'Well, anyway, looks like you were right,' he says, 'about Viki being some sort of sacrifice.'

'Oh? How's that, Detective?'

'Well, not a sacrifice to human love, as I think you meant, but for something very much bigger – a sacrifice for a, possibly misplaced, love for humankind.'

'Yeah. How about that. Thelma of all people. I only met her once, but she seemed nice enough, bit batty, praps—'

'Oh, she was far from batty,' he counters, recalling the keen eyes and the quick wit. 'All that "daft old biddy" thing was just an act. Dr Linsdottir was an extremely clever and calculating old woman. And one, it now seems, who was prepared to stop at nothing to achieve her ends.'

'Yeah, guess so.'

He waits for what seems an appropriate time before getting to his ulterior motive for coming today. On impulse he'd bought two tickets for the sundowner at Wild Waters tomorrow; weather conditions are set to be perfect: warm and dry and, particularly important, there's a full moon. Going to ask Lyse, as a thank-you for the songs (not that he's had any chance to put them to use yet, with all the publicity following the case). But he's not getting his hopes up. Likely it'll be too last minute. Or she'll have band practice – or another date, maybe even with the handsome singer.

He asks in a hesitant manner, but she needs no persuading.

44

WILD WATER

'Whew!' Lyse says, jumping into the slowly moving car. 'That looks more difficult than it actually is. Always think you're going to miss it somehow.'

'Yes, know what you mean,' he says as the doors close with a soft hiss behind them. 'But it can't leave without you.'

She sits back as the seat closes round her and the car begins to move more quickly under the overhead rail. Its domed roof and sides are of a transparent moulded material, giving maximum visibility and, as the speed of the vehicle builds, the sensation more of fairground ride than public transport.

'Magnets,' he says as she glances up at the free-floating rail.

'Oh right.' She grins, knowing that any further explanation would be lost on her. 'You just gotta believe, eh?'

He smiles and she can see excitement in his normally calm brown eyes. She'd agreed instantly when he'd asked – never been to any of the Wild Parks and the thought of swimming in natural water was just too enticing to turn down. And, has to admit, she very much enjoys the company of the clever detective. About anything more than that between them, she is curious, but emotionally neutral.

She looks around the car. Most of the other passengers are in their middle or late ages and all appear to be travelling on their own, access tabs firmly closed against unwanted intrusion. None react in any way when the car pulls out of the Citi port and picks up speed, their attention firmly other-worldly, but she's fascinated by the fast-changing social landscape as the bustle of the Banleus gives way to scrubby wasteland, littered with the ugly remains of Old-World technology and scarred by repeated attempts to extract value from the soil. She's surprised to see signs of still-active human settlement, with ramshackle dwellings assembled from all manner of practical, and manifestly impractical, materials.

'How can people live so far away from everything?' she asks. 'How can they even get enough water out here? All the rivers and wells dried up eons ago, didn't they?'

'*What are the roots that clutch, what branches grow; Out of this stony rubbish?*' he murmurs.

'Yeah, sounds about right,' she says, looking out at the desiccated landscape. 'Who said that?'

'Well, I just did,' he says, with a little smile. 'But originally? An Old-World poet called Eliot.'

'Oh, yeah. Queron liked that sort of thing…'

'But as to how people survive,' he continues, 'I can only conclude that human ingenuity is a powerful tool. We used to be able to live without all the trappings of so-called civilisation, so maybe it's possible to do so again. Get back to a simpler way of life. Must admit to a certain sympathy with the idea.'

She gives him a sceptical look. 'Really? I bet there's a few pleasures of modern life that even an upright enforcer of the law like you would miss, no?' He grins with an exaggerated shrug of his shoulders.

The car slows to a stop. *Avian zone*, a nearly human voice

announces. *Birding passes only*. A lone male gets out wearing full protective cover, strange gadgets hanging round his neck. The car pulls away more slowly this time and begins to crawl through an expanse of low-lying water and lush vegetation, crowded with wading birds. A small flock rises up into the cloudless sky, their soft bellies flashing in the sun.

'Never seen so many birds,' she says, keenly scanning the marshy landscape. 'Not all in one place, anyway. Didn't realise there were so many different kinds left. Look at those, there, the white ones – got beaks like spoons. And that big crowd of orangey-pink ones standing on one leg.'

The car slows again as it approaches the edge of a glade of tall trees. *Riparian swamp. No passes allowed*, the metallically prim voice intones as the car glides across the swamp. Wide-bottomed trees, hung with spectral strands of sliver moss, stand like alien beings up to their knees in the dark pond. Spikes of blood-red flowers spiral down from above the water, while waxen yellow blooms float idly across its green-coated surface. All is not Elysian, however; the stillness of the dark water is twitched, intermittently, by the sinister movement of something large underneath.

'Alligators,' he says, following her gaze. 'Swamps are teeming with them. See there,' he points to a raised mound of twigs and mud at the edge of the water, 'that's a nest. That's probably why they're not letting anyone out at the moment – eggs'll be hatching soon, and female alligators can be aggressive.' He gives a chuckle. 'Funny things, the babies. They're born with a little tooth on the end of their snouts to help them cut their way out of the egg and they give a little yell when they hatch.'

'What, like, *Yay!?*' She laughs.

'Yes, exactly so.' He smiles. 'Amazing creatures,' he continues. 'Living fossils, really. Been on Earth almost forever, hardly changing. We use them as a barrier between the human and the animal biospheres, but they're creeping in on us all the time. When the number of human casualties rises too much, the zoobots go in for the cull. Doesn't seem to set them back for long, though.'

'What a lot of things you know, Mr Detective,' she teases, impressed nevertheless.

'What, for a policeman?' he asks with a sardonic smile. 'Can't spend all my time in the gutter; need to see the stars occasionally. Talking of stars,' he turns and smiles at her, 'thank you for the songs. Really enjoyed them.'

'Especially mine, eh?' She grins.

'Especially yours, obviously!' He gives a short laugh. 'No, really, I do think you have a lovely voice, Lyse. You ought to get the band to let you do more.'

'Yeah. Working on it!'

As the car emerges from the swamps, the insipid blue of the late afternoon sky is turning pale yellow. They are crossing a vast open plain, peppered with spiky shrubs and low-growing trees, rimmed at its far edge by a spectacular mountain range. The rays of the sun are scorching the ochre earth and setting the distant peaks on fire. Frenzied spirals of dust dance alongside them, whipped by a merciless wind.

The car begins to slow again, and they can see a busy interchange ahead, tracks fanning out in multiple directions, with clutches of shiny oval cars hanging underneath like giant insect eggs. The platforms swarm with people getting in and out of the moving vehicles. *Animal Reserves*, the thin voice intones as the car pulls to a halt. *All passes accepted.*

'Most popular real-world destination,' he says, nodding at the scene outside. 'Well, actually the only still popular one. People used to come out here in hoards, swimming, climbing, trekking – even sleeping out. Used to be quite the thing – getting the fresh mountain air. But now,' he gives a short laugh, 'the air in the Citi's purer than out here.'

'And getting here costs time and coin that people don't have, I guess?'

'Yes. And most people seem to prefer their virtual worlds to the real thing, anyway. Seems we've just reached the tipping point where, at any given time on the Planet, there are more humans in virtuality than in anything you'd call reality. Some have even chosen to spend their lives there – "virtigration", they're calling it,' he says with a soft snort.

The car is streaking through the landscape now, as if trying to outrun the setting sun. But the light is already beginning to fade as they arrive at the Wild Pools. He squints at the sky, where a bank of steely cumulous is building from the west. 'Hope that doesn't spread too far,' he says, nodding at the skulking cloud. 'We need a clear moon if we're going to be lucky tonight.'

Before she can get to the meaning of this, the tinny voice cuts in. *Wild pool areas. Final destination.* The car slows to a stop and the doors slide open. *Please exit carefully. Magcar wishes you a pleasant experience but needs to remind you that IT IS IN NO WAY RESPONSIBLE for your health or safety once you have left the cabin.*

They leave the car, which floats off towards the park, and follow the signs to the pools. After touching in at the gate, they walk towards a large, immersive map of the complex. 'Let's try the small pool first,' he suggests, pointing at the far western edge of the map. 'It's one of the heated ones and it looks like we could have it to ourselves. Put your finger in – test the waters.'

She prods the watery image and pulls her finger out quickly with a grimace. 'Well, if that's a heated pool, I wouldn't want to try the unheated ones,' she laughs.

Once changed, they walk to the pool, awkward in the long, insulated gowns, passing very few people on the way. 'You're not wrong about it being quiet,' she says. 'Apart from that odd rumbling sound.'

'Yeah.' He grins. 'That's one of the things I like about it most. Sometimes it can seem as if you're the only person here – the only person alive on the Planet, in fact.'

They reach the small pool, which is actually quite large.

Soft-pulsing lights contour its uneven perimeter like a luminous necklace. She has never seen water so still. Or so dark – like obsidian. And the smell. She puts her head back and breathes in the earthy aroma: animal, vegetable and mineral rolled into one.

'One of life's true pleasures, is it not?' he asks, coming to join her. 'An undisturbed pool.' They stand together for a few moments, staring at the glassy water gleaming under the yellowing sky, its smooth surface etched with the shapes of trees and slow-shifting clouds.

She experiences a strong urge to dive in. 'Let's ruffle it up,' she says.

'Okay.' He smiles. 'But it's not exactly warm – as you found out. Heating only just takes the edge off things. You might want a quick dip in and out. It is the last run-off from the ice caps, after all.'

The cold is literally striking – almost forcing the breath from her body. She surfaces fast, sucking up air in deep gasps, then stills herself for a moment before setting off, less than elegantly she's sure, across the pool. By the time she reaches the other side, her breath is coming in hard. *Wow*, she thinks, catching hold of one of the slippery rocks. *Wow.*

He swims over to her, hanging alongside; misty breaths forming in the air. The warmth of his body is almost palpable. She shivers audibly.

'Had enough?' he challenges.

'No, I'll do some more,' she says. 'It's great. No, really it is.' She laughs. 'Now I'm used to it, anyway. Bit of a shock at first.'

The second hit is less dramatic. She swims more easily, more in control. The water slinks around her, dark but crystal clear. Its taste is clean, with a mineral tang; none of the cloying aftertaste you get in the artificial pools, or in the so-called 'mountain fresh' water sold in the Citi's bars. She swims fast for a while, generating a degree of body warmth. Before long, however, the cold starts to leech the strength from her limbs and her stroke becomes laboured. She strikes out for the steps.

'That's enough for me,' she calls as she climbs out of the pool. 'Off to warm up.'

Oh, my World, she thinks, as she sinks into the bubbling thermals of the hot tub – her head laid back and her eyes closed. *How wonderful is this?* Her skin feels tantalisingly sensitised, as if an infinitesimal layer has been stripped away, leaving it almost raw to the air. She breathes deeply, suffused with a powerful sense of Earthly well-being.

'So how was that?' he asks as he joins her.

'Yeah, great – now I'm in here, anyway,' she grins.

She is conscious of his body settling into the tub beside her and of the fact that her own appears to be operating on a higher, more febrile, frequency. As they sit, the whirl of the water seems, irresistibly, to draw their limbs together.

'First time there has been a full moon on the solstice since 2016 OL,' he is saying.

'Oh?' she asks, trying to focus on his words and not on the way the moonlight is highlighting the strong line of his neck and shoulders, nor the way small particles of water are nestled, glistening, in the dark hairs of his chest.

'Well, the summer solstice,' he continues, 'there's a winter one too, is the longest day – in our hemisphere at least. Solstice is from the old Latin – not that I know much of that, mind – meaning "sun-stopping"; the point at which the sun appears to stand still before reversing its direction. The ancient humans used to hold ceremonies of one kind or another on the night of the solstice. Sacrifices even…' He growls at her and she pretends to shiver.

The moon is now fully risen, bleaching the last of the yellow from the darkening sky. The threatening cloud of earlier has dispersed into wispy streaks of deep plum, paling to lavender as they drift across the face of the moon. She looks up at the glowing sphere. 'It certainly is beautiful,' she says, then laughs. 'If you can forget the mineral wars and the prison colonies, that is. And the endless stream of tourist ships.' She looks a little longer. 'Funny how people used to think you could see a face on the surface – the old man in the moon, wasn't it?'

'Yes,' he says with a soft snort. 'Old humans used to see their image – or those of their gods – in pretty much everything.'

She lies back, staring at the moon and the colour-changing clouds, enjoying the gentle pummelling of the water and, if she's honest, the proximity of his body.

'Guess things're going to be very different now,' she says after a while, 'with the suspension of the Program and everything.'

He nods at this. 'Yes, it'll depend on the outcome of the Conclave but, whichever way it goes, it's likely that entry restrictions will be reduced, if not removed,' he sighs, 'with all the public order problems that's going to cause.'

'World, yes. Can imagine. But at least the Vikis of the world will get their chance at Motherhood now?'

'Yes, maybe so. Once they break the link between sex and reproduction, there'll be many different kinds of Partnerships – between any of the sexes, or even between people of the same sex – with or without offspring. Be like stepping back. So, I was wondering,' he says as he starts up a gentle sculling and glances sideways at her, 'if you thought you might want to do that sometime in the future?'

'What, have offspring?' she asks, surprised.

'Well, yes, possibly that. But no, I rather meant take on a life-Partner; settle down with someone for the long-term.' He gives a small laugh, staring down at the bubbling waters.

'World, no!' She laughs. 'Couldn't think of anything worse.'

She thinks she sees his face fall slightly and wonders if he has taken this personally. She catches his arm, halting his sculling. 'If I wanted to settle down with anyone,' she says in as heartfelt a way as she can, 'you'd be my first choice, Coop, really you would. You're just the kind of man who'd be a great life-Partner. Any half-sensible woman would jump at the chance.'

'But not you?' he asks, starting up the sculling again.

266

'No,' she says in a firm voice, 'no desire at all to do that stuff – at least not for a long time. Want to try and make it with my music, if I can.' She looks across at him but, if he's disappointed in any way, he isn't showing it.

'Okaaay,' he says with a grin and a sudden burst of energy, 'you ready for the next bit? Need to keep an eye on the time; the last trans back to the Citi leaves at midnight. After that it turns into a pumpkin and we become mice or something.' He grins. 'But there's one last thing you have to see before we leave.'

'Another pool?'

'Yes, but that's not the main thing,' he says. 'Come with me.'

They pull their robes close as they make their way over to the rest of the complex, their breath just visible in the cooling night air. More people are milling around now, mostly elders, and most walking in the same direction as them. As they travel along the path, the rumbling noise she heard when she arrived has become louder and the air noticeably mistier.

They round the corner and the sight takes her breath away. A vast sheet of water, opalescent in the moonlight, is cascading down the face of the mountain, churning up clouds of roiling spray as it smashes off jagged outcrops into the pool below. Overarching the waterfall is a perfect bow of light – a pale reflection of its sunnier counterpart. The arc cuts a luminous swathe across the sky above the waterfall and glints of its ghostly spectrum dart in the steaming mists below.

'Wow,' she says, grinning at him. 'That's certainly a sight.'

'A moonbow,' he says, 'or lunar rainbow. One of very few places on Earth where you can reliably see one, but conditions have to be just right. Clear night, full moon.' He turns to her, smiling. 'Well, I think conditions have been pretty perfect tonight, don't you?'

'Perfect,' she says, with a feeling that she's somehow not managed to rise to the occasion, but not quite sure why.

45

INDEPENDENCE DAY

It's been a good day. She got an early bird in the pool despite a very late night *and* a bonus session when the next swimmer failed to show; then an extremely productive hour in the Virgim, followed by an intense mind-calming practice. Lyse feels remade and restored – ready for anything. She's off to find Seth now – relocated semi-permanently at his father's house since Queron's death. There's a little tune going round her head that could grow into a something, treated right, and she wants to run it past him before she gives it any more time.

Marcus gives her a warm welcome, saying Seth will be delighted to see her. 'He's down in the den – listening to music. What else!' He smiles, but she sees the strain in his usually placid face.

'Must've been a bit of a shock, y'know, about Thelma?' she asks.

'Oh my, yes,' he says, shaking his head. 'Known her for years and couldn't have imagined in the wildest of my dreams that she'd be capable of doing such a terrible thing. Not only to poor little

Viki, but nearly to Seth!' His eyes water and his age shows on his still-handsome face. 'All those years we've sat together of an evening…'

He looks so woebegone that she is moved to hug him, finding his large frame a lot frailer than it looks. He pats her back a few times then draws away.

'I'm all right, Lyse, thanks. I always knew Thelma felt deeply about things. And maybe in the bigger scheme of things—'

'Sacrifices have to be made?'

'Well, yes… no. Not human ones, anyway.' He sighs. 'Strange thing is, I'm going to miss her awfully. Card night was the highlight of my week. Sad, isn't it?' he says with a doleful smile. 'She was good company, you know, if you could keep her off the tirades. Not altogether sure how I'm going to fill my time now.'

'Didn't Seth say something about you joining a walking group?'

'Oh, that.' He grimaces. 'Yes. Well… I went once, but it was full of old gits like me moaning about their aches and pains. Or about life generally. How everything was much better in the good old days. That's not what I want, at all. One thing Thelma did teach me was not to live too much in the past. To try and move forward – embrace the future. I went out with those old moaners and came home more miserable than when I started.' He gives a short laugh. 'Anyway, for the moment I've got Seth to look after.'

'Yeah, course. How's he doing?'

'Not good, I'm afraid.' The old man shakes his head. 'Feels it's all his fault: Viki, Queron, the baby. Withdrawn into his music. Don't know whether to leave him alone or try to bring him out of himself. He seems pretty certain that the band's over, for one thing—'

'Oh no. We've got to shake him out of that, Marcus,' she says with feeling. 'The band's not going to fold. We can't let it. It's the only thing that will get him – and us – through all this. It'll be difficult to replace Queron, sure, but we can find someone. There's a lot of spare talent around. Viki's brother Naz, I've heard, for one, is a bit of a singer. We'll work up some new songs and then start the tour like Seth always talked about.'

'Well, you may be right,' he smiles, 'and I'll help any way I can, of course. Haven't got a lot of coin, but I'm quite good with my hands. However,' he shakes his head again, 'if you can get him interested, you're a better person than me.'

She finds Seth slouched on the sofa, earphones plugged manually into the ancient music system. He doesn't hear her enter the room and she regards him for a while. Seems very young, vulnerable, with his crumpled clothes and messed-up hair. Little boy lost. She feels the surge of an unfamiliar emotion that she hopes is not maternal. He seems to sense her watching and looks up, smiling as he unplugs himself and straightens up. 'Ly! Didn't know you were here.'

'No, well, how could you,' she grins, 'plugged in down here like a bot in a basement?' She points to the clunky ear-covers. 'What you listening to, anyway?'

'Some of the early stuff Q and I did together. Just to hear his voice, really,' he says with a weak smile. 'Wanna listen?'

'Yeah,' she says, settling close beside him on the sofa, taking up one of the covers and putting it to her ear. 'When was it?' she asks.

'Summer before last. We were support for another house band for a season. Just the two of us. Acoustic. Best time ever.' He lets out a strange noise: part human, part animal.

'Oh, Seth. I'm so, so sorry,' she says, putting her arms around him.

'Nah. It's me that's sorry, Lyse,' he says, pulling himself up and wiping his face. 'Just can't seem to stop this effin' rinse cycle.' He rubs his dripping nose with his hand.

She says all the things she's heard people should say: about things getting easier after a while; about taking one day at a time, but it all sounds hollow even to her ears, and how would she know anyway? When she was told, as a young teenager, that her father would not be coming back, she felt nothing. She knew the adults around her expected her to cry, so she cried; she saw they expected her to feel sad, so she fretted and moped and, best of all, she found they would tolerate significant misbehaviour, a situation she exploited for an enjoyable while. But really, she felt the best part of nothing then. Now, she misses him more each day.

Seth gets up to change the disc and she brings herself back to the point of her visit.

'Your pa says you're giving up the band?'

'Yeah,' he says with a morose shoulder shrug. 'Band's always been about Queron and me – right from the start. Just won't be the same.'

'But then it'll have to be different, won't it?' she says briskly. 'If it can't be the same, it'll have to be different. We can look for songs that work with other voices, find another singer. Won't be easy, I know,' she rushes on as she senses his detachment, 'but we can do it, Seth, I know we can. And I can sing more. I've got an idea for a song, actually—'

'Nah, Lyse,' he shakes his head, 'heart's not in it.'

She's not to be deterred. 'Well, not straight away. But promise me you'll start to think about it, least?' she cajoles. 'Talk to the boys, anyway; they're part of the band, after all. They need to know what you're planning.'

'Okay. Maybe. But just not yet, eh?'

'All right,' she says in a firm voice, resisting the little-boy-lost eyes. 'Not right now. But soon, Seth, or they – we – will all just give up and move on.'

He nods but says nothing, staring past her into the gloom.

'I've just been talking to your pa,' she starts up again after a further silence. 'He's worried about you. And sad – feels you're shutting him out. Wants to help but not sure how.' She takes his hand. 'He's grieving too, Seth. He lost his only so-called friend, after all—'

'Yeah,' he sighs. 'You're right. I'll talk to him. I'm staying here for a bit – months, prob. Already given up the pad. Only got the dal to live on now. Poorsville here I come.'

'Well, that's another reason to get back to the band, isn't it?' she presses. 'You'll need to start finding a way to make some coin. And I can't see you in a dead-end job, Seth. Even if the bots have left any.'

'Okay. I'll think about it, promise.' He gives her a shy grin, easing her towards him. 'Meantime, d'you want to come over here?'

*

Lyse returns home later to find Ida, Jai and Ammi sitting round the kitchen table; both the lighting and her family seem uncharacteristically subdued.

'What's this, a family conclave?' she asks, making a face as she approaches the table.

'Oh, Lyse, there you are!' Ida exclaims, rising to give her a kiss. 'I was just beginning to worry about you.'

'No need to worry, Ma. Keep telling you that. I'm a fully grown-up person now.'

'I know, but it's an old habit, not easily abandoned.'

'Well, is it?' she asks, looking round the table.

'Is it what, dear?'

'A family conclave. You all looked trey serioso when I came in.'

'Yeah, sort of, sis,' Jai replies. 'We're just talking about how things're going to change now; now the Program's been suspended. I was saying that Gencom's frozen all recruitment – so that's put paid to my planetary career.'

'Oh well, Jai, clouds and silver linings, eh?' she teases.

'So, what'll you do instead, Jai?' Ammi asks.

'Well, ultimately,' he says, not looking at Ida, 'travel. Get a bit of coin together first, though. There'll be loads of work in the new reversal labs that are springing up all over. Most of the males I know are planning to get themselves unsnipped, soon as.'

'But you're not interested?' she asks.

'Nah. Well,' he grins, 'not in the baby-making part, anyway – not for a long while.' He looks at Ammi. 'So, what's happening with your Program journey, Am? Are you staying on?'

'No, no, I'm not now.' Ammi looks round at the others. 'But I'm not too disappointed, to be honest.'

The others look back in surprise.

'Well, as I was saying to Lyse the other day,' she continues, 'the restrictions are awful – especially for females. Takes a certain kind of person to be able to put up with that level of control. And I've realised, in fact,' she gives a shy smile, 'I'm quite pleased to realise, I'm not that kind of person.'

'Well, it doesn't matter now, does it?' Lyse asks. 'People'll be able to get going on their own now, won't they, without the Program breathing down their necks?'

'Well, yes, in theory,' Jai answers, 'but it's a risky business giving birth and there'll be huge pressures on what passes for our public healthcare service. Even those with insurance won't get anything like the support the Program provided. And people off the system'll have to rely on their own resources.'

Ida nods. 'It's a long time since we've been able to give birth on our own. There used to be people that could help – "midwives", they were called – terrible name, I always thought. But there's been no demand since the Program took over, so nobody's got the skills anymore. They'll need to start training people up again.'

'Or find some new way to shut down the demand, more like,' she says. 'They're not going to let just anyone have babies, are they? There's gotta be some controls. Can't see Gencom giving up without a fight.'

'I'm sure you're right, Lyse,' Ida says, before turning to Ammi. 'So, you're sure about giving upon the Program, Ammi, dear? Seems a shame, as you were so keen.'

Ammi shakes her head. 'They said all those already signed up could carry on, but I just think it'd be too risky now, what with all the uncertainty – even if I had found the right Partner.'

'Which you haven't yet?' Ida asks.

'No, I haven't,' Ammi says, the slight flush showing again on her smooth, olive cheek. 'Although haven't been looking that hard, if I'm honest.'

'I know someone who would be great,' Lyse grins. 'Nice-looking, smart, fit bod.'

'Oh, and who's that then?' Jai asks with what sounds like a hint of jealously.

'The pol on Viki's case,' she says. 'Detective Cooper-Clark. He's definitely on the market. Told me so. Look here, got a pic. Always wears that hat. Sort of trademark.'

'Probably bald underneath,' Jai snides.

'No, he's got a fine head of hair, actually, now you mention it, Jai,' she rejoinders. 'Another of his good features.' She turns to Ammi. 'He's down the club a lot, Am. I'll intro you – if you'd deign to come down one night. Here,' she flicks up his image, 'remember him?'

'Ah yes.' Ammi smiles. 'From the Court. Does look rather nice, must admit. Okay, might just do that,' she says, avoiding Jai's gaze.

'So, where've you been anyway, Ly?' Jai asks, changing the subject. 'Haven't seen you for days.'

'Went to a Resomation on Sunday and out to the Wild Pools yesterday with a friend. Pretty cool; saw a moonbow.' She describes all the highlights of her trip to the Lakes – the swamps with the alligators, the flocks of weird birds, the mountains on fire and the tumbling sheet of water – omitting only one salient fact, the name of her companion. She's relieved when no-one notices the omission and when Jai asks about the Resomation.

'It was quite nice, really – if you can say that about a funeral,' she tells him. 'And quick – only about an hour. Not many there. The Detective was, though,' she gives Ammi a meaningful nod, 'which was a nice thing for him to do. Can't have known Qucron very well. And a strange woman who nobody appeared to know, blonde hair and red lips, seemed very upset. Some geeze welcomed us all and we took it in turn to play the stuff we'd brought. Seth and his father said a few words. I said a couple of things on behalf of the band. The strange woman didn't say anything. Otis, one of the boys, read a poem Q liked – something about how humans created death – then we launched his virtousia, named *Bright Star*, after one of his favourite poems – and listened to him sing one last song. Afterwards, we each said our goodbyes and took, I think I've still got them…' she burrows into her pocket and pulls out two sparkling stones, 'a little piece of him home with us.'

'Oh, grues!' Ammi says, turning up her pert little nose.

'Awes!' Jai exclaims, picking up one of the stones and squinting at it. 'What're you going to do with them, Lyse?'

'Set one in a wristband, I think, and maybe make the other into a necklet for Seth.'

'How nice,' says Ida, with a soft laugh. 'Used to be they just put you in the ground with a stone on top.'

'So, how about you, Lyse,' Jai asks, turning to her, 'has any of this changed your plans?'

'Well, yes, it has in a way. Not the Program stuff; that won't make any difference to me. But have finally decided to put off college.'

'Oh no, Lyse. Why would you do that?' Ida asks with a sharp intake of breath. 'You'll need qualifications to get on, won't you – even in music?'

'Well, yes. But trying to make it as a musician's gotta be better experience than any amount of studying. Learn more by getting out there and actually doing it than I ever could in front of a screen. And,' she smiles round at them, 'I've got a chance to do that now – one I might not get again. Seth's going to restart the band and I'm going to go touring with it. Good time to go: loads of clubs're looking for live music. And it'd be the best thing for Seth; he's been talking about going on tour ever since I first met him. His pa says he can help with equipment and maintenance and maybe sort out the transport. I can do the marketing. We could call it the *Sounds of the Sixties*—'

'Goodness, Lyse,' Ida exclaims. 'Seems like you've got it all planned. Just how soon do you see this all happening?'

'Oh well, just as soon as I've convinced Seth and Marcus and,' she laughs, 'the rest of the band. But none of that should take too long. In fact,' she gets up from the table, 'I'm starting right now. Only came back to pick up some stuff. Seth doesn't know it yet, but we're going to write some new songs – beginning with one for Queron.' She grins at her mother. 'Don't wait up, Ma. I'll be back late – if at all.'

She leaves the house and walks back to Seth. The setting sun is making a showy spectacle of lemon and green, against which the old moon's waning crescent gives little competition. Dark clouds are beginning to arrive on the scene, threatening action, and the air is cooler, with a tantalising hint of rain.

46

RED DIRT GIRL

Her stomach heaves as she retches; a string of bile trickles from the corner of her mouth. She lies there for a while, in the stinking dirt, bony arms wrapped around bent knees: a broken bird. Dazed, disorientated and overwhelmed by a powerful desire simply to cease to be.

The shuddering of her body begins, falteringly, to subside and the fog in her head starts to lift. Her gut clenches anew as the images hustle in: the sweaty face with its slathering lips; the acrid-slimed slug of a tongue; the bulging, pink-rimmed eyes. Deep disgust rises as the images intensify: the hot, flaccid body; the podgy, prying fingers; the whole revoltingness of him, panting like a dog as spats of his sweat hit her face like fat from a spit-roasting pig.

'Fuck!' She gasps at the volley of pain that strikes as she moves. 'Fucking, shitting, fuck!' She closes her eyes for a moment but recoils from the vicious flashes of glittering light she sees there. She breathes deep into her stomach, eyes held wide. How in the

World had she let herself in for that? Why didn't she run when she had the chance – before he got his hands round her hair and forced her against the wall? She feels the back of her head with hesitant fingers and cringes as they collect a bloodied clump of hair and foliage.

She struggles to recall the exact sequence of events, but it hadn't taken her long to realise her mistake. As if she would willingly have sex with a pathetic specimen like that – purely for his pleasure. Should have known better; she knows what Program boys are like. Heard enough stories. *Just thought that for once, for once in my shitty little life, lady luck had called.* She spits out the last of the bile with a sour smile. *Stupid mistake: red-dirt girls like me don't get the luck.*

Her anger gives her strength and she hauls herself up slowly, clutching at the ivy-covered wall, and stands, unsteady as a newborn calf, as successive waves of nausea crash through her. She grits her teeth and looks around. A half-moon is slung low in the dark navy sky, its mellow light giving a sepia tone to the scabrous wasteland. It's uncannily quiet and it must be very late. She has to get moving; he could come back.

She pulls together what's left of her clothing; hands trembling and bloodstained, nails torn. The skin on her shoulders is scraped raw and there's a terrible pain in her groin. One shoe appears to be missing. She steadies herself on the wall, trying to kick-start her deadlocked brain. Too late to get home, that's for sure – even if she could make it that far. Aunts will have locked up and taken her sleeps – nothing short of an earthquake would wake her now. Somewhere out of the blankness she remembers that Seth's father has a friend who lives down this way. An old woman, what's her name...? Thelma? Something Old-World like that. Some sort of doctor, gotta have something for the pain, and maybe somewhere to lie down for a while. She scans her surroundings. *Not far from here, down a little lane*, she thinks she recalls.

She walks in hesitant steps, the jagged stones of the path

tenderising her bare foot; each limping step prompts a new spasm of pain and several times she comes close to passing out. The night seems airless and she strains to draw down enough oxygen to propel herself forward. Her progress is almost unbearably slow, but eventually she finds the lane she remembers and gasps with relief as she sees lights on in the lone house at the end. *Thank World!* She takes a few deep, rasping gulps of the stale air.

Her bruised hands make little impact on the unforgiving wooden door and there seems to be no buzzer. She finds a large stone and raps it hard on the surface. Still nothing. Tears of frustration start to well in her eyes and she's just about to lie down then and there when she hears a shuffling noise from inside and a sharp female voice:

'Who's there? Stop that banging. You'll ruin my door.'

'It's Viki,' she calls as forcefully as her swollen throat allows.

'Who?' the voice calls back. 'Who did you say it is? Speak up.'

'Viki,' she rasps, 'Seth's girlfriend.' The door opens with a hesitant creak and she recognises the crumpled face with its bright-button eyes.

'Viki!' Thelma looks her up and down with consternation. 'Dear girl! What on Earth's happened to you? Come in, come in. You poor thing.'

She stumbles through the door, almost falling into the outstretched arms of the old woman. 'Sex attack,' she manages to get out. 'Shut out at home. Can I stay here for a bit?'

'Of course, Viki, dear. Come with me.' Thelma puts her arms around her and half lifts, half drags her down the corridor into a small room, where she helps her onto a chair by an unmade bed. She's surprised by the old woman's strength.

'Sit there for a moment,' she says, 'and I'll get some covers for the bed.'

'Can I wash first?' she asks. 'Really need to get his shit off of me.'

'Yes, I'm sure you do, dear,' the old woman nods, 'but you

need to rest for a while. Let things settle down a bit. I'll get you something for the pain. Then we'll clean you up.'

Thelma returns with an air blanket over an arm, a bottle of golden-brown liquid in one hand and a small vial in the other. She puts these items down as she helps her up onto the bed and places the blanket over her legs. 'Have a sip of this, Viki, dear,' she says as she pours a small cupful of the liquid. 'Help to calm you down.'

The drink burns as it runs down her sore throat, but she feels its disseminating warmth immediately and lies back on the pillow.

'Where does it hurt, dear?' the old woman asks.

'Mostly everywhere,' she grimaces. 'Back of my head mainly.' She leans up to show Thelma, who gives a loud tut. 'My shoulders are stinging a bit, too; and something's pretty grues inside—'

'Poor thing. Who did this to you? It wasn't Seth, was it?'

'Lor no! Seth would never do this.' The thought of him makes her tears start, and she pushes it away. 'Effin' repro, wasn't it? Wouldn't take no for an answer.'

'Oh yes,' the old woman says with a grim smile, 'I know the type. Don't suppose you got his name?'

'No. We didn't get on to first names, exactly! But I'd recognise him again anywhere: slimy fat grote.' She grimaces at the memory and lies back, closing her eyes.

The old woman opens the vial and shakes two of the blue and white pills onto her hand. 'Swallow these with a bit more of the whisky,' she says, drawing up the blanket and taking a chair beside the bed. 'They'll work fast.' They sit quietly for a while and she feels the worst of the physical pain – the thudding head, the screaming shoulders, the burning groin – begin to subside. The rawness of her emotions however remains undiminished.

'So, what happened, dear?' Thelma asks in a gentle voice. 'Can you talk about it?'

'Dunno really, all happened so quick. I'd had an argument with Seth and was walking home. Proggo must've seen I was upset, came over to *see if I was okay*.' She gives a harsh laugh. 'Should've known what he was really after. Shouldn't have been so stupid—'

'No, Viki, dear, you're not the one to blame here,' the old woman says in a firm voice as she refills her cup with the golden liquid.

'Yeah, course, I know that, but still should've known better. It just got out of hand really fast. Should have kneed him in his puny little bollocks,' she says, the alcohol encouraging her anger, 'but he was stronger than he looked. After a few minutes, I just kinda checked out. Seemed like it was all happening to somebody else, if you know what I mean – like I was looking on.'

Thelma nods and pats her hand. 'Probably saved you from getting any worse, dear. If that's possible, indeed,' she tuts.

'Then… afterwards, he pushed me to the ground and ran off. Don't know how long I'd been lying there, before I came round with my face in the dust. Lost my shoe…' She gives a weak laugh, pointing at her dirtied, reddened foot.

'You must report it, you know, Viki. He mustn't be allowed to get away with it.'

'Oh yeah,' she snorts. 'In an ideal world, somebody would care. But not this one. Banni girls deserve what they get, don't they? Nobody'll touch a golden Program boy. They'll just say I asked for it.'

'Mmm.' The old woman nods in agreement.

She leans back again and her eyes begin to close; the pills seem to be doing the trick. When she opens them, with difficulty, she sees Thelma regarding her intently.

'Was it a bad argument, the one with Seth?' the old woman asks, pouring each of them another tot of the whisky.

She wonders vaguely what this has to do with anything. 'Not really,' she lies, swallowing more of the burning spirit, her head beginning to spin.

'Was it about the baby? The argument with Seth?' Thelma presses.

Her heart wrenches at this. *Can't go there now. Not the baby.*

Not after all this. She screws up her eyes, wishing she could just disappear into a soft cloud of nothingness.

'I know you lost the baby,' the old woman is continuing, taking up one of her hands.

'You know? Seth told you?' She tries to pull her hand back, but it fails to obey and the tears she refused to spend on her attacker spring freely now.

'Yes, I'm so sorry, Viki,' the old woman says, stroking her hand. 'He told me how much you wanted that baby. You could try again, perhaps?'

'No, he's said he won't do it,' she splutters. 'Won't even help me do it on my own.'

'Well, it's not easy to hear,' the older woman says, 'but perhaps he's right, given the circumstances. You were lucky not to get caught last time; it would be very unwise for you to try it again.'

Despite her growing torpor, her hackles rise at this. *Why doesn't anybody ever take my side? Understand my needs, for once?* 'I could force him to do it, you know,' she cries as she finally succeeds in pulling her hand from the old woman's grasp. 'I could threaten to report him as an illegal. That would change his mind.'

'Oh, come now. You don't really mean that, do you? You're just upset.' The old woman retakes her hand and gives it a few quick pats. 'I shouldn't have mentioned the baby. Talk to him tomorrow and I'm sure he'll come round.'

'No,' she shakes her head as vigorously as she can, 'I know him. He won't budge now. Doesn't want me and deffo doesn't want any baby.' Anger and self-pity flood through her and she hears herself emit a low wailing sound.

'Sssh. There, there. You don't want to upset yourself anymore. Things will look different in the morning. I'm sure you don't really want to get Seth into trouble, do you? Such a nice young man.'

But her rage at her attacker has rekindled, fed by the slow-burning fuel of Seth's rejection – and the whisky. 'Seth this, Seth that. That's all anybody ever says. Well, what about me? What about what I want, for once?' She blinks defiantly at the old woman. 'If Seth won't have babies with me, I'll make sure he'll never have them with anyone else.'

'What, really?' Thelma frowns and, finally, lets her hand drop. 'You would turn Seth in? Even if it meant he would be reversed – or worse?'

'Yes, even that,' she says. 'Serve him right. 'He's a male, isn't he?' she sniffs, the force of her anger blowing itself out. 'They're all the same in the end. Heartless bastards.'

'Well, don't you fret about them now,' the old woman soothes as she gets to her feet. 'You just keep still for a bit while I run you a nice hot bath. I've still got one of those old-fashioned ones you can lie back in. It'll help soak away the last of the aches and pains. Then you can have a nice long sleep.'

When the old woman leaves, she thinks of Seth. *Would I really turn him in?* Even in her emotionally battered state she knows the answer: better to end her own life. She knows she's lost him. And that she can't keep him if he doesn't want to stay.

She closes her eyes with a long, deep sigh. The fight has finally left her and she is so overcome by the need to sleep that she's barely conscious when the old woman returns with a small chair on wheels.

'Bath's ready. Let me help you onto this contraption and I'll take you along.'

EPILOGUE

Well, someone's pleased to see me anyway. Arthur the catish is making his welcome moves: rubbing itself round his legs with a loud and repetitive meowing, tail stuck up like an exclamation. Coop picks it up by its neck and turns down the energy, getting an eyeful of umbrage (*'catfrontery' – that should be a word*) in return. The rejected haptic walks in a casual, cat-may-care manner over to the rug by the cooler, head high, and settles beside the GoGirl™, its rear end pointedly pointed towards him, its tail twitching. Coop looks at the near-deflated playdoll whose skin is now as wrinkled as an Old-Worlder and fancies he sees a hint of reproach in her lifeless eyes. *Needs to bag her up and send her back.*

Anyway, messages, messages. He pours a large glass of the enhanced aqua – *better start taking all this body-care stuff seriously now* – and opens his pinbox. Only two look remotely interesting. One is a medipin from the Program; *was expecting that – deal with that later.* The other is a message from a Marcus

Michelson marked '*Viki Jansdottir*'. There's an attachment and a short covering note:

Dear Detective Cooper-Clark,

I received the attached letter from Dr Thelma Linsdottir which may contain some information of interest to you in relation to the sad death of young Viki Jansdottir. Although no consolation, it was a relief to hear that her death was not a painful one.

I am sorry that the letter provides no forwarding address for Dr Linsdottir but, be assured, if I hear from her again, or get any hint of her whereabouts, I will not hesitate to get in touch.

World be with you,

Marcus Mitchson (Father of Seth Marcuson)

My Dear Marcus,

You will know by now that Viki died at my hand. She came to me on the night she was attacked, in a very bad state – mentally and physically. And very angry – at the man who attacked her and at men in general. But mainly at Seth for refusing to start another baby with her. So much so, she was threatening to report him to the authorities. I tried to talk her round, saying how dangerous it would be for them both, but the more I tried to dissuade her, the more adamant she became: if Seth wouldn't have a baby with her, she was going to make sure he would never have one with anyone else.

I realise that it may all have been just empty words, fuelled by her anger and pain. That she may well have thought very differently in the morning. In my heart of hearts, I felt she probably loved Seth too much to go through with it, but I simply couldn't take the risk. Not for Seth and not for the bigger prize. We had waited so long, and come so close, that it was unthinkable that we could fail at the last moment; simply too much – I truly believe it is no exaggeration to say the future of Humankind – was hanging on it.

So, I killed her as she lay in my bath. Intensive pressure on the vagus causing instantaneous neurogenic cardiac arrest, or sudden instant death, if you like – facilitated by her low emotional state and the mild intoxication of the whisky – your whisky! She didn't suffer, I can assure you. Helped by my little blue and white pills, her death was quick and quiet – almost peaceful. I don't think it is too fanciful to think that she might even have welcomed it, given how little she felt she had to live for.

Anyway, I washed her, dressed her in an old shift of mine (and her pretty scarf) and took her in my wheelbarrow to the edge of the bogs. I laid her body – she weighed so little! – in the ditch to speed decay and smeared it with a rue-based paste – mainly to deter the scavengers, but I was not unaware that rue, the 'sour herb', is also a sign of sorrow and repentance. Or, some say, comes from the ancient Greek 'to set free', and both seemed fitting somehow.

I knew it wouldn't be long before the charming detective closed in – he was as smart as he looked – but I hadn't expected Seth and his friend to find me out so quickly. I promise you that I fired only to frighten them, but his friend (who was not all he seemed, but I'll say no more of that) somehow got in the way of the bullet. It was a terrible, tragic accident. And, please believe me, one I would give anything to undo.

The execution of the plot, so long awaited, was faultless. The network mapped and amplified Seth's mutant genes, flooding the free market with zillions of synthetic copies. The carapace of Gencom's power was shattered in an instant. As you know, the politicians have moved swiftly to suspend the Program, pending the outcome of the emergency Conclave. While this may ultimately prove only a temporary cessation, it will give the scientific community time to assess the evidence objectively, and the global body politic an opportunity to reconsider the future of the Program and, hopefully, Gencom itself.

I am currently working with others on the vast cache of human biodata seized from the Life Program at its cessation. What I have seen to date is already showing, terrifyingly, the truth of the things I've long said to you about the adverse consequences of what is now almost half a century of selective breeding. On almost every key marker, from neonatal mortality to lifespan, the health of the species has deteriorated markedly. And worse, much worse, there is now irrefutable evidence of our direst fear: the systematic destruction of hundreds of thousands of 'not-quite-perfect' foetuses, many at a very late stage of development. Foeticide on a scale even I had not anticipated!

The work is challenging; the data hoard is enormous, and we have little time before the Conclave completes. But there are many of us and we are determined. When my contribution is finished, I will end my life (if they haven't caught me first, that is!). I won't be sorry when that time comes; living with the knowledge that I have killed two young humans is not easy. I wish, to this great Earth, that their deaths could have been averted. And that I could have avoided the pain and sorrow I brought to you and Seth.

I'm sure your heart is hardened towards me, Marcus, and I understand and accept that. But, if our friendship has meant anything to you over the long years, please believe I never, could never have, intended to harm your son. He is a fine young man, of whom you should be justly proud. I hope he manages to find some peace and move forward with his life. And please believe me when I say that I truly cared for you, Marcus. You brightened my life immeasurably. In another life, another time, we would be looking forward to a Thursday night grumbling about the state of the World over a tot (or two!) and a smoke. I will miss that more than anything.

That's all I wanted to say, my old friend. Please try not to think too badly of me. I did what I truly felt I had to do and I hope that in time you may be able to understand, if not bring yourself to accept, the actions I took.

Goodbye and World be with you.

Thelma

'Well, well, what do we make of that then, Arth?' he asks out loud of the catish which, still sulking, ignores him. 'The old biddy's ex-culpa, eh?' *Can't say I mind the 'charming detective' moniker and she's not wrong about Queron. Not as daft as she seemed – on either count. And thank the World the girl's death seems to have been peaceful, that's something at least. But what arrogance to suggest that she might have welcomed her death; that her life would have been worthless to her without a baby.*

He's sorry for the musician; losing two friends in the space of a month can't be easy. But then, he sniffs, he's probably got some consolation, hasn't he? He strokes the almost-fur of the catish, which starts up a conciliatory purring. He's heard through Ammi – whom he's met a couple of times now – that the band are preparing to tour, and that Lyse will be going with them. He's come to terms with her rejection, accepting, despite never quite believing, her assurances that it was all about her, not him, but he's newly disappointed at this turn of events. It was nice to be able to hear her sing at the club Friday nights, to pass her occasionally at the pool and, yes, to hold on to the hope that there might, even now, be something between them. *But this puts an end to that bit of pathetic self-delusion, doesn't it?* He snorts. Maybe this is his own personal Catch 22: the kind of female he would choose as a Partner, he would choose precisely because she's the kind of female who would never chose to be a Partner. *Get out of that one.*

Talking of which... He opens he message from the Program which informs him that the management of his 'PPP' (he has to look this up: *Personal Progenitor Pathway*, apparently) has been transferred to the SHS: the emaciated local remnant of the once-great example of human collectivism that was its national counterpart. Supposedly much-loved by the public – so much so that politicians couldn't touch it on the surface – but that didn't stop them carving it up under the waterline for the bottom-feeders of the global biohealth market. Nibbled away remorselessly, bit by tragic bit, until nothing was left but the bleeding core of emergency care. So, can't really say he's optimistic about his *Patient Journey* with the SHS, but least he hasn't got to watch all the porn. Daily usage to enhance self-mastering practice has been dropped from the Program induction; one of two less headline-catching outcomes from the Samson trial.

Attached to the message is the first of his twelve, monthly pills, designed to provide a gradual transition towards full restoration. Used to be given over twelve weeks, but the time extension was the second good thing to come from the Samson case. Before he can print the pill however he has to confirm he's read the *Product Warning!* and is prepared to accept any or all of the attendant risks, painstakingly detailed for him:

The PHYSICAL EFFECTS of this medication may change over the course of Reversal but may include over time some or all of the following possible side-effects: upset stomach, acne, nausea, sweats, blurred vision, raised blood pressure, exhilaration, dizziness, rash, back pain, muscle pain, stuffy, runny or bleeding nose, involuntary ejaculation, light-headedness and/or confusion.

The PSYCHOLOGICAL AND BEHAVIOURAL IMPACTS of the therapy are unpredictable and will vary between individuals. Common reactions can include unexplained mood swings, low mood or depression and heightened physical awareness of, and feeling of lust towards, one or more of the different sexes. Less common reactions include increased feelings of anger, aggression or self-hatred, the latter typically being displaced towards females.

He snorts. *Benefits had better be worth it!* He confirms his acceptance and a small, translucent pill rolls out from the printer. He holds it up to the window, its colour faintly blue in the stronger light. Blue: wasn't that the one for blissful ignorance; the red pill for the unpleasant truth? Wonder if the choice was deliberate? Unfortunate, if so: that's precisely the problem with the species at the moment – too many of its number spending too much of their time chasing blue pills in one form or another. Could all do with facing up to a few more unpleasant truths – himself included.

He places the glassy pill on the table and pours himself a beer (*one's not going to hurt, is it?*) returning, after a slow and satisfying glug, to consideration of the small, blue oval. Is this really what he wants: to change his body so radically, and possibly his character with it, everything he's ever known about himself, with no going back? What if he becomes the kind of sexpest that Lyse despises or, worse, an aggressor like Samson? And what if he goes through all these changes to body and mind and still doesn't find anyone? He'd be lumbered with his new, sexually active self until he dies of old age. Terrifying thought. He rolls the pill in his long brown fingers as he takes another swig of the beer.

A distant low rumble of thunder makes him glance at the window, where shy splashes of water have started to hit the panes. Looking out he can see people gathering in the street below, faces turned up, mouths open, to the iron-grey sky, soaking up the first rains of the year. Groups are forming, engaging in animated, real-world conversations. Drinks and small delicacies are being passed around and a band has started up. He puts the pill down, takes a further deep draught of the beer and goes out to join the party.

ACKNOWLEDGEMENTS

I would like to thank all those who helped this book on its way – particularly those who braved the early drafts – and who provided much-needed advice and encouragement. They include: Clare Croft-White, Ray Love, Marie McNay, Alex Noonan, Hilda Offen, Debra Okitikpi and Judith Swaffer.

I would also like to acknowledge the professional advice and support provided by Amanda Saint, from *Retreat West* and the *Jericho Writers* network.

Thanks too to my family, for enduring the process (it's not over!) and to my book club chums: Carol, Celia, Helen, Helga, Linda, Roisin and Ruth, for insights into what makes a good read. I hope they don't think this effort falls too far short.

Most of all, I have to thank my long-suffering partner Mark, who believed in the project from the start and who has supported it enthusiastically ever since.